A Tale of Two Russians

Christopher Arthur

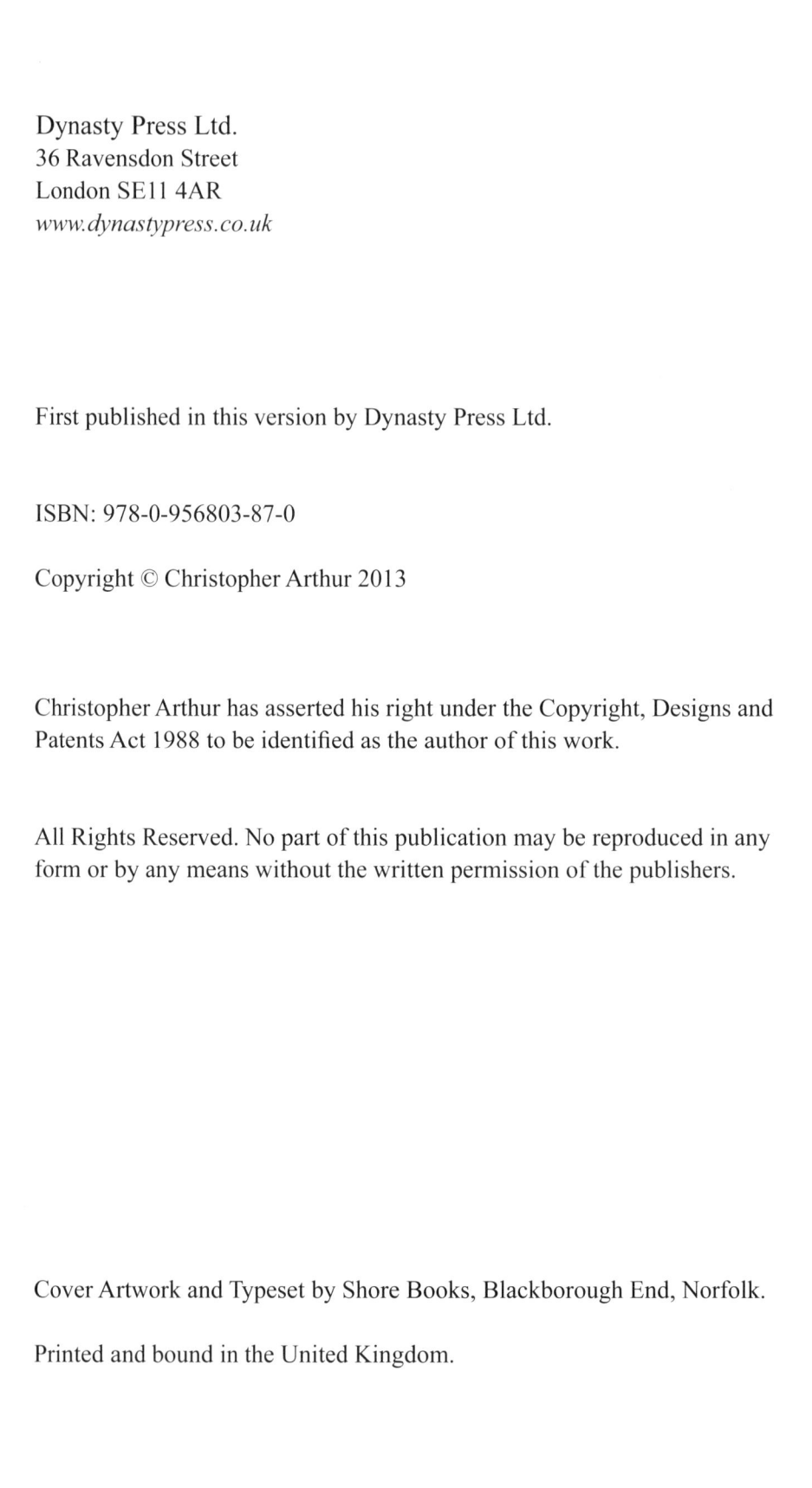

Dynasty Press Ltd.
36 Ravensdon Street
London SE11 4AR
www.dynastypress.co.uk

First published in this version by Dynasty Press Ltd.

ISBN: 978-0-956803-87-0

Copyright © Christopher Arthur 2013

Christopher Arthur has asserted his right under the Copyright, Designs and Patents Act 1988 to be identified as the author of this work.

All Rights Reserved. No part of this publication may be reproduced in any form or by any means without the written permission of the publishers.

Cover Artwork and Typeset by Shore Books, Blackborough End, Norfolk.

Printed and bound in the United Kingdom.

CONTENTS

Chapter One	The Symposium	1
Chapter Two	The Novgorod Master	17
Chapter Three	To Montenegro	55
Chapter Four	On the Beach	66
Chapter Five	Kotor	77
Chapter Six	Incident in Cetinje	90
Chapter Seven	London … at last	102
Chapter Eight	Viktor Arrives	112
Chapter Nine	A Fly in the Ointment	121
Chapter Ten	A Funeral and Plans for a Party	133
Chapter Eleven	When the Cat's Away …	143
Chapter Twelve	Preparing a Feast	150
Chapter Thirteen	The Housewarming	164
Chapter Fourteen	A Heady Mix …	174
Chapter Fifteen	A Private View	182
Chapter Sixteen	Father Christmas Calls and a Family Chore	190
Chapter Seventeen	Creative Aspirations and a Thickening Plot	204
Chapter Eighteen	And Thicker Still …	221
Chapter Nineteen	Cloaks and Daggers and an Unexpected Encounter	237
Chapter Twenty	Diverging Developments	250
Chapter Twenty-One	A Play Within a Play	267
Chapter Twenty-Two	More of the Same	291
Chapter Twenty-Three	Two Writers at Work	309
Chapter Twenty-Four	Peace in Our Time	322
Chapter Twenty-Five	The Balloon Bursts …	335
Chapter Twenty-Six	Washed Up on an Ionian Shore	352
Chapter Twenty-Seven	An Enigma Wrapped in a Riddle	370
Chapter Twenty-Eight	Viktor Forces the Pace	387
Chapter Twenty-Nine	Tale End	399

ACKNOWLEDGEMENTS

My thanks to Andy Rogers who led me down the dark paths of Cyberspace, so that my book safely reached its destination and thanks also to Mervyn Burleigh for his robust comments on my literary efforts and his generosity of spirit.

CHAPTER ONE

The Symposium

Nicko unlocked the door of the flat and quickly crossed the hall to switch off the burglar alarm.

"Quite safe now," he called back to Viktor who was already crossing the threshold and casting an eye about him.

"Casing the joint?" joked Nicko. "Do you know what that means?"

"Sure, I know," replied Viktor. "I was just checking for bugs, that's all." He spoke with an accent which was a pleasantly melodious blend of standard received English and Russian.

Olive skinned and rather thickset with dark wavy hair, Viktor Ilyich Nikishov was what is described as a New Russian. His family had made a fortune from the wreck of communism in the former Soviet Union and, out of the proceeds, had sent him to a leading English public school, which was where he had met his chum Nicko. Now, having both left school together in the summer, they had time on their hands before moving on to university or whatever after the obligatory gap year in Nicko's case.

Nicko liked to think that he was a Russian too - he even talked about his 'Russian soul'- but of a quite different vintage from Viktor. In reality, he was English, despite the family name of Orloff. His great-grandfather was indeed a Russian count of that name, who, having fought in General Wrangel's White Army against the Bolsheviks, fled to England in the early Twenties. Fluent in French and English and with a good number of well-placed friends in Paris and London, the Count had fared better than many of his fellow exiles at that time. A sound classical scholar, he had started life afresh as a humble schoolmaster teaching small boys Latin, but not for very long. He had fairly swiftly moved onto a higher plane where he had found an English wife, as in due course did his son and grandson. By the time Nicko was born the Orloffs were living in Sunningdale and Nicko had gone on from a fashionable preparatory school to a public school in the Home Counties. But, despite his exotic sounding surname, he looked as Anglo-Saxon as they come.

And it was at his public school that he had met Viktor, who had arrived straight from Russia. Ironically, it might have been Nicko's golden-haired, blue-eyed Englishness that had drawn Viktor to him in the first place, for like a lot of Russians, he carried in his head a stereotype of what he imagined quintessential Englishness to be - something that was associated with the idea of a gentleman - which Nicko appeared to fit.

Nicko laughed at Viktor's remark. "Wait 'til you see the rest of the place," he said, throwing open a door. "In here, for instance."

It was a small room, two walls of which were taken up by books. There was a heavy Victorian writing table over by the window and a well-worn Turkish carpet on the floor. But it was the shelves lining the walls that commanded the attention of any discerning visitor. For here was part of Uncle Frank's collection of fifth century B.C. Athenian red figure pottery. The pieces were carefully spaced and Nicko switched on a light to illuminate them.

"Wow," said Viktor, who was rapidly learning to appreciate such things. "But isn't it asking for trouble? I mean going away and leaving them standing on open shelves like this? Anyone could walk in and help themselves. That alarm wouldn't be difficult to fix."

Nicko laughed. "That's Uncle Frank for you. But you don't have to pass it on to any of your friends in the Petersburg Mafia."

Viktor grinned. "Tell me about Uncle Frank."

"He's not my real uncle. He was Father's old university tutor and my godfather. A retired professor of Classical Archaeology at Oxford to be precise."

There was a sweetish smell of pipe tobacco in the room, which supported this description.

"Married?" enquired Viktor.

"What Uncle Frank? No course not. He wasn't the marrying sort," said Nicko. "A confirmed bachelor."

The two young men looked at each other and smiled.

"You amaze me, Vik," said Nicko to his friend.

"Amaze you? Why?"

"How quickly you seem to latch onto the nuances of English life."

"Ludi, ludi," replied Viktor in Russian with a shrug. "People are people. Much the same wherever you go."

He crossed the room and took a small vase from the shelf that was different from the others, being painted white.

"A lykythos. It was placed in the grave with the dead," explained Nicko. "That's why it's that colour. But be careful with it, for Christ's sake."

Viktor pretended to drop it.

"For God's sake, Vik," his friend protested. "He'd have my head on a platter if that got broken."

Viktor eyed Nicko's golden locks with a critical frown. "I think not in your case," he said. "He probably likes it better where it is." He replaced the vase carefully and ran a finger along the shelf. "It could do with a dust."

"As you've probably guessed Uncle Frank isn't very worldly," Nicko told him.

"But not very Platonic either," replied Viktor.

They both laughed, thinking something clever had been said.

"You're such a bloody cynic," said Nicko. "You always think the worst of people."

Viktor grinned. "What do you expect- where I come from?

It was the middle of the afternoon on an early autumn day in Chelsea, and Nicko left the shelf lights on when he took his friend into the other rooms of the flat, which weren't large, but, like the study, rather faded. They smelled musty. The place had been done out in a neo-classical style- terracotta and ochre being the predominant tones- and the washed-out effect of the walls set the antiquities off well. Indeed, the threadbare quality might have been contrived, because everything came together so perfectly. It was as if the ancient artefacts themselves had been manufactured for the sole purpose of coming together in Uncle Frank's flat.

"How long's your uncle away for?" enquired Viktor.

"Another three weeks. He usually goes to the south of Italy or Sicily about this time - after the main tourist season has subsided."

"And he always lets you have the run of the place?"

"I keep an eye on things."

"If had this little treasure house I wouldn't go away for a month and leave it in the care of someone like you. That door and the alarm look too easy." Viktor shook his head.

In the drawing room was the piece de resistance of the collection. It stood by itself on a console table in the Empire style opposite the Adam fireplace.

"That is what's known as a krater," explained Nicko. "It held wine- mixed with water."

"Why spoil the wine by adding the water?" queried Viktor.

"It was the way the Greeks seemed to like it," said Nicko. "No doubt they made it strong enough to loosen their tongues without letting themselves get completely drunk. Think of those dazzling symposia."

"Symposia?"

"Supper parties. Strictly men-only affairs. You've heard of Plato's dialogues, haven't you? I should get Uncle Frank to tell you about them sometime."

Viktor frowned, unconvinced.

The krater was a magnificent piece, impressive to the eyes of even the most untutored layman, and Viktor, who was beginning to make progress in such matters, was accordingly impressed. It was tall, almost the size of a household bucket and shaped like an inverted bell with upturned handles at the shoulder above its base. There was a broad frieze of figures running round the main body of the vessel. The outlines of their muscles and the folds of their garments were applied with a vibrant delicacy on the red clay ground, while the blackness against which they acted out their drama added further dynamism to the scene.

"Now you can see why the Greeks were so special," declared Nicko. "No one else could touch them for their handling of the human form and for the sheer vitality of their art. I'm not sure anyone can, even now."

"What's it about?" asked Viktor. He squinted at the back of the krater but did not touch it.

"The death of Agamemnon," explained Nicko. "Murdered by his wife Clytemnestra as soon as he got home from the Trojan War. Strictly speaking, he ought to be in the bath when she killed him with an axe."

But in this version the King was toppling backwards in a chair, as an armed warrior wielding a sword, presumably the Queen's lover, grabbed his forelock, urged on by the lady herself, bearing a double headed axe. Agitated household slaves flapped their arms on either side.

"Uncle Frank informed me that it was the work of the Dokimasia Painter - whoever he was," added Nicko. "He did explain how he knows, but I'm afraid I can't remember what he told me exactly. There are small stylistic quirks that the experts can pick out."

"My God," exclaimed Viktor, turning to a group of objects the size and shape of shallow soup bowls. "What about these?" He picked one of them up.

"Please, Vik," pleaded his friend, as Viktor went through the pantomime once more of pretending to drop it.

"This one's too hot to hold," he joked.

And when he replaced the bowl on the table, his meaning became apparent. But for Nicko, who was familiar with the object, it required no elucidation.

"A drinking cup," he said. "You have to remember that this would be used at a blokes-only dinner party. That's what a symposium was."

An older, bearded man was penetrating a naked youth, who was bent double, from behind. The scene was surrounded by a 'Greek key' frieze, which neatly confined it within its circumference. Both the handles of the piece were intact and it appeared to be in perfect condition.

"Surely this must tell us something about your Uncle Frank," said Viktor who, in his blunt New Russian fashion, felt no compunction about speaking so explicitly to his friend.

"You can draw your own conclusions," replied Nicko tartly, "but it wouldn't surprise me if Uncle Frank is just a harmless old celibate. His kind usually are, and is that such a bad thing?"

Nicko felt that Viktor was pushing his insinuations after his godfather a little too far. Indeed the latter was rather taken aback by his sudden display of vehemence, when he had appeared to collude with him earlier in their shared innuendo about Uncle Frank's sexual preferences. Despite him being perfectly au fait with such matters, there was something engagingly old-fashioned about Nicko, who preferred not to probe too deeply into the inner urges of the people close to him.

They looked round the rest of the flat, even entering Uncle Frank's rather Spartan bedroom with its single bed and cane-seated chair which took the place of a bedside table.

"Not exactly a bordello," observed Viktor, trying to make amends for what he had implied earlier about its owner.

"The bedroom of a sober and shy university don- and therefore more like a monk's cell," Nicko declared. "There must be people like Uncle Frank in Russia too, surely? As you said people are much the same wherever they are."

"Kaneshna," returned Viktor. "Of course, there are." He smiled at Nicko, almost archly. His friend liked the way he slipped the occasional Russian word into their conversations.

They went back into the hall.

"Now what?" said Viktor.

"Now what?" repeated Nicko, slightly at a loss having shown his chum every room in the flat.

"I've got an idea - if Uncle Frank doesn't mind." Nicko eyed his friend dubiously.

"Only if he doesn't mind," insisted Viktor.

"How do we find that out? Ring him at his hotel?"

"That won't be necessary," said Viktor. "I'm sure he doesn't mind. By the sound of him he's an understanding sort of chap, who's tolerant of young people and their ways."

"What are you getting at, Vik?" retorted Nicko. He occasionally found the other's prevarication tiresome. "Stop beating about the bush."

Viktor repeated the phrase 'beating about the bush' in a low voice to retain it for future use.

"I'm sure your uncle wouldn't mind if we borrowed his flat for a little symposium of our own," he said. "He would understand that perfectly well, I've no doubt. Though of course we don't have to go quite as far as those two guys on the drinking cup."

Nicko still looked doubtful. "We'd have to be bloody careful we didn't do any damage."

"That goes without saying. Yes?"

"Yes, Vik, that goes without saying. You've got that one right."

"It would just be something simple. A few drinks and snacks in the Russian style- you know, nice fishy things- and lots of talk- in the Russian style too. What could be better- surrounded by all these amazing things?"

"That's what I'm worried about, Vik - drunkenness in the Russian style with its unfortunate consequences," Nicko pointed out. "I don't like it. It won't wash."

Viktor repeated 'it won't wash' under his breath. "I wish you'd stop doing that, Vik."

"Doing what?"

"Repeating things I've just said. You turn our conversations into English lessons."

Viktor laughed. "I'm sorry, Nick. But to go back to what we were saying. With so much history and beauty around us we cannot allow anything as squalid as a Russian orgy to take place in Uncle Frank's flat."

"Don't be so sure," replied Nicko. "You've heard the story of Peter the Great's visit to London, haven't you?"

"Kaneshna," said Viktor. "But if it makes you feel easier about it, we can use the kitchen. Simply to know that there's so much art and history close to us would be enough."

"But not too close."

"The kitchen would be perfect. That, after all, is the place where Russia's intellectuals have been meeting to share the mind's forbidden fruits for the past eighty or more years. And, Nick, we're both Russians, aren't we? Admittedly from different sides of the revolutionary divide, but together again and with so much to say to each other. And look at what else we've got in common, you and I; that special English thing - what do you call it in Latin? Our alma mater near Godalming, the Old School. That factory for the manufacture of gentlemen of the English kind, the public school."

Nicko smiled. "A great speech, Vik, but you do talk an awful of a lot of shit."

"Eighty years… more than eighty years," mused Viktor. "That's what it's been. I know we've talked about a lot of things already, but there's still so much and we've hardly scratched the surface of it. Yes?"

"Yes, Vik. We've hardly scratched the surface."

"We could go to a pub, of course or back to your folks' place in Sunningdale, but hell, why not here in Uncle Frank's kitchen? We will call it a symposium - in honour of our absent host. It needn't be a Platonic dialogue, of course, but it'll be a symposium just the same. I'm sure your uncle would approve: two intellectual young men holding a serious conversation in his kitchen. The situation is perfect."

"I'll buy it, you arsehole," said Nicko, "as long as we don't touch anything that matters."

Viktor proceeded to do the Russian thing: he pressed his friend close to his chest and kissed him on each cheek.

"Sit down, Nick," he ordered. "Or walk about if you want to, admiring all the wonderful things. This one's on me. Yes? My dad could buy one of your English football clubs any time he liked. But you provide - with Uncle Frank's help - what do I say? The class - which we Russians need so badly?"

"You're a snob," said Nicko.

"Probably I am," replied Viktor. "The way Tsar Peter was. I'll be back shortly."

He slipped out and Nicko could hear the lift descending to the ground floor. Going round the rooms, he picked up and examined some of the smaller objects as he had done many times before: the Roman oil lamps, a moulded ceramic Greek figurine - a temple offering, not rare and rather

7

crude, but interesting nevertheless for what it said about the small change of life in the ancient world. There was even a lamp done in the form of a gladiator's helmet - the Roman equivalent of present day seaside kitsch. In a way, these mundane objects brought him into a closer sympathy with the ancient world than the grander ones did.

Then it occurred to Nicko that he ought to be doing something to set up the kitchen for the forthcoming symposium. He had better get it done before Viktor returned with ideas about relocating it in a more exalted setting. Fishing around inside the kitchen cupboards, he found Uncle Frank's cheaper glasses and a selection of plates and bowls. These he set out on the kitchen table with cutlery from the drawer by the sink. Having completed the task to his satisfaction, he retreated to his godfather's study to browse among his books.

Three quarters of an hour later the doorbell rang, announcing Viktor's return. He was carrying three bulging supermarket bags, which he dumped on the kitchen dresser.

"Christ, you must have bought the bloody shop," expostulated his friend.

"Not quite," said Viktor, "but I did my best."

There were four bottles of champagne, an equal number each of claret and vodka- the proper Russian stuff, Nicko noted - as well as a mountain of cold snacks: salami sausage, rollmop herrings - indeed a whole range of fishy delicacies- black rye bread, butter and olives. Then, rummaging in his coat pockets, Viktor produced four jars: two of black caviar and two of red.

"That must have cost you something," exclaimed Nicko. "Where did you get it?"

"I have my ways," replied the other, making a pantomime of shiftiness.

"But you've bought so much. This isn't supposed to be an orgy, you know."

"It's a symposium," Viktor corrected him. "Is the freezer switched on?"

Nicko checked and Viktor placed the vodka inside and then the champagne in the main fridge compartment. We'll need to give the vodka plenty of time, but we can have the champagne first."

The spread covered the kitchen table and the adjacent dresser.

Nicko shook his head. "My God, Vik."

"Why 'my God'?"

"Are you quite sure I can't chip in?"

"Quite sure. You have provided Uncle Frank after all, and his priceless collection of Greek vases. So surely I can lay on a little caviar, can't I? And talking of which I really prefer the red stuff to the black. I know it should be the other way round, but it's a fact. Let's kick off - yes? with the wine. We'll have to give the champagne more time. Corkscrew?"

He uncorked a bottle of claret and filled their glasses.

"I hope there'll be enough," he said anxiously. "More than," responded his friend.

The symposium had begun.

"What are we going to talk about?" said Viktor. "Think of something suitable."

"Something Russian. You."

"Me? Why me?"

"You," Nicko repeated, "because I want to know who you really are. What your people actually got up to back in the Soviet Union and why you're here right now. You've told me some of it already, but there are still lots of gaps and it's all a bit vague. Kind of shadowy."

"You mean shadowy or shady?" Viktor grinned

"Very good Vik, your English is coming on by leaps and bounds."

"It's because I hear people like you speaking the best kind."

"Piss off, Vik. But your ancestors? What about them?"

"Yours were aristocrats."

Nicko nodded. "We know that."

"Were they big ones, like the Sheremetevs with vast estates and armies of serfs?"

"Hardly as big as that. But a couple of sizeable estates and sure they had serfs. But why are you asking me all this again, Vik? We've been over it before and you don't have to remind me that your great-great - however many greats - grandfather was shovelling pig shit while mine was blowing a fortune at the gaming tables in Petersburg and possibly shagging the Empress of All the Russias at the same time."

"What? On the gaming table?"

"Piss off, you know what I mean. It's you we should be talking about." Viktor grinned and raised his glass. "Nasdorovia!" he announced.

Nicko repeated the Russian toast.

"That champagne won't be ready quite yet," went on Viktor, "so let's carry on with the claret." He lifted a piece of salami sausage on his fork.

"You really want to hear the story of my family, do you?"

"I do," said Nicko. "What you've told me so far has merely whet my appetite- high ranking members of the Communist Party and asset strippers when the time came."

"In a nutshell. Is that right?"

"Is what right?"

"What I've just said- 'in a nutshell'."

"For Christ's sake, Vik. You know it is. We're having a symposium not an English lesson."

"Each time I talk to you it's an English lesson."

"You don't need me to teach you, so piss off."

"Well that's a very English word you've just used." He gestured at the contents of the table. "So tuck in. Mind, I said 'tuck'- not that other English word."

"Very droll, Vik."

They drained their glasses and Viktor placed the half-finished claret to one side, having decided to broach the champagne, sufficiently cooled or not.

"Fresh glasses," he ordered.

Nicko rummaged in the cupboard and found a couple of glasses that approximated to the champagne kind.

The cork popped and the bubbly frothed over their glasses' rims onto the table. Another Russian toast followed and Viktor smacked his lips.

"And now for the caviar," he announced.

A tin opener was produced and Nicko supplied some ice to serve as a bed for the delicacy.

"It was decent of your uncle not to turn off his fridge before he went away," Viktor said. "He must have understood that we would be holding a symposium in his flat."

Nicko helped himself to a generous spoonful of the caviar. He wasn't really sure whether he liked it or not, but took a second one partly to convince himself that he did.

"You never really told me," he said, picking up on their earlier theme, "what exactly your family got up to. Good Communists once upon a time and then they make a fortune and send you to a posh English school - buying into the very thing they were dedicated to smashing - social division and class privilege."

"I thought we'd been through that before, Nick."

"But you still haven't told me exactly what they did. You know the kind of things that went on in Russia for most of the last century. What part did your folks- the Nikishovs- play in all that? In Stalin's time for instance?"

Viktor laughed. "Your family had serfs, right?"

"Right."

"Well, so did mine - in a manner of speaking. Have I said that correctly?"

Nicko did not reprove him, but said nothing as he watched him swallow a mouthful of the red caviar this time.

"Perhaps we should keep that to have with the vodka. That's the proper time for the fishy things," Viktor said.

"Explain what you mean- about the serfs."

"Oh the serfs! Well, Russia is Russia- whoever's in charge of it. Certain things stay the same. Did we ever talk about Dalstroi?"

"Dalstroi? No, I don't think we did. What is it?"

"The Gulag," said Viktor. "You know what that was surely?"

"Kaneshna. Of course I do."

Viktor smiled. "Well, Dalstroi - or to give it its proper title, the Dalstroi Trust - was a part of the Gulag. It ran its operations in Kolyma - in eastern Siberia."

"Go on."

Viktor topped up their glasses with more champagne and insisted on another toast.

"Kolyma," he said, "in eastern Siberia, and the port of Magadan. That's where my grandfather, Nikishov, ruled. And I mean ruled. General of the NKVD and the boss. Tsar Josef was far away in Moscow. Dalyeko… dalyeko… far, far away." He intoned the words of the soulful Russian ballad.

"Tsar Josef being Stalin?"

"Of course. Who else? Josef Vissarionovich and a very terrible tsar too- every bit as bloody as Ivan IV, and with a much longer reach. What did people say? Ghengis Khan with a telephone. And Kolyma was run by the Dalstroi Trust as a part of the Gulag - its profitable part. Gold, you see. Mined by zeks, the prisoners who, in a nutshell - yes? were Grandpa's serfs. Like you Orloffs, he was service nobility. Is that right?"

Nicko nodded. "Quite likely."

"Communism or Tsarism - it comes to the same thing, doesn't it?

We're talking about Russia, after all. And what the Tsar gave he could take away again. Come on, Nick, eat up - there's a mountain of food to get through. 'In the North there is a mountain, covered o'er with frozen corpses, where the wild winds blow. Mother, dear, you'll never know, where your son lies buried…' A Gulag poem, translated from the Russian, but not by me. That's Kolyma for you. But it just a part of the story. There was gold, Nick, gold- lots of it and it needed slaves to dig it out. Anyway, what do you English say? Dig in? Eat up."

He filled their glasses with the last of the champagne, spilling some of it on the table.

"Tell me about Grandpa Nikishov then," said Nicko, having emptied his glass in a single draught.

Viktor nodded. "Every bit as exotic - yes? as your Orloffs. I'm sure of that."

"Why haven't you told me about him before?" queried Nicko. "You're not making this up, are you?"

Viktor looked affronted and put his hand on his heart.

"It needed the right occasion," he explained. "That's something you English are supposed to have, isn't it? A sense of occasion? Yes?"

"Yes, Vik."

Viktor dropped his voice almost to a whisper. "You see, Grandpa had got blood on his hands - plenty of it, no doubt. He was a chum of Beria, after all, and a senior figure in the NKVD who survived the Purges - which means only one thing. He had to put an awful lot of other people in the shit to keep out of it himself. And it worked for him. Like a cat - how do I say it? He managed always to land on his feet. He had nine lives and they never ran out. Yes?"

"Yes, Vik. I get the picture," Nicko said. "I'm a Russian too, don't forget."

"Da. Kaneshna, Nick. How could I ever forget your Russian soul?"

"Vik, eff off, will you? Just tell me more about Grandpa Nikishov."

Viktor shrugged and spread his hands. "Where do I begin? His limousines? His army of security guards? And the dacha with the wonderful view of the Pacific? That vodka might be just about ready." Viktor opened the freezer, felt one of the bottles and frowned.

"Not yet. Still a bit warm." He took two glasses and placed them in the freezer beside the vodka. "We nearly forgot to frost the glasses." He uncorked a second bottle of champagne. "Where were we?"

"The dacha overlooking the Pacific."

"Da, the dacha. Some dacha - more like a palace, though I daresay you Orloffs might think it… a bit over the top? Does that sound right?"

"Yes, Vik. Just get on with it."

"Fitted oriental carpets everywhere, bearskins, crystal chandeliers - and a luxurious dining room where he entertained with his wife…. Roast bear, Caucasian wines, fruits and berries flown up from the South… fresh tomatoes and cucumbers grown in his private greenhouses…."

"A true boyar," supplied Nicko.

"Or a Roman emperor … and vegetables quite foreign to it, grown for him in special hothouses and orangeries…."

A dreamy look had come into Viktor's eyes and he plied the champagne bottle once more.

"Steady on," Nicko said.

"Fuck off. Remember I'm called Nikishov as well."

"That's what I'm afraid of."

"Did the Orloffs have their own orchestra?" asked Viktor.

"They may have done. No one's mentioned one."

"Well Grandpa did. A serf orchestra. Or to be strictly accurate, a zek one - musicians who were prisoners in the Gulag. It comes to the same thing. They were just grateful to be kept out of the mines."

They polished off the bottle of champagne. A wistful expression suffused Viktor's face. "I wonder if that vodka's ready yet? To Hell!" He removed a bottle and the two glasses from the freezer. As he filled them some of the liquid slurped onto the table.

"Steady on," warned Nicko. "It's good stuff. Don't waste it."

Viktor sipped his glass. "Not quite as cold as it should be, but what the hell?" He threw the rest back.

Nicko sipped his more cautiously, though he too was feeling the effect of the champagne. Viktor meanwhile plunged into what was left of the caviar.

"I suppose Grandpa Nikishov had as much of that as he wanted," commented Nicko.

"Kaneshna. And carpenters to make his furniture…."

"You mean cabinet makers."

"Cabinet makers then… as well as fashion designers to dress his wife… some of the best."

"Were there still such people in Russia then? Very bourgeois," Nicko's words were beginning to slur.

"Kaneshna. And doctors… they were the best too… specialists from Moscow and Petersburg… whatever it was called then…" "Leningrad."

"That's it… Leningrad…"

"Fuck Lenin," Nicko said with feeling.

"Yeah, fuck him," replied Viktor, who was onto his third glass of vodka with his friend following manfully in his wake. "And the theatre," he resumed. "Did I tell you about the theatre?"

"No, Vik, you didn't."

"Well there was a theatre… with a front like a Greek temple… Uncle Frank would've liked that… in the park… a short distance from Grandpa's palace… all the actors were serfs. Did the Orloffs have any of those?"

"Actors? I've no idea. Maybe… quite possibly… yes, I'm sure they must have done…" Despite his increasing befuddlement Nicko felt the need to uphold the reputation of the Orloffs before this Soviet oik…

"The finest company of actors east of the Urals," went on Viktor. "They did all the great Russian classics… and Shakespeare too…"

"Shakespeare? In English?"

"In Russian…"

"Not the same thing…"

"Like Pushkin in English," rejoined Viktor.

"True," conceded Nicko. "And which of Shakespeare's plays did the Boyar Nikishov like the best?"

"Macbeth."

"I'm pleased to hear it," said Nicko. "It's my favourite one as well." Viktor replenished the glasses, spilling the vodka liberally across the table at the same time. Nicko ran a finger through the stream and licked it while Viktor opened a tin of red caviar and spooned half its contents into his mouth. He handed the rest to his friend who did likewise.

The vodka bottle was empty and the last tin of caviar broached. For a moment neither of them spoke, but Nicko was aware that there were still plenty of questions to be asked about Grandpa Nikishov. What had become of him after the party was over, for instance? Viktor had said that he'd had nine lives and didn't use them all up. He didn't like the sound of the man one little bit and resented the implication that he might be the equal of an Orloff. But, if what his friend had been telling him was true, he did have a point. After all, he liked to think that his Orloff ancestors had been larger-than-life Russians as well. And according to Nicko's own canon all true Russians were larger than life.

But now his brain was clouding and though clever-sounding things were pressing to be uttered, he was aware that he could no longer follow a logical train of questioning. Nicko was only eighteen, after all, and not nearly as good at holding his drink as he liked to think he was.

The same was equally true of his more worldly Russian friend and the symposium was rapidly disintegrating into a series of bombastic toasts and silly giggles. But there was no question of letting up. They were both young enough not to think that they needed to draw a line on it and call the thing to a halt…

"And the football team," mumbled Viktor. "Did I tell you about that? Stars from all the best Russian sides…serfs too… so when my dad buys Arsenal….or Chelsea…How do I say it?"

"Fuck it, Vik, don't even try."

One bottle of vodka remained, one of champagne and two of wine.

"Watering the wine…"

"Whayousay? Watering the wine?" Nicko mumbled. His head was now pillowed on his arms among the debris of the feast.

"This is a symposium, isn't it? So we should water the fucking wine…"

"Water the fucking wine…"

"That's what the Greeks did, isn't it? Watered the fucking wine…"

"The Greeks watered the fucking wine…"

Viktor lurched to his feet. "Water the wine…. Fucking water the fucking wine…." He rambled on in his native tongue as well, which, even if he had been sober, Nicko, despite his Russian soul, would never have understood.

"There's only one way to water the wine," said Viktor reverting to English, "and that's the Russian way."

"The Russian way," Nicko murmured from the kitchen table.

"Grandpa Nikishov's way."

"The Orloff's way."

Viktor staggered out of the kitchen, steadying himself in the doorway as he went.

Meanwhile Nicko closed his eyes, leaving the alcohol to take a complete hold. His eyes were fast shut when Viktor returned, carrying the Attic krater by one of its handles. He plonked it on the table among the detritus. Then, opening the freezer, he took out the remaining vodka and, ripping the metal cap off the bottle, poured its contents into the ancient vessel. It was followed by a bottle of wine and the last of the champagne.

Nicko had begun to snore and Viktor looked blearily round the kitchen, before staggering out once more. This time he returned bearing two drinking bowls- one depicting the act of sodomy and the other Oedipus and the Sphinx. He dipped the former into the krater and shoved it towards his friend, giving him a sharp nudge at the same time.

"Wake up, Nick," he mumbled. "Time to drink to Uncle Frank."

Nicko stirred, opening one eye. "Uncle Frank?"

"Drink up, Nick."

"To Uncle Frank, then… the old bugger."

Nicko blinked at the cup he was holding, but did not see anything amiss with it. He held it to his lips and slurped two large mouthfuls of the liquid before resting his head on the table once more. His friend dipped the Oedipus bowl into the krater and poured its contents down his own throat.

"Uncle Frank… the old bugger. Your turn, Nick."

"Oh shit," muttered the other. "Oh shit."

"That's not a toast," said his friend in Russian. "Come on Nikoshka," he added in English, "You're an Orloff!"

"An Orloff!" exclaimed Nicko suddenly seeming to wake up. "That's what I am - a fucking Orloff!"

"Just an Orloff, Nikoshka, not a fucking one." "And certainly not a fucking Nik… Nikishov…" "Not a fucking one of them either, Nikoshka…"

"If I want to say 'fucking' I'll fucking say it!" blazed Nicko. He sat right up and swallowed the fearsome liquid from his bowl which he dashed to the floor where it shattered on the tiles.

"Oh my God," murmured Viktor. "Oh my God." But then he followed suit, draining his bowl, before smashing it on the floor.

Nicko in the meantime had risen to his feet. "To Russia!" he yelled. "To poor fucking Mother Russia!"

He looked round in a confused way for a drinking vessel, now that his cup lay shattered on the floor. Then, lifting the krater, he raised it to his lips….

Early next morning the young men fled from the flat, leaving behind them the fragments of an Athenian red-figure krater and a pair of drinking bowls on the kitchen floor….

CHAPTER TWO

The Novgorod Master

For his gap year Nicko escaped to St Petersburg, where Viktor, meanwhile was wasting no time. Having turned nineteen and, feeling no particular need for further formal education, he was already pitching his stall. The time spent with the kind of upper middle class people he had encountered in an English public school had opened his eyes to the opportunities that might lie ahead in his own country. With a hefty financial back-up, he opened a boutique on the Nevsky Prospekt dealing in upmarket fancy goods and portable antiques.

For Nicko temporary exile was a necessary escape from the wrath of a parent appalled by the atrocity committed in Uncle Frank's flat. Naturally his father had done his best to make good the damage wrought by his son's outrageous behaviour, going to considerable expense in his efforts to do so, while Nicko had duly expressed his contrition in the manner of a medieval penitent. Then, stressing his Russian roots - of which Orloff Senior was himself proud - he had come up with the idea of taking a Russian language course in St Petersburg during his gap year, but being careful not to draw attention to Viktor's presence there, as he knew his father's opinions on the Soviet era in general and of the New Russian spivs who had settled like crows on carrion at its downfall in particular.

So Nicko, in the best tradition of a young radical of Tsarist times, went into exile, albeit an agreeable one, on the banks of the Neva. And it was no time at all before Viktor had made an appearance and offered him a generous supplement to his allowance for his services. Nicko's polished brand of Englishness was just what was required to get his enterprise up and running.

And it all went smoothly without any disasters of the kind that had occurred in Chelsea. Nicko, with his polished manners, helped sell the upmarket matrioshka dolls and hand painted lacquer boxes that Viktor was offering in his fashionable little boutique. There was a certain amount of carousing too, of course, with Viktor and his Russian cronies - young men on the make like himself - yet Nicko never once met any members of his family, who were, he was assured, tucked away safely beyond the Urals. Viktor had mentioned a brother, Semyon, who was a business man of a kind in Ekaterinburg, while his mother was dead and his father, having made a fortune during the decline and fall of the Soviet Union, had since become a recluse who seldom ventured from the house where he lived. It seemed strangely of a piece with Grandpa Nikishov, Nicko couldn't help thinking. And then when his time was up, it was back again to his own country to take up his place at St Andrews University in the following autumn, to read History.

A year later Viktor informed his friend of his marriage, but in all his four years at university Nicko saw his Russian friend just once, when he was on what he termed a fact-finding mission to the UK, to probe the art market. And then, apart from the occasional exchange on the Internet - which included plenty of schoolboy joshing - they had little direct contact with each other. Viktor once vaguely suggested it was time for his friend to come to St Petersburg, to meet Vera, his wife, and to see their baby boy, who was born shortly after the announcement of his nuptials. The child had been christened Nicholas, in honour of his father's old school chum, Nicko was informed, while Viktor also expressed a desire that he should take up the post of godfather. But then the family seemed to vanish completely, so that Nicko even grew concerned for their safety, knowing what things were going on in Russia at the time. He began to fear the worst for his friend, but there was nothing he could do about it, as he was trying to embark on a career of his own at the same time.

Then quite suddenly a breezy e-mail arrived out of Russia - seven long years after the two friends had gone their separate ways in St Petersburg: Viktor and family were settled now in Novgorod and were demanding a visit from their child's putative godparent! There were to be no ifs or buts about it: Nickolas Orloff was ordered to come at the first opportunity.

* * * * * *

The first thing that struck Nicko when he saw Viktor across the restaurant was that he had put on weight. For a man in his mid-twenties he looked a shade too comfortable, though it went well enough with his sturdy Russian build. And even before he reached his table Nick sensed that Viktor was doing well.

"Good to see you again, old boy," said Viktor in his agreeably blended plummy English and Russian accents as he hugged him warmly. "It's been a very long time."

"A lot of water has passed under the bridge," said Nicko.

"Say that again."

"Piss off, Vik. I think you know what I mean."

The Russian chuckled and squeezed his arm.

"Vera would have liked to have been here to meet you. But we felt that this was not really the place to bring a five year old malchik. You can't tear her from that child. Not with wild horses. Will that do?"

"It'll do nicely, Vik," replied Nicko. "The leopard hasn't changed his spots, I see."

For a second Viktor looked puzzled, then nodded.

"I'm dying to meet them both. Vera and Kolya," went on Nicko.

"Kaneshna. The malchik of course bears your name, as you know, the name of my dearest English friend."

"Thank you. I'm touched, but it's a common enough Russian one, surely?"

"Pravda," said Viktor. "But that's no reason for not giving my child the name of my favourite Englishman, is it? Oh, I apologise! My dearest Russian friend."

He pulled back a chair and placed Nicko at the table before sitting down himself.

"Yes," he resumed. "My dearest Anglo-Russian friend!" "You know something, Vik?"

"Try me."

"You're still full of shit."

They both laughed and Viktor squeezed his friend's shoulder affectionately. "What's it to be then- to kick off with? Vodka?"

"I think I'd better go easy on the vodka," said Nicko, "especially in your company."

"Oh dear, as bad as that, is it?" sighed Viktor. "And talking of such things, how is - what's he called? Uncle Frank? You told me that his precious vase had been glued together again and looked as good as new."

"He's dead."

"Oh dear. I am sorry to hear that. Poor old Uncle Frank! I hope his heart didn't break like his precious vase. Was he a very old man?"

"Not especially. In his later seventies."

"Old enough for a Russian, maybe, but these days you English are

19

expected to live a bit longer than that. And his collection? Including the what-do-you-call it?" He eyed his friend thoughtfully.

"The krater - the wine bowl. All gone - packed off to the Ashmolean Museum in Oxford. Lock, stock and barrel."

"Say that again, Nick."

"Piss off, Vik. The whole bloody lot. Every single piece. I don't think he trusted his own godson to look after it, not after our symposium."

Viktor laughed. "Our Russian symposium, you mean. And while we're on the subject, don't you think it's time we got - how do you say? stuck in?"

"What? Hold another Russian symposium right now, you mean? Here, in the restaurant? Well, I suppose we could trash the place. We are in Russia, after all. That chandelier might do for starters."

Viktor chuckled. "All the same it's sad about Uncle Frank's collection. To lose it like that, I mean. But it's water under the bridge by now, I guess. Did I get that right?"

"Vik, piss off will you?" Nicko gave him a gentle punch.

Viktor ordered a bottle of vodka - decently chilled - and a menu.

"I'm really looking forward to meeting Vera and the malchik," said his friend. "And yourself? Nothing, how do you say? Nothing to report?"

"Nothing to report," Nicko said. "But for Christ's sake, Vik, give me a chance, won't you? When I've reached thirty-five I'll start worrying about things of that sort. I have to make some money first. I don't have your knack for it. The stuff sticks to your fingers, but it doesn't to mine. I'm not exactly New Russian, as you know."

His old school friend said nothing, but raising his eyebrows, rocked his head from side to side, as if weighing up his statement.

* * * * * *

It was curious this friendship that had grown up in an English public school, between two products of Russia's turbulent twentieth century history: Nicholas Orloff, the great-grandchild of an aristocratic exile from the Bolshevik Revolution and Viktor Ilyich Nikishov, the scion of a Stalinist satrap who had once been the master of life and death in the Kolyma gold camps, Nicko, the aristocrat looking wistfully back on a lost past and the brash New Russian, who in so many ways reminded his friend of a flash character in a novel by Gogol.

The unfortunate affair of the smashed Athenian krater had sealed their friendship, yet to Nicko his friend was still something of an enigma. The source of his considerable wealth remained a mystery and, and he seemed to be oddly detached from the rest of his family, assuming that he still had one. He appeared to exist successfully in a post-Soviet business world and Nicko had not pressed the point. But ready-made wealth had not turned Viktor into an indolent lie-abed. He had a business bug coursing in his veins and the itch to trade was compulsive. His experience of an English public school had opened his eyes to a possible niche market for New Russians bent on the trappings of what might loosely be described as an English upper class lifestyle - anything from traditional country wear to household antiques. And the urbane upper-crust Englishman Nickolas Orloff, with his claim to Russian aristocratic roots, might have a part to play.

Nicko's father, who had made his views plain on the subject of Viktor and his like, would certainly look with distaste at any suggestion that his son might enter into a business arrangement with a Soviet upstart. And now that he had completed his degree, he was concerned that Nicko, who, unlike his sister, seemed to have no very clear idea of the direction his life should take, needed to be settled without wasting any more time. He had left university with a lower second and, having spent his gap year in St Petersburg with Viktor, he felt vaguely inclined towards something in the Fine Arts line. He had specialised in the Italian Renaissance for his degree and wondered if he possibly might make something out of that.

His father went quickly to work. He had an old chum in the in the antiques trade, who mostly bought up stuff at country house sales and the like which he sold on, so he approached him about Nicko.

Freddie Ryedale was what was euphemistically described as a confirmed bachelor who readily took to the polished exterior of this agreeable young man freshly down from university.

"I don't suppose I need to warn you about Freddie," his father cautioned Nicko.

"You mean I have to keep my bum to the wall, Dad?"

"In a manner of speaking yes, but I wouldn't have expressed it quite so vividly."

"Having survived an English public school I daresay I can handle that."

"As long as you keep it in mind, that's all. Actually I believe that Freddie's perfectly harmless. If he is a homosexual, it's almost certainly the repressed kind."

"A bit like Uncle Frank, you mean? He was gay, wasn't he?"

Nicko's father had not yet come to terms with the modern usage of the word 'gay', grumbling that it was a useful word whose meaning had been usurped.

"And another thing," he went on, ignoring the reference to Uncle Frank, "he won't be able to pay you a proper salary. It'll be pocket money to start off with and not much more."

Freddie Ryedale worked from a large old farm house near Aylesham in Norfolk, but his forays with a van sometimes took him as far afield as the North Riding of Yorkshire. He could be said to work the east side of the country and was prepared to take anything that caught his eye. And it was a pretty good eye too, especially for seventeenth century English oak furniture, as well as eighteenth and early nineteenth century topographical paintings and landscapes. He had committed one howler, though, when an early Constable had come his way, which had been properly identified only after he had passed it on for a tiny fraction of its true value. It was the kind of gaffe he swore never to repeat. His friends in the trade, looking at his relatively modest returns, tended to hark back to it among themselves, talking about 'Ryedale's luck', but Freddie did not repine as long as he could go on visiting the places he liked and mixing with the kind of people he found congenial. As a one man band he made just about enough to keep himself afloat.

And now, warming to Nicko's good looks and manners, he reined back whatever less than Platonic thoughts he might have been entertaining at the same time. As well as having an agreeable presence, Nicko was no threat to the tenor of Freddie's existence. He was given the spare room in his house and taken straight off on his first expedition. Nicko soon began to pick up a lot about old furniture, china and of course something of provincial landscape and topographical painting as well. He felt at home in the English countryside and enjoyed the work - except for one thing. He didn't earn a bean.

Already, three years into the job, he had sacrificed two summers to working with Freddie and, despite the satisfaction he found in the work, he felt in need of a break. He had no money put by from his notional salary to afford a holiday, while at the same time he hardly liked to go to his father, cap in hand. The ruined krater still cast its long shadow. So, perhaps inevitably, it came down to Viktor in Novgorod with whom he had renewed contact.

They had eyed each other's progress from a distance with curiosity, Nicko probably revealing more about his circumstances than Viktor about his. The latter was intrigued by his friend's attempt to get into the antiques trade, especially as it was the line he appeared to be most actively pursuing himself. Indeed, it was not difficult to guess why the young Russian entrepreneur might have been eager to keep in with his former school fellow. Nicko could see that himself, of course, but the romantic sentiments he felt for his lost ancestral homeland, still worked their magic. Moreover the Russian was rich while he was relatively poor. He badly wanted a holiday and Viktor offered him the chance of one - in Russia. And more than that, it was a chance to meet Viktor's wife for the first time and five year old Kolya.

And Vera was eager to meet him, Nicko was told.

He also liked the chance to visit Novgorod. He had only seen the place fleetingly in his original stint in Russia and a change from St Petersburg seemed timely.

Altogether it sounded like a good package and his flight was booked to Moscow from where he would take the night train to Novgorod.

The move had brought Viktor closer to Moscow and Novgorod was a pleasantly green, open-looking city with deep historical roots. Nicko had been left to find his way into the city, and the rendezvous in the fashionable restaurant was arranged for twelve o'clock on the day of his arrival. A reason, not disclosed, prevented Viktor meeting his friend at the station, but the directions to the restaurant in the kremlin walls had been clearly spelled out to him. After lunch they were to return together to the flat on the other side of the river.

* * * * * *

So Nicko left his case at the station and wandered through the park near the river, enjoying the warm sunshine, and stopping a couple of times for a cup of coffee and a beer, before going on to inspect Novgorod's great medieval kremlin. Eventually he made his way to the restaurant where he was to meet his friend.

It had occurred to Nicko as he approached Viktor across the dimly-lit, cavernous restaurant that the Russian had deliberately set it up this way: standing behind the table, with the snow white cloth and napery and the gleaming cutlery before him, with his arms half raised, ready to enfold his old school chum.

The vodka got things moving, while blinys and caviar followed with Georgian champagne, then a run of Russian dishes, whose flavours were not easy to identify, but which were subtle and a little mysterious - a bit like Viktor. In spite of his cautiousness - something he had managed to maintain even during his months in St Petersburg in the shocked aftermath of the notorious symposium - Nicko found himself drinking a good deal. Red wine followed the champagne while brandy arrived with the coffee. The bottle was left on the table for Viktor to ply his guest.

"When do we start playing monkeys on the chandelier?" he joked.

"My great-grandfather and his brother officers took pot shots at the with their pistols," said Nicko.

"My folk smashed a good few in their time too," supplied Viktor, determined to uphold the Stalinist service nobility's reputation for drunken vandalism against the claims of the more effete Tsarist officer corps.

They were giggling like a pair of schoolboys as fresh coffee arrived: the waiter was in no hurry to bring the bill, despite the fact that it was almost the middle of the afternoon. Viktor had seen to everything.

"Now," he said, placing an affectionate hand on his friend's shoulder, "tell me all about it."

"All about what?" asked Nicko. The drink had made him expansive, but had not yet clouded his wits completely. It was enough, however, to make him just a shade reckless.

"Your work, buying and selling nice things, the places you visit, all those old houses in the beautiful English countryside."

"I'm still learning, Vik, even now, after what? Three years. Building up the knowledge slowly. It's the only way to do it, not to force feed myself. I suppose Petersburg gave me an appetite for it. I have you to thank for that."

Viktor dipped his head in acknowledgement, in a mildly patronising gesture on the part of one who was the same age as his friend.

"But…"

"Ah! But…"

"There's still no bloody money coming in - for me at least. Don't get me wrong, Freddie's a great guy, but he can only pay me a pittance."

"Tell me about Freddie."

"About my father's age. Perhaps a few years younger. Unmarried. Lives for his work."

"Maybe a little like Uncle Frank?"

"Possibly, but a bit more down to earth than him, I guess."

"I see." Viktor did not expand the thought that appeared to be developing in his mind.

"He loves his work, but never has any fucking money, or so it seems, anyway. Mind you, he once could have done - if he hadn't let it slip through his fingers."

"What did he let slip through his fingers?"

"A Constable. You know Constable? One of our two finest nineteenth century landscape painters."

"And he lost it?"

"Dead right he did. Sold it on for practically nothing before anyone knew what it was. He's never had another break like that - or so he claims."

"Poor old Freddie. Even worse luck than Uncle Frank's vase being smashed, I guess. At least he was left with the pieces." "Shut up about the vase."

"Is he 'Uncle' Freddie?"

"No, of course he's not."

"Just plain Freddie, then. Who could do with a bob or two? Have I said that right?"

"Do I have to labour the point?"

"And you're fond of Freddie?"

"He's a nice enough guy."

Viktor frowned thoughtfully and reached for the brandy bottle.

"Steady on," Nicko warned him. "Remember I've still got to meet your wife and the malchik."

"I'd rather like to meet Freddie," mused Viktor, "but then perhaps that might not really be necessary."

"Oho? You have a cunning plan?"

"Do you feel up to it?"

"Up to what, for Christ's sake?"

"You mentioned… who was it? A painter."

"John Constable."

"Constable."

"Freddie Ryedale's blackest hour."

"Freddie deals mostly in pictures?"

"Not at all. He does other things mostly - probably that's why he screwed up."

"We must think more about this," Viktor said. "It's possible I could help - both of you." He looked at his watch." But now it's time for you to meet the Tsarina and the Tsarovich, Nickolas!"

He called for the bill, which he settled with his credit card, leaving the waiter a generous cash tip at the same time.

"Are you steady on your feet?" he asked Nicko.

"I think so."

"We'll take a taxi anyway. Your things?"

"At the station."

The girl at the cash desk rang for a taxi and they wandered down the wide staircase that led to the entrance built into the side of the kremlin wall.

Having picked up Nicko's luggage, the taxi took them across the river, skirting the religious heart of medieval Novgorod to a pleasant street of nineteenth century stuccoed houses. Little gardens lay behind them, rather unkempt in the Russian manner that Nicko liked. By now it was late afternoon and the street was empty. Viktor led the way through the big double door of one of the houses that gave onto the broad pavement. "We live on what you in England call the first floor," he explained, "the one above the ground."

"I like the look of this," Nicko said, looking down the street with approval as they entered.

"It's not the whole story. Yes?"

"Yes Vik. You mean there's more to it?"

"Kaneshna. Tomorrow I will take you to see our dacha."

"You have a dacha? I might have guessed. You're not letting the grass grow under your feet. Now work that one out." Nicko gave his friend a playful nudge.

"Piss off, Nick."

Despite the house being spacious and predating the Khruschev flat building era, its stairwell was dingy with the rather sour smell, common to so many Russian stairwells. Viktor was conscious of the anomaly.

"The usual thing," he told his friend. "We Russians don't change. We don't - how do I say? lift a finger to look after the what-do-you-call-it, the shared space?"

"That's one of the things that make you so exotic in western eyes. The squalor on the outside and lo, the opposite once you're inside."

"Russia in a nutshell?"

"Quite so, Vik."

"We curl up in the warmth and comfort of our homes away from the nasty world outside. Like a return to the womb?"

"Which is fine until the knock comes on the door at two o'clock in the morning."

Viktor sighed and shrugged his shoulders. They had stopped outside a large door on the first floor with a finely carved frame. Viktor rang the bell.

Slippered footsteps approached and Vera opened it.

"Welcome," she said, addressing Nicko in English.

"Try him in Russian," said Viktor, giving his wife a peck on the cheek. "He likes to call himself one." This was also said in English for the benefit of the guest,

Nicko gave Vera a peck on the cheek as well.

Viktor meanwhile slipped off his shoes and Nicko did likewise. "Try these for size," said Viktor, offering him a pair of slippers. Nicko shuffled into the flat through its ample vestibule and into the living room, the double glazed doors of which Viktor threw open before him with a ceremonial flourish. It was good deal larger than the rooms Nicko had seen in other Russian flats, with a high ceiling and a cornice from which several oil paintings in heavy gilt frames were hung by cords. The floor was polished parquet with several Turkish rugs distributed about it. A large round mahogany table with a lace-fringed cloth stood near the window, where the light was filtered through the lace curtain which stirred in a slight draught. There were a couple of deep leather upholstered sofas and several chairs covered in throws with pleasantly faded oriental patterns. On a bulky, almost baroque, dresser stood a massive samovar. An ikon and a lamp were set in one corner of the room.

"What do think?" asked Viktor.

Nicko nodded his head appreciatively.

"It's not bad for a New Russian, wouldn't you say?" Viktor slyly lowered an eyelid.

"I wasn't going to say that."

"But you were thinking it. Anyway, it was Vera who set it up," explained Viktor.

"She has a good eye. I'm impressed." Nicko looked round for Vera who had not followed them into the room. "Where is she, by the way?"

As he spoke she appeared in the doorway, leading a little boy by the hand.

"Meet Kolya," she said. "Kolya meet your uncle Nicko."

The child eyed Nicko critically for a second and smiled.

"Pleased to meet you, Kolya," Nicko said, offering him his hand. He looked at Vera.

"Should I speak in Russian?"

"English will do," she said.

"Where did you learn to speak your English? It's excellent."

"In the Pedagogical Institute in Petersburg," she replied. "And I worked as a tourist guide after that. I've done a couple of trips as well."

Viktor rumpled the child's flaxen mop of hair. "His mother's colour," he said.

"Tea?" asked Vera.

"Kaneshna," said her husband.

"Kaneshna," she repeated as she left for the kitchen.

Viktor lifted Kolya up and pretended to toss him up to the ceiling. The boy gave a little squeal of pleasure. When he returned to earth he looked at Nicko with a steady curious gaze.

"He's enchanting," Nicko said. "I'm trying to work out which of you he's most like. He's got his mother's colouring."

"His mother," said Viktor. "More like himself, I'd say."

Viktor pushed the child Nicko's way.

He told him in Russian to make friends with his uncle, which Nicko understood.

Nicko sat down on a sofa and placed the boy beside him, where he gazed at him with his thumb stuck in his mouth.

Vera meanwhile returned with the tea and a large bowl of raspberry jam.

"I see you've made friends," she said.

"You must be very proud of him," Nicko gushed.

"Kaneshna," said the boy's father.

"May I take him back to England with me?"

Both parents laughed as Vera poured the tea, before giving the child a spoon loaded with a generous dollop of jam.

She fired questions at Nicko about England: his university and what he was doing now. Then, leaving the boy with his father, she took him to his bedroom, pointing out the bathroom on the way.

"You must be tired," she said. "I can never sleep on trains."

"I'm all right," replied Nicko, "but I nearly fell out of the bunk."

"It was a hard carriage?"

"I'm afraid so."

"When you return to Moscow we must make sure that you have a better one," she said. "But it's so good to have you here with us. Vitya has told me such a lot about you."

Nicko laughed and made the conventional reply, hoping that it was only the good things.

"Kaneshna - of course. You're old friends."

"This room looks comfortable," said Nicko. "It much bigger than the ones you see in most Russian flats."

"The house is old and was the home of a bourgeois. I love the big rooms. Would you like a rest?"

"It might be nice to stretch out a bit, though I don't suppose I'll sleep. It was a big lunch."

Vera looked at him and nodded knowingly. "Rest for as long as you like," she told him. "There is no hurry here."

Nicko lay down, but a few minutes later Vera put her head round the door.

"Not sleeping?" she said.

"I'm afraid not, but your bed is very comfortable."

"Shall I draw the curtains?"

"One of them, but leave the other. I like the light at this time of day."

He looked at Vera as she crossed the room, really for the first time.

She was the opposite of Viktor, who was square and dark and already running to fat. Vera was also Slavic, but in a different mode. For a start she was slim, fair-haired and blue-eyed with a slightly repoussé nose and the high cheekbones, typical of many Russians. Nicko approved of the way she was dressed. There was nothing showy about it. He liked her muted lilac slacks, which came to just below her knees, and her chunky pale grey sweater. She wore a discreet pearl in each ear lobe and no make-up. She didn't need any.

"Feeling better?" she said, turning back to Nicko. "I'm sure Vitya gave you too much to drink."

"I'm feeling fine." Nicko caught himself pondering the contrast between the man and his wife.

"Don't let him give you more than you want," she admonished him.

"I think I know Vik well enough."

"Hm." She added nothing more. "Finish your rest," she told him from the door.

Nicko lay there woolgathering. Though he still knew virtually nothing about Vera or even where his friend had first met her, he found that she was filling his thoughts to the exclusion of anything else. She had a simplicity which was pleasing, as well as seeming to be acute. He wanted to try her out on Russian literature - something he had never been able to do with her husband, who in Nicko's eyes partly redeemed himself by appearing like a character out of its pages. But with Vera he felt that he might actually be able to discuss artistic questions without attaching monetary value to them - or at least that was the impression she had given him on this first encounter.

He took a book from his case and read a little as the light faded, thinking it best to wait until his hosts summoned him. And sure enough, when his watch told him that it was seven o'clock, there came a tap on the door.

"Yes?" Nicko called.

It was Viktor this time who stuck his head round the door. "Not - how do you say? in a state of nature?"

"It wouldn't matter if I was. You've seen me like that often enough before."

"All boys together - like in our Russian banya. Do you fancy one? We'll get it going up at the dacha."

"I'm on," Nicko said.

"Good. We will eat in a few minutes."

"God, I don't know where I'll put another meal."

"Tomorrow you can walk it off with some sightseeing - before we go to the dacha," Viktor informed him as he slipped away.

Nicko put his feet into the slippers - which were at least two sizes too big for him - and shuffled into the vestibule. It was getting dark, but there was a light on in the living room. Viktor was alone, poring over his laptop.

"Come and sit down, old boy," he said, reaching at the same time into the dresser for a couple of glasses.

"Golly," said Nicko. "I don't think I can handle any more drink. I'm sure Vera is a wonderful cook, but I hope she isn't preparing a big meal. We can leave that 'til we get to the dacha, can't we?"

"What kind of a Russian are you?" laughed Viktor. "But Verochka understands. She won't give you too much. As a matter of fact she tells me that I'm getting too fat."

"She's right, Vik. You're going to spoil your good looks if you're not careful."

"Fuck off, will you?" Viktor said it in a whisper out of deference to his wife, who presumably wasn't out of earshot.

He went out of the room and returned with what looked like rollmop herrings on a plate and a decanter of chilled vodka.

"You bloody man. You're quite impossible," his friend groaned.

Viktor charged the glasses, right up to the brim. "Nasdorovia!" he declared, downing his in one. Nicko sipped his.

"Now," said Viktor. "About Freddie."

"What about him?"

"He buys pictures, and sells them on, right?" "Right."

"That's where I might be able to help him. What I mean is that I could make a lot more money for him than he's making now, if what you say is true."

Nicko frowned and his friend eyed the mistrust in his face.

"Look old boy, it isn't very difficult. There are plenty of people I know here who would be only too willing to pay a hell of a lot more for the sort of thing he has to offer than he gets in his own country. Believe me, Nikoshka, I do know my own kind."

"I wouldn't dispute that for one second, Vik."

"I've been thinking- quite seriously. But maybe we should talk about it at the dacha - after the banya. He topped up the glasses, throwing back the contents of his own in one. "Nasdorovia!" he said again. "You're not drinking, Nikoshka." He put a hand on his friend's arm. "Don't worry. Take your time."

Vera appeared and spoke to her husband in Russian. "Would you like to eat?" she asked Nicko in English.

"You should really try him in Russian," interposed her husband. "He knows much more of it than he lets on. But I know my Nikoshka from the old times. He's a lazy boy. You must be strict with him."

Vera and Nicko exchanged a smile.

"I'm sure it'll be lovely, but I don't think I've got room for very much," he told her.

She smiled and nodded and Viktor lead the way into the dining room.

Vera had got it right. Instead of loading her guest with a lot more food, she had scrambled some eggs which she served up with dark rye bread. This was followed with a good old-fashioned compote.

"My babushka's recipe," she informed Nicko.

"And how can you improve on that?" he enthused. "Grandmother's recipes always turn out to be the best. God save the Tsarovich Kolya!! He declared turning to the boy sitting between him and his mother and raising his glass with the remains of his vodka.

Vera looked wistful and sighed. Nicko had recalled to her the fate of the last Tsarovich, the child called Alexis, son of Nicholas, and murdered in cold blood by Bolshevik thugs. And his sisters too. It was an unhealed wound running through Russian life, which still occasioned maternal sighs.

They did not sit about for long. Tomorrow would be the right time to open out in the proper Russian fashion.

Vera took the boy in hand. He had said little while they were eating, but had gazed at their guest with a steady curiosity.

"Bedtime," she announced in English, before repeating it in Russian. "Kiss your Uncle Nicko." The instruction was repeated in the boy's mother tongue.

The boy stretched out his arms and hugged Nicko close. He did not appear the least bit shy and the latter felt flattered.

"Now your Papa," Vera said in Russian.

The ritual was gone through once more, though Nicko could not help feeling that Viktor's response was a little more perfunctory, a matter of routine.

"An early night?" suggested Viktor and his friend concurred.

"Have you everything you need, Nikoshka?" his wife said, having returned from putting the child to bed. "You don't mind if I call you that?" "Not in the least. I'd be pleased if you did."

"With two Nikolais we can't have two Kolyas," she said. "Nikoshka suits me fine."

Vera followed him into the spare room, but instead of going straight out again, she sat down on the bed and, locking him in her arms, hugged him tightly, before planting a kiss on his lips.

Nicko's head swam and he prolonged the kiss as their tongues joined, releasing a further charge.

"You're such a beautiful boy," she whispered. "I've been looking forward to seeing you so much!"

"And you're a beautiful girl. I should try saying that in Russian, shouldn't I?" he murmured.

"I hope my Kolya grows up to be just like you." "He's beautiful the way he is. Like his mother."

Viktor shuffled into the kitchen opposite and Vera got up from the bed. Without a word she kissed her guest once more, on his forehead this time, and left the room, closing the door behind her.

Nicko switched off the light and lay back. That he might be cheating on his old school chum never crossed his mind.

It was a while before he slept. In the matter of girls Nicko was unfashionably, innocent. He had kissed them enough times before, but had always fallen short of the final consummation. It had felt fleetingly pleasurable, but this time something lingered. It was if Vera was still in the room, her head resting beside his own on the pillow. He turned to caress the place where it should have been.

Eventually he drifted off to sleep with Vera hovering on the margin of his dream, never quite at its heart, but a presence still, colouring it.

When he woke it was Viktor and the boy looking down at him. The child reached down and brushed aside a lock of hair that fallen across his face.

"Thank you, Kolya," Nicko said.

Viktor lifted the child from the bed onto the floor.

"What time is it?" Nicko asked, sitting up.

"Not late. It's turned eight o'clock. Verochka's preparing breakfast."

Nicko could hear someone singing softly in the kitchen.

"She's got a nice voice," he said. "A woman of parts."

He felt he should have expressed that differently somehow, but any innuendo seemed to have been lost on Viktor.

As the two men dawdled their way through breakfast in the kitchen, Vera busied herself in the living room where she sang softly or spoke to the boy in a mixture of Russian and English.

"I'll show you some of Novgorod," Viktor informed his friend. "We can have a kebab for lunch and go to the dacha in the afternoon. I will need to light the fire."

"I like the look of Novgorod," said Nicko. "It was a good idea moving down here."

"I've still got the shop in Petersburg," explained Viktor, "but it's quieter here - and more private."

"I want to see more of it after we've come back from the dacha," Nicko said.

"You shall. And in the meantime we must put our heads together while we're there. Yes?"

"Yes Vik."

Vera was still in the living room and her husband dumped the breakfast things in the sink. Kolya appeared in the doorway and was swept by his father onto his lap.

The child giggled and poured out a mixture of Russian and English while his father tickled him.

"He'll have to make up his mind," pointed out Nicko. "Whether it's to be Russian or English. But then it's not a bad idea to grow up with that choice. I wish it had happened to me."

"Your Russian soul, locked in an English prison," said Viktor in mock commiseration. "You unhappy malchik!"

Nicko mouthed "fuck off" back at him.

Meanwhile Kolya joined his mother in the living room, still talking his head off.

"He's not usually as talkative as this," his father said. "You seem to have loosened his tongue. And I haven't heard Verochka sing quite so much- not for a long time."

Nicko blushed and did not reply.

Taking their leave of Vera, they went out and strolled back towards the river and the kremlin. In the park Viktor lead his friend off into what was known as Yaroslav's Court. It had once been old Novgorod's market, as Viktor explained, but all that remained of that now was a seventeenth century arcade fronting the Volkov River. It stood alone, looking pointless, in an open space.

Nicko was struck by how green and spacious the place looked under the benign summer sky. A soft breeze gently eased along a scattering of clouds.

"You did well coming here," he told his friend.

Viktor took him into the Court Cathedral of St Nicholas. "Your very own saint," he said. "It's all that's left of the palace of the Princes of Novgorod."

It had recently been restored and they looked at the fragments of the twelfth century frescoes, including the one of Job covered in boils while his wife passed his food to him on the end of a pole.

"I hope my wife might do the same for me one day," joked Viktor.

Then they crossed the footbridge that took them to the main east gate of the Kremlin.

At the end of the bridge opposite the gate was a café tent which was selling beer and kebabs. They went inside and sat down at one of the tables.

"Let this be on me," said Nicko.

But of course Viktor wouldn't hear of it. "Later," he told him, "before you leave."

Nicko didn't argue.

"Tell me," said his friend, taking a pull at his beer, "what do you think of Verochka?" Viktor eyed him closely as he spoke, but there was nothing in his tone to suggest any misgivings about what might have passed between his wife and her guest.

"Impeccable taste on your part," Nicko assured him, trying to make light of it in a bluff fashion. "I couldn't have done better myself. As for Kolya, he's a gem too. You're a lucky old sod, Vik!"

Viktor nodded and beamed complacently. "Yes, I suppose I am. She's really an orphan you know. Both her parents were killed in road accident just outside Petersburg when she was only a year old. A drunk ploughed into them head on, but Verochka was in the back and escaped. Her grandmother brought her up and gave her everything she needed, but above all made sure of her education. She's a lot better read than I am."

"That wouldn't be difficult."

"Piss off, Nick. Anyway her babushka passed away a couple of years ago and now she's just got me and the kid."

Despite having had breakfast not long before, they each had a kebab and then wandered into the kremlin itself, but did not go into the Cathedral of Saint Sophia, Viktor suggesting that they store it up until they had got back from the dacha. Instead they ambled under the trees in the extensive park that lay along the river bank. Stopping at a small open air café, they drank coffee before Viktor lead his friend into the streets beyond the kremlin.

"It's so quiet here," declared Nicko. "It's making me feel quite sleepy."

Eventually they turned back to the footbridge, where they paused to gaze along the wide Volkov river where it flowed south through a grassy plain scattered with copses of birch and other deciduous trees. The golden cupola of a church was catching the sunlight a short distance from the river's bank in the middle distance.

"A cliché, almost, of Old Russia," mused Nicko. "Stari Russye. Levitan might have painted this very scene. In fact, I'm pretty sure he did."

"Most likely," replied his friend. "And while we're on that subject…." He paused and looked thoughtfully at Nicko, but did not continue.

They drifted slowly homeward, where Vera had been busy, packing up for the couple of days at the dacha. She had loaded two big plastic containers with food and drink, which her husband opened again and inspected.

"What's wrong?" she said. "I haven't forgotten your vodka." She smiled at Nicko as she spoke. "We Russians!" she said with feigned exasperation.

"Careful what you say," her husband warned her. "He's a Russian too, don't forget. A Count Orloff, no less!"

The conversations between them while he was around were carried on in English, Nicko could not help noticing, a language that they seemed to be at home in almost as much as their own. Part of him regretted it and he reproached himself for not making a more determined effort to speak Russian. But then he was hardly being allowed to.

Together they loaded up the car, Nicko carrying down a large bag holding Kolya's things. They included a teddy bear and again he reproached himself, this time for failing to bring the child a present from England. Something he wouldn't forget in future.

The car was in a lock-up at the end of the street and Viktor went to fetch it. Vera climbed into the back with Kolya and Viktor joined his friend in the front. Viktor set off at speed in a southerly direction along the embankment.

"Don't drive so fast!" his wife admonished him from the back.

He winked at Nicko and slowed down slightly. "We're out in the country," he explained. "I don't like being too close to other people."

"A poor communist you'd have made," Nicko said. "And me too."

The dacha stood on its own, screened on two sides by copses of birch.

"Pure Levitan!" announced Nicko, hoping to strike a chord with Vera.

"You know Levitan?" she asked.

"Kaneshna. I love his work."

"You have visited the Tretyakov?"

"Once, but I mean to go back - many more times."

"We must go together, then."

Nicko wondered if 'we' included her husband.

But now he was climbing out of the car and admiring the dacha. It was spanking new, but not built by his own hands, Viktor informed him. "I know some people do," he said. "But I'm not one. If I can pay someone to do it for me I will."

It was built in the traditional style of a Russian isba with elaborately carved and gaily painted window frames, a steeply-pitched roof with wooden shingle tiles and finials over each gable. But, unlike most isbas, it had two storeys and an outside staircase leading up to a balcony, also rendered in a folkish style.

Nicko wasn't quite sure about it from close quarters, but managed to come out with the right thing. "Most impressive," he said.

"It needs more time," Vera said. "Things always look better when they've grown older."

"Exactly so," enthused Nicko. "That's what I think too. In two or three years' time it's going to look great! It'll be real Levitan by then."

"The garden's round the other side, at the back," Viktor said.

He led the way up the stairs onto the balcony.

There was a central fireplace in the open living area. A table with chairs, whose backs were carved in a folkish style similar to that of the windows frames, took up one side. A sofa with a Turkey rug pinned to the wall behind it and a couple of armchairs were on the other. There were a couple of lesser rooms leading off from it. The place had an air of calculated simplicity about it.

"The kitchen is downstairs and there is a cellar," Viktor explained. "Oh and the loo- I'm afraid you'll have to go outside for that. We live very simple lives in the country." He shrugged cynically.

"And the banya?"

"Across the yard."

Nicko offered his services in getting it started, but Viktor insisted on doing it himself.

"You stay and talk to Verochka," he said. "She likes to practise her English and it mightn't do you any harm to try speaking Russian for a change." He dug Nicko playfully in the ribs,

"Kaneshna - except that I'm never allowed to."

"Perhaps the Orloffs only spoke French."

"Fuck off, Vik."

"Now say it in Russian!"

Viktor set off to light the banya while Nicko wandered down to chat to Vera in the kitchen. Kolya was fishing in the cupboard and piling its contents on the table.

"I like this," Nicko said.

"You do? Really?"

"Of course I do and the surroundings are good too. "

"I love the nature too."

"The countryside." It was the first time he'd had to correct her English. "The countryside. But I'm not so sure about Vitya. I think he's really a city kind of a person."

"He seems to enjoy playing with his banya."

"Oh he's very Russian, in spite of his education. He loves doing Russian things. That's the reason you like him, isn't it?"

"One of the reasons. There are others as well."

"But I mustn't forget - you're a kind of a Russian too,"

The boy had his head in the cupboard so she took the opportunity to stroke Nicko's hair - almost as if he was her second child.

Nicko laughed. "I'm really a bit of a fake."

"You're not a fake," Vera told him emphatically. "I think I know what a fake is. I ought to by now."

She did not elaborate and Viktor, who had set his fire, entered in search of a light.

"Having a good gossip?" he said in English.

"I'd like to watch you do this," Nicko said.

"Come along then and you might learn something every real Russian should know: how to fire up a banya."

Vera nodded at Nicko, as if granting him leave to go, and he followed his friend out into the yard.

Viktor had filled his furnace with small kindling logs from the woodpile and with newspaper. He had also added a touch of paraffin.

"Ready?"

"Fire away," Nicko said.

Viktor put his lighter to the paper which flared up.

"It draws well," commented Nicko.

"Which reminds me."

"Of what?"

"Of your friend Freddie and his pictures."

"Very droll, Vik."

"I'm being serious. There's a lot in this for him, you know, and for you too. But we'll talk about it later and then, when we're back in town, there's someone I'd like you to meet."

"You're being very mysterious."

"Remember where I've come from. I'm not a bloody Count Orloff" Viktor grinned and punched Nicko playfully. "But come on, let's have a beer while the water's warming up."

They went back indoors, where Viktor collected several bottles of Baltika Number Nine, and then up the stairs at the front to the balcony.

"This is the strong stuff," pointed out Nicko.

"Kaneshna."

Viktor expertly removed the cap of a bottle with his teeth and handed it to Nicko, then providing one for himself, he clinked it against his friend's. "Nasdorovia!"

They pulled at their bottles in silence for a few seconds until Viktor spoke.

"I'm waiting, Nick, for you to ask me some questions."

"What kind of questions?"

"Things like what I'm selling and what kind of a profit I'm making." He made an expansive gesture over his shoulder.

"I think I can guess- without having to ask."

"Can you really? Are you sure I'm not trafficking pretty Natashas into the U.K.?"

"Fuck off, Vik." Nicko raised his bottle in a toast.

"And you too. But you know I'm interested in pictures - seriously interested."

"And that's where Freddie comes in?"

"Kaneshna. But it's not just English pictures. They can be French or Dutch or German ones as well. From anywhere in fact."

"Can I ask you, Vik? Do you know very much about pictures?"

His friend shrugged. "Not a lot, but enough - for what I want, anyway."

"And what do you want - apart from the dosh?"

"That of course, but I want the sort of things that the people I sell to want. My New Russians." He grinned broadly, almost provocatively.

"But that's enough for now. I'll take you to meet someone when we're back in town. He's rather interesting. But no more 'til then."

"You're not going to tell me about him now?" "Nyet. So you can piss off."

He pushed another opened bottle Nicko's way.

They finished the remaining bottles before descending to the banya at the back of the house and the steppe ritual of cleansing. Viktor had everything laid on - the heated stones, for generating the steam, the birch twigs and jugs of cold water. When the time came for it, he plied the birch twigs on Nicko as he stretched naked on the slatted bench. Viktor was adept, the twigs passing crisply from the base of his friend's thighs and up to his shoulders. It felt good, and Nicko wished that he could have performed as well for his chum, but Viktor, after his cautious essay, took the twigs from him and beat himself down effectively. Afterwards the pair of them sat in the steamy heat and reminisced about their schooldays, their talk consisting mainly of smutty appraisals of how their former peers had looked in the showers. Nicko felt a slight twinge of guilt at this regression into adolescence, but enjoyed it nevertheless.

Finally Viktor dashed cold water over him and he returned the favour. It was supper time.

The two days at the dacha passed peacefully. Nicko walked out a couple of times with Vera and Kolya, but while their talk rattled along very happily, they did not repeat their brief intimacy. Vera's English was well-nigh perfect and she was not given the kind of pedantries that Viktor was inclined to. It went without saying that Nicko's Russian was making no progress whatsoever.

Otherwise Nicko played with Kolya, who was a communicative child, happy to mix the two languages together. And there were expansive chats with Viktor about large questions such as the long term future of Russia and the nature of its government. Viktor talked about his own plans in a general kind of way, but for the time being was keeping off the topic of Freddie Ryedale and the buying in of English pictures. Nicko talked wistfully of his Orloff ancestors, Viktor listening with a gently indulgent smile. They had two more banyas and of course drank far too much Baltika Number Nine, of which Viktor appeared to have a limitless supply.

* * * * * *

It was an overcast day when they returned to Novgorod, but pleasantly cool. Nicko liked the grey tones that the landscape had assumed. Grey had always been his favourite colour - for its subtle gradations and for the way that it set off other, brighter, colours.

In the afternoon Viktor walked with him to a street not very far from his own. It was close to the church of the Apostle Philip, running off Ulitsa Nikolskaya. By now the sun had started to break through the clouds, sending out ray like beams. It was a magical effect.

The little side street seemed to be completely deserted. Its houses and the fencing that separated them had that unkempt look which Nicko thought of as typically Russian and admired, as if the Russians were somehow spiritually superior to the Germans with their neurotic neatness. Near its end Viktor pushed open a wooden gate which scraped noisily on the pavement and led the way into a courtyard. At the same moment the sun sent out a burst of light which irradiated the scene in front of them.

"This is the real Russia!" exulted Nicko. "What's the name of that painter, Vik?"

"You're not still talking about Levitan?" Viktor smiled and shook his head dismissively.

"No! No! Polyenov! That's the guy, Vik! You must know that marvellous painting of his!"

Viktor eyed the scene before him and clicked his tongue reflectively. "Come on! You know the one I'm talking about!"

"Do I?"

"Of course you do, Vik." Nicko swept out his arm, taking in the yard with its dusty patches and vivid green grass; its shrubs growing against the wooden fence at the side of the house. Everything the yard seemed to be lit up from within. In the middle of the scene two grubby children with vivid straw-blond hair were playing in the dust.

"Polyenov!" exclaimed Nicko once again. "Polyenov!"

"If you insist," Viktor said. "But come to think of it, I see what you mean."

"It might be that wonderful picture of his in the Tretyakov!"

"Russia in a nutshell, you could say?"

"Piss off, Vik, but yes, you're right. It is Russia in a nutshell."

Viktor approached the two children playing in the dust and asked them if Leonid Antonich was at home.

"Da," replied a flaxen-haired cherub, pointing in the direction of an open door.

"Is it Leonid Antonich that we're going to see? "Nicko asked. "Are these his kids?"

"No," said Viktor. "They belong to his landlady. Oksana Andreevna."

Beyond then open door, on the ground floor of the house, was a cluttered kitchen with a vast fridge of Soviet dimensions where a young-middle-aged woman was slicing vegetables. She nodded at Viktor in a familiar way and pointed to the worn wooden staircase leading to the floor above.

"Spasibo, Oksana Andreevna," Viktor intoned as he started up the stairs without bothering to introduce his friend.

On the landing a door was ajar, past which a shaft of sunlight filled with of dust specks thrust its way onto the dark landing. Viktor put his head round the door. There was a whispered conversation before he turned back to Nicko. "Come," he said. It was a large room with a north-facing window and another to the west where the sun was just starting to sink through a now clear sky. A couple of paintings were perched on a pair of easels while a large work table was spread with colour photographs- mostly close-ups of trees, Nicko noticed. There was a piece of board serving as a palette with different pigments arranged round its perimeter and jars of oil, and clumps of brushes of different sizes.

Viktor introduced his friend to Leonid Antonich, speaking of course in Russian with occasional English offerings thrown in Nicko's direction.

Leonid was short, with an untidily-cropped grizzled beard. He wore a large apron, made of what looked like sailcloth and covered in daubs of paint. Smiling pleasantly at Nicko, he revealed a gold front tooth, and dipped his head graciously as Viktor introduced his friend, not forgetting to mention his aristocratic Russian roots, which seemed to make a favourable impression on the artist.

Nicko's eyes wandered to the easels and the pictures on them. One was an exquisite rendering of a stand of birch trees in a forest glade. They were catching the late afternoon sun, which seemed to be possessed of the same degree of luminosity as he had just witnessed in the yard outside. He nodded his appreciation to the artist, who smiled back and returned his nod. Then he looked at the other easel and saw what was quite clearly an old picture. At a glance it could have been a Dutch or Flemish landscape - flat, with clumps of trees, like parkland almost, retreating into the distance under billowing clouds. There was the telltale windmill and a few cattle grazed in the middle distance, while a pair of figures appeared to be fishing on a canal bank in the foreground. Of its kind it was a little jewel and Nicko could not say which of the two works he liked the best.

"Do you understand?" asked Viktor.

"Two very good pictures," Nicko replied, "but no, I don't quite."

Viktor smiled and exchanged a glance with Leonid. "I'll explain it to you, then. But I think it's fairly obvious."

"Not to me it isn't, but I'm listening."

"Are you familiar with the works of Shishkin? "

"A nineteenth century Russian painter who specialised in woodland or forest scenes. I've seen his work in the Tretyakov."

Viktor nodded in the direction of the painting on the easel.

"Is this one a Shishkin?" said Nicko. "It's a gem whoever painted it." Viktor nodded in the direction of Leonid who appeared to be following what they were saying, despite their conversation being in English. The painter smiled and shrugged his shoulders in a self-dismissive manner.

"You mean…?"

"Yes I do mean. He painted it."

Nicko looked at the picture closely. "It's beautiful. But…Couldn't that make it a forgery…technically speaking?"

Viktor shrugged and raised his eyebrows. "Why should it? It's a matter of opinion, isn't it? It isn't an exact copy of another picture, if that's what you mean by a forgery. Painted in the manner of Shishkin, that's all. And if it's as good as a Shishkin and people want to believe it's one, who gives a damn apart from a few experts?"

"But saying it actually is by Shishkin is a lie, surely? Will you sell it as one?"

"If it's that what people want to think. If it makes them happy to believe it's by him and they are prepared to pay me a decent price for it - which makes me happy. This talk about forgery is just a game for a few experts."

"An interesting point of view." "A sensible one."

"What does Leonid himself think?"

Viktor spoke to the painter softly in his own language and the man shrugged his shoulders, spread his hands and smiled broadly. He uttered the Russian word for 'money' which of course Nicko knew.

"I think you got that," said Viktor.

"He's a bloody good painter all the same," Nicko said. "Isn't he wasted playing this sort of game?"

Leonid Antonich, who appeared to understand, shook his head. "There's your answer," Viktor said. "He's perfectly happy that people believe his paintings are done by Shishkin and admire them for that reason, when all the time he knows that they are really the work of Peshkov. It amuses him."

Leonid was nodding vigorously and chuckling at the same time.

"Well, I suppose it tells you something about art critics," observed Nicko.

"It certainly does."

Nicko lifted the picture, which was about eighteen inches square, from the easel and turned it round.

"This is already an old picture!" he exclaimed as he examined the back. "At least the canvas and the stretcher look as if they are."

"Sure it's an old picture - but with a few adjustments to meet the market. You can take it from me Shishkin's in great demand these days - as you might imagine- especially with Russians of the newer kind. They might be new, but they like pictures that look old."

"Very droll, Vik. And this one?" Nicko pointed to the Dutch landscape. "You're surely not going to fuck this one up too, are you? Really, you mustn't touch it, Vik."

Viktor put on a token display of being affronted. "Leonid here would be very distressed if you accused him of fucking any picture up," he protested. He explained what had just passed to the painter who chuckled loudly.

"I grant you he's done a superb job with the er Shishkin," conceded Nicko, "but it would be sheer vandalism to alter the other one in any way!" He flourished a hand at the easel and nearly dislodged the precious painting.

"You should see what Leonid Antonich can do to cows." Viktor went on. "He's a real magician and turns them into bears and even camels if he wants to. A real magician! A shaman from the old times!"

Nicko shook his head.

"What's the matter? Most painters down the ages have been prepared to touch up and even paint over an earlier work if the money's right, haven't they? However good it was supposed to be. Even I know that. Pay them enough and they'll do anything! You see, Old Boy, every time it comes back to that word - denghi."

He had used the Russian word for money, but Leonid Antonich was taking it all in anyway. It was, after all, exactly what he was up to.

"And I'm sure you're chum Freddie Whatsit is no different from anyone else when he smells the stuff," Viktor went on. "And you, Nick? What about you?" He poked him in the ribs slyly.

"So what do you want from me?" Nicko asked.

"Now we're getting somewhere. Nothing very difficult, Nick, nothing that might dirty your conscience - you smelly White!"

Leonid Antonich, who understood, discharged a guffaw.

"You can see for yourself," went on Viktor, "how good our friend here is. I defy you to say that his version of a Shishkin is any less good than one done by the man himself. It might be better even."

"But all the same, don't mess around with something that's already good." Nicko pointed again at the little Dutch landscape.

"All right. For the moment I accept what you're saying to me. But you agree with me about the Shishkin and the Peshkov?"

"What's he's doing may be good, but it's still a Peshkov, not a Shishkin - which is not the same thing."

"Sure it's a Peshkov, but does that make it any less good? You still have some way to travel, my White friend, if you're serious about selling pictures."

I'm not sure that I want to travel down that particular road."

"Do you have any idea how much this is likely to sell for?"

Nicko shrugged. "Not a clue."

"It could be as much as forty thousand dollars and in roubles that works out at…You work it out, Old Boy."

"And some sap of a New Russian will take your word for it that he's buying the real thing?"

"Sure he will. If he wants it badly enough - as most of them do."

Nicko laughed. "You really are a bloody crook, aren't you Vik? A bloody cheat and a liar! But a clever one. I have to give you that."

Viktor threw back his head and guffawed, joined by Leonid Antonich.

"But to be serious for a moment, Nick," went on Viktor, "I will - how do you say? lay my cards on the table? All I ask is this. If you and your friend Freddie can push a few pictures in my direction I'll pay a decent price for them. They don't have to be very good ones. In fact it would better if they aren't. I do understand your feelings about this Dutchman, believe me. But they need to be old and-well- adaptable. Leonid here will probably make them into better pictures than they were before. Take that Shishkin - or Peshkov. It was quite frankly shit before he worked on it, but look at it now. I can see you like it."

No translation was needed for Leonid Antonich who nodded in agreement and dipped his head in acknowledgement of the compliment that he had just been paid.

"He's a bloody good painter," conceded Nicko. "There's no question about that and I can honestly say that I admire his work."

Leonid Antonich seized his hand and shook it warmly.

Viktor put an arm round the man's shoulder. "The Novgorod Master," he said.

Nicko dipped his head in acknowledgement. "The Novgorod Master," he echoed.

They fell silent, looking at one another, waiting for the first to speak.

"All the same I'll have to have a word with Freddie first," Nicko came out with at length. "I can't take him for granted. We mustn't get too carried away." "Kaneshna."

"And getting the stuff out to you is going to be a bit of a problem, isn't it? Pretty dodgy as a matter of fact."

"Leave all that to me. I have ways."

"Of course you do, you old cunt. There's no stopping you once you've got the bit between your teeth, is there?"

"Say that again."

"Piss off Vik."

They glanced at Leonid Antonich to see if he could make anything of their school banter, but he merely looked back at them with a smile that almost celestial. Before they left he took them to a bench at the far end of his studio behind which was a collection of small vats, rather like a canteen serving unit. Each one contained a different pigment.

On the bench were bottles containing different coloured powders, some with what looked like small pieces of rock, and a glass mortar and a pestle. Viktor picked up a fragment of what looked like dark blue glass.

"The lapis lazuli stone," he declared. "The precious ultramarine from beyond the Caspian!"

Leonid Antonich explained something in Russian which Nicko was able to understand.

"He's saying that he was a chemist before he switched to being a painter?"

"Exactly so," Viktor said, "and a museum - how do you say? conservationist?"

"Conservator. So he really does know his stuff?" Nicko dipped his head to the painter in homage to his undoubted skills.

"What's this for?" said Nicko pointed at what looked like an oven door set into the wall. "Does he cook his pictures as well?"

"In a way he does - to provide - you should know - you've studied the thing, haven't you? Craq…."

"Craquelure," supplied Nicko.

"Your French is better than your Russian," said his friend.

"It means the network of tiny cracks that forms over the surface of an oil painting as it ages. I take my hat off to you, Vik."

"Say that again. Take your hat off to me?"

"You know perfectly well what I mean, so fuck off."

* * * * * *

When they got home and after they had eaten Viktor suddenly announced that he had some business to attend to on the other side of town that same evening and would be taking the car. He would not be back before the morning.

"A little sudden, isn't it?" Nicko said.

"It's the way these things happen," his host explained. "But I'm sure Verochka will look after you. And you can always talk to Kolya in English. The sooner he learns to speak it the better."

"Can I ask- what kind of business?"

"The kind that has to be washed down with a good deal of vodka. That's why I don't want to drive home before the morning."

Vera looked on and said nothing.

"Good bye, darling," he said to his wife in English, pecking her on the cheek as he left.

"Well, well," said Nicko as a way of picking up the thread. "He never stops, your Vik, does he? Always on the move."

Vera sighed. "Sometimes I wish he'd settle down, but I don't suppose he'd make so much money if he did. But is it really worth it? You're not a bit like him, are you, Nikoshka? Do you mind if I call you that?"

"Please do. It makes me feel like a child."

"Does it really, Nikoshka? But isn't that what you are - a little boy?" Leaning over him where he sat at the kitchen table, she gently passed her fingers through his hair.

"I like you doing that."

"Do you, Nikoshka?" She kneaded it again and gave it a sharp tug.

47

"Ouch!"

Vera went into the living room and switched the television on for Kolya so that he could watch a fairytale. She closed the door as she left.

"Tea?" she said to Nicko in the kitchen.

"Please. And some of your delicious jam."

Soon it was all on the table. Nicko dipped his spoon into the jam greedily and Vera gently rapped the back of his hand.

"Don't be greedy, Nikoshka," she admonished him.

Nicko sipped his cup noisily. "This is the best way of drinking tea that I know."

Vera placed a hand on his knee and they drew closer.

"It's nicer this way," she said. "By ourselves."

Nicko shifted back an inch, which did not go unnoticed by the Russian.

"You must stop thinking of Vitya," she told him. "He's not jealous. He's not that kind of a person. He's too busy making money and anyway if the mice like to play sometimes, he can be a very naughty pussy-cat!"

"That's something he's never talked to me about."

Vera stroked the bridge of his nose. "You're so English, in spite of your Russian name."

"What do you mean by that, exactly?" Nicko retorted.

"Don't be cross," she said. "It's what I like about you. It's the thing that makes you sexy."

Nicko took another large sip from his cup. "I like my tea hot. Very hot."

"Is that English too?" Vera took a large dollop of jam on her spoon and pressed it against his lips. "Open your mouth, Nikoshka. Wide."

He did as he was told. She pressed two more spoonfuls home. "Good boy."

Nicko leaned across the table, rested his head on his hands and closed his eyes while Vera got up and approached him from behind. She started to massage his shoulders and he purred like a contented pussycat.

"You like that, don't you?"

He simply purred his contentment.

"A good little English boy - or are you really a Russian one? A malchik?"

"Both."

"My little Nikoshka!"

He let her rub his shoulders, while not quite knowing what was expected of him. But then he didn't really need to. Vera handled him with the tender firmness that a mother might use on her own child, which suited him perfectly.

* * * * * *

It was the middle of the following morning when Viktor returned, by which time the two naughty mice were up and about and he found the boy sitting in Nick's lap in the living room.

"Quite the dad," Viktor said. There was not the slightest hint of jealousy in his voice.

"He's a delight, Vik. You must be very, very proud."

"We'll have to make a man of him," Viktor declared. "He mustn't be spoiled."

"I'm sure that won't happen."

"He must go to his father's old school - and his Uncle Nicko's." "What does Verochka think?" He knew the answer already, but felt he ought to hear it from Viktor.

"She wants him to be an English boy. She has very definite ideas about what English boys are like. As I think you might have discovered by now." He grinned at his friend, who glanced away.

For the time being nothing more was said about the piece of business that has been broached in Leonid Antonich's studio. Nicko sensed that his friend having planted the seed was giving it time to germinate.

Together the pair of them visited more of the churches that dotted the old city and drove with Vera and Kolya into the neighbouring woods for a picnic. There were a couple more banyas and barbecues out at the dacha and they went fishing on the river where it flowed into Lake Limen. Viktor was a competent fisherman, but Nicko, who had fished for salmon on a Scottish river once or twice, was able to hold his own and though the catch was meagre and strictly of the coarse variety, he felt that he had outfaced the New Russian on one occasion, at least.

The fortnight passed happily with Viktor staying away for a couple more nights, leaving the mice free to play by themselves, which they did with increasing abandon. Vera revealed to Nicko her hopes for her child to an extent that he suspected that she never did with her husband.

"I do so want him to grow up an English boy," she kept insisting.

"Just like his father?" said Nicko. "He had a good English education."
"No, not like his father," she said. "He's a New Russian. Kolya mustn't be like that."

"But without New Russian money such things wouldn't be possible, would they?"

"Kaneshna. But I think you know what I'm trying to say to you, Nikoshka." She pinched his ear and stroked his hair. "You're so gentle," she said.

They sank back onto the pillow and said no more.

* * * * * *

Before leaving for home Nicko sat down with Viktor and together they drafted a letter to Freddie Ryedale, which only Viktor signed. He would be in London in October when they ought to meet. Effusive compliments were heaped on Nicko, which he managed to tone down. Despite his time in England, Viktor had still not quite got the hang of English understatement.

Nicko knew that he would need to tread carefully. Freddie certainly stood in need of a bob or two, but shady cross-border deals had never been in his line. He could be described as a guileless snob - affable, happy not to push his luck too far as long as he could go on moving in the kind of circles he liked. It was small wonder that he had missed out on the Constable. Nicko reckoned that it would probably be better not to put him wise to the fate of the pictures he dispatched to Russia. He merely needed to be told that in Russia there was a hearty appetite for English landscape painting.

Viktor, having discussed him with his friend, had made a shrewd guess at Freddie's character, it went without saying.

And so it turned out. When Nicko, back in England, quoted the kind of sums that really very modest works fetched on the Russian market, Freddie was drawn. He had a residual reluctance about selling homegrown works of art abroad, the dispersal of what he termed 'our island heritage', but at the same time he approved of the idea of disseminating Englishness among foreigners who were receptive to it. Freddie Ryedale was an old-fashioned armchair imperialist. He could be quite hardheaded and drive a decent enough bargain at a local level if he needed to, but he was distinctly fuzzy when it came to thinking of a wider world. For one thing, he seldom took a holiday abroad.

Nicko explained the Russian market and Freddie tugged at his bowtie and assumed a thoughtful expression. He always tugged his tie when he was trying to convince someone of his expertise. In front of him was Viktor's letter.

"Your Russian chum seems to think pretty highly of you," he observed.

Nicko shrugged his shoulders. "Russians tend to lay it on a bit thick," he replied. "It's all or nothing with them."

Freddie frowned in a businesslike manner. "Are they really as interested in English landscape painting as all that?" he asked.

"It would seem so," said Nicko. "They are very romantic about all things British. You know, Big Ben, Scotsmen in kilts, the Queen, that sort of thing."

"Would they like some highland cattle? I get loads of them and I'd be only too glad to shed a few. Most of them are just wallpaper."

"I'm quite sure they would."

"Good," said Freddie in a show of decisiveness which combined banging the table and giving his bowtie a final jerk. "I think we might do business with your Russian chum, don't you? Providing we can sort out the paperwork, of course."

That morning he had received a statement from his credit card company and the amount of interest due was terrifying.

Freddie was introduced to Viktor in London - an occasion that tied up a number of loose ends - and trade opened with a batch of highland cattle which Viktor assured them that he was likely to sell for a moderately good price, because there apparently was a demand for them, but landscapes with rivers and trees were the kind of thing he was really after. These, of course, could be most readily modified for the Russian market - something that was not explained to Freddie, it went without saying. The names of Shishkin and Levitan were the ones most frequently mentioned to Nicko, who, having seen Leonid Antonich's skill at running up a Shishkin for himself, was ready to take the bait - especially after the dispatch of a very commonplace nineteenth century Midland landscape - the work of an obscure provincial painter he had never heard of. Viktor e-mailed him a photo of it in its transformed state: it had been turned into sweeping view of wooded steppe and water, which was passed off as a Levitan. Its provenance was rendered sufficiently plausible by the upheavals the Revolution which created the necessary obfuscation. Viktor was able to provide such cover for his transactions, though, as he pointed out to Nicko, it was astonishing the number of clients who did not even bother to ask for it, their desire for what he was offering them far outweighing such technicalities.

Viktor kept his side of the bargain and paid Freddie promptly. When it came to paintings of the nineteenth and early twentieth century the Russian naturally had first refusal. Usually Nicko would e-mail a snapshot of the work with a few covering comments and wait for his response which was seldom slow in coming. Viktor in his turn would later send back a photograph of the same work after Leonid Antonich had worked his magic. And Nicko's admiration for the Novgorod Master grew by leaps and bounds. But he never passed these images on to Freddie, who continued to believe that the things he dispatched to Russia were being sold in their original state and were meeting a rather touching desire for English things. Nor did the people from whom Freddie acquired the works ask any awkward questions either, trusting his home grown manner as they had always done, and accepting the valuations he placed on them in the English marketplace.

So Freddie was able to pay off his credit card debts sooner than he had expected, while his visits to house sales extended into fresh territory. Indeed, he grew to relish the hunt and started to shed some of his old languor. His associates noticed the change and most of them put it down to the young thruster he had taken on as his assistant. Ryedale's luck seemed to be on the turn.

It was almost too good to be true and eighteen months on from that first dispatch of highland cattle, Nicko was packing up three or four canvasses at a time to be transported by the channel that Viktor had discreetly arranged. He left the selection to Freddie, adding only the occasional passing comment. The truth of course was that Nicko was still somewhat green and had some way to go in judging the merits of English provincial landscape and topographical painting by himself. But he loved Leonid Antonich's transformations that Viktor passed back to him and continued to be amazed at the way in which the man could turn an English thatched cottage into a Russian isba. It was managed with such finesse that he felt that no violation had taken place - quite the opposite if anything. It was a wonderful piece of magic - a frog being turned into a prince.

One day, when autumn was drawing to a close, and the first real chill of winter was in the air, Freddie approached his assistant with a worried frown. He had an ancient saleroom catalogue in his hand.

"Nicko? I turned this up by chance. I found it in a job lot of books I was going through." He pointed at a colour photograph of a woody landscape.

Nicko glanced at the title page of the catalogue which dated it to the mid Fifties.

"Do you recognise it?" Freddie went on. "It looks familiar, doesn't it?"

"It certainly does. It went off with the last consignment. It'll be in Russia by now."

"Is there any chance of getting it back?" asked Freddie anxiously.

"Is there a problem? It's a bit late in the day, but I could e-mail Vik and find out whether he's sold it or not."

"I wish you would," said Freddie. "You see who it's by, don't you?"

"Not another bloody Constable, for Christ's sake?"

"No, not this time," said Freddie miserably, "but just as bad. I can't think why I didn't spot it."

"Gainsborough," said Nicko. "We mustn't let that one go. I'll get onto Vik straight away."

"God," groaned Freddie. "It'll be worth a bomb - far more than they'll ever give me for it! There's not a moment to lose!"

Although Nicko recognised the picture from the catalogue, he recalled that it had not struck him as anything particularly special when he had first set eyes on it. It was a modest oil sketch and had come out of a tied cottage on a large Lincolnshire estate, where it probably had been a kind of thank-you gift to a retiring housekeeper or someone of that ilk. But the Fifties catalogue was quite specific in attributing it to Thomas Gainsborough.

Nicko e-mailed Viktor in Novgorod, enquiring about the picture and a day later had a reply from Vera, saying that her husband was in Novosibirsk and it would be several days before he would be back. "A good time for the mice to play, my little Nikoshka," she cooed. "I'm sad that you're not here."

Nicko explained the hold-up to Freddie, who wrung his hands miserably.

"I simply can't believe it," he complained. "I fucked with a Constable and now I've done it again with a Gainsborough."

It was very unlike Freddie to utter profanities of that kind.

"It was easy to miss," commiserated Nicko. "After all, it didn't look much. Very much a minor work I'd say."

"That's hardly the point, is it? It's one thing to export all that dross, but minor work or not, this is a work by one of our greatest painters. It's a part of our national heritage. I feel I'm a traitor."

"It might find a good home," suggested Nicko, hopefully. "Someone who cherishes it. And anyway, all is not yet lost. Viktor might send it back."

"God, I hope so," moaned Freddie. "Bloody Ryedale's luck! Have you sent him another e-mail?"

But Nicko did not need to. When he got home there was a message from Viktor already waiting for him which described his visit to the Siberian capital at considerable length where things were really opening up. "You said something about a picture," he eventually got round to saying. "I'm not sure which one you mean. You need to tell me a bit more. Let me have a photograph. You've got one, surely? And here are a couple more Peshkovs for your approval, by the way. Verochka sends her naughty English boy her love. I wonder what I'm meant to make of that?"

Two of Leonid Antonich's works were appended for Nicko's delectation, one of which was a woodland scene in the manner of Shishkin and it took Nicko no time to work out what almost certainly lay hidden beneath its surface. English ash trees had been transformed into birches and a shepherd, in the best shamanistic fashion, had become a mother bear, a couple of his sheep her cubs, while the rest of the flock had been spirited into nothing. It was a magical transformation and Nicko was in doubt which version he liked the better. But then, of course, Nicholas Orloff had a Russian soul…

CHAPTER THREE

To Montenegro

Nicko was impressed by the sight of Kotor as they passed its old walls on the way to the bus station on the far side. To the right, on the bay's margin, the yachts and motor boats of the rich were moored and alongside them, a vast cruise liner - more like a block of flats than a seagoing vessel. But the old city stood as it had done, since the Middle Ages, enclosed by ramparts that appeared to mount almost vertically up the slope behind to the fortress on the crest of the ridge. Along the stretch by the road was an arcade filled with market stalls and thronged with people, and not just tourists, it seemed to Nicko, taking it in cursorily as he rode past. Already in Montenegro he felt that bit closer to the East than he had done in his brief stop in Croatia.

The bus swung into the station and drew up at one of the platforms. A crowd was expecting it, including women with cards offering rooms in three languages. As the passengers descended, these pressed forward, picking out the tourists, most of whom were backpackers, with a practised eye. Glancing around for his friend having unloaded his bags, Nicko politely spurned their offers.

Where was Viktor? He could see no sign of him or of his family. There surely couldn't have been a mix-up with the date or his time of arrival? That was not like Viktor. Then he saw him, standing in the doorway leading out of the ticket office. He was dressed in a pair of baggy shorts and a striped t-shirt, not unlike the ones worn by the Russian military, Nicko could not help noticing, and a baseball cap. He was eying the crowd by the bus, but appeared reluctant to enter the fray. Then Vera emerged from the ticket office, leading Kolya by the hand

"Vik, you old tosser!" Nicko called out. "I'm over here!"

Viktor advanced through the now dispersing passengers and hugged his friend against his chest. For a few seconds neither of them spoke.

"It's been a while, my Russian brother," Viktor came out with at length. He repeated it in Russian.

"It has indeed," Nicko responded, "and much water has passed under the bridge in that time."

Viktor grinned at him, mouthing the f-word.

"And you too. What is it? Three years? I can't believe it's been that long!"

"Three this summer - since Novgorod."

"And how's it been? I mean since we stopped sending you pictures? That business of the Gainsborough broke poor Freddie."

Viktor sighed. "Uncle Frank… then Freddie…"

"But I still think you made a better picture out of it."

Vera was hanging back with her son, leaving the old school chums to complete their ritual, but Viktor took up the bags and dumped them beside her at the end of the platform. Kolya stepped forward and, with a broad smile on his face, hugged Nicko round his knees, while his mother kissed his forehead.

"You can do better than that, Verochka!" joked her husband.

She kissed him on the cheek this time.

"You're looking so well, Nikoshka," she said. "Really well!"

"And you too… and Kolya. He's shot up. How old are you now, Kolya?" he asked the boy in English. He knew the answer, but wanted to try him.

"Eight," the boy replied in the same tongue.

"The car's outside," Viktor told them.

He led the way to a small side street outside the bus station.

"It's wonderful to have you with us again," said Vera once they were settled. "I can't say how much Kolya has been looking forward to you coming. Isn't that right, Kolochka?"

"Da."

"Da," repeated Nicko pulling a poker face.

"His English is getting better all the time," Vera informed him. "I want you to speak to Uncle Nicko in English, Kolochka. I told you that." Nicko had been placed in the passenger seat beside Viktor, with the malchik and his mother in the back.

"This is a smart number," Nicko said to his friend. "Have you hired it?"

"Kaneshna."

They swung out onto the main road to the south, leaving Kotor's outskirts behind.

"Where are we going?" Nicko asked. "You haven't told me anything yet."

"To our place, the Villa Nikishov."

"Is it your own? Or are you renting?"

Viktor glanced at him and winked. "Renting. How do you say? In a manner of speaking."

Nicko nodded but did not comment. As usual Viktor appeared to have some deep-laid plan.

"Are you a long way out? Of Kotor I mean?"

"A bit," Viktor said.

"I only caught a glimpse of it, but I like the look of it." There was a hint of regret in Nicko's voice.

"The place is new," Viktor explained. "Only just built. Between Tiva and Budva." "Ah."

Vera who caught his tone leaned forward.

"Don't worry, Nikoshka," she said. "You'll see plenty of Kotor. I know it's your kind of a place - and mine too," she added. "Vitya prefers his boat."

"And Kolya?" asked Nicko, turning to the boy. "What do you like doing?"

"Papa's boat is fun," he declared formally in English. "It's a speedboat."

"And you like that?"

"Da, kaneshna - I mean yes. Of course."

"That's better," his mother said.

"I would be perfectly happy to hear some Russian spoken as well," Nicko told her.

She punched him playfully in the back.

In half an hour Viktor turned off the road and into a short driveway to the villa, which Nicko was relieved to see stood at a distance from its neighbours and was not overlooked. But, like the others, it was painted a gleaming shade of white and had a first floor balcony with ostentatiously - bulging balusters, reached by an outside spiral staircase. In front was a small paved courtyard with a garage for a car. Hardly my kind of thing, he told himself, but clearly it's Vik's.

"I still don't understand. Do you own it outright or are you simply renting?" he asked his friend.

"That's little complicated," Viktor said.

"It always is with you. You're as straight as a corkscrew."

Viktor turned to him and mouthed "piss off!" Then out loud. "What do you think?"

"I'll tell you once we're inside when I've had a chance to take a proper look."

The large downstairs living room was spacious. It was fitted with expensive-looking modern furniture which appeared comfortable yet dull at the same time.

Nicko nodded and smiled. Viktor seemed gratified by his friend's immediate reaction, but his wife gave him a searching look, as if expecting a more critical response. She caught his eye and he nodded in a way that was non-committal, but nevertheless suggestive.

"Your room," said Viktor taking up his bags again. "Oh and you must meet Ludochka?"

"Who's Ludochka?" "Ludochka- Ludmilla."

"You didn't tell me about her."

"No I didn't. I was storing her up. She's from Petersburg, a student, travelling by herself. She's interested in last King and Queen of Montenegro- for some reason."

"So what's she doing with you?"

"We ran into her in Tiva. Her money was running a bit low so she offered her services."

"What kind of services?" Nicko eyed his friend suspiciously. "Helping Verochka and acting as our guide, that's all! She has been here before and knows the country pretty well."

Looking at the villa, for a second Nicko found himself thinking wistfully of the apartment in Novgorod - which seemed to him so much more agreeable than this rather flashy, holiday home.

"So you're pretty well covered, aren't you?" he said. "Kaneshna."

They ascended the spiral staircase to the balcony where Viktor pushed open a door. The room with its single bed, and en suite shower and loo was neat, and like the one downstairs devoid of character, but a perfectly comfortable hotel bedroom.

"I'm afraid it doesn't run to air conditioning, but there's a fan if you need one," explained Viktor.

"It'll do me fine," Nicko assured him. "You sleep further along?"

"Kaneshna. Verochka and myself are next to you. Kolya's in with Ludmilla further along."

"And she's happy with that?"

"Why shouldn't she be? She's shared a room with a brother for most of her life."

"And where is the fair Ludmilla now? At least I assume she's fair."

Viktor laughed. "I expect she's in the kitchen or maybe she's reading on the beach. She's a great reader."

"Does she join in the fun? "

"Sometimes. Would you like a shower? It's all there. When you're smelling of roses, come down for a drink. There's plenty of vodka in the fridge, but perhaps you'd prefer to start with a beer."

Nicko showered and in a quarter of an hour presented himself in the sitting room, smelling of roses. Kolya was putting together a rail track on the floor and as none of the other adults was present he got down, determined to show the boy how to set it up in a complete circle instead of merely adding the pieces together. Vera found them on the floor together.

"My two boys," she said.

Nicko stood up. "I think you understand, Kolya," he told the boy. "I want to see you make a complete circle."

"Everything all right, Nikoshka?" asked Vera.

"Perfectly. I had a lovely warm shower. You run a good hotel."

A dark girl who looked to be in her late teens or early twenties had followed Vera in from the kitchen.

"This is Ludmilla- from St Petersburg," Vera said.

"Dobre veche," said Nicko with a dip of his head. "Ochin priatne!"

"Very good!" Ludmilla replied in English. "So you speak Russian? Ochin priatne!"

"He ought to," Vera told her. "He's an Orloff - from one of the oldest boyar families in Russia."

"I'm afraid my Russian has never had much of a chance," explained Nicko. "It can't compete with the English you all speak so well."

Ludmilla smiled, a rather watchful smile.

"What do you do?" Nicko asked. "I mean when you're not slaving for the Nikishovs."

"I'm a student."

"Of what?"

"Literature. English literature."

"Perhaps you can teach me a thing or two. You Russians seem to be powerfully well-read in our own classics. I only got to read Scott after coming to Russia,"

"I'm interested in twentieth century literature mostly," said Ludmilla, "especially some of the American writers."

"And the Montenegran Royal Family? "

"And the Montenegran Royal Family."

"Does Kolya give you any trouble?"

"Not much. He's a boy. I have a brother."

"Do you talk to him in English?"

"Of course she does," put in Vera.

"You all make me feel terribly guilty- about not speaking to you in Russian," said Nicko.

"Nonsense Nikoshka!" protested Vera. "Your English is exactly how it should be spoken. We love to hear you using it. I want Kolya to speak it the same. Do you hear me, Kolochka?"

"Yes, Mama,"

"You are to learn to speak English the way Uncle Nicko does."

"Yes, Mama."

Viktor came in through the main door from the garage.

"Drinks," he announced. "Nick's tongue is hanging out. Yes?" He glanced at his friend.

"Yes, Vik, it'll pass," Nicko replied, following it with a mouthed f-word.

Vera and Ludmilla left for the kitchen taking Kolya with them, followed by Viktor who returned a minute later with several bottles of beer and plates of nuts and crisps on a tray.

"My God," protested Nicko.

"The beer will do to start with. We can get down to the real stuff later." He placed the tray, opened the first two bottles and plonked himself beside his friend on the sofa.

"Now, Nick, tell me everything. You no longer work for Freddie - whatwasisname? Ryedale. Is that right?"

"I haven't worked with him for over a year now. I fear the mishap with the Gainsborough, especially after the Constable business a few years earlier, has pretty well finished him off." He picked up a bottle from the tray and wagged it under Viktor's nose. "But he was always quite ready to kick off before six o'clock."

Viktor looked at his watch. "It's not half past five yet."

"Mind you," Nicko went on, "I still think the picture looked better after Leonid's makeover. Did it find a good home?"

Viktor scooped up a handful of nuts, "Eat up," he said. "I don't know whether you'd call it a good home or not. A bloke in Novokuznetsk bought it for his mum. They say they like it."

"What did he pay for it?"

Viktor swallowed another handful of nuts. "Buggered if I can remember," he said.

"I wish you wouldn't talk that way," said Vera who had come back from the kitchen and placed herself on the arm of the sofa next to Nicko. "It makes you sound - how do you say it? common."

Her husband ignored her and went on talking to Nicko. "So you don't work for Freddie anymore. Have you got something else?"

"Kaneshna."

"Selling pictures?"

"No, I'm teaching."

"Teaching who or what?"

"Kids. I've got a job in a prep school. Kids between Kolya's sort of age and fourteen. Then some of them might even go on to our old alma mater - among other places."

"Christ. That's a bit of a comedown, isn't it? It sounds like a woman's work to me."

"I don't think so. The money's bad admittedly, but I'm quite enjoying It - for the time being at least."

"I like it, Nikoshka," put in Vera. "Teaching must be very rewarding and I'm sure you're very good at it."

Viktor shook his head.

"Take no notice of him," said Vera.

"It's nothing very special," Nicko explained. "Young kids in a small independent school - a prep school, we call it," he explained to Vera. "Vik knows what that means. Mostly they're children from families, with enough money to spend on education, so they tend to be well motivated. Vik's right of course. In one way it is a bit of a comedown. The money is lousy - especially for someone living in London."

"It sounds the right kind of school for Kolya," Vera said.

"There are a couple of Russians there now, as a matter of fact," said Nicko. "It's in a quite a posh part of town - white stucco terraces, that sort of area. Pretty outrageous, I suppose, if you're burdened with a social conscience."

"Which you're not," put in Viktor. "The Orloffs always looked down their noses at the lesser members of the human race."

"Take no notice of him," Vera said.

"I'm only a New Russian oik." Viktor laughed gently as he spoke as if to show that he felt no bitterness about it.

"It's hardly very demanding academically," Nicko went on. "I'm not teaching Physics to aspiring cosmologists - though some of them may end up as that for all I know. It's just basic English and History."

"It sounds good. Can we send Kolya there?" Viktor said, while Vera nodded eagerly.

"It's not a boarding school. You'd need to base yourselves in London. Like the Khlebnikovs."

"The Khlebnikovs?" Viktor pricked up and relaxed again. "No, I don't know anyone called Khlebnikov - but it's a common enough Russian name. It's the same as your Baker."

"It's a pretty traditional type of school - old fashioned some people would even say - which I think is no bad thing," Nicko said. "There's a proper school uniform for one thing - green blazers, caps and grey flannel shorts for the boys, with a striped school tie and green tops to the stockings."

"It sounds what a school ought to be like." Vera turned to her husband. "Vitya, we must send Kolochka to Nicko's school!"

"As I said it's not a boarding school," Nicko reminded her. "We can find a way surely?"

"I could talk to the Khlebnikovs - with Vik's permission of course. We don't want any business wires getting crossed." "Say that again."

Nicko wanted to tell him to eff off, but in the circumstances had to let it go.

Meanwhile Ludmilla had arrived from the kitchen with the child in question and was listening to the conversation.

"What do you think, Ludochka?" Viktor asked her. "Think of what?"

"About Kolya going to his Uncle Nicko's school in England."

"What does he think?" She turned to the boy.

Though the conversation was being carried on in English he appeared to understand everything that was being said.

"Fine," he said, "but England is far away. I couldn't fly in aeroplane to school every morning."

Nicko laughed. "No, you couldn't, Kolya. You'd have to live in London." He glanced at Viktor.

"Would you like to live in London?" the boy's father asked.

"Morjna byt," the boy said. "Perhaps. I have to think about it." He went on, speaking to his father in rapid Russian

"Maybe, we will," Viktor answered him in English. "Mama would like to, I'm sure."

Vera had said nothing, but was watching the boy with maternal pride.

Viktor took her hand. "I think he's ready for his English education," he said. "What do you think Ludochka?"

"Does it matter what I think? It's something you must decide for yourselves." Her tone was almost listless. "You must excuse me." She went out of the room back into the kitchen,

Viktor frowned and winked and raised an eyebrow at Nicko.

"A dark horse - yes? is our Ludochka. Her moods change like the English weather. You must try her on literature."

"She says she likes twentieth century Americans. I'm not too hot on them."

"You might learn something from her then. If you never learn to speak Russian properly at least you might try to read American."

Kolya was sitting cross-legged on the floor taking it all in, but Vera got up and summoned him away.

"Papa and Uncle Nicko want to talk," she told him.

"I want to hear them talking," said the boy.

"Maybe you do, Kolochka, but it's men's talk. And it's your bathtime. If you don't hurry up there won't be any ice-cream. Morozoniye neyt."

Reluctantly he followed his mother out while his father topped up a couple of glasses.

"I'm impressed with Kolya," Nicko told him.

"We'll have this to start off with," Viktor said.

"And he pronounces the words so well. He's absolutely clear. Is his Russian as good?"

"Better than yours, you windy old fart!"

"Thanks for that. So then, tell what you're really getting up to. After we stopped sending you pictures, you went very quiet."

Viktor raised his glass and touched Nicko's. "Cheers!"

"Are you going to tell me? Or does it stink too much?"

"It doesn't stink, or at least not in the way you think it does."

"How do you know what I think?"

"This is a fine spot. A beautiful little country and a loyal friend of ours, from the days when it had its own king and we had a Romanov tsar. You're not drinking."

Nicko drained his glass and Viktor, whipping off a bottle cap with his teeth, re-charged it. He their talk veered back to his son. The idea of sending him to school in England seemed to appeal to both parents, but Nicko wondered how they were going to set about it. The idea of a boarding school would not be acceptable to the mother for one so young, but Viktor appeared to have a more robust Spartan attitude- like many British parents - and the idea of a boy being cut loose from his mother's apron strings at seven or eight did not bother him.

Vera called them through for their supper when the beer had almost all been drunk. They ate in a dining area which was part of the kitchen. Kolya freshly bathed and in his pyjamas, was already at the table. Ludmilla placed a large bowl of spaghetti before them and started ladling it onto the plates. Viktor, meanwhile, went to a wine rack and selected a bottle of red.

Vera directed the talk into the things that Nicko was keen to know. He expressed his urgent desire to look at Kotor and she assured him that there would plenty of time for that, and for other sightseeing too, during his fortnight's stay. Viktor, meanwhile, promised him a run in the speedboat that he kept moored on the nearby beach, while Ludmilla talked about her interest in Montenegro and its royal family. Nicko mentioned that his own great-grandfather had met the country's last king, which impressed Vera at least.

"In that case," declared Viktor, "we need to go to Cetinje. We haven't been there ourselves yet, but it's a good drive up with some stunning views, I'm told."

"We will visit the royal palace," said Vera. "I believe it's very small and hardly a palace at all, but charming."

Nicko recalled that she had once been a tourist guide in St Petersburg,

"I'm on," he said enthusiastically. "When can we go?"

"There's no great hurry," Viktor pointed out. "You've got two whole weeks ahead of you. Tomorrow we can do the boat, the day after that Kotor maybe, if it's what you want, and Cetinje any time after that. Da?"

Supper passed off agreeably and after Kolya had gone to bed - his mother was quite strict about such matters - giving his godfather as well as his parents a kiss, they lingered an hour in general chat until Ludmilla announced that she too was ready for bed and, having cleared the table with Vera, she departed.

Vera left shortly afterwards, kissing the top of her husband's head as she went. "Don't be late," she said as she did the same to Nicko.

As soon as she had gone, Viktor was on his feet and opening the fridge freezer. He carried a bottle of vodka and a pair of frosted glasses through to the living room. They were followed by a large pile of caviar, two plates and forks and a sliced lemon.

"Oh my God," groaned Nicko. "Here we go again."

"We have to celebrate you being with us once more, Nick. It's been such a long time," Viktor said. He filled a glass and pushed it towards his friend. He filled the other for himself and raised it. "Nasdorovia!"

"Nasdorovia!"

Nicko's sip was cautious, unlike his friend's gulp, and he had to admit that the vodka was good stuff.

Then Viktor began to fill him in on what kind of things he had been up to. He still traded the occasional imported artwork, he said, but property- real estate- was now the thing. And that was what had brought him to Montenegro a year ago- which came as no big surprise to Nicko.

But while he explained it, his voice dropped almost to a whisper and he even glanced over shoulder once or twice as if some unseen person might be listening. Having outlined his interest in the holiday home market- without giving away any names- he talked about London. This was where the real money was to be made still and he added for good measure that it was something that might tie in rather well with what they had been saying earlier on about Kolya's schooling.

By the time they had polished off the bottle Nicko was more than ready for bed.

CHAPTER FOUR

On the Beach

Nicko slept soundly and woke with a clear head. Glancing at his watch - he saw that it was almost seven o'clock. He could hear Kolya's voice and Ludmilla's sleepy replies. They were speaking in Russian and she sounded irritated. From Viktor and Vera he heard not a sound. There was no hurry to get up, but as he was now wide awake, Nicko picked up the paperback copy of an English classic which was his invariable travelling companion. On this occasion his choice of book was 'The Three Clerks' by Anthony Trollope which had lain half-forgotten at the back of a linen cupboard in his mother's house, until one day he had picked it up on a whim. He liked Trollope and the very Englishness of Barchester, for example, provided an agreeable antidote to whatever foreign place he happened to be in at the time.

But his escape into nineteenth century London was not to last long. He had barely completed a page when the door burst open and Kolya threw himself onto the bed and started to bounce on his chest. Any shyness that the boy might previously have shown had vanished and Nicko, despite having his reading rudely interrupted, was touched.

Kolya rattled away in a mixture of Russian and English, the gist of which was that they were going for a spin in Papa's speedboat, though his mother would not be joining them.

A moment later Vera put her head round the door.

"I hope he's not being a nuisance," she said.

"Not at all. He's telling me about today's programme."

Vera picked the paperback up from the floor.

"I know this man," she said. "Didn't he write those stories about a cathedral?"

"The Barchester Chronicles."

"I've read one of them. Who was that priest who upset everyone so much?"

"The Reverend Obadiah Slope."

"He was like a snake, if I remember. Come away Kolochka. You must let Uncle Nicko read his book. I know how annoying it is when someone stops you reading."

She lifted the child off the bed.

"Breakfast is in half an hour," she told her guest. "But there's no hurry. After that I'm afraid you'll be racing in Vitya's boat. It's not something I enjoy, but I'm sure you will say the right things about it."

She reached out and stroked his cheek before she left the room.

At breakfast the boy was bubbling with excitement at the prospect of the coming trip, while his father fed him with engine noises and descriptions of dramatically tight turns.

"Eat your breakfast, Kolochka or you won't be going," his mother ordered him.

The boy pouted and his father winked at him.

Ludmilla, meanwhile, engaged Nicko on the subject of the Montenegran royal family and the Orloff connection with them.

"My great-grandfather knew the princesses, the ones who were living in St Petersburg," he explained to her. "They all made good marriages, but none of them to an Orloff, I'm afraid."

"But they were really just Balkan bandits, weren't they?" Ludmilla pointed out.

"Isn't that how most royal dynasties start out? They came later to it than others, that's all. Anyway we might be able to find out more in Cetinje."

Breakfast over, the three males set out for the beach: shorts and T-shirts being the order of the day. On the way Viktor collected three life jackets from the garage.

"We mustn't lose the Tsarovich," he said to Nicko. "Especially as one day he might be your star pupil."

The speed boat was moored to a small jetty. It was an elegant machine with a streamlined hull and a curving windscreen which reminded Nicko of his friend's designer sunglasses.

"Has it got a name?" he asked.

"Not yet. Can you think of one?"

"It should be something Russian, shouldn't it?"

"How about a famous general or an admiral? Can you think of one? Or shall we leave it to Kolochka?"

"Perhaps it should have a woman's name. Most ships do."

67

"We could call it Vera."

Nicko shook his head. "What do you think, Kolya?"

The boy came up with the name of a character from a Russian children's television programme whom Nicko had never heard of.

"I don't think so," the boy's father said decisively. "We'll settle for Anna. It sounds right for a boat."

"Oughtn't we to have a naming ceremony?" suggested Nicko.

"Sure, but not right now. I'm going to show you what she can do first." Viktor tied his son into his lifejacket and helped Nicko into his.

Then he took the steering wheel, fired the engine and ordered Nicko to cast off. The boy sat close to his father as they roared out into the open water of the bay, with Viktor issuing loud Cossack yells and his son laughing excitedly. Nicko clung on, keeping his head low, but raising it occasionally to feel the breeze in his face. It was his first experience of a speed boat and he was finding it exhilarating.

Viktor continued to make his yells and drove in a wide arc out to sea. There were several other craft doing the same and one was towing a water skier. As they picked up speed, Viktor pulled the boy into his lap and placed his hands on the wheel.

"You're the captain now, Kolochka," he told him in Russian.

The boy tried to turn the wheel, but his father held onto it firmly.

"Would you like to have a go?" he asked Nicko over his shoulder.

"I'll leave it to Kolya," Nicko replied. "He's a more experienced sailor than I am."

Viktor meanwhile started to do tighter and tighter turns and Nicko hung on for dear life, half-expecting to be flung overboard. The volume of the Cossack yells mounted as the driving grew more reckless.

"Steady on," Nicko called. "Hold your horses!"

"You're not feeling sick, are you?"

"Not yet, but I soon will be. And anyway, I don't want to end up in the drink."

Out in the open water the other boats were being driven just as wildly, skimming the surface and sometimes almost leaping free of it altogether.

Then Viktor set his course straight for another boat, anticipating its line of turn. The idea seemed to be to nip across its bows, at the very last possible second. He looked back at his friend, a gleam of devilry in his eye.

For the first time Nicko felt seriously scared. "For Christ's sake, Vik, what the hell are you doing?"

The boat tore on, set on a collision course with the other, which seemed oblivious of what was bearing down on it like a bullet.

"Vik, are you mad?" yelled Nicko. "Think of the child, if nothing else!"

The other boat came on, joining in the game.

"For God's sake!" roared Nicko. "You're crazy!" He leaned forward and seized the boy from his father's lap.

And then, when the disaster seemed inevitable, both craft swerved, each to its own starboard, and cut speed immediately.

The boy was clinging to Nicko's neck, trembling.

"You fucking idiot, Vik," Nicko called out. "You might have killed the kid!"

Viktor in the meantime was exchanging greetings with the driver of the other boat in Russian, each uttering yells, redolent of the Steppe. They drew up alongside and Viktor introduced Nicko to his fellow-Russian as if their little dalliance with death had never taken place.

Which character in Russian literature did his friend resemble most? Probably Dolohov, the reckless psychopath in Tolstoy's 'War and Peace'…. Nicko lowered Kolya onto the bench, where he lay with his eyes shut. Then the boy grabbed Nicko's hand.

"It's all right, Kolya," his godfather said to him softly. "You're safe now. Your dad just wanted to give us a bit of a fright, that's all."

Viktor turned away from his fellow Russian and looked at his passengers. For a second a scornful smile played on his lips.

"What the hell did you think you were doing?" Nicko protested. "It's your own flesh and blood, for Christ's sake!"

"A lesson for life. I want him to grow up to be a man."

"Bollocks!" Nicko snorted. "You bloody nearly killed him!"

"But I didn't." He lifted the boy up. "You're a brave boy," he said in English, before repeating it in Russian. "And I'm proud of you."

Nicko felt that it was better to leave it there. It wasn't really his business anyway.

Viktor executed a few more sweeps, slow and graceful ones this time, before steering the boat back to its moorings.

"Well that was quite an adventure," Nicko said in a restorative kind of way.

"I think Anna might be a good name. Do you think we need to smash a bottle of champagne on the whatsit? The bow?" said Viktor.

"Not if it's any good. Georgian would do, I daresay. I hate to see decent stuff wasted. Racing drivers always annoy me when they do that."

"Racing drivers are hardly your type, are they Nick?" Viktor grinned, almost triumphantly, at him. "Probably not."

They went back up the beach to the house and sat at a table outside. The day was warming up and Ludmilla, in a bathing costume, appeared with a large jug of lemonade.

"Had a good time?" she enquired in a perfunctory manner.

"Papa drove the boat really fast," Kolya told her.

"He always does. Too fast for me."

"And me too," Nicko said.

"What about you Kolochka?" enquired Viktor.

The boy said something in Russian and Viktor glanced at Nicko,

"He says it was great," he said. "That's two against one."

Ludmilla went back indoors and for a while the group at the table sat in silence.

"I think we should have a swim before lunch," Viktor came out with at length. "And then just take it easy when it gets hot."

A haze was settling out to sea, taking the edge off any views.

"Sounds fine to me." Nicko drained his glass. His recent adventure had made him thirsty.

"That's what's so good about this place," mused Viktor. "Nothing has to be done in a hurry."

Their talk was subdued after what had passes between them and Nicko pondered, as he so often did, on the nature of their friendship. They were really quite different. It was just this Russian thing that held them together - the romantic idea he clung to of his own ancestral past, which was gently ridiculed by the New Russian. And with it went the urge to cast Viktor as a character out of Russian fiction. It could be Chichikov in Gogol's 'Dead Souls' or, as now, Dolohov in Tolstoy's 'War and Peace'. There were paradoxes, of course: his delightful family, Verochka and little Kolya, being the most obvious one.

"Time for that swim," Viktor declared, breaking in on his thoughts.

They changed into their swimming costumes and after Vera and Ludmilla had joined them with their towels, they trooped down to the shingly beach. Viktor carried a large picnic basket. Their recliners were already down there, Viktor informed his friend, kept safely under lock and key. It occurred to Nicko that an English beach might have been better for the boy. With bucket and spade he would have enjoyed helping him to build a sandcastle.

There was an established routine that went straight into action. Viktor fetched the recliners and a canopy with poles- which was a relief to Nicko who was wary of exposing his fair skin to too much direct sun. Ludmilla was carrying a small bucket of fast-melting ice, which contained a bottle of white wine and a couple of juice. Out of the picnic basket Vera produced four books, one of which she handed to Ludmilla, another, a book of Russian folktales, to her son. The other two were a copy of 'Wuthering Heights'- in its original English- and Nicko's own copy of 'The Three Clerks'. Nicko noticed that Ludmilla's book was 'The Talented Mr Ripley' by Patricia Highsmith. There was nothing for Viktor.

Nicko took the book from Ludmilla's hand and raised an enquiring eyebrow. "I have yet to read any of her work," he said. He glanced at the blurb on the back.

"I will lend it to you when I have finished it," she replied. "We can talk about in then. You need to read it first."

"Race you into the sea, Kolochka!" called out Viktor to his son.

They raced to the water's edge, where the former plunged in before turning back to the boy who was holding back, dabbling his toes in the water. He spoke to him in Russian, but Nicko caught the drift of it. Kolya waded cautiously towards his father.

"It's cold!" he protested in Russian.

"Not for long," his father said in the same language. "You'll feel warm in a minute."

He waded across to the boy and took hold of him, then drew him out to where the water was deeper, walking backwards and giving him a swimming lesson. He explained to him what he should do with his legs while the child tried to obey his instructions.

"Don't drown him!" Vera called out from the shore. She waded out to join them.

"You're doing well, Kolochka," she told the boy in English. "You're learning fast."

Ludmilla in the meantime stretched out on her recliner, lifted up her sunglasses and picked up her book.

"What else of hers have you read?" Nicko asked her.

"I have read 'Strangers on a Train' but none of the Ripley stories. This is the first," she said.

"There is an excellent film about Ripley," said Nicko. "He's an utterly plausible monster who gets away with his crimes. Murder is just a practical necessity for him - a bit like Stalin. When you kill someone you're simply getting rid of a problem. Mind you, there're some good moments when he nearly gets caught, but his luck holds and it never happens. Justice is never done. Not exactly a moral tale, but then that's how life so often is."

"You mentioned Stalin, but there are plenty of Russian characters like him who're walking free today." She opened the book.

"When I've read it we'll talk about it," Nicko said. He watched the family splashing about in the sea and got up to join them.

As he waded a little gingerly into the water, Kolya splashed him cheekily and Viktor started to as well.

"Ouch!" Nicko said and returned the fire.

He dipped his body below the surface and began to enjoy himself.

"Isn't Ludochka coming in too?" asked Vera.

"She's busy with her book. I could see she wanted to read and took the hint. 'The Talented Mr Ripley' by Patricia Highsmith. It's a crime story. They made it into a very good film."

"I've never heard of it," said Viktor.

"I don't suppose you have. Highsmith's an American crime writer, and her characters might put some of your Russian chums in the shade! Ripley rubs out anyone who gets in his way and thinks nothing of it."

Viktor splashed him, silently mouthing the eff-word," and then said aloud. "You'll be the first!"

They swam a short way out together before returning to Vera and the boy.

She had been continuing with his swimming lesson.

"He's going to represent his country in the Olympics one day," said Viktor;

"Which country?"

"His own. Russia, of course."

"Verochka might have other ideas."

Viktor laughed. "We'll see about that."

He waded ashore and wandered over to where the boat was moored.

"I'm still thinking about that name," he said.

"I thought you'd made up your mind," said Nicko, who had joined him. "Isn't it going to be Anna?"

"Verochka!" Viktor shouted at his wife. "Nick thinks we should call the boat Anna. Any objections?"

"It sounds all right to me - for a boat."

"We were wondering if you might be offended if we didn't call it Vera."

"I don't want my name on a stupid boat."

Viktor raised his eyebrows and winked at Nicko.

"We need to break bottle on it," he continued. "Perhaps we can leave it 'til later."

He and Nicko strolled back to the others where Vera had started to read a folktale to her son in his native tongue. Ludmilla meanwhile seemed to be completely engrossed in 'The Talented Mr Ripley'. She did not even look up as they approached. Viktor threw himself down on a recliner and closed his eyes.

"This is the life," he murmured.

Nicko mumbled something in reply, knowing that he would soon be getting bored. Then he remembered that Vera had remembered to bring his book. But for the moment he did not feel like reading, so he closed his eyes, and opened them again to look across at Ludmilla.

"You seem to read English very easily, Ludochka," he told her.

"Of course," she said absently, without lifting her eyes from the page.

Nicko felt that it would annoy her if he interrupted her again.

"You know something, Vik?" he said to his friend.

"Hm?"

"There must be some beaches here with a decent amount of sand, mustn't there?"

"Maybe."

"If we can find one I could show Kolya how to build a castle."

"Hmm?"

"We'd need a bucket and spade as well as the sand."

Viktor did not answer, so Nicko got up off the recliner. "I think I'll go for a walk," he said.

"Don't go far," Vera told him. "We will eat shortly."

"I need to work up an appetite."

He walked along the short strand to where he could see the old town of Budva behind its walls.

It must once have been so much nicer here, he told himself. I've been born out of my time. Now the place is heaving with people and their tacky villas.

He climbed up onto the road that skirted the shoreline and walked a short distance along it, eying the people packed like sardines on the beach just below. It struck him as odd that people who were trying to enjoy themselves on a beach never really looked as if they were.

A bit like Christmas, he told himself. That's always a bloody letdown.

He wandered back to the others. Viktor was still lying with his eyes closed and Ludmilla was deep in her book.

"Come and tell Kolochka a story," Vera called to him.

"What kind of a story?"

"Anything you like. You're a teacher, aren't you?"

"I'll tell him something from English History," said Nicko. "How about the Gunpowder Plot?"

"That sounds exciting," Vera said. "Kolochka, your Uncle Nicko is going to tell you a true story. It is a true one, isn't it?"

"Yes it's true," replied Nicko. "It's exciting and gruesome at the same time." "Gruesome?"

"Yes. Torture and execution. Like Russian History. "

"I hope it's suitable."

"Kids love it."

Kolya had been listening and appeared to be following, even if, like his mother, he was unfamiliar with the word 'gruesome'.

Nicko placed himself on the recliner beside him.

The boy, sitting next to him gazed at his face with big blue eyes - like his mother's.

Nicko spoke slowly. He remembered an account of the plot to blow up King James and his Parliament he had read as a child himself in a Nursery History of England and got straight to the point. Needless to say he was flattered by the rapt attention the eight year old was giving him. He explained a few things like gunpowder and its destructive power and provided a short description of what people looked like at the time, while making a high drama our of Guy Fawkes' capture in the cellar below the Parliament chamber. Then he launched into the grim process of his torture and confession, followed by the trial and execution of the plotters. The boy wrinkled his nose, but listened fascinated, interjecting the description with comments in English and Russian like 'that must have really hurt!' and 'why were they so cruel?'

When the disembowelling of the traitors began, Vera intervened. "I think that's probably enough for now," she said. "But our own tsars did things that were just as cruel. People were much more cruel in those times."

"Like impaling," put in Viktor who had sat up and was listening.

"What's impaling?" asked the boy.

"A very nasty way of killing people by driving a stake through their bodies and then leaving them to die slowly," explained his father.

"I think that's enough for now," said Vera firmly. "Now Kolochka it's time for another swim and then we must eat. Go with your father."

With a mild show of reluctance Viktor climbed to his feet and went with his son to the water's edge.

"You told that well," Vera said to Nicko. "He was interested."

"They all love the torture and execution."

Vera shrugged. "We'll have to try something gentler next time and see if that's just as successful."

She spread a cloth and started to lay out the lunch. There were other people on the beach, of course, but it wasn't crowded, so their space did not feel overlooked. Nicko adjusted the awning to provide some shade. Ludmilla, meanwhile, remained engrossed in Ripley.

When the cold meat and chicken were laid out, Vera put out the plates, knives and forks and plastic cups.

"Come and eat, you boys," she called out in Russian to her husband and son.

They munched in silence and the food disappeared rapidly. Ludmilla nibbled at hers and read her book at the same time.

"He's caught you, Ripley, I mean," Nicko said to her.

"Da," she replied absently.

"It must be a very good story," Vera said.

Ludmilla nodded and turned a page.

Vera frowned, feeling that she was not setting a very good example. "Leave it," she admonished her, "and eat properly, Ludochka."

Reluctantly Ludmilla turned over the top of a page to mark her place and set the book aside.

"Are you going to tell me another story, Uncle Nicko?" asked Kolya.

"Tomorrow maybe."

"What's it going to be about?" He added something in Russian.

"You want another true story? One from History?" said Nicko, catching his meaning.

"Da - I mean yes."

"Try to speak English, Kolochka," his mother told him.

"I'll tell you about the Two Princes in the Tower," said Nicko.

"Is it - what's the word?"

"Gruesome? No, it's not gruesome, but it's mysterious and sad. It's a kind of historical detective story. Ludmilla might be interested."

She smiled. "I think I know it already."

"Tell me now," ordered the boy.

"Tomorrow," said his mother. "You mustn't be greedy," she added, repeating it in Russian.

Nicko picked up the empty ice bucket. "You know something, Vik?" he said. "Try me."

"If we could just find a decent bit of sand I could show the boy how to build a castle. We've got the bucket. And you might it find it useful to know as well."

"If you think so. But can't it wait until another day? There'll be plenty more."

The search for suitable sand was postponed and the languid afternoon was passed between reading and dips. Ludmilla was the exception: she did not go near the water and scarcely lifted her eyes from her book.

Viktor glanced at his watch.

"Four o'clock," he announced. "Time for a little refreshment,"

Nicko concurred. It was earlier than he was used to, but then he was on holiday. He and Viktor packed away the recliners and the awning, leaving Ludmilla behind, engrossed in Ripley's crimes.

CHAPTER FIVE

Kotor

Nicko slept soundly after his day on the beach and woke with the comfortable thought that it was the day appointed for his visit to Kotor. He and Vera were to go together while Viktor had opted to take care of the boy and Ludmilla, who was wrapped up in Patricia Highsmith, had elected to go with them to the beach- which was a kind of a relief to Nicko who recalled all too well Viktor's reckless performance of the day before. He felt that Vera would be an ideal person to poke around the city's old streets with. She had been a tourist guide, and was obviously more aesthetically sensitive than her husband. Viktor baffled Nicko in this regard. Despite extensive trading in the art market, he seemed to take no pleasure in such things. Indeed, how many of his alleged oligarch friends were very different, despite the millions they splashed out on works of art? Nicko could understand someone lusting to possess something by Shishkin, but one by Damien Hurst? He caught himself thinking of 'Vanity Fair' and the need people have to score over their fellows in every possible way. Despite his relative youth, Nicko tended to think the sober thoughts of an older man, while Viktor preferred his motorboat and tacky villa- which came down to the same kind of thing. Better that, perhaps, and less pretentious, than collecting Damien Hirsts. Nicko respected his friend for at least not claiming to be other than what he was.

He lay in bed, mulling over the coming day until his thoughts were interrupted by Kolya storming into the room and jumping onto the bed. Nicko felt flattered by the child's obvious affection. Trust, after all, was the nicest compliment that a child could pay you.

But the boy having already been appraised of the day's programme was not entirely satisfied with it. Possibly the business in the motorboat had unsettled him.

"I would like to go with you and Mama to Kotor," he declared in English.

Nicko noted once more the child's readiness to slip into English.

"We'll go together another day," he assured him. "You're going to have a great day with your dad."

"I hope he won't drive the boat so fast this time. He nearly killed us."

"You weren't frightened, were you, Kolya? A Russian boy like you? And, anyway, Ludmilla won't let him drive too fast."

"If she isn't reading her book." He mumbled something more in Russian, the meaning of which Nicko did not catch, apart from its sulky tone.

The boy snuggled up against Nicko, putting an arm round his neck. A few moments later a knock came at the door and Vera looked in. She saw the two of them lying together, Kolya with his eyes shut.

"Is he being a trouble?" she enquired.

"Not in the least. He's cross that he's not coming to Kotor with us, that's all, but I've told him he's going to have a great day with his dad."

Vera gave an impatient sight. "That boat."

"I'm sure Vik will be careful this time. He got a bit carried away yesterday. Probably showing off to me." "I'm never sure about Vitya."

"Ludmilla will be there too."

"She'll probably want to read her book. Time to get dressed, my malchik," she added to the boy in Russian as she lifted him off the bed.

A few minutes later Nicko was downstairs, followed shortly by Viktor fresh out of a shower and clad only in a bath gown. Ludmilla in shorts and T-shirt followed a minute later. Kolya was in a sulk and Nicko hoped that there wasn't going to be scene.

But few words were spoken. Conversation at breakfast was seldom a good idea, Nicko felt.

He went upstairs to fetch his Rough Guide to Montenegro as soon as he had finished his bowl of cereal and his coffee. For a moment or two he lingered in the bedroom, locating the description of Kotor and by the time he came down again only Vera and Ludmilla were there, clearing away the breakfast things.

"Can I help?" he asked conventionally.

"No of course not," Vera told him. "You wouldn't know where to put the things."

With Vera driving, they set off up the road to Kotor. Despite the proliferating villas, Nicko could still appreciate the grandeur of the bay as they approached the old town, most of which was contained, medieval fashion, inside walls that appeared to climb almost vertically up the hillside. The marina in front of the main gate was crowded with expensive-looking motorboats and yachts while a vast cruise liner was also berthed there. Vera cut down a small alleyway and parked the vehicle on a piece of waste ground, with which she was familiar.

"I feel this place is going to agree with me," declared Nicko, "in spite of its claims to being a World Heritage site."

"I do hope so," Vera said. "It's full of tourists, of course, but then you have to expect that at this time of year, don't you? Somehow it doesn't really spoil it and there are plenty of nice places to eat."

They went through the old main gate into the square by the clock tower. It was thronged with people, mostly visitors by the look of them, though by no means all foreigners. Several restaurants and cafes filled up the open space in front of the warm Korcular stone buildings with their tables. And it was refreshing to be in a place that excluded motor vehicles.

Vera had a small tourist map of the city, so they decided to sit down at a café and to study it together. She knew her way around, but, ever the conscientious tourist guide, she wanted to put Nicko fully in the picture.

"I can never do this kind of thing with Vitya," she told him as they sipped their espressos.

"It's not really his scene, is it?"

Vera shrugged and laughed. "We are here," she said, pointing the map.

Nicko meanwhile opened his guide book at the right page.

"The Catholic Cathedral of St Tryphon is probably the best place to begin," he suggested. "And after that we should visit St Nicholas's - the namesake of both your son and myself - but of course I'm in your hands."

"I have to go there anyway," said Vera. "Something I promised to do for Vitya."

"Oh? I didn't think he was particularly religious."

"It's started just recently. He's asked me to light a candle for him."

"Well, well, that does surprise me. If he was anything, I would have said Vik was as godless as his Communist grandfather."

Vera looked away with a little shrug.

"An interesting development, anyway," went on Nicko, "and one I'm quite pleased to hear about."

"I'm not so sure. Could it just be a kind of magic? Is he afraid of something?"

"We can lose nothing by doing what he asks," Nicko said, "but in the meantime let's begin with St Tryphon." He started to read aloud from the guide book. "'St Tryphon- a goatherd from Phrygia. Martyred as a young boy for refusing to make an offering in front of the statue of the Roman emperor…' Oh, and the patron saint of gardeners as well," he added. "How that fits in with the goatherd bit, I don't quite see."

He paid for the coffees and they set off down the narrow street to the Trg Ustanka Mornara. On the opposite side was the Romanesque west front of St Tryphon's. It was sturdy without being particularly grand, certainly not in the French manner, Nicko reflected. A later balustraded arch, spanning the porch and linking the bell towers, had been added after the earthquake of 1667. This was surmounted by a handsome rose window. Before paying their dues and going inside, Nicko read out what the guide book had to tell them about the exterior and they spent a minute or two studying some of its details.

Once inside, they examined the scenes from the saint's life carved on the ciborium of the high altar, trying to figure out its programme. Nicko felt very content doing this kind of thing with Vera, whereas Viktor would have made him feel the need to push on. They took their time, each being tuned to the other's wavelength, and, nearly half an hour later, they were still consulting the guide book and discussing the thing they were looking at.

On the way out Vera selected a fridge magnet from the ticket booth which Nicko insisted on paying for. From there they went slowly in the direction of the St Nicholas Cathedral, admiring such recommended highlights as the Gothic windows of the Drago Palace on the way. They decided to postpone a visit to the Maritime Museum until another day, preferring simply to let their surroundings work on them.

"It's important to let a place speak to you in its own voice," stated Nicko.

He wondered if he was sounding portentous, but Vera agreed.

In the Orthodox Cathedral she bought and lit a candle, which she placed on the tray beside the others, then she crossed herself and even whispered a short prayer while Nicko stood discreetly at the back.

"All done?" he said as they left the building together.

"Da."

Next they decided to take the bull by the horns and climb the winding path up to the Fortress of St Ivan on the ridge high above the city. So they paid their two Euros each and started the steady plod up through the houses and onto the ridge. Nicko had a rule for such occasions: to keep going without stopping at a slow and regular pace and not to talk. Vera fell in with this regime and they were shortly overhauling groups of sweating tourists- mostly Americans- from the cruise ship in the harbour, some of whom appeared to have taken on more than they had bargained for, and were making frequent stops to draw breath.

A fairly decent class of tourist, at least, decided the snobbish Nick.

The view from the ruined fortress was well worth the climb. The old Byzantine town lay below them, crammed inside its walls, with a fine view across the harbour and the bay. A soft murmur rose from the jumble of rooftops, while in the open space between the main gate and the harbour the shifting of tiny particles was all they could make out of the crowds milling about. It was cooler up here with a light breeze. Sitting on the fortress wall, they admired the spectacle in silence. Nicko reached out and took Vera's hand.

Five minutes went by and then, as if by mutual consent, they both stood up and started back down the path as the toiling Americans finally made it to the summit.

"Time I think to eat," Nicko said. "Do you know somewhere good?"

"I think so." Vera gave him her hand again as they made their way down the slippery well-worn path.

They reached a restaurant with a shady outdoor space not far from the Orthodox Cathedral. Thankfully Vera sat down. "I'm ready for a drink," she said.

"Me too."

Nicko ordered chilled beers and a menu. Glancing around, he saw that a few of the tables were occupied, but since it was early still the place was by no means full. They could take their time. A party of young Russian men was drinking beer at a nearby table.

"Russians," he said.

"Of course. Montenegro is full of them." Vera eyed her fellow-nationals with distaste.

The men were talking quietly and there was nothing about their behaviour or appearance that anyone could complain of. They were dressed in grey or dark blue tracksuit bottoms and T-shirts. Two had their hair cropped fairly close to their skulls, but none of them were wearing ear studs and there were no shaved heads or visible tattoos to make them menacing.

"There are too many Russians here now," declared Vera. "They are taking over this country. Buying it up and building everywhere." She gave a short, impatient sigh. "Vitya's doing that too, of course."

"I would be surprised if he wasn't. But, speaking honestly, Verochka, how do you feel about it? Do you really like it here? Apart from Kotor, that is?"

"It's a good place to bring Kolya - maybe for a year or two. But then we ought to think about somewhere different." She eyed the Russian party scornfully.

"I get the feeling that you want a bit more from life than a comfortable villa near a beach in a warm climate. But I suppose there are worse things than that."

"London. That's where we should be, with Kolya attending a proper English school like the one you teach in."

Nicko laughed. "We'll need to work on that. No doubt Vik will be able to fix something."

"I do hope so," said Vera. "But, honestly, Nikoshka, I'm worried about him. Really I am. He seems so much less certain about things than he used to be. And…" she raised her glass and pointed to it.

"Is that really a problem? He could put it away since I first knew him, but then he's a Russian, isn't he?"

"Except that he doesn't do it in a nice way."

The waiter arrived with a menu and for a moment they were taken up choosing from it. Seafood seemed to be the obvious order of the day.

They began with a hors d'oeuvre of a selection of different meats, following it with fried kalamari and spinach. A local white wine followed their thirst-quenching beers. Ice-creams succeeded the kalamari and Nicko ordered cognacs with the coffee. They were agreeably fatigued after their climb to the fortress and in no hurry to move. As the place began to fill up they ordered fresh coffees.

"I wonder how the beach party's getting on?" Nicko came out with at length.

"I hope it's going fine. Shouldn't it be?" "Kolya wasn't too keen on that motor boat."

"I suppose he'll get used to it and anyway Ludochka will keep Vitya in order. She can be quite strict. Certainly with the boy she is, so why not with his father as well?"

The conversation drifted onto books and Vera pressed Nicko about recent English novelists- a subject he was not too hot on as he was still working his way through the Classics himself. He steered their talk in the direction of Dickens and Trollope, before launching out on his own great favourite, Thackeray's 'Vanity Fair' which Vera had also read.

"That's one thing I like about your Russian education," Nicko pointed out to her. "Your respect for the Classics, something which our trendy permissive system is afraid of, in case the kids get bored, so we settle for something that's too easy for them instead."

It was a favourite theme of Nicko's, one which Vera warmed to, getting none of it from her husband, and it carried them through a fresh round of cognacs into the middle of the afternoon. Meanwhile the Russian foursome also seemed inclined to linger. The restaurant was one of those easygoing establishments that did not pester its customers with a bill, despite getting rather full. Nicko wondered whether the four young men were discussing such an elevated a topic as he was with Vera. Unlikely, he decided, judging by the sounds they were making. And in any case they hardly looked intellectual types.

"Good day to you!" Nicko called out to them in their own language when he and Vera had at last settled their bill.

The young men looked startled for a second, but chorused back cheerfully. Vera offered a rather frosty smile.

"They seem pretty harmless to me," Nicko assured her. "Not like some of our football fans."

"Ours too. They're animals."

They took each other's hand and returned slowly to the Square of Weapons, where they admired the Clock Tower, before going out through the Main Gate to wander along the quay, looking at the shipping.

"There's a hell of a lot of money here," remarked Nicko.

"Most of it's Russian." Vera sounded dismissive. "And not earned honestly."

"It's not all like that surely?"

She shrugged and said no more.

They went back through the arcaded market, stopping at some of the stalls, which were selling household bric-a-brac, including some quite decent prints, one of which Nicko fancied. It appeared to be a nineteenth century view of the city from the opposite side of the bay. Vera, speaking in Russian, with a few words of the related Serbo-Croat added, negotiated it down to a reasonable price, which was a fraction of what it would have cost at home, Nicko reflected. She insisted on paying for it.

"It's my turn," she said emphatically. "You bought me the fridge magnet."

Nicko tried to protest, but quickly conceded, pecking her on the cheek and thanking her in Russian.

They returned to the car, saying little on the way, each immersed in private thoughts. It had been a perfect trip, but now a cloud seemed to building up above them.

* * * * * * *

The beach party had returned by the time they got back and they found Ludmilla reading by herself on the terrace- not a Highsmith novel this time.

"Was Ripley too much for you?" Nicko asked her.

"Not at all," she replied. "He's a monster, of course, but a great creation. I need to read the other books about him."

"I'll see what I can do when I get home."

She smiled her gratitude and returned to her reading.

Vera wanted to know where her husband and son were and was informed that Kolya was watching a children's cartoon on the Montenegran television service and Viktor was showering upstairs.

"Have you had a good day, Ludochka?" Vera asked, speaking in English for Nicko's benefit. "No dangerous moments in the motor boat?" "Kolochka was happy," Ludmilla explained. "Vitya drove very carefully this time."

"We've had a great day," Nicko said. "Kotor's a stunning place."

The three of them went indoors and found Kolya glued to the television.

Vera frowned and spoke to him in Russian, informing him that there were better ways of passing his time, while Nicko sat beside him, pretending to show interest in what he was watching, a Walt Disney cartoon, dubbed in Serbo-Croat. He felt that the boy's mother was being just a trifle hard.

"Do you understand what they're saying?" he asked him.

"Most of it," the child answered. "It sounds the same as Russian."

Vera meanwhile had gone upstairs. A couple of minutes later she was down again. Her face was clouded and she did not speak.

"Anything wrong?" Nicko enquired.

She frowned and went into the kitchen where he followed her.

"He's been drinking," she said, "since he got back from the beach."

"Is he drunk?"

"Not completely. How do you say it in English? Aggressive?"

"Not violent, I hope?"

"No, just rude and using bad language. And wanting to know what we got up to in Kotor."

Nicko sighed. "Bloody fool. I suppose he's got the wrong end of the stick."

Vera was unfamiliar with the idiom, but picked up its meaning.

"I'm afraid so."

"Shall I have a word with him?"

"Would you mind, Nikoshka?" There was a look of pleading in her eye.

Nicko went upstairs to confront his old school chum. Something serious must be eating him, he thought.

He knocked on the door of Viktor's room, but getting no reply, went straight in where he found him stretched on the bed, gazing at the ceiling with a glassy look in his eye. Nicko sat down on the bed beside him.

"I hear the boat ride went well," he said.

"Sure. Kolochka enjoyed himself."

They looked at each awkwardly until Viktor turned away.

"We had a great day in Kotor," offered Nicko. "A pity you couldn't have been there."

"Piss off. You know perfectly well I'd have been in your way." He produced a sleepy yawn. "No you wouldn't." "Piss off, will you?"

"Well Kotor's a great place," went on Nicko rather desperately. "We saw some fascinating things and even climbed up to the Fortress. I'm glad you asked me to come out, Vik. Really I am."

Viktor only grunted in reply.

"What's the matter with you? You can say it to me, can't you? Fuck it, I've known you for long enough."

"It's nothing you can do anything about."

"You're sunk in a Russian gloom, if you ask me. By the way Verochka lit a candle for you in the Cathedral."

"That was kind of her. What made her do that?"

"She said you wanted it. She worries about you, Vik. Really she does, and she loves you too. And I worry about you as well. After all, we managed to get through an English public school together, didn't we? Life ought to be pretty plain sailing after that."

"Fuck off, Nick." Viktor smiled. It was the schoolboy joshing they normally went in for, but with an edge to it.

"No I won't, but tell me something. You can be quite open with me. I won't reveal any state secrets. Have you got business problems? You're involved in quite a big way out here, I suspect. You're not in the shit, by any chance?"

"Who's been telling you I was in the shit? Not Verochka by any chance?"

"Not Verochka, Vik. All she said that you were doing a lot- probably too much- and not quite your old self."

"And what's my 'old self'? Stupid woman." Viktor reached down beside the bed and lifted a bottle of vodka and took a large pull at it.

"Give me some of that." Nicko took the bottle from his friend's hand and took a swig. It was a local brand. "It's better when it's chilled," he said. Wincing from the large intake, he placed the bottle on the floor again.

For a minute neither of them spoke.

"How am I going to put this?" Nicko came out with eventually.

"Don't ask me. I've no idea what you're trying to say to me." Viktor lifted the bottle and drained it completely.

"Piss of, Vik, just answer me this: have you found God, in a manner of speaking?"

"You mean the candle she lit for me?"

"The candle she lit for you, Vik."

Viktor heaved a large sigh. "I suppose, like a lot of Russians, I've never really lost Him. I know my grandfather was a big fart in the Communist Party and I was brought up not to believe in any of the old superstitions, but now when things get difficult and even a bit nasty it's something you fall back on. Sorry, that doesn't sound very profound, does it? "

"That's hardly the point, Vik. Are you in any kind of danger? I mean serious danger? There must be some pretty ugly characters piling into this neck of the woods right now, each wanting a bite of the cherry."

His friend sat up suddenly and seized Nicko's hand, the rush of emotion, amplified by the quantity of vodka he had consumed- the best part of a bottle.

"You can tell me, Vik, you know you can. It's business, isn't it? You are in the shit, aren't you?"

Viktor lay back again with a brief sigh and said nothing.

"It's true, isn't it?"

"Sure. Of course it's bloody true. I'm never out of it! I'm a fucking Russian, aren't I?"

"And someone wants to stamp on you?"

Viktor grunted by way of assent.

"Anyone in particular? Anyone you can talk about?"

"I've got a pretty good idea." "Are you going to tell me?"

Viktor yawned, he was starting to get sleepy. "A guy called Dobrinin," he mumbled. "His yacht's just tied up at Budva."

"Not the best time for you to have brought the family out for a holiday, was it?"

"He may not even know that I'm here- at least not yet anyway."

"Let's hope it stays that way."

Viktor yawned, again, shook his head vigorously and lowered his feet onto the floor. He stood up and wobbled towards the basin where he put his head under the cold tap.

"Time for a proper drink!" he announced as he dried his face on a towel. "I can see your tongue's hanging out!"

"For God's sake, Vik! Just eff off, won't you?"

Viktor put out his own tongue and examined it in the mirror.

"Are you sure you want your son to see you like this?" Nicko said.

"He's a Russian, isn't he? It won't be the first time and anyway, he's got to get used to it." The statement was clear, while the voice still thick and slurred.

But the cold water seemed to be having its effect, and Viktor was achieving an approximation of sobriety. He went to the wardrobe and rummaged for a fresh shirt.

"Now run along like a good boy and tell Verochka that I'm on my way and I won't say anything to make her feel ashamed."

Nicko left to carry out his order.

A couple of minutes later Viktor was downstairs, with his wife eying him anxiously as he went into the kitchen to prepare the drinks.

"I only want an apple juice," Vera called through. "I don't know about Ludochka."

"The same," said Ludmilla from her corner, where she was curled up with her book.

"Nikoshka needs something stronger," called Vera again.

"He's just drunk half a bottle of vodka," Viktor called back.

"He's liar," said Nicko.

Viktor put his head out of the kitchen and stuck out his tongue at his friend. He arrived with the tray a minute later. As well as the drinks for the others it included a large bowl of mixed nuts, a glass of orange juice for Kolya and cans of beer for Nicko and himself.

"So then," Vera said. "The day after tomorrow- Monday- how about a trip up to Cetinje?"

Viktor looked at his friend. "You'd like that, wouldn't you?"

"I'd like nothing better." A visit to the old Montenegran capital was at the top of Nicko's list when he had decided to join his friends on their holiday.

"Good. That's settled. Monday in Cetinje. All right for you, Ludochka?"

"Kaneshna." The girl uncoiled herself and put aside her book. "I feel like a walk," she said.

"Don't be late," Vera told her. "We eat in half an hour." "I won't."

"What strange times she chooses," commented Vera as the door shut behind her.

Talk of Cetinje set them onto the Montenegran royal family and then the usual schoolboy banter between Nicko and his friend about their Russian roots - Tsarist and Stalinist- with Nicko mounting his high horse about his family's links with the Montenegrans during their days in Russia.

Vera listened with easy tolerance - she had heard its like before - and then went into the kitchen. Kolya, who had sat silent listening to the adults for a while, crept back to the television.

Almost exactly half an hour after she had left, Ludmilla returned and swept apologetically into the kitchen to make her apologies for not being back sooner to help with the supper.

Viktor seemed to have regained his composure - Nicko marvelled at his recovery rate - and they discussed the prospect of Monday's visit to the old capital, Ludmilla regaling them with her knowledge of the subject. The byways of Balkan history clearly attracted her.

In due course Kolya was packed off the bed with the promise that Uncle Nicko would come up and read to him. When he came down again, Nicko found Viktor alone in the sitting room, at a low table in the corner studying what looked like correspondence. He took it as an excuse to slip off to bed himself.

"I'm fagged out," he said. "It's been a long day, but a bloody good one."

His friend mouthed the f-word and called "sweet dreams" after him. With the prospect of a visit to the Montenegran capital in a couple of days' time and the more immediate one of Trollope, Nicko settled happily in bed.

CHAPTER SIX

Incident in Cetinje

Another day had passed uneventfully on the beach and now Nicko was in bed, absorbed once more in 'The Three Clerks'. It had passed midnight, but he couldn't let it go. And it was to be Cetinje in the morning, with the whole family this time….

Viktor had been rather subdued all day. He had taken the boat - freshly christened 'Anna' in a brief naming ceremony that same morning - for a spin just once. They had all gone with him and he had indulged in no fancy driving. He had then retreated under the awning, out of the sunlight….

Eventually Nicko dozed off, sleeping until the now customary arrival of Kolya broke his dream apart. It had been a vivid one and shreds of it remained with him afterwards. In it he had been back at school, playing in a house rugby match. Viktor was playing also, but the game had been stopped because the Russian boy was accusing the referee, who was one of the masters, of trying to kill him. Vera, meanwhile, was standing on the touchline with a golden Labrador on a lead, looking blissfully unconcerned about the rumpus taking place on the pitch.

Then Kolya's arrival replaced the incident's denouement. The boy flung himself down on the bed in the way that was becoming habitual, and put an arm round his godfather's neck, resting his head against his shoulder. He uttered not a word, but closed his eyes as if he was settling down to sleep.

"Move over Kolya, you're choking me," Nicko complained gently.

The boy mumbled something and slightly shifted his position.

Shortly afterwards came the expected knock at the door.

"Both my Nikolais," ordered Vera, "it's time for you to get up."

Nicko glanced at his watch. It was past eight o'clock.

"On our way," he replied, heaving the boy to one side.

When he went downstairs, he found Viktor already busy with the car. He had taken it from the garage and was stretched on the ground, examining its underneath with the aid of a flashlight.

"Anything the matter?" enquired Nicko.

Viktor stuck his head out. "I don't think so. Just checking for an oil leak, that's all."

He climbed to his feet and opened the bonnet. Shining his torch into its darker recesses, he scrutinised the engine. Finally he pulled out the dipstick and wiped it on his handkerchief in a nonchalant fashion.

"Verochka won't like that," his friend told him.

Viktor tested the oil and replaced the dipstick. "All clear," he announced.

"Messy bugger."

Viktor grinned. "Sod off."

He locked the vehicle and went back into the house.

Breakfast completed, Vera and Ludmilla stacked the dishwasher and they set off shortly after nine o'clock, Viktor having done a quick check of the engine one more time. It was another fine day, but with several large cumulus clouds assembling on the opposite side of the bay. Nicko liked a bit of cloud cover and also the light breeze that promised to take the edge off the day's heat. The clouds also provided a pleasant tonal variation to a view that might otherwise have been too washed-out and hazy.

Nicko sat in the front beside Viktor with the two women and the boy behind them. It was a comfortable vehicle with a generous amount of legroom. Viktor switched on the radio which was playing a Balkan folk ballad.

"Do we have to listen to this?" Vera complained in Russian.

Viktor turned to Nicko. "What does our guest want?"

"For a start, you don't have to treat me as your guest. But I'm easy. In a way it suits the place we're going to. I'm afraid I'm a bit of a sucker for the old Balkans. As I think you know, I was born a hundred years too late."

Viktor turned down the volume so that it didn't drown their conversation.

They drove first towards Budva and then started the climb the broad highway that twisted up the slope to the interior of Montenegro and its old capital.

"There are really two capitals," explained Viktor. "Cetinje is the old royal one and a former communist dump called Podgorica - at the foot of the mountain, which is what the name means."

As they turned one of the bends in the road, Nicko looked back in the direction of Budva whose old town behind inside its heavy fortifications projecting into the bay was an impressive sight.

"There's a big boat moored down there, a billionaire's gin palace, by the look of it," he remarked. "Could that be?..." He did not finish his question.

Viktor glanced in the same direction and nodded.

They reached the plateau above, with its pale karst limestone gleaming in the sunlight. Shrubs and cypresses grew among the rocks. Nicko was pleased to see that they were in open countryside at last, away from the blight of holiday villas.

Reaching a straight stretch of road, which was empty before them, Viktor suddenly braked.

Vera and Ludmilla exclaimed angrily in Russian, while he sat staring into his rear mirror at another vehicle which had stopped immediately behind them.

"Sorry about that," he said, "but that bastard's been sitting on my tail for at least ten minutes." He slid his right hand into the shelf space beside the steering column and kept it there, while he continued to gaze into the rear mirror.

"Anything the matter?" enquired Nicko, looking back over his shoulder.

The vehicle behind was a small Fiat with a young man in dark glasses at the wheel. With him were a couple of passengers, also young men. He was making no attempt to back off. Instead his companion in the front had opened his door and was starting to climb out. But Viktor moved again suddenly, putting his foot hard down on the accelerator, while keeping his right hand in its place beside the steering column. The other car was left far behind with its passenger scrambling to get back on board.

Protests in Russian came from the back seat, which Viktor ignored. When Nicko looked back again, the Fiat had been left a long way behind.

"Why do you have to make it into a race?" complained Vera, in English this time.

"Because I don't like people driving directly behind me," replied her husband. He removed his hand from the shelf space and replaced it on the wheel.

In another three quarters of an hour they were in Cetinje.

The first impression that Nicko had of the old Montenegran capital was how agreeably small it was, with no intrusive holiday homes. It nestled in rough karst hills, much as it must have done a hundred years earlier when a Montenegran dynast was sitting on his throne. Viktor drove quickly through to the far side, glancing continuously in his rear mirror, then swung round and doubled back before parking in the shade of the trees not far from the Hotel Grand. Getting quickly out of the car, he looked up and down the deserted street and seemed satisfied.

"Let's go," he said.

They strolled towards the centre of the town, in a leisurely manner. It looked prosperous and quite modern, not at all rundown, yet Nicko felt that somehow it had held onto some of the Ruritanian quality that he had been hoping to find still in the Balkans. It was refreshing, for instance, to see signs written only in the Cyrillic script, and not in the ubiquitous English provided on the coast for foreign visitors. There was an abundance of cash points, but not many tourists about. Above all, it was the place's small scale that Nicko appreciated. You could see the surrounding karst hillsides at the ends of its tree lined streets.

"I like it here," he told Vera, who concurred.

"We must go at once to the palace," urged Ludmilla, who seemed eager to get stuck into the Montenegran royal family.

Having walked the length of the Ulica Njegoseva, they returned to the main square and the State Museum which had been the Royal Palace. It was a modest building, but with a handsome porch projecting into the open square, where once had been the town threshing floor. Opposite was the Ethnographic Museum which had formerly housed the Serbian Embassy.

Like the rest of the town, it was the humble scale of the once Royal Palace that appealed to Nicko.

"Wouldn't it be nice if the whole world was made up of small kingdoms like this one once was," he mused, "each of them ruled by its own monarch living among his own people?"

Viktor emitted a scornful laugh.

"Of course the likes of the Nikishovs with their empire of slaves in Kolyma could never have settled for anything so ridiculously innocent," retorted Nicko. "They always have to screw up the world with their grand schemes."

Viktor mouthed the familiar expletive.

Meanwhile Ludmilla had made a beeline for the Palace and was waiting impatiently for the others in the porch. They arrived at their more leisurely pace. She seemed to have taken the Last King of Montenegro, or his family at least, completely to her heart, making an interesting contrast to the Talented Mr Ripley, Nicko reflected.

Inside they found that they could take a guided tour in a number of European languages, which their case might be English or Russian. In deference to Nicko, they settled for English, which Vera felt would also be good for Kolya. The guide was a cheerful girl who had recently worked in London. Vera observed her critically, without letting on that she had once been a tour guide herself.

Though small, the salons and bedrooms had been restored to something close to what they had been in the days of King Nikola at the start of the twentieth century.

"Another Nicholas," pointed out Vera. "There'll soon be far too many of them."

Many of the original contents of the Palace had been looted during the Second World War, but its restoration looked sympathetic. Among other things there were displays of arms and decorations, including a company standard, which had been riddled with bullets in a battle against the Turks at Vucji Dol in the nineteenth century. Montenegro's role in the frontline of Christendom was proudly spelled out. Kolya enjoyed the weapons especially, which his father explained to him in Russian, while it was the collection of sepia photographs of the royal family that interested the others, Ludmilla in particular. She bombarded the guide with questions, hardly letting her answer one before firing off the next. The royal daughters, newcomers, upstarts even, among the royalty of Europe, interested her most since they had married into some of its greatest houses. And here they were, alongside the Tsar of All the Russias himself, yet another Nicholas, with his portrait hanging there, in the former royal residence of Cetinje.

But in Nicko's case it was the Balkan aspect of the display that struck an immediate chord.

The pictures of the Montenegran clan chiefs in their traditional costumes, rather Turkish-looking, with their dashing pillbox caps- worn also by the king- their belts or sashes bristling with daggers and pistols, their proud moustaches and matching postures - these were the things that caused him to regret that he had not been alive a hundred or more years earlier, before the arrival of holiday villas and the efforts to turn this once sturdy mountain kingdom into a glitzy Adriatic Riviera.

"King Nikola was an amazing pistol shot," their guide explained to them. "He could shoot a cigarette from a man's mouth at a distance of twelve paces."

The ideal monarch for a proudly embattled nation on the frontier of Christendom.

The tour ended in the museum shop, where Ludmilla bought a book of photographs of Montenegro - which also contained a short account of the dynasty's rise from tribal chieftains to royal status, while Vera added two more fridge magnets to her collection - portraits of King Nikola and his spouse. As well as buying a copy of the same book as Ludmilla, Nicko also bought a toy soldier for Kolya, which pleased him. Viktor meanwhile was scanning the square impatiently from the shelter of the porch.

"That girl was good," Vera called to him. "Come back and give her something, Vitya."

"Did you get big tips in Petersburg?" he asked her in English, as he began to fish reluctantly inside his wallet.

"Sometimes," Vera replied, "and I never refused them. But I don't give my praise lightly. I know the Royal Palace of Cetinje is hardly the Winter Palace, but she was good. She told all the right stories. Nikoshka, who's a teacher, will understand what I'm saying."

Though her reply had been in Russian, Nicko had picked it up. He consulted his guide book and they went on to the court chapel built by King Nikola on the foundations of the original Crnojevic Monastery at the back of the Palace. Here the mortal remains of the king and his queen, Milena, had been laid to rest with great ceremony when they were finally returned in 1989, an event signalling the end of Communism in their country. Entry was two and a half euros for adults and one and a half for the child, all of which Nicko insisted on paying. Inside Ludmilla went at once to the modest-looking royal tombs and, standing before them in silence, crossed herself, just a shade too ostentatiously, Nicko felt.

"She really does seem to have been carried away by the Montenegran royals, doesn't she?" he whispered in Vera's ear.

"I think she wants to write a book about them. About the girls who lived in Russia, at least." Vera smiled. "It's not such a bad idea. It might make a good story."

"All clear- I think," announced Vik, looking around the square.

95

"Why's he's so jumpy? Said Nicko

"And there was that funny business with the car coming up."

It was hardly the moment to be discussing it. Vera looked at him with a shrug and raised her eyebrows.

They crossed the square to the museum, which was still known as the Biljarda. It had featured colourfully in Montenegran history. Built in 1838 for Petar II Petrovic Njegos, the poet/playwright prince, it held the manuscript of his famous verse play, 'The Mountain Wreath'. But it had taken its name from the billiard table which he had brought back as a souvenir from his travels in Italy. It had to be hauled up the precipitous mule track from Kotor, the only available route from the coast to the capital at that time. All this information Nicko solemnly passed on from his guide book before they went inside.

They stopped first to look at the relief map of Austria, which was housed in a glass pavilion connected to the main building. Created by the country's Austrian occupiers during the First World War for strategic purposes, Nicko's guide book compared it to a crazy golf course. In its faded, muddy-looking way, it was impressive enough and worth a few minutes' attention. The effect, though, was somewhat diminished by a brightly-coloured sweet wrapper which had come to rest near its centre.

Another small group, of three young men, was ahead of them, studying the curiosity from the opposite side. They spoke in whispers so it was difficult to place their nationality.

Viktor was staring hard at them, when suddenly he turned on his heel and left the pavilion. Without saying a word to the others, Nicko followed him out.

He met his friend at the foot of the stairs, leading up to the first floor galleries.

"Get the others out of here - at once," Viktor hissed. "Think of something, any bloody thing you like, but get them out, right now! Especially Kolochka!"

He started up the stairs, but as he was speaking the party of three emerged from the pavilion and loitered in the foyer. They talked to each other softly and barely gave the figure retreating up the stairs a glance.

Nicko returned to the map room.

"Where's Vitya gone?" asked Vera. Her face wore a strained expression and she was clutching her son's hand tightly.

"Upstairs," Nicko told her. "I don't think he liked the look of our company. He nodded in the direction of the spot where the three men had been standing. "And he wants you out of here too."

He did not pass on the particular reference to Kolya in his instructions. He felt it might be too alarming and superfluous anyway.

He went back out. The three men had disappeared and there was no sign of Viktor either. "Wait," he told the others, "I'll go and find Vik."

He started up the stairs. First he went into the room which contained the famous billiard table. It was a modest affair and looked the worse for wear. But there was no time to linger and to ponder on the poet/prince of Montenegro. The room led onto a succession of galleries with blown-up photographs on the walls. A fascinating record of the old Balkan kingdom, no doubt, Nicko felt, as he passed them by, but he had to find Vik.

The place appeared deserted, one gallery leading on to the next, producing something like the recessional effect created by mirrors when they face each other.

"Vik," he called out softly as he advanced. "Are you there?"

No answer came and he seemed to be entirely by himself - which was unsettling. But there was no sign of a posse of young men either.

"Vik," he called once more. "For Christ's sake, Vik, where the hell have you got to?"

He reached the final room in the line, which a glance told him contained recent material from the Second World War, then looking out onto the adjacent landing, he glimpsed a movement, while at the same time a shadow cut off the sunlight in the direction from which he had just come. It was gone again in an instant and the sunlight streamed back once more. But it was the movement on the landing ahead of him that gripped Nick's immediate attention.

"Vik?" He looked around, advancing cautiously. And then he saw him with his back pressed against the wall.

The look of relief on Vik's face was palpable when he realised who it was.

"Vik, for Christ's sake, what are you playing at?"

"Thank God it's you, Nick."

Nicko noticed that his right hand was in his trouser pocket, pressed against something bulky.

Of course, he reflected, it has to be like this. These Russians are, after all, of the New kind, and that's how they do business. For a moment pity and contempt mingled in him and he enjoyed a sense of English moral superiority.

"We've got to get out of this place," he told Vik.

"If they'll let us."

"For God's sake, I know you're in the shit, Vik, right up to your neck, and I can guess the kind of reason you are. But we can't hang about. No way."

He tiptoed back into the room he had just left and looked back down the succession of galleries. There was only sunlight reflected off glass cases and the parquet floor.

"I don't think we'll have to go out the same way," he told his friend.

A staircase led down from the landing to the ground floor.

Taking cautious steps, with Nicko going ahead, they set off down, stopping a number of times to peer over the rail and to listen for any sounds. Like the galleries above, it seemed unnaturally quiet.

"Where've they all gone?" whispered Viktor. "There's nobody about." Nicko did not reply, but when he reached the ground floor he walked swiftly through a gallery to the ticket office.

"All clear, Vik," he called back softly to his friend, as he went back part of the way to meet him.

The foyer was empty apart from the woman in the ticket office.

Nicko went over and, addressing her in English, enquired about the rest of their party. She understood enough to tell him that they had left the building. Her relaxed manner did not suggest that she had witnessed anything suspicious. Before he turned back to his friend, who had emerged into the foyer, Nicko took a quick look into the map pavilion which was also deserted.

Outside he could not see them at first, but then he noticed the others standing in the shade of the trees on the path that led up to the Ulica Njegoseva. He waved, giving them a thumbs up, and Vera waved back.

"I've found him," he called.

Vera crossed over to him, leaving Kolya with Ludmilla.

"Where was he?" she asked

"In a galley upstairs. He thought someone was following him. Those guys who were in the car behind us - and were here just a few minutes ago - they're the same ones. Have you seen any more of them?"

Vera shook her head.

He looked around the peaceful, almost somnolent, space and went back into the museum to fetch Viktor.

They emerged together - Viktor sheepishly, not a bit the cocky New Russian.

Vera did not reproach him, but merely sighed and shook her head. "Where is all this taking us?" she asked Nicko.

"We mustn't stand around here," he told her. "They are probably watching us right now."

Viktor crossed swiftly to the other two standing under the trees, where he lifted Kolya off his feet and hugged him. But he remained alert and was determined that they should stick together as a group.

"Time, I think, for an ice cream," he announced in Russian. "You'd like one, wouldn't you, Kolochka?"

The boy nodded.

They walked back to the main square and went quickly into a café on the side opposite to the Royal Palace. There were plenty of people about, and, in front of the outside tables, several small boys were riding in hired pedal cars.

Viktor was determined to resume charge. He placed them discreetly in the shade of a large umbrella where he ordered espresso coffees and ice creams, casting an eye over the other tables at the same time. He appeared satisfied and Nicko, who was doing the same thing, also felt reassured.

The tension eased as they ate their ice creams and sipped the espressos.

Nicko suddenly jumped to his feet. "Kolya," he said, "How about a drive?"

He had noticed the boy casting envious glances in the direction of the other boys in their pedal cars.

"Isn't he too big?" objected Vera.

But Kolya shook his head vigorously.

"Let's give it a go. I'll keep an eye on him," Nicko said.

The pair of them went out to where a man was hiring out the cars. They selected a red one, which Kolya, despite being eight years old, still managed to squeeze into.

"Don't drive too fast and keep over on this side," Nicko ordered him.

But some of his father must have been in the boy, who started pedalling madly towards the middle of the square

"Kolochka!" Vera yelled from the café while Nicko tore after the car. There was a sharp crack and something spat into the paving immediately in front of him. He halted in his tracks for a second as a figure dashed out from the far side of the square and ran towards the boy in the car.

Vera screamed something from behind and a second shot rang out, which fell just wide of Nicko who was racing towards the boy.

He just made it before the other and, snatching Kolya up, staggered back with him, zigzagging his way to the café where everyone was on their feet.

No more shots were fired as he plunged in among the tables, sending one flying as he did so. Then a bullet whined past his ear and into the café window, which shattered. Viktor rushed forward and grabbed the child from his arms and together they joined the scramble to relative safety inside the café.

Vera was waiting just outside the door, being pushed back in the rush. She grabbed the boy from her husband and ducked with him into the café and behind the counter where she thrust him onto the floor.

In the panic Nicko could not help noticing Ludmilla, as cool as a cucumber, taking a vacant seat at the back of the room, where, incredibly, she opened the book she had bought in the Royal Palace and start to read it. Ripley couldn't have handled it more phlegmatically, he concluded.

Meanwhile he and Viktor crouched down among the other outdoor customers in the doorway. More people arrived and tried to push past them and there was a babble of panicky chatter. The café owner was shouting into a phone at the counter. Everyone was still in this position when, with commendable speed, Nicko felt, a couple of policemen appeared.

The story was soon told, with Viktor doing most of the telling. Neither policeman seemed particularly surprised by it. They listened almost wearily, nodding from time to time, while one of them jotted down a few notes. Looking at it historically, Nicko could not help thinking that shootings on the streets Balkan capitals were hardly occasions for great surprise.

Several more policemen arrived in the square and, when he emerged from the café, Viktor was asked further questions. The conversation went on in a rapid mixture of Russian and Serbo-Croat which seemed to be working well enough.

It ended with Viktor leaving his address and telephone number in Tiva and the entire party being bundled into a pair of police cars to be driven back to their own car near the Hotel Grand. A detailed inspection of the car followed and only when it was pronounced clean was the party allowed to board. With a police car fore and aft, they set off down the road back to the coast.

When they arrived they were met by more police, waiting at the gate of the villa, allowing their escort to return to Cetinje.

Hardly a word had been spoken during the entire journey, but now, home once more, the tension broke. Vera was hugging her son tightly- indeed, she had not let go of him for the entire journey back except for once when he had pleaded to be allowed to relieve himself by the roadside- an operation closely supervised by two of the policemen. Now Nicko embraced mother and son, then drew Viktor into the huddle. Only Ludmilla, who had remained largely silent on the way back, stood to one side.

Viktor broke away for a conversation with the police in the kitchen, supplying them with generous shots of cognac at the same time. Eventually they departed, but left one of their number behind in the porch. Vera provided him with coffee and a large plate of biscuits, cutting off her husband's attempt to supply him with still more alcohol.

Viktor explained the arrangement to Nicko and threw himself down on the sofa. "Christ, I don't know about anybody else, but I'm ready for a drink."

Then, as if he had suddenly remembered something, he got to his feet again and crossed the room to his wife and child. Clasping them both to his chest, he burst into sobs, which the others joined until all three of them were blubbing away like mad. Nicko shed tears too, while Ludmilla tiptoed into the kitchen.

CHAPTER SEVEN

London … at Last

The first that Nicko heard about the move to London was when Vera telephoned him from Moscow a couple of days before flying out. She was coming to look at a house in Chelsea and bringing Kolya with her. Viktor had told his friend none of this. He had heard from him a couple of times since they had fled from Montenegro - a couple of hasty phone calls, in which he had been careful not to reveal where he was ringing from, and Nicko, having asked him once, realised that it was better not to press the matter. He sensed that his friend was just relieved that he and his own were still alive. That was two months ago and in the meantime Nicko was back at work, teaching history to small boys and girls. When Vera rang she said little, but told him that she would contact him from her hotel in London and that if he had time he might help her buy a house! No, she would find her own way in from the airport and he was not to try to meet her.

It was Friday evening when she rang from a hotel near Regent's Park, and Nicko came in from his Finchley flat on Saturday morning.

Vera was waiting for him with Kolya in the foyer. As soon as he saw him, the boy rushed over and hugged his Uncle Nicko round his legs, practically toppling him over. He was followed by his mother who held him to her breast.

Held fast by both Russians, Nicko lurched towards a small settee and managed to sit down with the boy still clutching his knees. Vera sat beside him

"It's wonderful to see you, Nikoshka!" she said.

"And you," he replied," and to know that you're all safe." He cast an eye round the foyer at the same time. It was empty, apart from the porter on duty. "And Vik? He's all right, isn't he?"

Vera nodded. "He rang last night from Petersburg. He's staying with a friend and sounded fine."

"No nasty follow-ups from our Balkan adventure?"

Vera crossed herself. "Please God, no."

"And the plan is to settle here in London? Will that be safer?"

"It's not only Vik. We're thinking about Kolochka." She hugged the child as she spoke. "Remember we were talking about him going to school here? But what about you Nikoshka? I feel terrible about the way we've dragged you into our trouble, our gangster culture, I mean."

"You forget that I'm a Russian too. A kind of a one, anyway."

Vera laughed. "Your famous Russian soul! But you're not a bit like Vitya, Nikoshka - as I've said to you before. Not the same kind of a Russian at all. He's a gangster which you're not."

"That's a bit harsh, isn't it?"

"It's true."

Nicko updated her on his rather uneventful existence since his abrupt return from Montenegro.

"I'd love to see the school where you teach," Vera said. "And I'd like to bring Kolochka, if I may."

"I'd need to make an appointment with the head. But that should be no problem - he's used to Russians. How long are you going to be here?"

Vera shrugged. "As long as it takes to find a house. Vitya's heard about a place in Chelsea."

"That'll cost him a bob or two."

She looked puzzled, so he explained the unfamiliar idiom to her.

"He'll be paying millions of pounds. Has he got that much?"

Vera shrugged. "He seems to think so. I've arranged to see the place at three o'clock this afternoon. Would you come with me?"

"Perfect. Today's Saturday so I'm free."

"Bless you, Nikoshka! But let's have lunch first, shall we? Have you any ideas?" She leaned across and kissed him on his cheek and then dabbed the boy's forehead too. "Bless you both!"

Nicko felt that he ought to offer to pay, despite his very modest income and the cost of living in London. He realised, too, that they would need to find a place that was child-friendly, so he suggested that they should take the Underground into the West End where he knew a reasonably priced Greek restaurant in St Martin's Lane.

It was a year or so since he had last been there, but they were made welcome, especially with a child. Now was the time to get some lowdown on what Viktor had been up to since his rapid exit from Montenegro, though obviously Kolya's presence called for discretion.

They had moved house, but remained in Novgorod for a while. Bodyguards had been hired from a security firm and the place watched around the clock. Viktor, it appeared, having got his fingers scorched in Montenegro, had moved out property speculation and was back into the art market, but reading between the lines of Vera's account, he was not out of the woods yet. Revenge merging with a pragmatic Stalinist requirement to be rid of a potential as well as an immediate threat, left him a marked man. He had, after all, made a heap of money. But he seemed to know who most of his enemies were and was managing to keeping ahead of them, for the time being at least.

All this Nicko was able to infer from the rather veiled and circuitous account that Vera felt able to give him. As she spoke, he found himself casting the occasional glance around the restaurant as if some of her husband's enemies might even be there. After what had so nearly happened to them in Cetinje, Nicko was acutely conscious of the dangers faced by the wife and child.

They had enjoyed their moussaka and Kolya was stuck into a huge chocolate ice while the two adults sipped cups of Turkish coffee. The first real chill of autumn could be felt on the streets outside and with the waiter pressing fresh cups on them, it would have been tempting to pass the afternoon in chat, but of course the appointment in Chelsea with an estate agent awaited them. Having settled the matter of Viktor for the time being at least, Nicko asked about Ludmilla and her literary plans.

"I've only seen her once since we got back to Russia," Vera explained. "She did not tell me anything about her literary plans then. Perhaps she did not think it was the right time to discuss them, so soon after what had happened."

"Not even Patricia Highsmith? She was hooked on Ripley."

"She did mention that once and I've promised to bring her back more of the stories when I return to Petersburg. She's doing - how do you say? post-graduate work at the university there now."

"A clever girl, but ... during the business in Cetinje she seemed so relaxed, somehow."

Vera eyed him quizzically.

"And when you first ran into her in Montenegro was she by herself?"

Vera nodded.

"The introspective type."

Kolya was scraping out the last of his ice and starting to listen attentively to what they were saying. They fell silent.

Nicko frowned and shook his head. He looked at his watch. "Christ, is that the time? We mustn't miss your appointment."

He called for the bill and insisted on paying it.

"Is that not too much?" Vera said.

But he shrugged and helped her into her coat. They said nothing more until they were in the street and heading for the Leicester Square Underground station to take them on to South Kensington.

The house which they were to look at was an early nineteenth century one in Thurloe Square, rendered in white stucco like the others, and not far from the station. They mounted the short flight of steps to the front door. Nicko was familiar with the square, from the pavement at least. He sometimes used the small Polish restaurant, the Pilsudski, near the Underground station and liked to walk that way into Knightsbridge. They entered the Doric style porch and rang the bell. It was the sort of house Nicko would have liked for himself if he had the means. But he did not repine: his parents, after all, lived in a substantial pile in Sunningdale which in the fullness of Time might be traded for something more suited to his own taste. In the meantime he was helping Vera.

It was a handsome house on the outside and appeared to be in good condition too, but was it not in too conspicuous a location, given Viktor's need to keep his head down?

"It looks nice," Nicko said, "but…"

"But what?"

"Vik, I mean. Might it not just be a little too conspicuous? Shouldn't he be looking for something more discreet?"

Vera gave a, nervous sort of laugh. "Let's see it first, shall we?"

At that moment the door opened and a man who looked about the same age as Nicko welcomed them in. He had reddish, crinkly hair and spoke with a mildly plummy accent. Nicko could not help noticing the quality of his dark pinstripe suit and the shoes that might have been purchased in Jermyn Street.

"Mr and Mrs Nikishov? Or should I say 'Gospodin' and the other thing…'Gospida'?"

"Not quite right, I'm afraid," Nicko replied. "This is Mrs Nikishov and her son Nikolai. I'm an English friend - also called Nicholas as it happens - Nicholas Orloff."

For a second the man looked bemused, hearing Nicko's Russian sounding surname.

"Dobra dan," he came out with to Vera, adding in English. "Pleased to meet you. I'm Tim Mumford. Come right in."

He led the way into the house, where they paused in the hall for him to switch on a light. It was empty of any furnishings, but the paintwork and the walls were in a good state, showing signs of a recent and caring occupancy. Vera immediately started to ask questions, mostly of a practical nature, about things like the central heating, while Nicko, left to admire the stuccoed cornices and moulded ceilings, was attempting to point out some of their finer features to Kolya.

He rather warmed to Tim Mumford. He was not pushy and indeed seemed more like a gentlemen showing guests round his own house than an estate agent trying to sell one in a pricey part of town. In his way he reminded Nicko of some of the more upmarket types he had met working in the art and antiques trade alongside Freddie Ryedale. He was tempted to ask him which school he had been to, but realised that it would have looked snobbish. And anyway, he had to think of Vera first.

He liked the house with its spacious rooms, their marble fireplaces and moulded cornices and ceilings. There was plenty of space at the back too- with enough of a garden to offer a quiet retreat on a summer's evening. Vera meanwhile was keen to examine the kitchen, its cupboards, larders and the like.

But despite the well-bred charm of Tim Mumford- which was clearly having its effect- he was managing to make himself agreeable to the child as well - one question still nagged in Nicko's mind. Was it secure?

"What about the neighbours?" he suddenly asked Tim.

Tim smiled. "Quiet sorts by all accounts," he said. "And as far as I know perfectly civilised, as you might expect. I've heard no complaints about any of them, though I can't speak for all the properties." He shrugged his shoulders. "If any of them are big-time crooks, word hasn't reached me yet."

Nicko and Vera exchanged glances, while Tim cast a discreet glance at the toes of his Jermyn Street shoes. He was dealing with a Russian, after all, and the less said about such matters the better.

"There's a chap who's quite well known a couple of doors down. He's a trade minister in the Government." He looked at Nicko. "Lord Isaacs, no less, not long back from exile in Brussels and restored to the Cabinet from which he fell from grace a few years back - as you will no doubt recall."

"Of course. A highly oleaginous gentleman by all accounts. A leftie in his student days - even a member of the Communist Party, I believe - and now a peer of the Realm. The P.M. hates his guts, but apparently needs his skills to fight a general election - the black arts of an experienced witchdoctor."

"The Universal Spider," added Tim. "But, to mix my metaphor, like many of his sort an exotic bloom as well - if that's the kind of a neighbour you like. I can't offer you anyone else I'm afraid. He's the only celebrity immediately to hand that I'm aware of."

The tour continued up to the attics and down into the basement, which held out the possibility of being converted into a separate flat. Vera nodded her approval at what she was being shown, though of course could not commit herself without consulting her husband first.

After an hour they parted from Tim on very friendly terms and Nicko even suggested that the might meet up for a drink some time quite soon. He did not let on that he working as a prep school master, but instead preferred to talk about his time in the art and antiques trade. Tim nodded approvingly, but confessed that he had never heard of Freddie Ryedale, adding, perhaps tactfully, that maybe he should have done.

After they had parted from Tim on the pavement outside, Nicko turned to Vera. "What do you think?"

"I like it, but of course Vitya has to decide. You two seemed to be good friends," she added.

Nicko shrugged. "I'm used to his sort. We can rub along."

Vera nodded, unsure of the idiom, but guessing its meaning.

"Anyway," resumed Nicko, "you liked it?"

"Very much, but as I told you, Vitya has to agree."

"Can he afford it?"

They had been given a figure which seemed fairly representative of the current state of the market.

"I think so. He can afford most things if he wants them badly enough. But as you know he has to think of other ones too."

"Sure he does. I've seen it for myself, haven't I? But that's something Vik's going to have to face wherever he chooses to live. And another thing, this isn't far from Kolya's new school which you have to see for yourself next week, by the way, before you fly back to Mother Russia."

"You'd like us to buy this house, wouldn't you, Nikoshka? You and Mr Mumford are friends, plotting to make a fortune out of some stupid

New Russians who have far too much money to spend. I understand you now, Nikoshka! Naughty Nikoshka!" She tapped him on the bridge of his nose, which he liked.

Kolya, meanwhile, with this play going on between his mother and his English godfather, was admiring a handsome husky dog which a man was leading up the steps of a house a couple of doors away. The man was lean with a pronounced forward-projecting chin and longish dark hair, flopping down over his brow.

Nicko followed the boy's gaze and recognised the man at once.

"That's Lord Isaacs - the Government Minister, the one that Tim was talking about," he said.

"Is he important?"

"He certainly thinks he is and so does the BBC which eats out of his hand." Nicko glanced at the child and lowered his voice. "He's gay of course, but I don't think he's any kind of danger to small boys. He presumably wouldn't be in the Government if he was - though of course you never quite know with some of them. He's said to have a Mexican boyfriend living with him. Don't let any of this put you off buying the house, by the way."

Vera laughed. "I think we could live with all of that."

They went into the Pilsudski restaurant near the Underground station where Kolya consumed another massive ice cream. He was very taken with the husky.

"Can we have a dog like the one I saw?" he demanded of his mother in Russian.

"Maybe we can, when we are in our new home," she replied in the same language. "And try to speak in English. You are in London now, Kolochka," she added sternly.

Nicko left them back at their hotel and promised to ring as soon as he had spoken to his headmaster, Dick Trubshaw, to arrange Vera's appointment.

The following evening, Sunday, she was on the 'phone to Nicko. She had spoken to her husband about the house in Thurloe Square and he had liked the sound of it, but wanted to see it for himself before closing. That it had a basement was important to him, so he instructed Vera to hold her fire until he could fix a visa to come across himself. He hoped to join her before the end of the week, if his contact in the Consulate delivered as he normally did.

Monday came and Nicko spoke to Dick Trubshaw about Kolya and Vera's proposed visit. There was no problem: she could easily be slotted in on Wednesday afternoon. He had an earlier appointment at two, so how about three? It suited Vera and Nicko as well, because it coincided with a free period when he could meet her. He did not particularly want to be observed by her taking a class. Though the work was rewarding in many ways with polite, well-motivated children being taught on traditional lines, he still had the sneaking feeling that it wasn't quite a man's work. He dreaded being stuck with such a role to the point where he was given the label of a 'confirmed bachelor' and what the euphemism tended to imply. Still, it would be an ideal school for a bright boy like Kolya and besides, he would not be the only Russian in it either. There already were young Evgeni Khlebnikov and his sister Eleni.

Bailey's was in Knightsbridge, just a station ride from South Kensington and could also be reached easily on foot which would be ideal for a family living in Thurloe Square. So, come Wednesday, Nicko met Vera and her son at the school's big double doors on the dot of three and took them straight through to meet Dick Trubshaw.

As they went down the passage a bell rang for a changeover of classes and the children emerged from the classrooms in files. The boys were wearing green school blazers and grey flannel shorts with green-topped stockings. The girls were dressed likewise, but of course in skirts rather than shorts. They all sported the yellow and green school tie. Seeing a visitor in the company of one of their masters, they each said a punctilious 'Good afternoon' as they passed.

Vera was impressed. "You see how smart they look and how polite they are!" she whispered to her son in Russian.

Dick Trubshaw emerged from his study to meet them in the passage. He was a man in his late thirties with a breezy subaltern's manner. He greeted Vera and her son warmly while Nicko left them, saying that he could be reached in the small common room if and when he was required. He preferred to leave the sales pitch to Dick whose easygoing charm, laced with the right degree of headmasterly gravitas, generally proved an effective formula for winning prospective parents round. Nicko settled into one of the elderly leather armchairs that were the principle furnishing in the Spartan common room. The head would ring through when he was ready.

It was three-quarters of an hour later when Dick rang and Nicko went down to find the party standing on the threshold of the head's study having returned from their tour. Kolya was talking volubly in his native tongue to Evgeni Khlebnikov - the Russian boy already in the school. He was three years older than Nikishov, but they appeared to be hitting it off.

Sensible of Dick to have fished Evgeni out of class to meet his fellow Russian, thought Nicko. Vera meanwhile was nodding vigorously at something the head was explaining to her. The body language of both suggested that things had gone well.

"Ah, there you are, Nick," said Dick as he rolled up.

"All well?" asked Nicko.

Dick Trubshaw chuckled. "You'll need to ask Mrs Nikishov that one."

"All very well," confirmed Vera, her eyes glowing with satisfaction.

Dick Trubshaw saw his visitors onto the step at the front door and, after shaking hands with mother and son and receiving an effusion of thanks from the former, he left them with Nicko.

"What do you really think?" Nicko asked.

"It's a lovely school. The classes are small, the children properly dressed- the way school children ought to look - and very polite. They seemed to be well taught too. And I like Mr Trubshaw your director- or should I call him your head teacher?"

"The second'll do, but 'headmaster' is the term he likes best. Dick's a great charmer, but he runs a tight ship - as we say in English. He's sympathetic, but stands no nonsense."

"All children need discipline," said Vera. "Kolochka's no different."

"What do you think?" Nicko asked the boy. "Do you like this school?"

"It's different from my school in Russia, but I think I will like it. There are not too many kids and I like Evgeni."

"Who are the Khlebnikovs?" Vera wanted to know.

"Yet another Russian family - like you, living in London and wanting the best for their kids. I believe he's something big in fish products- but you never quite know, do you?" He laughed gently and Vera smiled with a shrug.

"You make him sound fishy."

Nicko groaned at the feebleness of the pun and they laughed at it together.

"I hope I'm allowed to make bad jokes too, Nikoshka," Vera said.

"I think mine are better bad jokes than yours. Or do I mean worse? But seriously, I thought Evgeni was a nice boy and might make a good friend for Kolochka. Mind, he must find some English ones too."

"You and Vik have got a lot to talk about," said Nicko. He looked at his watch. "But I'm afraid I've got to go and earn my daily bread. Would you like a taxi?"

Vera assured him that she could find one for herself. "Tomorrow I'm taking Kolochka to the zoo," she said. "He's been good and earned a treat."

"I'd like to come with you, but I'll be working." He pecked her on the cheek.

"I'll ring you later, at seven o'clock," she told him as she and the boy set off down the pavement.

Which she did, exactly on the hour. She had already talked to Viktor who was due into Heathrow in two days' time.

"What did he think?" asked Nicko.

"Interested- in both the house and the school, but you know the kind of things he has to think about."

"Could I forget?"

"Tomorrow it's the zoo. And if Kolochka's still being good, we might go to Hamley's, the toy shop, after that. You couldn't join us there, could you?"

"Alas not - but the name Hamley's revives many a wistful memory of my childhood."

"But you're really still a child, aren't you Nikoshka? I mean it in a nice of way."

"Of course you do. But think of me while you're there - and let me know as soon as Vik's arrived. And my love to Kolya in the meantime."

"He's never stopped talking about Evgeni."

"Ring me tomorrow, Verochka."

CHAPTER EIGHT

Viktor Arrives

Nicko heard nothing the next day and wondered if he ought to ring Vera instead, but decided to leave the ball in her court. In his vaguely diffident way he felt that he might be pushing things too far if he rang first. The following day was a busy one when he had to take a game of football with the younger boys, a weekly chore he disliked, and it was nearly seven when he got home to Finchley. He was hardly through the door when the 'phone rang.

It was Viktor, who had arrived in the hotel only ten minutes earlier and sounded breathless.

"Tomorrow evening, Nick? About this time? You will join us here in the hotel."

"I'll try to be there."

"Not good enough. You will be here. Prikaz."

"Piss off, Vik. I said I'll try."

"Seven o'clock. There's a lot to talk about. And I'll have someone you should meet."

"Oh God, have you really?"

"He's a friend - a kind of one anyway."

"What's that supposed to mean? I'm not sure if I want to meet your kind of friends."

"You and Alyosha'll get along fine."

"Anyway. What news? No trouble in Moscow?"

"None at all. It all went like clockwork - the visa, everything."

"I suppose Verochka's told you about the house? And Kolya's new school?"

"I'm seeing the house tomorrow and Kolochka's told me about the school - he seems to have made up his own mind about it. But, Nick, it's great to hear the sound of your voice! So seven o'clock and don't be late. I know Russians are meant to be, but we're in England now and I never thought you were a real one anyway."

"Piss off." Nicko put down the 'phone.

It appeared as if the Montenegran nightmare already was water under the bridge- but that was the way with Viktor's kind. They shrugged the thing off and passed on to the next episode in their lives. Nicko was intrigued by the mention of a friend, Alyosha. He probably wouldn't take to him- especially if he was some kind of a hired heavy, but then he might provide an interesting addition to the plot. And that was the truth of it: the whole affair was beginning to look like a piece of fiction to Nicko- especially after the recent Balkan adventure- so any new character might enrich an already rich tale still further. But at the same, time, he told himself, I mustn't lose sight of some of the apparently more marginal ones- Ludmilla Mikhailovna, for instance….

* * * * * *

Shortly before the appointed time, Nicko arrived at the hotel in Prince's Gate and was met by Viktor in the foyer. He wasn't alone. Beside him was a man who looked about the same age, but leaner and with a crisp military-style haircut. Nicko was relieved to see that at least he did not have a shaved head like a club bouncer - a fashion which he found distasteful. He was soberly dressed in a plain dark suit and wore a silk tie with a discreetly striped shirt. While he looked tough, it was not in a thuggish kind of way, and nor did he look particularly Russian either. He could have passed for an officer in the Royal Marines.

"Hi, Nick," said Viktor, jumping to his feet. "It's great to see you again!" He took his chum's hand and shook it warmly. "Meet Alyosha."

The other dipped his head and taking Nicko's hand, pressed it firmly in his own. His broad smile revealed a single gold incisor- a Russian trait.

"Ochin priatni," said Nicko.

"Ochin priatni," the other replied.

"You can say it again in English," Viktor pointed out. "It might be better if you did."

"This isn't your first time over here then?" enquired Nicko politely.

"Not at all. I have come many times." The man nodded and grinned in a relaxed manner.

"And dare I ask," Nicko went on, "what you do exactly? What's your job?"

Alyosha looked at Viktor, who patted Nicko on the shoulder and chuckled.

"I'm surprised you bother to ask that question, Nick," he said.

"Alyosha's my accountant or book-keeper if you prefer that term." Alyosha smiled and nodded in agreement.

"And Verochka?" asked Nicko. "She'll be down soon?"

"You know what women are like," said Viktor in his male chauvinist way. "You must be ready for a drink. Alyosha and I certainly are."

"Nothing heavy," answered Nicko. "A dry Martini'll go down nicely at this stage."

At Viktor's suggestion they moved to the bar and as they did so, Vera emerged from the lift with Kolya.

The boy was full of his recent trip to the zoo and to Hamley's and launched immediately into an account for the benefit of his godfather. At the zoo it seemed that his interest had been divided chiefly between the giraffes, an orangutan who had gazed soulfully back at him from his cage, and a tarantula lodged safely behind a stout pane of glass.

He rattled on, speaking fluently in English for the most part, as they settled at a table in the bar. Alyosha took the order for drinks and carried it to the barman, who arrived with them a minute later. Viktor and Alyosha both joined Nicko with a dry Martini with ice and a slice of lemon, while Vera and her son stuck to Coca-Cola.

Eventually after a few token questions from the boy's father and Nicko, the account of the visit to Regent's Park drew to a close. Vera looking rather proud of what her son had just achieved in the way of spoken English, squeezed Nicko's arm warmly.

"Has Mr Trubshaw spoken to you?" she asked.

"I haven't seen him all day," Nicko replied

"Well, he rang me to say that he would be very happy to take Kolochka in two weeks' time - at the half term."

"That's great news," Nicko said.

"But he wants him to sit a small examination first - in his English and his Mathematics."

"I'm sure he'll pass with flying colours. Won't you, Kolya?"

The boy looked a little mystified by the unfamiliar idiom, but grasped its meaning quickly enough.

"Kaneshna. I mean 'of course'. I'll do my best."

His mother hugged him. "I'm so proud of my Kolochka!" she murmured.

The boy edged away, slightly embarrassed by this outburst of maternal pride.

"Pass with flying colours?" Viktor repeated ponderously. "That's one of your military metaphors, isn't it?"

Nicko mouthed a noiseless 'fuck off' in his direction.

"You'll do fine, won't you Kolochka?" his father said. "Especially in Mathematics. You have been well taught already."

"And tomorrow we buy his uniform and then he'll be a real English schoolboy," announced his mother. "And after that we'll go to see the house."

Viktor meanwhile had settled into a whispered conversation with Alyosha, who was nodding and interjecting an occasional 'da'. Vera gave them an irritated glance and turned again to Nicko.

"He must make up his mind quickly," she said, loud enough for her husband to hear. "I wish you two wouldn't talk in Russian," she added crisply.

Alyosha gave her an apologetic glance, while Viktor pouted in a sulky fashion before joining in the general chat which his wife seemed determined to keep going.

As the following day was a Saturday, Nicko promised to join the party at the end of their house-viewing. They could then go and eat at the Pilsudski or find an Indian if they preferred. With that settled, the talk turned to the present state of Russia: Putin's schemes and gas supplies to Europe. Vera, Nicko could not help noticing, was especially scornful, talking of 'Tartar Politics', an expression that made Alyosha smile.

When they went to eat, Nicko cut away. He had some marking to do and wanted to clear it out of the way before the weekend.

* * * * * *

The inspection of the house in Thurloe Square had been arranged for half past two, so Nicko contrived to appear an hour later. He had timed it well, because the party was just emerging as he arrived. Viktor nodded to him over Tim Mumford's shoulder. Vera was leaning on her husband's arm, smiling, while Kolya was stroking a large husky dog whose owner had stopped on the pavement to talk to them. The boy was firing questions at him, which the man was attempting to answer with a show of easy good nature. Indeed, he had the relaxed air of a practised politician - which of course was what he was, being none other than Lord Isaacs of South Shields. Alyosha stood to one side of the group, with a benevolent smile on his face.

When he saw Nicko, Tim greeted him like an old friend.

"How did it go?" enquired Nicko.

Tim dipped his head, smiled and shrugged. "That's hardly for me to say," he said.

But Viktor nodded and made a thumbs up sign. Vera continued to smile, while Kolya went on talking dogs with Lord Isaacs.

"Actually he's a Russian, the same as you," the Government Minister was explaining. "He's really a Siberian and he he's got a Russian name. He's called Igor. What's yours, by the way?"

"Nikolai or Nicholas," answered the boy. "But most people call me Kolya."

"Nicholas or Nikolai," said the Minister. "The name of the last Tsar of Russia!" He let out a short sigh. "But I like Kolya. So we might be neighbours?" he added, addressing Vera.

"It seems so."

"How very nice. I'm Mark Isaacs, by the way." He did not wait for a reply, but dispensing a friendly nod all round, he glided up the steps into his own porch, two doors away, the dog following obediently in his wake.

"A Siberian husky," declared Kolya in an awed voice. "Cool."

"Well?" said Nicko looking from husband to wife. "Or is it Tim who has to break the news to me?

"We're taking the house," Vera told him. "The Master is satisfied."

Viktor and Alyosha nodded in unison. "There will need to be a few alterations," the former said, "but hopefully not too many."

Nicko risked a wink at Tim, who nodded in his turn and smiled back, clearly pleased at the swiftness of the settlement.

"Some happy bunnies," said Nicko. "It's cause for celebration."

"I'll leave that to you," said Tim. "We'll be in touch tomorrow." He looked at Viktor. "All that paperwork. Legal stuff- it's a bit of a pain but it has to be done."

"It's easier in Russia," Viktor replied. "We don't bother with paperwork - or not so much of it anyway. So you won't join us now?"

"Thank you, but not today. I'll give you a ring tomorrow- about ten. Here's my mobile number, by the way." He handed him a card and having shaken hands all round, including Nicko's, he set off down the street.

"What do you think of your new neighbour - Mr - or rather Lord Isaacs?" asked Nicko.

"His dog's really cool," effused Kolya.

Nicko pursed his lips at Vera who frowned slightly.

"How do I say it?" he said. "Oleaginous? Do you know that word?"

"I think I can guess."

"A creep, in a word. Then I would say that. I can't stand the man's politics."

"God save the Tsar!" announced Viktor facetiously.

Nicko mouthed the f-word at him in the usual manner.

"Is he a socialist?" asked Vera.

"He pretends to be - or at least did once. It's the first time I've seen him in the flesh, so to speak. But he's hardly ever out of the news and he has the BBC eating out of his hand. He's really one of their own. He oozes charm, mixed with a great deal of poison. Don't let me put you off the man, by the way. They say he can be very amusing, both him and his young Mexican friend. "He turned to Viktor. "I'm ready for that drink, aren't you? And there'll have to be an ice cream for Kolya!"

"Can we have a Siberian husky too?" Kolya demanded of his mother. "You'll have to ask your father about that," she told him. "But not straight away. We have to move into our new home and you have to start your new school first."

"I liked Mr Isaacs," the boy said.

"Did you? But remember he's not called Mr but Lord Isaacs."

A brief snort came from Nicko, but no further comment.

Nicko suggested the Pilsudski, not far from the Underground station, where they might enjoy a celebratory drink and meet Kolya's needs at the same time. Nicko liked its Slavic ambience. It took its name from the Polish leader who had trounced the Bolsheviks when they invaded his country in 1920 - a single shaft of light in those dark times when the Socialist Revolution seemed to be sweeping all before it and his own family had been dispossessed. The Orloffs had had a soft spot for Poles ever since.

The party settled at a corner table near the street window, a procedure that Alyosha discreetly took in hand. The Russian, Nicko could not help noticing, placed himself on the banquette with a good view of the street door, while the boy was wedged between his parents and Nicko sat with his back to the door.

Alyosha ordered vodkas and Coca-Cola for the mother and child. It seemed that Viktor was quite happy for him to run the occasion, which he proceeded to do with an almost pedantic precision. He insisted on the best vodka that the house had to offer, which had to be properly chilled, and accompanied by the right kind of herring snack. A large chocolate ice was brought for the boy at the same time and a glass of white wine for Vera to join in the toasts.

It was Alyosha who called them to order, with a few words in Russian. Glasses were raised and the toasts given in two languages. Viktor laughed cheerfully, happy, it seemed, to have found such a good master of ceremonies. The vodkas were thrown back and Alyosha ordered a bottle for the table. Nicko meanwhile caught the waitress's eye as if to tell her that, he would not let it get too rowdy. She nodded at him in a conspiratorial fashion, while Alyosha saw to the formalities in the best Slavic manner. Nicko's mind flew back to that symposium in Uncle Frank's flat.

The talk grew more animated, with a mixing of languages, to which the boy added his pennyworth about Lord Isaacs' dog. More toasts followed, one to Nicko and another to Alyosha's folks back in Yaroslavl. Viktor even let out a couple of whoops like the ones he uttered behind the wheel of his motor boat in Tiva. But Vera drew the line at that and dressed him down severely in Russian. He seemed oddly chastened, more like a small boy than an assertive Russian man of business. There was a power in Vera which was palpable. Excessive displays of Slavic conviviality - especially in public places - were a feature of her native culture that she disdained. As she spoke, she glanced anxiously at the scattering of late afternoon customers at the other tables.

Nevertheless Viktor and Alyosha managed to get off a few verses of the Song of Stenka Razin, sotto voce, and Nicko could not help noticing that the latter had a good baritone voice. He noticed, too, that for all his show of conviviality, the man remained alert to who was coming and going through the door, also glancing over his shoulder from time to time into the street. While Vera eyed her husband with mounting disapproval, Alyosha was careful to consume only one shot of vodka to every two of his. Indeed when Viktor loudly announced a toast to the new home, revealing its address to the restaurant at large, he nudged him, putting a finger to his lips at the same time, and Nicko was glad to see that his caution was heeded. Vera meanwhile was attempting to distract Kolya from his father's behaviour by drawing him and Nicko into a separate conversation about his new school.

It was Alyosha who called a halt to proceedings and asked for the bill. Nicko took the boy down to the men's lavatory on the basement floor, where there was a second dining room, while Vera sought the ladies' kind. By the time they got back Viktor and Alyosha were standing in the doorway waiting to leave. As soon as Nicko arrived Alyosha went ahead into the street.

"You must give me some gen on your friend from Yaroslavl," Nicko whispered to Viktor.

"What do you need to know?" His tone was a trifle defensive.

"Obviously he has to be clean."

"Of course he's clean! What the fuck do you take me for?"

Nicko glanced at the boy who did not appear to be listening to them. Meanwhile as Vera appeared Alyosha stuck his head back in through the door, giving a brief nod.

As they filed out, Nicko recalled the scene in the Billiardo in Cetinje and its immediate aftermath. He assumed Viktor had a fairly good idea who was friend and who foe in the murky world he appeared to inhabit. He seemed to have made some pretty impressive enemies, including the owner of the yacht standing off Tiva. It was a mark of his upward progress, Nicko supposed, and might even be construed as a badge of honour. Its lethal aspect was, of course, of a piece with his family's past in its Stalinist heyday. But unless he took good care, he might be dead meat himself, which would be a shame, of course, though it would be even worse if any harm came to those who were closest to him....

As they started down the pavement towards where Alyosha had stopped a taxi, Viktor squeezed his friend's arm apologetically. "Sorry," he said. "We can't talk about it now."

"Piss off, Vik," Nicko whispered in his ear. "I'm sure you've got it everything in hand. I don't want anything to happen to you, that's all."

"Piss off." Returning the compliment, Viktor grinned and pressed his arm again.

Nicko left them boarding the taxi and turned towards the Underground station.

"Tomorrow, at five o'clock then. Teatime," Vera ordered him from the cab. "First we go to Madame Tussaud's. I don't suppose you want to do that, but come to the hotel."

Instead of going down into the station, Nicko wandered back in the direction of Thurloe Square and Knightsbridge. He stopped outside the new home to admire its handsome Doric porch. While he was gazing up at it, a taxi drew up and a small man carrying a laptop jumped out and ran up the steps of Lord Isaacs' house, two doors down. He rang the bell and the door opened and shut behind him immediately.

The ceaseless press and drama of High Office, thought Nicko.

He wondered about giving Tim Mumford a ring. It would good to have his perspective on the recent purchase, while he could not ask him for any breach of confidence, needless to say, a little background on the state of the market in the West End and the nature of some of its main players would be of interest. There was no doubt that it was all beginning to look more like a work of fiction all the time, perhaps a piece of virtual reality, with Nicko standing outside, yet being drawn inexorably into its plot….

CHAPTER NINE

A Fly in the Ointment

Nicko rang Tim from home. He knew nothing about him, apart from the fact that he worked for an upmarket estate agency, Bainbridge and Murton, in a fashionable part of Town, but his voice and his manner suggested that he was hardly a barrow boy and might be an agreeable and informative companion to have a drink with.

The background sounds indicated that Tim was in a room full of people. A brief word and a tentative suggestion for a meeting were all that was called for, but Nicko had difficulty making himself heard and he had the impression that Tim was letting his hair down and putting work out of his mind. Nicko roared his message: he reminded Tim of their brief acquaintance and suggested a meeting at a mutually acceptable location for a drink and a chat. Tim agreed in principle and said that he would get back, apologising for cutting short their conversation. It was his girlfriend's birthday, he explained, and a commanding female voice could be heard in Tim's immediate neighbourhood, which brought their talk to an end.

But the principle of getting together to pool their impressions of the Russian market in particular was clearly an agreeable one. Nicko could fill Tim in on the Nikishovs and the art scene, while gleaning things from the estate agent that might possibly be of benefit to his friends. And, anyway, it would be nice to relax with Tim, since they appeared to belong to the same tribe.

Tim's call came through at nine-thirty on Sunday morning as Nicko was sitting down to a piece of toast and a cup of coffee. He began by apologising for sounding so peremptory the previous evening and Nicko assured him that he had understood the situation perfectly and that he hadn't sounded the least bit peremptory. He described his own background and the nature of his friendship with Viktor without touching on its more dramatic moments.

Tim, who was used to dealing with oligarchs looking for homes in the

West End, took him up eagerly, making it clear at the same time that he was interested in Russia and its history anyway, being familiar with St Petersburg and a number of the towns and cities of the Golden Ring. They left it there for the time being, having fixed to meet in the Cock and Hen in St Martin's Lane, a place that Tim occasionally patronised.

It was a satisfactory start to the day which was to be a lazy one, browsing in the Sunday papers until it was time to go out and join his friends for tea. The news was all economic doom and gloom, with the added threat of war in the Middle East. One other thing caught Nicko's eye, however: a feature about a Russian oligarch, who had recently bought a house in South Kensington for close on seven million pounds. His name was Oleg Dobrinin.

"Oh God," groaned Nicko. "That's put the cat among the pigeons."

There was a picture of the house; a handsome Palladian affair standing on its own, white-stuccoed and with a generous driveway for a town house, with a brief biographical sketch of its purchaser. It was the familiar story: a vast fortune made out of minerals in the carve up following the collapse of the Soviet Union. Viktor no doubt would know all about it, as would Pavel Khlebnikov. And probably Tim as well. There was a photograph of Dobrinin beside the one of his new home. He looked meagre, even ratlike- hardly the sort of man to summon up assassins by a flick of his fingers or a word whispered in an ear. But it rang a bell in Nicko's mind. He had the feeling that he had seen the man somewhere before, not in Tiva, but somewhere closer to home though he could not think where it was. But, now, for him to put himself down in London, of all places, was not good news and Nicko wondered how it might affect his friends- Vera especially, who had set her heart on the move, mostly for the sake of her son, who seemed to matter to her so much more than her husband.

Nicko arrived at Prince's Gate early and found Alyosha sitting alone by the big revolving door at the entrance to the hotel. He sat down beside him and the Russian patted him on the shoulder in an affable manner.

"Where are the others?" Nicko asked.

"They'll be down in a minute," replied the Russian. "Mrs Nikishov has only just got back. She and the boy are changing."

"Not for me I hope."

Alyosha laughed. "You must wait and see."

"And Viktor? You are allowed to call him that, aren't you?"

"Of course."

"He's pleased with his new home?"

"I think so." There was a hint of a qualification in Alyosha's tone, while at the same time he was eying a man entering through the revolving door.

"Do you spend all day sitting here?" Nicko asked. "Checking who comes through that door?"

Alyosha laughed but said nothing.

"What do you think of the house? Would you spend all that money on it?"

"How much money?"

"I can't say exactly, but I know it's a hell of a lot. A goldmine at least, I'd say. But tell me something else, Alyosha, what do you know about Oleg Dobrinin?"

"He's a very rich man. An oligarch."

"It seems that he owns at least half the mineral wealth of Russia. Anyway he's just bought himself a house here in London, as you probably know. Bigger than Viktor's it goes without saying."

"He's a much richer man."

"It's your job to, isn't it? To keep an eye on things of that kind?"

Alyosha grinned, shrugged, but said nothing. The arrival of Oleg Dobrinin in London did not appear to be fazing him.

"Sometimes I feel we Orloffs might have left Russia too soon," mused Nicko. "We should have hung on until the Bolshevik house came crashing down and made a fresh fortune for ourselves - like Mr Dobrinin's. But I expect we would all have been shot long before that could have happened."

Alyosha said nothing, but patted him sympathetically on the shoulder again.

"We would have been bumped off at the very start - like those members of the Moscow Tennis Club." Nicko laughed. "But what about you, Alyosha? You're not an aristocrat, by any chance, are you? One whose people slipped through the net?"

Vera's arrival with Kolya cut short their dialogue.

"Nikoshka!" she exclaimed, seizing Nicko and giving a big hug as if she hadn't seen him for months. She kissed him in the middle of his forehead and then pushed him gently back. Standing to one side, she proudly presented her son. "What do you think?"

Nicko was looking at a Bailey's boy, Kolya, his hair neatly trimmed and with a smiling face. He was wearing his new school uniform and looking very proud of it: a green blazer, a striped tie, grey flannel shorts with green-topped stockings, and in his hand he carried a school cap, the same colour as the blazer and the tops of his stockings. He was every inch an English schoolboy, of the Bailey kind.

"A Bailey's boy," declared Nicko. You look great, Kolya!"

"Thank you sir."

"And you sound just like one as well. But you can keep 'sir' for school."

"I'm very proud of him," his mother said. "But you must remember to work hard, Kolochka."

"Indeed he must," his godfather said. "But all work and no play makes Jack a dull boy. There must be some fun as well. Where's his father? He must feel proud of him as well, surely?"

"I think he does. He'll be down in a minute."

"A real English schoolboy- at last, and we owe it to his Uncle Nicko, my other Nikoshka!"

"I'm not paying for it. And one other thing, Kolya. You may be an English schoolboy now, but you're still a Russian one. You mustn't forget that." Nicko felt he was sounding a little portentous.

Then Viktor emerged from the lift, and mouthing the silent four letter word at his chum, led the way to the dining room with Alyosha bringing up the rear.

"What do you think of your son?" Nicko asked him

"He looks great. How about an English tea for our English schoolboy?"

It was a cheerful occasion, with Kolya starting off as the centre of attention. His mother fussed over him, making sure that nothing was spilled on his lovely new blazer, which made Nicko smile, knowing as he did how indifferent most schoolboys were to such niceties. Their plumage was a matter of little moment to them.

Talk wandered on to the new house with Kolya once again saying his piece about Lord Isaacs' dog. When he referred to 'Mr' Isaacs his mother admonished him, and insisted that he referred to him by his proper title- which inevitably brought a smile to Nicko's face.

Viktor made a paternal speech about the need for hard work and the hopes he had for Kolya to follow in his own and his godfather's footsteps by going on to their old alma mater near Godalming. He grew quite maudlin when he talked about the bond of friendship that had sprung up between the two schoolfellows there. The boy listened dutifully to everything that he was being told. The speech was in English- deliberately because the occasion was intended to be a celebration of the family's adoption of its new life in England - a slight pity, Nicko thought, as he felt that there should have been a place for their Russianness too - though arguably the very nature of the occasion itself provided a bit of that. He was hoping that something might come of the Khlebnikov link. Indeed, he approved of Pavel Khlebnikov's retention of the mellifluous Russian accent in which he spoke his fluent English. The boy, Evgeni, was already speaking the same standard received as his classmates and no doubt Kolya would shortly be doing the same.

No mention was made of the arrival of Oleg Dobrinin on the London scene, however, and nothing seemed to be detracting from Viktor's apparent enjoyment of the event. Obviously he and Alyosha, who remained silent for most of the meal, had the situation under review and measures were being worked out. Alyosha's being stationed at the hotel door when Nicko arrived had made that pretty clear. Nicko left promising to see them all again in a week's time.

* * * * * *

Meanwhile he met Tim Mumford in the Cock and Hen on Wednesday as they had agreed. On the dot of seven Tim appeared, wrapped in a heavy grey overcoat and a muffler, almost as if he was trying to conceal his identity. He spotted Nicko sitting at a corner table with a pint of beer. Stopping at bar he ordered another for himself and arrived with it in his hand.

"We can move onto other things later," he said to Nicko. "Don't get up," he added as the latter was climbing to his feet.

"Good to see you," Nicko said. "That's a magnificent scarf, you're wearing."

"My grandmother knitted it."

"Did she indeed? I wonder how many people have still got grandmothers who do that sort of thing. Not many, I suspect."

Tim unwound the muffler and settled himself beside his new friend and in a moment they were getting along famously, just as Nicko had anticipated they might. It took only fifteen minutes to establish which public school each had been to and which university: in Tim's case

Cambridge and in Nicko's St Andrew's. Subsequent careers were touched upon, though Nicko was somewhat cautious about explaining what had taken him out of the world of antiques and fine art into one of prep schoolmastering. Tim's trajectory appeared to have been more straightforward, moving with a degree in History to postgraduate Business Studies and then to his present situation with Bainbridge and Murton, the West End estate agents.

But what intrigued Tim most about Nicko was his Russian family name and what lay behind it. Nicko launched into the story he had often told before of his great-grandfather fighting in the White Army under Wrangel against the Reds and his subsequent arrival in Britain.

"I've always felt that part of me was left behind in Russia," he explained.

"So you've got a Russian soul, have you?" There was a good-humoured twinkle in Tim's eye.

Nicko laughed. "You said it, not me. I get mocked by my Russian friends whenever I make claims of that sort. But seriously, I do feel drawn to the place and its people. Call me a deluded romantic, if you want to."

"And that's why you're tied up with the whatsits? The Nikishovs?"

Nicko nodded and went on to explain his friendship with Viktor. He described their sharply contrasting histories - aristocratic White and Soviet parvenu. But it was the Russianness of each that had led to and sealed their friendship. He even used the term 'service nobility' when referring to the role played by Viktor's grandfather under Stalin.

The historian Tim knew what he was talking about. Apart from his degree, he was well read in the nineteenth century Russian classics and common ground was swiftly established between them. Together they roamed widely among the works of Tolstoy, Turgenev and Dostoyevski, showing, perhaps, more enthusiasm than critical insight. Meanwhile they had progressed from pints of beer to malt whiskies, which better suited the quality of their discourse.

"Tell me about Oleg Dobrinin," Nicko said, changing the subject suddenly.

For a second Tim looked as if he had been caught off his guard, as if Nicko had introduced the name of a writer he had never heard of, but should have done. Then he smiled and nodded.

"He's not one of ours," he replied. "He's not on our books."

"You know about him though, and that place he's just bought in South Ken?"

"Of course I do."

"According to the piece I read in the paper he owns half the nickel mines in Russia. So he's got to be a big time crook, hasn't he?"

"Naturally."

"He makes Vik look like a down-and-out. But looking at the picture of the guy in the paper, you'd never guess it. He looks such a runt."

"That's probably why he gets away with it. He looks sod all and keeps his head below the parapet."

"And splashes out on one the best houses on the London market?"

"That's the reason for making a fortune, isn't it?" pointed out Tim. "That and maybe buying a football club as well. But better not to shout about it. Though he can hardly expect to keep a lid on it for long."

"I suppose the place'll be stiff with CCTV cameras and security heavies."

"No doubt."

"You know what it could mean for Vik?"

Tim shook his head. "Not really, but I can guess."

Nicko then proceeded to give him an account of the events in Montenegro, at which Tim showed no great surprise, but widened the discussion into one about the mores of New Russians in general, at the same time drawing a comparison with their historical forebears.

But at the end of it, and a couple of tumblers of malt later, Nicko felt glad that he had taken Tim into his confidence. And when he was home again, he suddenly remembered where he had seen Oleg Dobrinin before. Of course, he told himself, bloody fool that I am, that's no great surprise, is it?

* * * * * *

Vera in the meantime was determined to go full steam ahead with the house. Money being in sufficient supply, she intended to waste no time, though she was curiously unsure of her own judgement. Nicko reflected on the apartment in Novgorod where she had seemed to strike exactly the right note, but now that she was away from her roots her confidence seemed to fail her. Not that Viktor had much to offer apart from the necessary means. He took such matters for granted, preferring to leave his spouse to line the nest. He was, in any case, away in New York for a large part of the succeeding month, leaving Alyosha, who was already housed in the basement flat of the new house, with his wife and child.

Nicko of course came forward with ideas and accompanied Vera on her trips to various antiques emporia and galleries. It suited both parties, needless to say. Nicko enjoyed spending someone else's money on things he liked, even if he could not actually own them himself. He liked the ambience of such places, where he could air the bit of knowledge that he had picked up in the trade. And of course it impressed Vera.

Kolya, who had started at Bailey's after the half term break, would sometimes come with them too. Things seem to be working very well for him. He had taken readily to the disciplined environment of a traditional English preparatory school and was already making friends. Evgeni had taken him under his wing, but nationality was soon ceasing to matter.

So under the watchful eye of Alyosha, her son happily settled and with Nicko to help her, Vera was enjoying herself while her husband went about his business across the ocean.

"I know that Vitya has been involved in the business before and would like to return to it, but he really knows so little about Art. He has none of your understanding of it, Nikoshka," said Vera.

"Are you sure about this, Verochka? I mean letting me off the leash to spend your money?"

"I trust you, Nikoshka."

"I wonder what the Isaacs house is like inside?" he mused. "I have a feeling it's either rococo-fussy or state of the art minimalist."

"Why do you think that?"

"Either way suits his politics, I guess. Oh and did you know that he seems to be a friend of Dobrinin's? I saw the man paying a call here a week or two ago. I had no idea it was him until I saw his picture in the paper."

"That's bad news," she said.

"Vik needs to know, of course. But with Isaacs such a close neighbour it might make things easier. It could tie his hands."

Vera gave a short laugh. "Oh you really don't know us Russians at all, do you, Nikoshka? We just wait for the moment and then choose the right place. He doesn't have to spill blood on Lord Isaacs' carpet."

"And when you invite Lord Isaacs here he doesn't have to bring any of his other Russian chums along with him, does he?"

"I wouldn't expect him to."

They went into a gallery in Duke Street. Nicko had been there once or twice before and knew the people slightly. It was typical of him in its way - knowing a fair spread of people without being on particularly close terms with any of them.

The gallery dealt mostly in modern works, but of a kind that Nicko appreciated: such as the more disturbing examples of German Expressionism and early essays in Abstraction. This time something in particular caught his eye and held it.

"My God," he whispered in an awestruck voice.

"What's the matter? Have you seen a ghost?"

"In a way I have. This is a Schwitters."

Vera looked puzzled. "So?" She eyed the work, which was about eighteen by twelve inches square, and glanced back at Nicko.

"Have you heard of Schwitters?"

"No. Should I have done? Is he important?"

"He certainly is. Kurt Schwitters - a German painter and a member of the Dada group. One of the first people to work seriously in collage. You could almost say that he invented it."

Vera continued to gaze at the picture, which was a collage assembled from newsprint, old tickets of one kind or another and pieces of shredded cardboard, held together by a discreet yet bold brushwork, whose tones were mild and a little sombre; blues, greens, different shades of grey and ochre...

"Do you see this?" Nicko said, pointing to a scrap of paper near the heart of the picture.

Vera looked at it closely, then turned to him for elucidation.

"Merz," Nicko read. "It's the last part of the name of a German bank, the Kommerz Bank. It's a motif Schwitters used in a number of his collages. He tears off the rest of the label and keeps only the last syllable - Merz. So they are referred to as his Merz pictures and are worth more than most of his others, it goes without saying. This seems to be one of them. I wonder what they're asking for it?" He scrutinised the picture again at close range. "It looks O.K. and there's a signature on it - the usual K.S. for Kurt Schwitters, though that's not difficult to fabricate, but I don't think it's by Vik's chum - the Novgorod Master." He winked and grinned at her, while Vera went on studying the picture, trying to puzzle it out.

"Why do you like it so much?" she asked. "What's special about it?"

"There's a bit of family history attached to it. My family history.

"Tell me about it, Nikoshka."

"Well, it was before the War - in the Thirties and my grandparents were touring Norway in a motor car when they met Schwitters in a small hotel near Trondheim. He had been denounced as a decadent by the Nazis and rather than toe the line had exiled himself to Norway where he was scratching a living, running off landscapes mostly. Neither of my grandparents knew much about art - they were my mother's people incidentally - certainly not the avant-garde kind - and it went without saying they had never heard of Schwitters either. But apparently he completely won them round. He charmed them with his anarchic humour, especially with his account of his service in the German Army."

"I don't suppose he was a natural soldier."

"Well, for instance, he told them that every time he was addressed by a corporal his mouth would drop open. It had to be a corporal. It couldn't happen with any other rank."

Vera smiled and looked again at the picture. "In a way I can see some of that here," she said. "It's a bit crazy."

"Anyway," resumed Nicko, "that's how it went. And despite being persona non grata with the Nazis, he managed to wheedle a bottle of whisky out of the officers' wardroom of a German warship that was in Trondheim harbour at the time. Among other things he took Granny and Grandpa to visit an ice cave in a glacier. I suppose he was feeling lonely. But when Granny said she wanted to buy one of his pictures, he wouldn't hear of it at first."

"I would have thought that was just what he would have wanted."

"Quite the contrary. He thought she was only doing it to be kind - which I suppose in a sense she was - but that wasn't entirely the reason. She insisted that she liked the work that she saw - which of course was large loosely painted landscapes and not the kind of experimental stuff we've got here. Anyway, he relented and they mounted an exhibition in the hotel lounge and the entire company staying there helped to choose my grandmother's picture."

"And what did they choose?"

"A view of Molde harbor - a potboiler you'd have to call it."

Vera was unfamiliar with the term 'potboiler' which Nicko had to explain to her.

"He hadn't bothered to sign it- he was pretty casual about things like that - but it was unmistakably his work, painted on a piece of board rather than a canvas, with very bold brushstrokes in the German Expressionist manner and a rather clever use of the grain of the board in the sky - a Dada touch. Probably he ran it off in a single session."

"Did your grandmother pay much for it?"

"I don't know what she paid, but it certainly wasn't much. But he seemed grateful."

"Where is it now?"

"In my parents' home. They've still got it."

"And it'll be yours one day?"

"One day- I hope. But we should be talking about now, Verochka. Do you really not like this picture?"

"I thought I didn't, but after what you've just told me I'm not quite so sure. I could get used to it."

"Then please try. Because I want you to have it. It's seminal. It represents one of the turning points in Twentieth Century European Art. Sorry to sound like an exhibition catalogue, Verochka, but it's true. And anyway I like it… really I do. It's Schwitters, at his most pure and undiluted."

"Then we must buy it if you like it so much, Nikoshka, and I will learn to- for your sake." She kissed him on the cheek. "You have to teach me, Nikoshka. You must tell me more about this amazing Kurt Schwitters."

"The story isn't quite over, regarding my family and Schwitters, I mean."

"Tell me the rest and then we will talk about the cost of the picture."

"Well, when the Germans invaded Norway in 1940, he fled to this country. He took the Shetland Bus."

Vera looked mystified. "He took a bus?"

"A boat, that ferried people secretly across the North Sea to the Shetland Islands from occupied Norway," explained Nicko. "It was called the Shetland Bus. And then when he got here he was locked up, as a possible enemy alien."

"And after that?"

"He wrote to my grandfather, asking for a reference- which of course he provided. They were my mother's people and their name couldn't have sounded more English - Bowyer-Smythe - so there were no suspicions aroused in Intelligence circles that might have been the case with a Russian-sounding one at that point in the War when Stalin was still sharing a bed with Hitler."

"So Schwitters was released? Thanks to your grandfather?"

"Kaneshna. He settled in the Lake District, in the North of England."

"And did your grandparents ever see him again?"

"Only once - here in London, when he was mounting an exhibition shortly after the War. He had wanted to come and live with them, but they fought shy of it - they were hardly the kind of people to handle a bohemian artist for any length of time - especially in wartime. A pity in a way. But at least they opened the door for him and I believe he felt grateful for that."

"You must buy your Schwitters, Nikosha. I order you to."

"It's your picture and could be expensive."

"Tush!" She pressed a finger over his lips. "Vitya's paying for it, isn't he?"

Nicko shrugged and looked for somebody to ask.

He found a young man, who reminded him in a way of Tim. Having done his homework on Schwitters and the Dada Movement in general, he was eager to demonstrate his expertise. Nicko repeated the gist of the story that he had just been telling Vera, which slightly took the wind out of the young man's sails.

The picture was marked up at £6000, which struck Nicko as very reasonable, considering its place in the canon of twentieth century art. The one owned by his family, though a larger work, would probably have fetched a good deal less.

Vera, however, did not bat an eyelid and wrote out a cheque, while the young man undertook to see the picture delivered to Thurloe Square in a couple of days' time.

It was Nicko's first serious art purchase on behalf of his friends. Vera, he realised, had indulged him and he knew that next time the choice must be truly hers. But the kind of thing she really liked, he still had to find out.

CHAPTER TEN

A Funeral and Plans for a Party

When he got home, Nicko found a message left by his mother on the phone. Her voice was almost sepulchral. She told him nothing, but asked him to ring her back straight away.

He had a bit of a conscience about his elderly parents in Sunningdale. Since his return from Montenegro he had been dilatory about making regular trips down to see them. His father had suffered a mild stroke two years earlier, but seemed to have mended well, while his mother continued in formidably good health. She, of course, had poured much oil on troubled family waters at the time of the krater incident, when his father had hit the roof. Perhaps she felt that smashing Attic red figure vases was the kind of thing that a spirited young man ought to be getting up to. But generally, she was the more intimidating of the two. She felt that with the education he had received, her son's career should have been on a steeper trajectory and was inclined to speak her mind on the subject whenever they were together. So the weekend trips out of town had grown rather sporadic and the telephone conversations, though reasonably frequent, more reproachful.

All the same, Nicko felt he ought to return this call straight away. His mother's tone had indicated that course. He rang and she answered immediately, as if she was sitting next to the telephone waiting for him.

"You rang, Ma?"

"I did."

There was a pause.

"Something you wanted to tell me? Is Pa all right?"

"He's dead."

"You don't mean it!"

"Of course I mean it."

"My God! When did it happen? Was it sudden?"

"Mercifully yes. We had got back from Sainsbury's. He sat down in the drawing room with the paper. He wasn't complaining of anything, but when I took him a cup of coffee, he… he was gone." Her voice faltered for the first time.

"Oh Ma, I don't know what to say. I'm terribly, terribly sorry for you and I….. I feel it too."

"It was very quick. All over in a moment."

"I suppose he was lucky, but it's hardly the moment to say that, is it? Are you by yourself?"

"Kate from next door is with me now. She's being very kind."

"Listen Ma, I'll get down tomorrow - as soon as I can. This is a terrible shock and of course arrangements will have to be made. Does Debbie know?"

"I spoke to her on the phone. She'll be over in two days."

"Really Ma, it's a terrible shock…But as you say it was quick at least… the best any of us can hope for. I'll come straight up from the station as soon as I get there."

"That's good." The voice was steady and matter-of-fact.

"Bugger that," Nicko said to himself, having put down the phone. "Why does he have to drop off the twigs now?"

He hoped he had said the appropriate things to his mother - it was impossible to know, people and circumstances were so variable. His mother was behaving as he would have expected her to - chin up, all that sort of thing. And then, though he had no known heart condition, his father was at that time of his life when such things were not entirely unexpected. There had been the mild stroke two years ago, after all.

But Nicko's own feelings were more ones of frustration and boredom with what the death of his parent entailed than anything else. It was curious, though, that he had been describing his grandparents' adventure with Kurt Schwitters that very afternoon. That was an age away and the generation coming after them was now beginning to drop off the twigs…

It set him thinking of his own mortality - but in a detached kind of way. He was not grief-stricken. It was not as if he was a small child losing some one very close and dear to him, after all. He had flown the nest and his father had shed his mortal coil reasonably ripe in years. And his mother? There was no bond sufficiently strong between them for him to repine greatly on her behalf. He would go through all the right motions, it went without saying, and the dragon would inevitably cope. She was the coping kind. And Debbie would not let the side down either. She was living in Italy, for the time being at least, but she knew where her duty lay... no, Nicko, reflected, it was a necessary chore, but one of those moments in life which have to be seen through with appropriate decorum and then left behind. When he went to bed he lost no sleep brooding.

When Nicko went down to Sunningdale next day - conveniently it was Sunday - he found things as he had anticipated. His mother was perfectly in control of herself and the situation with Kate Mainwaring-Burton, her neighbour on hand, fussing over her with cups of tea. Nicko was taken to see his father laid out as decently as circumstances permitted on the drawing room sofa, awaiting the arrival of the undertaker's team. The idea was to place the open coffin in a small anteroom that was referred to as the breakfast room.

But as the remaining man in the family, Nicko felt it was incumbent on him to take the matter in hand. He rang Dick Trubshaw who immediately gave him leave of absence, promising to cover his classes himself, and then Vera, who expressed her sympathy to a degree that Nicko felt was excessive. He did not prolong the conversation with her, but promised to get over to see them the following weekend.

Kate left him alone with his mother and, after a light supper, they retired to her small upstairs sitting room, leaving the drawing room in the possession of the late Count Orloff - as Nicko had inwardly styled his father.

It was a relief when his mother decided to switch on the television after they had discussed the logistics of the funeral: the arrangements for the event itself, the informing of scattered kin and family friends, the church - it was to be an Anglican burial - the notice in the papers and so on. Nicko was to get in touch with the undertaker again first thing in the morning.

All this was quietly gone through, before switching on the television for the News, which, among other items, included one about a Russian investigative journalist being gunned down on the stairwell of an apartment block in Moscow, which seemed uncannily close to the circumstances beginning to unfold in Nicko's own life.

Shortly afterwards he saw his mother to bed with her customary hot milky drink and, kissing her formally on the forehead, wished her goodnight, remarking to himself how utterly English she seemed to be, despite the name she had consented to make her own.

Debbie arrived the following day on a flight from Rome, having left the two children in the care of another Embassy wife. She and her brother saw little of each other, so they had plenty to talk about. Debbie was intrigued by the Nikishov set-up, while referring at the same time to the recent killing in Moscow in a half-facetious manner. It was only when her brother revealed to her what had what had happened in Cetinje that she adopted a less lighthearted tone. She handled her mother briskly, possessing the same bossy streak as her parent. While her brother dealt with the undertaker and the vicar, Debbie looked after the other arrangements, but left Mrs Orloff or 'The Dowager Countess' as Nicko now rather flippantly described her, to fuss over what to lay on in the way of hospitality following the funeral.

It was a suitably sombre event as it turned out, under a drizzly sky, with a decent showing of friends and relatives, but hardly a grief stricken one. Given the age of the man and the nature of his passing, there were no tears shed. But among the mourners leaving the churchyard, Nicko noticed Freddie Ryedale, who had not shaken his hand in the porch at the end of the service. Later, he saw him once more at his mother's home, but when he crossed the room, feeling that he ought to make his number with him again, Freddie slipped out into the hall and through the front door, muttering a brief word to Mrs Orloff in passing. Nicko thought of calling to him, but something held him back. He wondered why the man had bothered even to attend the funeral feast, but then he remembered that Freddie was not one to miss the right sort of party, while at the same time having to talk to Nicko, with the painfully knowledge that they shared, was probably more than he felt up to. For one in his line of business, Freddy was pretty thin skinned.

Nicko stayed until the following morning while Debbie was to remain in Sunningdale for two more days after that. She urged her mother to come to Rome the following month and she would welcome to stay on until after Christmas.

"The children will love it," Debbie told her.

Mrs Orloff did not agree. "I'm not so sure they will after a couple of weeks of me," she retorted. "But there should be plenty to look at in Rome for a day or two at least."

Nicko kissed her on the forehead, which was his token of homage, and simultaneously pressed her hand in recognition of the solemnity of the occasion. "Look after yourself, Ma," he told her. "I'll pop down again on Sunday, if you'll have me."

Heaving a sigh of relief, he headed back to town. There were only two working days left in the week, but he felt he ought to go in the following morning to relieve Dick. He would see his mother again on Sunday and no doubt a regular pattern of visits would have to be devised, now that his father was dead and his sister and the grandchildren were living abroad. It was not something he relished, but it couldn't be ducked. Meanwhile he was eager to check the safe arrival of the Schwitters in Thurloe Square and to discuss its placement with Vera.

* * * * * *

When he rang, it was Viktor who answered. He had just got back from the United States and Nicko felt a pang of disappointment: He had been enjoying his expeditions with Vera and her reliance on his judgement for furnishing the house. But his friend was brimming over with schoolboy cockiness and ebullience. He started by expressing his condolences for the death of Nicko's father, the scion of a Russian boyar house who had disdained him as a Bolshevik upstart, and, having performed that ritual, turned to his own affairs.

The time in America appeared to have been usefully spent. As Vera had said, he had plans for getting back into the art market, having burned his fingers and put his family in danger with his efforts to muscle into the Montenegran property boom. Since his retreat from the Balkans, he had so far managed to keep out of the clutches of his enemies - the full account of which Nicko had still to hear - and had arrived in London with his family and a sufficient fortune to set them up in a fashionable part of town.

The move to London by Oleg Dobrinin, almost in his wake, had cast a shadow over it, however. The effects of the Montenegran property speculation might not yet be fully played out and who knew what fresh perils lay ahead in the anticipated return to the art market? Alyosha was now settled in the basement and had certainly been assiduous in attending to Vera and Kolya's needs. No doubt further precautions were in the pipeline, while in their fairly brief conversation Viktor sounded remarkably insouciant. He airily informed Nicko that he was now in the business of trading in modern art works, though he knew very little about them.

He had found a useful contact in New York, however - the son of

Ukrainian immigrants - who was eager to find a way into the Russian and Ukrainian markets where the demand for avant-garde Modernist works was on the increase. Post-modernist works were also in demand, though it seemed to be the Abstract Expressionists of the Fifties and Sixties that were the most desired.

In Nicko's eyes it looked a pretty tall order: running Rothkos and Jackson Pollocks to earth, after more than half a century, during which time both painters had acquired something of the cachet of Old Masters, which, needless to say, meant a lot to the kind of purchasers that Viktor's new associate, Boris Babko, had in mind.

Nicko smiled to himself at the mention of Rothko. Probably easier to run off than Shishkin, but the main problem being that they were rather bulky, so where had they been lurking all this time? He put that one to Viktor.

Viktor chuckled. "That's one for Boris to work out. Provenance is his field."

"But it needs to be pretty bloody watertight, you daft cunt. You should know that by now. You're not likely to be dealing with the likes of Freddie Ryedale."

"How is he by the way?"

"He was at the funeral, but fled before I could talk to him. Rumour has it that he's working with an auction house somewhere in the Scottish Borders."

"Close to his source of comfort, at least."

"Seriously, Vik, knocking up Rothkos might sound easier than Shishkins, but it could be a lot more dangerous. Think of the type of guys buying into that kind of market for a start. They'll be very big boys with acres of wall space to fill, looking for the right backdrop to set off their dolly birds - something that's a bit more flash than a Turkey rug."

Viktor clicked his tongue dismissively, "Boris has been into all that. He's been playing the game for a few years now and is no chicken, but times are getting harder and he needs some working capital and- how do you say? fresh fields to sow? Yes?"

"Yes, Vik, you're getting to be quite a poet in your old age. And you oligarchs don't feel the pinch like the rest of us?"

"That depends what you mean by a pinch."

"But all the same be bloody careful. And keep right away from Jackson Pollock. All that nifty wristwork - hellish difficult to match.

Damien Hurst, mind you, would be easier. But the problem there is that he isn't dead yet."

Viktor chuckled.

"Don't get ideas," Nicko added. "But in the meantime, piss off. I'll be over later. Have you seen the Schwitters, by the way?"

"Hmm," his friend mumbled something in a non-committal kind of way.

When Nicko got to Thurloe Square, they examined the new purchase together while Vera was busy in the kitchen.

Viktor showed only mild interest in Nicko's account of how the purchase had been made, but seemed satisfied with the way his friend was helping Vera to furnish the house. Despite all his wealth, he was pretty indifferent to such matters. He was always pleased to see his family again after one of his absences, but quick enough to delegate some of his parental duties to others. Alyosha, for instance, had been assigned to take Kolya to watch Chelsea - a role that the former Russian spook was only too happy to fill. Kolya's new Russian chum, Evgeni, and his father sometimes went along with them too, which made a jolly foursome.

Viktor's line with the Schwitters was quite simple: if you like it and Vera does too, which, after all, is what matters most, that's fine by me. The price was all that seemed to interest him, but he did not query it.

When they rejoined Vera in the kitchen, she announced her intention of throwing a party for the friends that they were beginning to make. The house was more or less in shape by now, with Nicko's help, and Kolya was happily settled into his new school, so she felt that the time was right. After all, that was half the point of living in a fashionable part of town, wasn't it? to make interesting friends. Viktor did not disagree, but in his case he saw the practical aspect of it, the advancing of his business interests whatever turns that they might take. Meanwhile he slipped off to make some phone calls, leaving Vera to consult Nicko about a guest list - who felt a good deal less useful in this capacity than he did as an artistic advisor, not being gregarious by nature. Nor did he particularly enjoy parties, preferring to slink off into a corner and to watch the play from a distance. One to one meetings with an interesting topic of conversation suited him much more. His now regular get-togethers with Tim Mumford were the kind of thing that he enjoyed most.

His advice to Vera in the matter of her list was to keep it short, not that she had much choice.

"Don't ask too many people," he warned her, "at least not to your first party. You'll gradually get to know more people, but take it slowly. Start with the ones you feel most comfortable with." He felt a bit of a fraud offering such sage advice.

Vera was looking to him, sucking her ballpoint, with her notebook open in her lap.

"You can put my name down first, at the top of your list."

Obediently she wrote down 'Nikoshka.'

"Now. Who else?" he frowned, pretending to give the matter profound consideration. "Mr Dobrinin?"

"Stop being naughty, Nikoshka!"

"Perhaps it might be better to leave him until another time. The Trubshaws, of course. I'm sure Dick and Imogen would love to come."

"That's a good idea." She wrote their names down.

"And while we're thinking of Bailey's, why not ask the Khlebnikovs? They can bring their kids to keep Kolya company. But that should do for the Bailey crowd - unless you can think of anyone else. I'm not sure Kolya's form teacher would fit in, somehow."

"That's only five people. It's not enough."

"Well the big fish could be Isaacs of course. But he might not be very easy to pin down. Being a member of the Government I expect he's got a pretty full diary."

"We should still ask him," Vera said firmly. "He is a neighbour."

"And don't forget his Mexican partner. You can't leave him out."

Vera frowned and wrote the Government minister's name on her list, then paused.

"You know about Miguel, I suppose? You must, surely by now? It's common knowledge. He's supposed to be a charmer who knows how to behave himself. His Lordship wouldn't allow him to do anything else."

Vera put the word 'partner' down on her list.

"Good. It would be nice if they both could come. It would add to the gaiety of nations." Nicko glanced at Vera as he said it, but his sickly pun had failed to find its mark. "Anyway it might be interesting to see how Miguel hits it off with Imogen Trubshaw - and the senior partner with her husband, for that matter. And I'm sure Kolya would welcome the dog as his special guest."

"Vera put 'dog' down on her list,

"He's called Igor. He's another Russian, don't forget. From Siberia - or least his breed is."

Vera wrote 'Igor' next to the word 'dog'.

"And Tim of course? After all, without him you wouldn't have the house."

"Kaneshna. Tim."

"He's got a girlfriend. It might be a good idea to ask her as well. I'm sure he'd appreciate it."

"Do you know her name?"

"Elspeth, do you want me to spell it? But that should be enough to start off with, I must say I like the idea of mixing the Isaacs party with the Trubshaws. If he comes, Miguel should add some Latin spice."

Vera leaned over and kissed him.

"As long as there're not thirteen of us," Nicko said. "Check the number and choose a good date. I suggest a Friday in the middle of next month. It'll give them time. Two weeks before Christmas? I trust Vik will be at home then?"

"I'll make sure."

"But don't waste time. It's important to get your invitations out as soon as possible."

Vera accepted the package whole and the invitations were sent two days later.

* * * * * *

Dick Trubshaw informed Nicko that he and Imogen would be only too delighted to be asked to the Nikishovs' housewarming and she wrote Vera a friendly reply. They were used to mixing with the parents of their pupils socially and a number of them were personal friends. Nicko mentioned the possibility of Lord Isaacs being at the party, knowing that politically-speaking that where Dick was concerned, the man's politics were a red rag to a bull, but on this occasion the idea was taken on board.

"I've heard that the man's a colossal snob," Dick said. "Like many of the left wing brethren."

"He might bring Miguel, the Mexican housemate," Nicko warned him.

"Bring it on!" Dick emitted a hearty laugh. "Make sure he does! Imogen would love to meet him. It will add to the gaiety of nations!" Dick Trubshaw also had an aptitude for lousy puns.

And then on the following Saturday morning, Nicko ran into the great man himself, in the street outside his house with both his pets - Miguel and Igor. Isaacs recognised him and introduced his companion in a relaxed fashion.

Miguel was undeniably a stunner, his features a perfect blend of Spanish and native Mexican - a flawless mestizzo specimen. His figure was slender and on the short side. And he looked to be in his late teens or early twenties. His dark ever-so-slanted Indian eyes were graced with long, almost girlish lashes, yet his nose was classically straight. When he spoke, after being introduced, it was with a soft North American accent. There was nothing of the rough trade about this boy, nor was there anything overtly effeminate - only perhaps the flirtatious eyes. His jet black hair was cut short, rather like a schoolboy's. He was wearing a light grey tracksuit, identical to the one that Isaacs was wearing.

"We met briefly when your friends were looking at the house," said Isaacs to Nicko, "though you'll have to remind me of your name."

Nicko supplied it and the introduction to the Mexican god went ahead.

"Miguel is a dear friend of mine," Isaacs explained smoothly. "He has come all the way from Mexico."

It seemed that Nicko posed no kind of a threat to him and his manner was completely relaxed.

"An Aztec? Or are you a Maya?" joked Nicko, drinking in the boy's beauty at the same time. "Or might you be an Olmec or even a Toltec?"

The boy laughed a soft silvery laugh. "I see you know all about my country. Have you been there?"

"Alas no, one day perhaps. But tell me," Nicko went on, "are you coming to the Nikishov bash next month? I know they'd like you both to come. And the dog too, Kolya insists on that."

"We'll certainly do our best," said Isaacs. "My name's Mark, by the way. You can forget the other thing - it's just political."

"Mark it is then." Nicko laughed. The man despite his reputation was remarkably easy.

"And one other thing," Isaacs added in a more confidential tone. "Igor here." He jerked the lead and the dog looked up at him, "Igor is about to become a father. It's all quite above board and we should have a fine litter of thoroughbreds. Young Kolya might like to know."

With a graceful bob of his head, he passed on to his own front door, while Miguel cast a smile back in Nicko's direction and winked.

CHAPTER ELEVEN

When the Cat's Away …

A week later Nicko found Vera giving Kolya his tea. The boy got to his feet as soon as he entered

"Sit down Kolya, you're not in school now."

"Thank you, sir."

"And you don't call me 'sir' at home. You only do that at school."

Viktor was away - in New York yet again, where, according to Vera, he was looking at an important picture. She sighed and shook her head.

Nicko shook his head sympathetically, but did want to comment in the hearing of the boy.

"Is Isaacs coming?" he enquired.

Vera nodded. "He left a note this morning."

"Is he bringing Miguel?"

"Da."

Nicko rubbed his hands and smiled.

"Why's that important to you, Nikoshka?"

He nodded in the direction of the boy by way of reply.

"You can go and watch the television, now Kolochka," his mother said.

"I hope he brings Igor," said the boy, getting to his feet.

"He may be becoming a father," said Nicko,

"Who? Lord Isaacs or Igor?" asked Vera.

Nicko laughed. "Igor of course. It's not exactly Isaacs' line, is it?"

Vera looked nervously at her son, hovering in the doorway.

"Are there going to be puppies? Is that the English word for them?" He looked to his godfather to confirm his use of English.

"Quite right, Kolya. I've forgotten what the Russian word is."

"Shchennok. Can we have one?" the boy demanded of his mother.

"First of all, Kolochka, they haven't been born yet and anyway we'd have to ask your father."

"I'm sure Papa will let me have one."

"Run away Kolochka and remember, tonight's your bath night."

The boy gave a sulky shrug and left the room.

"Sorry. I shouldn't have mentioned the dog," Nicko said.

"Vitya will have to agree. I can make no promises and anyway Isaacs may not want to sell us one."

"But what's Vik up to? He's back in the art market. He told me something about Abstract Impressionists."

Vera gave an exasperated snort. "Vitya knows nothing about art - nothing at all - only how to make money from it. And you know the way he does that. He'll get hurt one day, Nikoshka, I can feel it."

"I don't think he trusts his own judgement."

"He hasn't got any to trust."

"He needs to authenticate a Rothko - one of the New York Abstract Expressionists. He says he's got a Ukrainian chum over there, who can handle it."

"Oh my God."

"We'll find out more about it when he gets back. When's he coming?"

"He said Wednesday. But he keeps changing his mind. Alyosha will know."

"How is he, by the way?"

"Fine. He's got a girlfriend - another Ukrainian."

"Is she safe?"

"I think so. Vitya seems quite satisfied with her. Her name's Tsina. Alyosha and Kolochka are very good friends. They're great Chelsea fans."

"We'll try to forgive them for that, I suppose."

Nicko stayed for supper and listened to Kolya talking about football, before he went to bed. He wasn't the slightest bit interested in it himself, but he tried to put on a reasonably convincing show for the boy's sake. At the same time he steered clear of school topics, though if the lad had shown a readiness to talk about History or Art even, he would have been happy to dilate on either of those.

Vera had prepared a large Russian meal, starting with a borsch, which Nicko liked. It was followed by a stew with sour cream and a salad - indeed, he thought that salads were what Russians did best. Potatoes, of course, and, as a finale, a torte - a mountainous chocolate and cream edifice, horribly bad for the figure, yet irresistible. All these Vera had made herself and confessed that she had been working on the last item since the middle of the week. Nicko had been told to make himself free of Viktor's cellar, such as it was, where he had found a very passable Bordeaux.

If the fatted calf had been slain, it wasn't to honour the homecoming of the Master of the House. Feeling a little too well fed, Nicko sank into the sitting room sofa while Vera, having dispatched her son to bed, made coffee which arrived shortly afterwards with a very large brandy.

"My God, I'll never get home if I drink all that!" he protested. "You're as bad as Vik!"

"Stay here then," she replied. "You're welcome and can borrow a pair of Vitya's pyjamas."

Nicko hesitated for a second, then succumbed. "The spare room's up and running?"

Vera answered with a kiss on his cheek. She poured the coffee and settled on the sofa beside him, slipping out of her shoes at the same time. Nicko took a pull at his brandy and placed an arm round her shoulder. Vera passed a finger down the bridge of his nose and nestled closer. He pecked her cheek with a kiss of his own and took another pull at his glass.

For a while no words were spoken, as they lay on the sofa, enjoying their shared warmth and pecking at each other's cheeks, in a manner which was affectionate, but hardly passionate. Eventually Vera shifted her position and Nicko sat upright.

"My malchik," she murmured.

She wasn't talking about the child upstairs in bed. Pressing her back onto the cushions, Nicko kissed her squarely on the lips this time, searching out the tip of her tongue with his own.

"Come to bed," she said.

"Hmmm."

"Bedtime, Nikoshka," she told him sternly.

Getting to her feet, she put out a hand to help him up. For a second he felt unsteady and everything suddenly seemed to go far away.

"We'll clear the things in the morning," Vera said. "Come now, Nikoshka."

She led him by the hand to the door of the room. He followed submissively and they went upstairs to the landing where she peeped into the boy's bedroom. His regular breathing could be heard. Softly she closed the door, putting a cautionary finger to her lips as she glanced back at Nicko. Then, holding him by his wrist, she led him across the landing into her own room.

She started to undress at once and Nicko rather meekly followed suit. Neither of them said a word, until they were standing naked and looking at one another.

There was something slightly boyish about Vera, especially as she had started to wear her hair shorter. But her body was every bit as good as Nicko remembered it from Novgorod.

Vera eyed him up and down, seeming to appraise him. Then she nodded her approval.

"You still look good, Nikoshka."

"Thank you, Verochka, you do too - more than good. I love the way you've cut your hair, by the way." His words tumbled out.

Vera smiled. "I didn't have to take my clothes off for you to see that."

"But it matches the lines of your body so perfectly," he said. "That's why I'm saying it now."

"You're such a funny boy, Nikoshka." She stretched out her hands and drew him towards her until their bodies were pressed together.

The drink had blunted his inhibition and Nicko's cerebral faculties were sufficiently off their guard to allow his instincts a freer passage. It wasn't something that came easily to him, but by now Vera had got his measure.

Her body rubbed against his, setting a surge in motion, and feeling its warm pressure, his penis took its cue. It stiffened, as a tremor ran through his body into hers.

She did not need to draw him down onto the bed. Nor did he have to think what to do because the primal urge was asserting itself, leaving no time for self-analysis, and the pair of them coupled,

And yet, on the very cusp of his satisfaction, something odd happened. Instead of Vera's face he seemed to be looking into a different one - one that was olive-skinned, with a classically straight nose and dark, almond-shaped eyes…

But then, as they drew apart, emitting little grunts of satiety, the intrusive features vanished and Nicko, turning his head on the pillow, saw Vera's once more. He kissed her on her forehead, while she, as was her way, ran a finger down the bridge of his nose.

"Happy?" she murmured.

"Da. Kaneshna."

"Sometimes I think 'da' and 'kaneshna' are the only Russian words you know, Count Orloff! But for now they're enough." Nicko, although in his late twenties, felt an adolescent pride in his achievement, despite it not being his first essay in lovemaking. The duck had been broken already, but since that time no further runs had been scored. He liked the cricketing metaphor because at school it was the only game he had enjoyed.

They turned off the bed light and kissed each other again in the dark, when once again that second face seemed to be the one that Nicko was addressing. But eventually they drifted off to sleep and it was still dark when Nicko sensed Vera getting out of bed and heard the key turning in the door.

"All right?" he whispered as she climbed back in beside him.

"Kolochka," she answered. "Sometimes he wakes early and comes in before I'm up. I don't think he should find us like this."

"Then I'd better leave before he does," said Nicko, sitting up and swinging his feet onto the floor.

"Nonsense, Nikoshka. It's Sunday and you don't have to go to work. You must stay and have your breakfast. I'll deal with Kolochka. I can manage you both perfectly well, as you know. And Vitya too," she added as an afterthought.

"You're an amazing woman, Verochka."

"Sarcasm doesn't suit you, Nikoshka."

"I'm not being sarcastic. I mean it."

She got in beside him again, but they did not try to go back to sleep. Instead they snuggled against one another and chatted in a desultory fashion. Then at seven, Vera's alarm clock went off and she climbed out once more.

"Stay where you are," she ordered Nicko. "I'll look after Kolochka. Would you like a cup of tea?"

"I'll make it," he said, "so you stay where you are." He pushed back firmly.

"You won't know where to find anything."

"I'll manage."

"You must put something on." She climbed out of bed once more and took a silk dressing gown belonging to her husband from a cupboard. "We can't have my son seeing his history teacher with no clothes on."

Nicko put on the dressing gown and went down to the kitchen, where he quickly put together the means of making a pot of tea. Meanwhile he could hear Vera's voice on the landing where she was talking to Kolya. He heard a door shut and a moment later she had joined him in the kitchen.

Observing the tray neatly set out with mugs, a bowl of sugar - which neither of them took - spoons, a jug of milk and a couple of digestive biscuits - she was impressed.

"Vitya never does this for me," she said.

"Shall I take it upstairs or are we having it here?"

"Here. Kolochka's awake now, but I've told him to stay in bed and read his book."

They sat at the table to drink tea before Nicko went upstairs to wash and get dressed. Vera offered him a shower, but he declined. "That can wait until I get home."

Vera meanwhile prepared the breakfast - which consisted mostly of the leftovers from the previous evening's meal - a thrifty Russian habit which she had retained, in spite of her marriage to a man with ready money.

When Nicko returned to the kitchen he found the boy already sitting at the table.

"Good morning, Uncle Nicko," he piped. "Is it all right if I call you that?"

"Of course it's all right, just keep 'sir' for school, that's all. And a very good morning to you too, Kolya. Or should I say Nikishov?"

"When's Papa coming back from New York?"

"Probably on Wednesday," said his mother.

"I hope he brings me something nice. He promised he would, but that it would be a surprise. I'd like a dog."

"You can't bring a dog into the country. It isn't allowed," Nicko said.

"Why not?"

"Because sometimes they bring nasty doggie diseases in with them - like rabies."

"What's rabies?"

"A disease which makes you mad." Nicko tried to explain the effects of rabies on both humans and dogs as far as he knew them.

"So stop thinking about dogs," the boy's mother admonished him.

"It's difficult to stop thinking about them when you want one. But I don't want one if it's got rabies."

Nicko stood up and announced his departure.

"You must come and stay with us again, Uncle Nicko," Kolya said.

"It's the first time anyone has stayed with us."

"I'll stay with you again if your Mum and Dad ask me to," replied Nicko, tactfully making sure to include Viktor.

"You needn't worry about Papa," the boy assured him. "He's always somewhere else."

CHAPTER TWELVE

Preparing a Feast

Viktor returned, as Alyosha had stated, on Wednesday. On Tuesday he had sent Vera an e-mail, telling her not to meet him at the airport or the city terminal as he had a little business to attend to before reaching home. Alyosha, without saying anything to Vera, had undertaken to meet him and returned with him to Thurloe Square shortly after seven o' clock that evening.

Viktor telephoned Nicko, when they exchanged their usual puerile banter with its expletives and creaky innuendoes. Both were men approaching thirty, yet they still needed to talk to one another like a couple of seventeen-year-olds.

But there was a new note creeping into Viktor's banter, a slight lessening of the old cockiness and replacing it a hint of melancholy, as if somehow he was looking back to a land of lost content from which life was dragging him remorselessly away. Until the scrape in Montenegro, it had all gone pretty smoothly for him, but now it involved considerable stress, danger, even, to himself and his family. His own family roots had been severed shortly after he had set himself up in Novgorod, mainly by a combination of death and distance, and he was effectively the sole proprietor of his business interests, but he understood that if he was ever to reach a ripe old age, he must know when to pull out, not least for the sake of his wife and child.

Having worked through their obligatory schoolboy talk, he seemed anxious to press Nicko on the subject of Kolya. How was he getting on at school? And what hopes were there that he might make it one day to their own alma mater? It was a rather sentimental, chip-off-the old-block, kind of stuff; with the lad following in his father's footsteps. Indeed it struck Nicko as ironical, considering Viktor's roots in the Stalinist system, that he should feel this way.

"Vera's updated you about the party?" Nicko asked him.

"Kaneshna."

"Well then, are you happy about it? It looks as if you might even have a Peer of the Realm gracing the event - Lord Isaacs of South Shields, no less. And his duchess too, who, rumour has it, is pleased to have received an invitation."

"I might be bringing an extra person - but it's not certain yet."

"Oh? Am I allowed to ask?"

Viktor laughed. "It's in the line of business."

"Muddying the waters already, are you? You're an incorrigible cunt, Vik. And talking of business, since you stoop to mention it, how many Rothkos have you managed to flog so far?"

"Something's already in the pipeline, but we won't talk about it right now, if you don't mind. Walls have ears - is that what you say?"

"Yes, Vik, that's what we say. Especially Russian ones. I'll pop over on the Friday evening before to give you a hand if you like."

"Verochka would appreciate that."

"My love to her." "Da. Kaneshna."

"Dobre veche and f-off."

"You too."

Viktor had sounded somewhat downbeat about the forthcoming event and Nicko was curious to know who his extra guest was going to be. A prospective buyer of a picture, most likely. His first Rothko sale? A sitting duck with the ready cash? Anyway it would serve the bugger right and his flashy tart too, who wouldn't have the faintest clue what art really is anyway….

* * * * * *

Nicko came on from school on the Friday evening and was cordially welcomed by his friends. Viktor offered him a bed for the night and a pair of his own pyjamas, probably the ones that Vera had offered him on his previous stopover. It made Nicko smile and wonder if his friend had any inkling of what had taken place in his home while he had been away. He remembered that night in Novgorod when Viktor had absented himself, almost on purpose it had seemed, and Vera had taken him in hand, vastly raising his self-esteem in the process. He had never looked back with Vera since, but he was intrigued, nevertheless, by the part, if any, his friend might possibly have played in it.

Nicko declined the offer of a bed, but with the help of Alyosha, who emerged from the basement flat, he set about shunting tables and chairs around. The arranging did not take much time, since the guest list was not a long one, but Vera was nevertheless choosy about the placing of furniture and, although it was to be a buffet, she was particular about the positioning of chairs and the laying out of napery and her cut glass- most of it purchased recently with Nicko's help. She came from the kitchen to inspect the situation in the dining and sitting rooms, nodding her approval of what she found there, while adjusting the odd napkin or glass here and there as a token of her role as chatelaine.

Viktor had ordered the drinks - the greater part consisting of champagne - which had been delivered shortly before his friend's arrival. In the best Russian tradition he had not stinted and there looked to be a lot more than was likely to be needed.

This was certainly the view of Alyosha, who was keeping a beady eye open for what might remain unconsumed. He hinted to Nicko that at the end of the day they might, as their due, each receive a generous division of the spoils. As he unpacked the cardboard boxes, placing some of the contents in the fridge and others on the steps leading down to the cellar below the basement, where it was relatively cool, Nicko's thoughts went back, as they so readily did, to the symposium in Uncle Frank's flat. Viktor had also laid on a plentiful supply of vodka for this occasion, but, despite Nicko's spending spree with Vera, there was nothing in the house that offered quite the same temptation to a drunken wrecker as an Athenian krater had done. Kurt Schwitters' 'Merz' picture was a possible candidate, but fell a long way short of a Fifth Century Greek mixing bowl in either presence or monetary value.

Kolya meanwhile took off his handsome new blazer to lend Nicko and Alyosha a hand. He showed a particular penchant for setting out glasses, which, for some reason he wanted to stack in pyramids, until his mother and Alyosha intervened, while his godfather applauded his creativity and hinted at other possible configurations that might put the glasses in less peril.

Viktor had slipped away, leaving it all to his wife and her team. Having laid in the drink, it seemed that nothing was left for him to do until the time came to receive his guests. For much of the evening he could be heard making phone calls. In fact he was hardly ever seen these days without a mobile or a blackberry in his hand. Nicko found these appurtenances of modern business practice disagreeable and even felt uneasy about using a mobile, while his friend, it went without saying, had taken to it all like a duck to water. To Nicko the attraction of gizmos was one more thing that seemed to be coming between his old friend and himself.

Only occasional snatches of Viktor's conversations reached Nicko, who, to be fair, was not trying to listen to them. But he noticed that the bulk of the talk went on in Russian, which, at Viktor's end at least, grew quite heated at times. Was this to do with his entry into the North American art market? It struck Nicko, in his impractical way, that works of art should not be commodities to be argued over in such a hardnosed fashion. Murders might be committed in the pursuit of them, but then, he reflected, in Viktor's world murder, too, was a commodity with its price. Anything at all was a commodity as long as someone was willing to pay for it. Such ruminations fluttered through his mind as he helped Vera with the flowers.

The newly set-up sitting and dining rooms looked very pleasing by the time he went home. While the small breakfast room made concessions to Modernism - the Schwitters, still without a frame, had been placed there for the occasion- the others were devoted, if anything, to Arts and Crafts, the handsome medieval-looking candelabra, over the dining room table, providing a good example. When he had persuaded Vera to buy it, Nicko had managed to steer her away from a more conventional crystal chandelier - a significant victory, he felt. The dining room walls, papered in a William Morris pattern, were hung with several late nineteenth-early twentieth century English rustic scenes. Nicko had taken full advantage to his friend's funds to indulge his own predilection for works from the late Victorian and the Edwardian periods.

The main sitting or drawing room had yet to be fully furnished, but the thoughtful distribution of sofas and chairs with cleverly-hung drapes provided an appropriate atmosphere. Flowers were deployed throughout and Kolya's serpentine arrangement of the cut glass looked well on the snow white cloth, covering the dining room table. A separate table had been placed on one side for serving the drinks for which Alyosha was taking responsibility.

Needless to say, it went ahead without any intervention on the part of the Master of the House, who remained occupied with his telephoning, no doubt creating the wealth that underwrote it all.

So everything was set nearly twenty-four hours before the event. Nicko, inspecting the rooms, felt satisfied with his own part in it. Over the past few weeks as he had been helping Vera to put the house together, an idea had been germinating in his mind: the possibility of becoming a fulltime designer of interiors whose owners would give him a free rein in choosing the objects to fill their rooms. Despite his own preferences, he felt he could launch into entirely new waters and even work in a modernist idiom if necessary. New Russians with unformed taste, but aspirations to High Art, were an obvious place to start, especially if he had a business card with 'Count Orloff' stamped on it.

He was thinking along these lines as he was passing through the lobby, when the telephone on a side table rang. He picked it up.

"Hullo," he said. "The Nikishovs."

The soft-sounding American-accented voice that replied told him immediately whom he was speaking to before a name was given. "Nicko, isn't it?"

"That's right. How did you know it was me?" His voice fell to a confidential whisper.

"Your lovely upper class English voice. I'd know it anywhere." A warm chuckle followed.

"Thank you for that. Can I take a message or fetch Vera?" "You'll do fine."

"Fire away then. It is Miguel, isn't it?" It was a superfluous question.

"Sure it is. You know me."

"How would I forget you?"

"Just to confirm finally to the Nikishovs that Mark and I will definitely be coming to the party tomorrow and that we're both looking forward to it."

"I'll pass that on to Vera. She'll be pleased."

"And I'll be pleased, too. Been nice talking to you, Nicko. See you there then. Bye-bye."

Nicko replaced the receiver and went through to give Vera the glad tidings. And, when he finally left that evening, he danced a little jig on the pavement outside, without asking himself what he was doing it for. Matters seemed, to be going rather well.

* * * * *

It was Saturday morning and no school - only coaching for the children about to take their Common Entrance, which did not involve Nicko. He lingered in the bath until the water had grown cold and it took an effort of will to haul himself out. Breakfast was a glass of grapefruit juice, followed by a slice of toast and marmalade, with a cup of instant coffee. Then a stroll to the newsagent to buy a couple of papers, though he found the weekend editions tiresome with all their extra supplements when all he wanted were the news pages, TV listings and book reviews.

He planned to take a walk on Hampstead Heath in the afternoon, before coming home to ready himself for the Nikishov bash. The guests were invited for seven o'clock, but he intended getting there sooner to make himself useful, although he wasn't quite sure how. Everything seemed to have been set in order the night before.

Once back with his papers, he settled down to browse through them in his small sitting room. And there on this day of all days, the one of the Nikishovs' housewarming, on the second page of the paper he was reading, was a big spread about Russian oligarchs in London. Several were named, but fortunately not Viktor- probably he was not a big enough fish- not yet, at any rate- but Oleg Dobrinin and his new residence featured in a large way. His photograph, taken in a street somewhere and one of his house, were included. The man in the picture seemed to be unaware of the picture being taken of him, but looked as if he was in a hurry and was almost pointedly inconspicuous. It was the man Nicko had seen scuttling into Lord Isaacs' house.

The article talked about his nickel fortune, something that was already generally known, and made the almost ritualistic references to his likely links with the Russian underworld and key figures in the Kremlin itself. There was nothing very startling about any of it, but one thing did hold Nicko's attention. The piece mentioned that Dobrinin had 'friends' in the British Government, but named no names. There was also mention of links with members of the European Commission, but again no names. Nicko wondered how much Viktor knew of any of it. Surely he must be up to speed on everything that the piece mentioned - and a lot more besides. His path would not be crossing Dobrinin's again, with any luck, now that he was reverting to his old line of business in the art market, so hopefully he should be out of any immediate danger. At the same time Nicko still could not put Cetinje out of his mind.

It was a sharp clear day on the Heath - with low winter sunlight and long shadows. By the time he got home to prepare for the party, Nicko felt braced. He decided to put on a suit - a pinstripe number - though he was ready to strip off his tie and to stuff it into his pocket if it turned out to be that kind of a do. But having played a part in inviting the guests and helped set the place up, he sense that this was not going to be a laid-back affair- while what Viktor may have got up to in the provision of drink left a door open to some interesting possibilities.

Vera's intentions were clear when he arrived to be greeted at the door by Kolya, in his green school blazer and grey flannel shorts. His shoes were freshly polished and his hair brushed. He said 'good evening' politely and, as Nicko entered, offered to take his coat and scarf. Nicko approved: he preferred children with old-fashioned manners and who behaved and looked the way children should, which at the same time did nothing to dampen their spirits. Vera, he was pleased to see, felt the same and Kolya appeared perfectly content with his lot.

"Well done, Kolya," he told the boy. "You handled that nicely. I'm sure Mr Trubshaw would be very impressed. Make sure you do the same for him when he arrives."

"Thank you, sir."

"And leave out the 'sir'- for me at any rate. Remember what I told you."

The boy grinned. "No sir."

Nicko noticed a mildly impudent glint in the boy's eye, which he also approved of.

Vera meanwhile had approached him across the hall from the kitchen. She wrapped him in her arms and kissed him while the boy looked on, seeing nothing untoward in his mother's outbreak of affection.

Nicko fished in his jacket side pocket. "I've brought you this. It's for Vik as well, but above all it's for Kolya. I hope such things will interest him one day."

The boy craned his neck to see the small package Nicko was handing to his mother.

"Oh, Nikoshka, you shouldn't have done it! You've done so much for us already!"

"In a way it's not much, but it belonged to my great-grandfather and came out of Russia in his coat pocket."

"But that's the very reason why you shouldn't give it away," Vera objected. "I don't think I can take it."

"Open it."

She untied the package and under a layer of tissue paper was an ikon of the Virgin and Child.

"Don't let Vik sell it. That's the only thing I ask. And make sure that it's passed on to the boy."

Kolya took the ikon from his mother and looked at it. He was curious and a little bemused.

"It probably doesn't mean much to you yet, Kolya," his godfather said, "but one day it will."

The boy looked at it again, rubbing a finger over its surface. "You know what it is, of course?" Nicko said.

"Kaneshna. It's an ikon. We had one in our house in Novgorod and I've seen them in the churches as well."

"And you know who it's a picture of?"

"Mary and Baby Jesus."

"Full marks, Nikishov! You'll be an expert one day!"

The boy frowned, not completely convinced by the flattery and handed the ikon back to his mother.

"I think you'd rather have a dog," said Nicko.

The boy nodded.

Vera did not speak, but gazed at the object in her hand.

"Where's Vik, by the way?"

"Business. It's always business." She hugged Nicko. "Really, Nikoshka, you shouldn't have done it."

"I hope Vik likes it too. But I'm not quite so sure about that."

Vera laughed.

"Speak of the Devil and he appears!" exclaimed Nicko as Viktor walked through the front door.

The two men mouthed the customary four letter expletive at one another, then Viktor kissed his wife and ruffled his son's neatly brushed hair.

"Are you ready for tonight's event?" Nicko said. "We'd better not refer to it as a symposium."

Viktor grinned. "We could still smash some of those glasses. That's no problem."

"Be quiet, Vitya," his wife ordered him. "I don't like it when you say things like that. Look at what Nikoshka has just brought us."

Viktor took the ikon and eyed it closely, aping the attitude of an expert, before looking at his friend, for an explanation.

"The Stroganov School," explained Nicko. "It might even be the work of the great Chirin himself. My great-grandfather brought it with him out of Russia when he went into exile, so no Bolsheviks got their dirty paws on it- not until now, at any rate." He gave Viktor a playful punch. "And don't try selling it either. It's meant for the boy."

"But you, Nick? A family heirloom like this should be kept for children of your own, when you have some, surely?"

Nicko shrugged. "I have no thoughts of that kind, not immediate ones anyway, and Kolya here is my godson and he's a Russian, so it might mean something to him."

"You understand that, Kolochka? Your godfather's giving you an ikon - possibly the work of one of our finest painters - which once belonged to one of the noblest families in Russia."

"It came to me from my father - in his will - and I want it to go home, to a Russian home." Nicko looked at Vera. "You must look after it in the meantime and see that Kolya gets it when the right time comes."

Viktor gave him a cynical smile and what was almost a wink, while his wife kissed him on the cheek.

"By the way," said Viktor. "Something I need to tell you. There'll be one more guest tonight. But it shouldn't make any difference."

"Who's that?" asked his wife.

"A business friend, that's all. Nobody special. He won't be any trouble, I promise you."

Vera uttered an impatient sigh. "I suppose we'll have to have him as you've asked him."

Viktor said nothing and went off with Nicko to inspect the other rooms and Alyosha's arrangements for the drinks. He glanced at his watch. "Alyosha should be coming up from his lair shortly. I'll leave it in his hands. He knows what to do."

He poked under the table and produced a bottle of red wine and handed it to Nicko.

"I think we might get ahead of the game - just you and me. Yes?" he said.

"It's a bit early, isn't it? Oughtn't we to wait?" "It's never a bit early."

"Stuff it, Vik. We can't get ourselves pissed before any of your guests arrive."

"Maybe you're right. But we can have something nearer the time. The vodka might be decently chilled by then. Better than this stuff, anyway." He put the bottle back under the table.

"Who's your business friend, Vik? The one you've just asked?"

Viktor winked. "Wait and see."

"Like that is it?"

"How do I say it? In English, I mean. He's a big cheese - yes? who thinks he's into Abstract Art - or at least that he should be."

"Have you got anything to show him?"

Viktor shrugged his shoulders dismissively.

"I suppose he's a Russian?"

"Kaneshna."

"Kaneshna," repeated Nicko with a sigh.

Alyosha arrived in the room so quietly that neither of them heard him coming. It reminded Nicko of something he had once read about Stalin - the story of the hapless aide whose spouse had made him a pair of slippers so that he could move about his master while he was asleep on his couch, without disturbing him. One day, as he approached the couch, as silently as ever, the Great Man opened an eye and cried out in terror, thinking that he was about to be assassinated. The aide became another Gulag statistic. Nicko wondered where Alyosha might have acquired his skill for unobtrusive movement.

"I'll leave you to it," Viktor said. "Alyosha, don't let him get pissed before anyone arrives, You can't trust him to be left by himself with it."

Alyosha reviewed the bottles of wine under the table. "There's no need to hurry. We won't take the stuff out of the fridge before anyone comes." He looked over the napery and glasses. "That boy's clever," he remarked. "The glasses look very good."

"Tell me, Alyosha, who's the guy Vik's bringing along? The one he's just asked?"

Alyosha. "Oh? Has he has asked someone else? He didn't tell me."

"He should have cleared it with you first, shouldn't he? But knowing Vik, it was probably done on the spur of the moment, if you know what I mean. Someone he might be selling a picture to."

"A Rothko, maybe?" Alyosha shook his head. "What's your English for it? Not my cup of tea?"

"Not mine either."

Alyosha put his hand into his jacket pocket and pulled out a quarter bottle of vodka. Unscrewing the cap, he handed it to Nicko.

"There's a long time before anyone shows up," he said. "I think we'll need it."

Nicko politely rejected the bottle. "I don't want to make an idiot of myself. By the way, is Tsina going to be here? She is called Tsina, isn't she?"

"Sure. She's downstairs."

"Ukrainian, isn't she?"

"Kind of. Her father's a Russian- separated from her mother. She grew up in Poltava."

"The place where Peter won his famous victory over the Swedes?"

"Da. The same."

"So what's she doing in London? Apart from living with you, I mean."

"The usual thing. Studying- English literature."

"I wonder if she knows Ludmilla Mikhailovna who was with us out in Montenegro? She was studying English Literature, as well as being crazy about the Montenegran Royal Family."

"I didn't know there was one."

"Indeed there was. Great friends of the last two Tsars and my great-grandpa as well, as it happens, or so I've been told."

Alyosha nodded, but did not look over-impressed by Nicko's namedropping. "I'll introduce you," he said'

"Thanks. I'd like that."

It was too soon to start shifting the champagne, so they went to the kitchen where the snacks to be served to the guests with their first drinks were being set out. Alyosha took two plates of blinys with anchovies and carried them through into the dining room. Meanwhile in the breakfast room near the front door, Kolya had turned on the television.

When he returned to the kitchen, Nicko met a sturdy-looking girl with vivid straw blonde hair. She was bending over the pans on the stove.

"It's Tsina, isn't it?"

"That's me. And you must be Nicko."

"The same."

They chatted about Alyosha's den in the basement, then about her home town, Poltava. Nicko assumed that she must be clean since she had been allowed to move in with Alyosha.

She told him how Alyosha had been born in Poltava as well, not long before his family had moved to Yaroslavl, but he was too young to remember anything about it. He and Tsina had met in London and were both perfectly attuned to life in the English capital. Her spoken English seemed to be every bit as fluent as Alyosha's, but she made no comment on the way he was earning his living and Nicko did not press her.

Like Ludmilla, Tsina was interested in English Literature, but appeared to like a different kind of book to Ludmilla. She was mostly interested in the great nineteenth century classics, with a special place for Jane Austin in her canon. Nicko ventured into his own favoured territory- Anthony Trollope and William Thackeray- and though Tsina had read none of the former yet, she had enjoyed the latter's 'Vanity Fair'. Of the moderns she had not even heard of Patricia Highsmith and in some respects hers was a reading list of the late Soviet era- which Nicko confessed he preferred.

They chatted for a good twenty minutes, while Tsina tended the pans. Vera re-appeared in a black silk dress with a diamond brooch. Her fair hair was platted and coiled on the back of her head in what looked to be a traditional Slavic fashion. Simplicity is what she had set out to achieve and she had succeeded.

"I don't want to look like a football player's wife," she explained when Nicko complimented her on the result.

"You'll never do that," he told her. "And anyway at school Viktor was useless at football. Though, he wasn't bad at cricket."

"But that's such a slow game."

"And a very subtle one that requires patience. In a way it's a physical kind of chess, so it ought to appeal to Russians - and Ukrainians too, of course," he added for Tsina. "Vik was a pretty accomplished leg-break bowler."

"That sounds aggressive - whatever it is. But I'd like Kolochka to play cricket. He must play as many English sports as possible."

"Dick Trubshaw's your man then. He was a Cambridge blue." He proceeded to explain to both the women what a blue was. If anything it seemed increase still further Vera's determination that her son should press ahead with his English education.

Alyosha wandered into the kitchen and, creeping up behind Tsina, as she was bending over the stove, placed a kiss the back of her neck. She squealed in mock protest. He mumbled to her in Russian while she ticked him off playfully. Vera in the meantime was inspecting the dishes and starting to transfer the ones on the stove to the hotplate. There was a borsch, a plate of blinys and various sauces, fish and otherwise, to go with them. Sour cream - smetana- was produced from the fridge and a selection of salads - which Nicko had already decided would be the best thing.

Vera glanced at the clock and stopped what she was doing. "We're much too early," she said. "In Russia everything's done at the last minute."

Nicko slipped off to join Kolya in the breakfast room where he was watching 'Robin Hood'.

"You know all about him?" his godfather asked.

"Yes, of course." The boy nodded impatiently and Nicko said no more.

He looked at his watch; another half hour at least until any of the guests started to arrive, but he could think of nothing useful to do with himself in the meantime. It occurred to him that Viktor was probably upstairs changing. Hopefully he had stopped telephoning and since Vera was busy in the kitchen he felt free to go up and pester him.

"Don't forget to listen for the door," he told Kolya, "but probably you won't have to worry for another half hour. Most of them will be late. It's the polite thing to do in England. In Russia you don't have to try." He gave him a playful slap on his knee and left the room.

Viktor was knotting a large silk tie, one that he had brought back from New York, when his friend entered the room. Nicko eyed it critically.

"A bit over the top, isn't it?" he said.

"Piss off. I bought it on Fifth Avenue."

"So? That makes it all right, does it?"

"I said 'piss off'"

"Did you bring Verochka anything nice? And what about Kolya?"

"I got him a racing car which works by remote control."

"And he likes it?" Kolya hadn't told Nicko about the car.

"Of course he likes it. What boy wouldn't?"

"He still wants a dog."

"Bugger the dog."

"So you're not going to get him one?"

"I don't want the boy to get spoiled."

"That's hardly spoiling him. It'll be good for him to look after. I believe the Isaacs beast might have sired a litter. I mean the dog, of course."

"It might be asking a bit much of the man himself." Viktor grinned at his own reflection in the mirror. "But he'll be here tonight, so I'll ask him. By the way, tonight's extra guest says that he knows Isaacs."

"You're not telling me his name?"

"You'll find it out when the time comes."

"Why be so bloody mysterious about it, if all you're doing is trying to sell him a picture? But I suppose any friend of Isaacs is going to be a bit iffy."

Nicko went back downstairs to locate Alyosha. It was time to shift bottles up from the cellar.

He found him, assisted now by his girlfriend arranging bottles of red wine on the table as well as ones of cognac and Madeira.

"For Christ's sake, who on earth's going to drink all this?" expostulated Nicko.

"There are Russians coming," Alyosha explained.

"But we're not expecting Tsar Peter. Though it might be fun to watch a member of the British Government making an idiot of himself."

As the hour approached bottles of champagne were brought from the large fridge in the pantry and a couple of well-chilled vodka ones were primed and ready. Viktor appeared and offered Nicko and Alyosha a glass each of the latter, which accepted and rapidly dispatched.

Then exactly fifteen minutes after the time of commencement stated on the invitations, the front doorbell rang and Kolya sprang into action.

CHAPTER THIRTEEN

The Housewarming

He opened the door to find his headmaster and his wife on the step. Imogen Trubshaw was holding a small present wrapped in bright paper.

"Come in sir!" exclaimed the boy.

"Thank you, Kolya. My word, you're looking smart tonight, aren't you? I hope it isn't specially for us?" said his headmaster.

"Not just for you, sir. My mother wants me to look smart."

"Well you're a credit to her and to your school, Kolya."

"Thank you, sir. But please come in. I will take your coats."

Nicko was waiting with Viktor as they entered the hall.

"Dick Trubshaw, "said the guest to his host. "I don't think we've met, but I know your wife and of course Nicko here. This is Imogen, my wife."

"Viktor Ilyich Nikishov," Viktor replied. "Ochin priatni, as we say in Russian." He took Imogen's hand and kissed it.

"It's a while since anyone did that to me," she said.

Viktor stared at Dick Trubshaw's tie. "Good Heavens…which house was it?"

"Enderby's and you were in Aldridge's, along with Orloff here, so I've been told. But that was a bit after my time. Quite a Russian mafia, I believe."

Viktor let out a polite guffaw.

"You may remember my mug," went on Dick. "if you were interested in cricket. There's a photograph in the pavilion."

Viktor looked a little unsure of himself.

"Dick was the vice-captain of the First Eleven back in Nineteen-eighty," provided Nicko, "And Vik, here, bowled leg-breaks for the house team."

"Not quite in your league, I'm afraid," said Viktor, "but then I'm only a Russian. Chess is more our game." He turned to Nicko. "Why didn't you tell me Dick was one of us?"

"I guess too much else was going on and you're hardly ever here to tell anything to."

"But it's great to know," went on Viktor. "I want my boy, Kolya, to go on to Stanford and Aldridge's too. And to be captain of the First Eleven, if he can manage that as well."

Vera meanwhile had approached Imogen whom she already knew.

"It's lovely to see you. "

Imogen presented her gift. "Just a little something for your new home."

Vera kissed her on the cheek and thanked her. "I'll open it later if you don't mind. I'm sure it'll be something nice."

"Kolya's looking very smart tonight," Imogen said. "And he greeted us perfectly. His English is spot on."

"Did you know that Dick is an Old Stanfordian?" Viktor announced to Vera. "I've only just found out. He's one of us!"

"I suppose we ought to have a special handshake," joked Nicko.

"Actually there is an Old Boys' lodge," said Dick, "but I'm not a member of it myself."

"In Russia the Freemasons are back in a big way," said Viktor.

The bell rang and Kolya rushed to his post.

It was the Khlebnikovs this time- father, mother, Katya, and the children, Evgeni and Natasha. Kolya addressed them in Russian and they responded in the same.

Viktor also welcomed them in that tongue. Though he had not met them until now, he had read the situation. Hugs were exchanged with Vera and Kolya.

"This is starting to look like a Bailey parents' bunfight," remarked Dick as he helped Katya out of her coat.

Little Natasha approached Vera with an offering in bright paper and was kissed in return, while Kolya and Evgeni immediately started rattling away with each other in a mixture of their two tongues.

"Genia, you must speak English," his father admonished his son sternly.

"Sorry, Dad, we're talking about Chelsea," the boy replied.

"I know you are, but you must say it in English. I'm sure Kolya's father agrees with me."

"Quite right," concurred Viktor with a solemn parental nod. "Remember that, Kolochka."

165

Once their point had been made, the two fathers retreated to the other end of the hall where they began their own animated conversation in Russian.

Meanwhile Alyosha had appeared along with Tsina and champagne was handed out while Nicko produced a plate of anchovies on cocktail blinys. For the moment the chat centred on the mutual topic of Bailey's. Vera praised the uniform to Imogen.

"Some people say that it's old-fashioned," she replied, "but that's why plenty of others like it, and interestingly enough the children do as well. It's better than being turned into miniature grown-ups. In a way they sense that and appreciate it. A role model for boys, Dick always says, should be Just William. Childhood is short enough as it is."

Naturally Vera wanted to know something about Just William and Dick was happy to fill her in.

The bell rang once more and Tim and his girlfriend, Elspeth, were admitted.

Kolya took charge of their coats, bearing them into the breakfast room, while Tim offered his tribute to Vera, earning himself a kiss on the cheek in return.

"You're so very kind," purred Vera in a husky voice. "It's like Christmas or my birthday."

"Why aren't you opening your presents, Mama?" demanded Kolya, in a reproving tone.

Alyosha was discharging the champagne and replenishing empty glasses as the party moved down to the far end of the hall, breaking up Viktor's Russian conference with Pavel Khlebnikov. The talk was lively and it was clear to Nicko that these people were getting on well with one another. He observed Tsina and Elspeth hitting it off too. The latter had read English Literature at Durham University, so a mutual topic was assured.

Pavel was introduced by Viktor to Tim in a robust Russian fashion, with much shoulder slapping and mirth.

This is working, thought Nicko. It's a good mix.

They were all talking so hard and the champagne was busy doing its work, so that no one, not even Kolya, who was describing a Chelsea goal to his chum, heard the bell ring. It rang a second time, more insistently.

"Kolya, do your job!" his godfather called to him.

The boy broke away and raced to the door.

It was Lord Isaacs this time, with his 'duchess', the former full of silken apologies for arriving so late. Having come from a few doors away, neither of them was wearing an overcoat. They wore dark suits, Isaacs with a discreet silk tie, Miguel with no tie at all. Nicko felt that Isaacs' quiet number compared favourably with the brash affair that Viktor had acquired for himself on Fifth Avenue. Miguel wore a gold chain with his open-necked shirt and a couple days of stubble graced his olive cheeks and chin.

"Where's Igor?" Kolya demanded to know. "At home, guarding the house, like a good dog," purred the Government Minister.

"I want one like him."

"Well, we'll have to see about that, won't we?" The man stroked the boy's head as he passed on into the hall.

Isaacs made no attempt to explain his relationship with the Mexican boy, but went smoothly about, introducing him to the company. The gossip columnists, needless to say, had prepared the ground for him, while the setting seemed to be suitably cosmopolitan. Indeed it was Imogen, whose husband was the headmaster of a fashionable London prep school, who appeared the most eager to meet the Mexican favourite. He took her up immediately.

"Is Kolya here - it is Kolya, isn't it? one of your lovely Bailey boys? Are they all just as lovely as him?" asked Miguel.

"He's a fairly typical specimen," replied Imogen.

"It must be like being in Heaven, to be surrounded by so many angels."

Imogen laughed. "Don't be taken in by their sweet faces. Some of them are little devils behind their masks." It came from her easily, but all the same she was glad that her husband was not within earshot. He was busy discussing house prices with Tim, who was listening to him with a mildly glazed, yet attentive, expression.

Little Natasha Khlebnikova, having been taken by Tsina into the kitchen, her mother was deep in conversation with Viktor and Lord Isaacs about dogs. The Khlebnikovs had a pair of boxers and Isaacs his Siberian husky, which had just sired a litter of fine pedigree pups. He produced a colour snapshot of the newborns suckling at their mother's teats. There was a second one of Miguel holding a blind puppy up in each hand. He was pressing them against his cheeks and grinning broadly.

"He looks as if he wants to eat them," joked Katya Khlebnikova.

Isaacs issued a tinkle of laughter. "I hear that your boy wants a puppy," he said to Viktor.

"He never stops talking about it."

"Well there's one way to put him out of his misery- to give him one. I'm sure that Mrs Khlebnikov would agree."

"Our children love the dogs," she said, "and the house feels so much safer with them."

"And you're here for the foreseeable future?" Lord Isaacs said.

"Da. London is our home now. We love it so much here and it's so good for the children. Mr Trubshaw has such a wonderful school."

"Well, how about it, Viktor? - may I call you that?"

"Kaneshna- if I can call you Mark."

"Of course you can. So how about it?"

Viktor shrugged his shoulders and left him to continue.

"It's perfectly straightforward. The boy wants a puppy and I can get him one."

"How much would you or the mother's owner want for it?"

Isaacs assumed a faux-conspiratorial manner. "Nothing at all," he whispered in Viktor's ear.

"No, no," protested Viktor. "I can't possibly allow that. Dogs aren't cheap- especially ones with good pedigrees."

"I insist, absolutely insist. Think of it as my present - our present - to celebrate your coming to live here, among us."

"Well it's too kind of you. The boy will be… how should I say?"

"Over the Moon?"

Isaacs smiled while for a second Viktor looked bemused.

"Our children were over the Moon when we got Sasha and Strelka," Katya said.

"Which would you like? A dog or a bitch?"

Viktor shrugged again. "I don't suppose it matters, does it? But a dog would probably be easier."

"A dog it shall be then. There's a dear little chap I know who's looking for a home in Chelsea right now."

As they were talking Viktor's eyes kept wandering in the direction of the front door - something that was not lost on Lord Isaacs.

"Are you expecting anyone else?" he asked.

"Just a business acquaintance who said he might drop in, but maybe he's not coming."

"I think we ought to arrange for Father Christmas to deliver the little fellow on the right night, don't you?" resumed Isaacs.

"That would be great!" Viktor said. "I hope the others find good homes too."

"That's not a problem." Isaacs pressed Viktor's hand warmly.

There was a hesitant ring at the door which only Nicko heard. Kolya was no longer at his post.

"Door, Kolya!" Nicko called

The boy rushed back to his station and admitted a small man in a drab brown raincoat who Nicko recognised at once.

The man looked around, seeking the assurance of a familiar face. He glanced in the direction of Lord Isaacs and lifted his eyebrows, but pursing his lips in a barely discernible cautionary movement, the latter turned aside to whisper something in his host's ear.

Viktor, while listening attentively to the Great Man, had nevertheless observed the fresh arrival.

"Excuse me for one moment, Mark," he said and went down the hall to greet the man who was shedding his coat.

An almost relieved look of recognition crossed the man's face and he and Viktor hugged each other in a display of Russian bonding, the visitor looking a little startled by the effusiveness of his host's behaviour.

"Let me introduce you to my wife," Viktor said, speaking in English, "and to my other guests."

Vera meanwhile had disappeared into the kitchen, so Viktor felt beholden to present the man to his grandest guest first.

He had of course been made aware that Oleg Dobrinin and Lord Isaacs already knew one another, but he led his fellow-Russian to where the latter was standing with his back to them all the same. He tapped the Government Minister on the shoulder.

"Mark," he said. "I believe that you and Oleg already know one another."

Isaacs turned and a shadow crossed his face for a second, to be followed by a welcoming beam. "Oleg! Well fancy that! Running into you here, of all places! Ha! Ha! Ha! Life is full of surprises, isn't it?"

The rest of the company in the meantime retreated into the doorway of the dining room, leaving the protagonists on stage by themselves, a situation that the Government Minister looked a little uneasy about.

"Tatiana, not coming tonight?" he enquired. Realising that the company was aware that he and the Russian oligarch already knew one another, he kept up his jocular tone.

"She has a headache."

"Oh dear, I'm sorry," gushed the Minister. "What can we do to make it better? Have you any ideas, Miggie?" he said, turning to his housemate who standing beside him.

"Would she like a puppy?" the young Mexican suggested.

"What a good idea! Would she like a puppy? It might work wonders with a migraine." Isaacs threw back his head a little way and discharged a short burst of silvery laughter.

The Russian shrugged. "Maybe she would. I'd need to ask her."

"It's a Russian breed," Isaacs went on, "a Siberian one, like yourself. I can show you a picture." He produced the two snapshots from his pocket again.

The Russian made a rather guttural sound to express his appreciation and handed the pictures on to Imogen who had meanwhile approached the pair from the wings.

"They look lovely!" she exclaimed. "Can I have one too?"

"Hang on a minute, dear," protested her husband. "In case you've forgotten, we've already got a dog."

There was a round of slightly awkward laughter as Vera rejoined the party and Alyosha pressed a glass of bubbly into Dobrinin's hand. Viktor beamed on the company at large, while Isaacs patted the oligarch warmly on his shoulder.

"That was a great trip in the Adriatic last summer," purred the Minister. "Miggie and I talk about it all the time. We argue about which places we liked best - Dubrovnik or Kotor. Personally, I'm a Kotor man. And then there was Corfu, of course."

The champagne was slipping down fast, the glasses replenished by the assiduous Alyosha as the Government Minister got more garrulous.

"Are you off somewhere exciting next year?" he demanded to know. The Caribbean would suit me rather well. Who knows, I may even be out of Government by then, and have a bit more time to play with! Ha! Ha!"

Nicko was chilled by what he was hearing. Had Isaacs been a guest on board Dobrinin's floating gin palace at the time the shots were fired in Cetinje? He turned to see Miguel gazing at him with rapt dark eyes. A fluttered lid and a raising of the chin suggested a retreat to a more discreet location.

Nicko lead the way to the breakfast room where he found Kolya and his school chum tucking into a plate of canapés which they had purloined.

Nicko dismissed them, suggesting that Kolya might take his guest upstairs to look at the car that his father had brought him from New York. They left without demur, but were careful to carry off the plate of canapés with them.

"What lovely boys. I like the blond ones best," remarked Miguel. "Both of them are Russians?"

"Both. But Mark isn't blond," Nicko pointed out.

"He's not a boy, is he?"

"You wanted to say something to me?"

Miguel smiled and gave a shrug. Then suddenly lunging forward, he planted a kiss on Nicko's lips. The latter felt the Mexican boy's stubble rub against his own smooth-shaven cheeks and enjoyed it.

He stood back and Miguel looked at him with a mock penitent expression on his face, while appearing to suppress a giggle at the same time.

"Steady on," Nicko said. "Let's sit down, shall we?"

"A pity those little buggers walked off with the canapés," said Miguel. "They're both boys in your school, aren't they? You must beat them for it."

"Is that what you would do?"

Miguel laughed out loud. Anything seemed to go with him.

There was a pause of a few seconds.

"I believe that you and Mark Isaacs were on board Dobrinin's yacht last summer, cruising in the Adriatic?" ventured Nicko.

"Right. And very nice it was too. Not quite- what-do-you-call-it? the celebrity 'A' List, but quite good enough for a poor little Mexican boy like me."

"What sort of people were they?"

"Business ones mostly. Some British, Russians, of course, and a couple from Brussels, old friends of Mark's. A few politicians - from both sides of your Parliament - but Mark was the only big one."

"And how did he get to know Dobrinin?"

"From Brussels, I guess. But you'll have to ask him about that yourself. You know something, Nick? I'm dying of thirst. Aren't you?"

"I was in the Adriatic in the summer as well. In Montenegro."

"Were you? Did you go to Kotor?"

"Yes."

"A nice place, but I liked Dubrovnik better. Rather full of people, though."

"That was my impression. I was in Cetinje as well."

Miguel looked puzzled. "Where's that?"

"The old capital of Montenegro." Nicko looked hard into the other's face.

But Miguel appeared not to register any curiosity. "What was it like? A nice place or a dump?" "Quite a nice place."

"Christ, I'll drop down dead if I don't get that drink! Haven't they got anything stronger than champagne? They are Russians, aren't they?"

"How about some vodka? There's a good supply of that."

Nicko got up to leave the room and Miguel held his hand for a second, as if reluctant to let him go.

He was still sitting there when Nicko returned.

"Dobrinin's going great guns," he informed the Mexican boy. "He's insisted on serving Imogen Trubshaw with her supper and he's asking her all sorts of questions about their school. Could he possibly be thinking of sending a child of his own there one day? He might do a lot worse. But, now, tell me more about your idyllic summer afloat with all those B - or was it C? list celebs, though I don't expect I'll have heard of any of them. And what of Mr Dobrinin and Mrs Dobrinin - if that's who she really is?"

"Well there was Mark and me. And a couple from your main Opposition party and a dealer in diamonds from Amsterdam…"

"What was he doing there?"

"That's obvious, isn't it? Decorating the tree. Hanging decorations on Tatiana Yurievna."

"It sounds a pretty chav or WAG set-up if you ask me. You know that expression?"

"Sure I do. Mark's always using it."

"He's a snob isn't he? And yet he's meant to be a socialist politician."

"Do you mean he's a phoney?" Miguel laughed, savouring an idea which clearly was hardly new to him.

"I didn't quite say that. Only I don't share his politics."

"You English do love your class."

"Stop being pious." Nicko tapped his nose, the way Vera did to him.

Miguel had little more to say about Tatiana Yurievna except that she was no longer slim, but blonde and a lot younger than her husband, if indeed that was what he was. Apparently she had been a small-time TV actress in Kiev when Oleg had taken up with her.

The remaining celebrities on board the Dobrinin yacht were, needless to say, people Nicko had never heard of - apart from one very passé soap star. Instead he turned to a matter which interested him much more; the part that might have been played by any of that cast in the Cetinje incident. Nicko felt that there was no need to be reticent with the Mexican boy.

There were armed security men on board the ship, it went without saying, but their presence was discreet. They never showed off their weapons and kept in the background, so if any of them went ashore it was not remarked upon. But of course everyone on board knew why they were there and would not have expected it to be otherwise.

All this Miguel explained to Nicko, who went on to tell him what had occurred in the square in Cetinje.

The Mexican merely shrugged his shoulders and registered no surprise. After all, it was the sort of thing that went on all the time in the country where he had been born. Could Lord Isaacs have known anything about it? The boy shrugged again and said that they never talked about such things. The only question that had really exercised them was a controversial exchange that occurred between Isaacs and a leading member of the Opposition front bench in a Corfu restaurant which had found its way into the British newspapers shortly afterwards.

It seemed like a dream: There was Viktor, inviting into his own home, as a guest, the very man who had probably tried to murder his child only months before....Nicko prided himself on having a Russian soul, but this he could not fathom. Maybe in it was a clue to so much that had happened in that troubled land during the past century.... Glancing at his watch, Nicko realised that he was neglecting his duties, whatever they were supposed to be. He got to his feet, but Miguel immediately pulled him back down and planted a slow kiss on his lips before releasing him.

CHAPTER FOURTEEN

A Heady Mix …

The rest of the party was in the dining room, tucking into the fare, either at the table or with plates balanced on their knees round the sides of the room. Vera was looking a little anxious, but her face lit up as soon as she saw Nicko enter the room.

"I was wondering where you were hiding, Nikoshka," she said to him

"Doing a little research on your latest guest," he told her.

Tsina meanwhile filled a bowl of borsch for him and he grabbed cutlery and a napkin before setting out to the far end of the room.

"Have you seen Miggie?" Isaacs asked Nicko as he passed him and Viktor talking together.

"He's taking a short break- in the breakfast room. Dying of thirst, he told me. He needs vodka, plenty of it and quickly."

"Is he by himself?" Isaacs scowled.

"He was when I left him just a moment ago."

"I hope he's not having one of his sulks. It's his Latin temperament."

"Does he have lots of them - sulks, I mean?"

"He's very capricious. Perhaps I'd better go and have a word with him."

In a corner of the room Dobrinin and Imogen Trubshaw were sharing a small occasional table, locked in what appeared to be an intense conversation. The Russian was making sweeping gestures with his hands and his froglike features were alight. Meanwhile Dick, the Khlebnikovs, Tim Mumford and his girlfriend had formed a cheery, more relaxed-seeming party at the end of the main table. Alyosha was attending to glasses and none of the children could be seen.

For a second Nicko hesitated, unsure of where to park himself. He chose a spot next to Tim, but within earshot of Dobrinin and Imogen. Nudging Tim, he indicated with a flick of his head the couple behind him.

"I know," whispered Tim. "I've been flapping my ears like mad and have picked up scraps of it. There was a great deal of talk a few moments ago about schools and what's being taught in them. And comparisons between Russian schools and English ones- especially about the teaching of Maths - which our Russian chum takes very seriously. Mrs Trubshaw - what's her name again?"

"Imogen."

"Imogen said that she'd be delighted to have a twinning arrangement with a Russian school. Then they switched to property values, which sounded a bit too much like work, so I broke off. Anyway, how's Isaacs' young chum? You seemed to be having a bit to say to one another in the breakfast room."

Nicko frowned at him. "I was doing some research on you-know-who," he whispered back.

"Did you find out anything?"

"Not so far, but Isaacs and his boy are the ones to work on. They were on that ship in the summer, as you know, when we had our spot of bother in Montenegro."

"Tell me more."

"Later on I will, Tim, but not right now. Only this - that Isaacs and Dobrinin are as thick as thieves - going back to the former's Brussels days. But I guess you knew that already."

The guests meanwhile had started to select their desserts.

"I can recommend the torte," Nicko informed the group. "It's something they do particularly well in Russia." He nodded affably at the Khlebnikovs as he said it. "Where are the children, by the way? They mustn't miss out on the cake."

As if on cue, the children arrived, but Tsina was on hand to issue them with instructions that the grown-ups were to be served first. She appeared to have taken on the role of nanny. Meanwhile a rather thoughtful-looking Mark Isaacs slipped quietly back into the room, followed by Miguel, with his hands thrust deep into his trouser pockets and a sulky pout on his face.

"Hullo. Hullo," Nicko whispered into Tim's ear. "I think we may have just had a lovers' tiff." "You said it not me."

The possibility was somehow satisfying to Nicko.

Viktor immediately collared them and helped them load their plates, after which they settled at the far end of the table, away from the rest. A couple of minutes later Viktor left them and sidled over to Dobrinin, where he apologised for breaking into his conversation with Imogen, which had resumed once they had been served with their dessert. Nicko observed the fleeting look of irritation which crossed the oligarch's face, but which disappeared as soon as he set off with his host to join Isaacs.

"Come and join us," Nicko said to Imogen, "and tell us all about Mr Dobrinin. You looked as if you were plotting some kind of a deal."

Imogen hooted in her rather horsey manner.

"What would you like me to tell you? There's a lot more there than meets the eye. He looks like a toad, but he's passionate about education."

"So was Tony Blair, but we'll let that one pass."

"He thinks that they do things much better in Russia- especially Maths."

"Are there any kids?" asked Dick who joined them.

"Back in Russia there are," Imogen informed them. "But they're grown up and at university. The spouse he has here is his second- or third. Tatiana Yurievna, however you say it in Russian. Pavel might put us right on that one."

Pavel, who had sidled up with Dick, spread his hands. "Or the fourth? Or the fifth? Or the sixth even? Who really knows? Maybe he's like your King Henry VIII?"

"He's not a bit like our King Henry VIII," put in Dick. "He's more like a toad or a lizard than a Tudor monarch. All the same, I'd love to know how he's made all his money."

Imogen raised a cautionary finger to her lips as she sensed that their talk was getting uncomfortably loud, unlike the Dobrinin party whose members were leaning across to one another, with their heads almost coming together in a conspiratorial huddle

Nicko felt that it was the moment to locate Vera, who had left the room, and to see what he could do for her. She was in the kitchen with Tsina and the kids, who were blissfully engaged in gobbling up what was left of the torte. Alyosha wandered in to take a fresh bottle from the fridge and filled Nicko's empty glass. The latter, pressing a hand on his shoulder, forced him to sit down at the table with the others.

"Harasho?" Nicko enquired of Vera in her own language.

"Ochin," she replied. "But I don't know what we would have done without Tsina here."

"Did you get any warning about who your mystery extra guest was going to be?"

Vera shrugged. "None, but I might have guessed."

"After last summer's affair it can't be easy welcoming him into your home- if you think he really was behind it."

"But that's Vitya, isn't it? And it may mean we're safer. It's Kolochka I think about first."

"Alyosha and Tsina are a great help - a bit of a change from Ludochka in the summer," pointed out Nicko. "Have you heard from her, by the way?"

"Not since we came to London."

"I wouldn't be surprised if she showed up one of these days. She said she would like to study here."

He glanced at Tsina, who smiled back at him, while instructing Evgeni Khlebnikov in the civilised way to hold a spoon.

Loud guffaws suddenly erupted in the next room, amidst which Isaacs' silvery tinkle could be picked out. There followed loud exclamations in colloquial Russian which caused Vera to shake her head.

"I hope Vitya isn't drinking too much - especially with that man," she said.

Meanwhile Miguel slipped into the kitchen, with catlike stealth, and pressed his hands on Nicko's shoulders. "Always politics," he complained. Mark is such a bore."

A minute later Dick followed him. "So this is where you're all hiding."

"What have you done with Imogen?" Nicko asked him.

"Left her with Elspeth and Tim. "Discussing school fees."

Vera chased the children into the breakfast room and the new arrivals squeezed in at the table.

"This is very English," Dick explained to his hostess. "You lay on a splendid party in your best rooms and yet we all pile into the kitchen."

"Where the things that really matter get aired," added Nicko. He turned to Miguel. "Spill the beans," he said.

The Mexican boy looked guarded.

"Miguel here was on the Good Ship Vcnus in the summer," Nicko explained. "With Dobrinin and Lord Isaacs."

"There are no beans to spill really," Miguel said. "Just a lot of rather boring talk about people they both knew in Brussels and Moscow, but none of it is very interesting. Just tittle - how do you English say it?"

"Tittle-tattle."

Nicko reached for a bottle of bubbly and filled a glass for the Mexican boy.

"I'm afraid it's a bit warm," he apologised.

Miguel lowered an eyelid at him over the rim of the glass as he took a sip.

That he could provide little of interest to tell them about the relations between the former European Commissioner for Trade and a Russian oligarch was hardly surprising. Clearly Isaacs liked to keep his affairs in separate boxes. Any serious business would be conducted out of earshot. Miguel was perfectly aware that, like his dog, his job was to supply the sweetness in the great man's life.

"They were talking about dogs and Lubya's litter," he said.

"Is that the bitch's name?" enquired Dick.

"She's a Russian bitch," Miguel said, with a mildly apologetic glance in the direction of Vera. "Mark wants to sell Dobrinin a puppy. His offer is perfectly reasonable, but he's not letting him have it for nothing, like he's doing for Viktor. Dobrinin is not too happy about it."

There was more loud laughter from the next room

"It seems to take a long time to wrap up a deal about a dog," observed Dick.

"There was some talk about a picture as well, but I only caught the tail-end of that," said the Mexican boy. "Dobrinin seemed more interested in the dog."

"Your field Nicko," Dick said. "The picture, I mean, not the bitch."

"Viktor said something to him about a Mark Rothko, but as I say, Dobrinin only wanted to talk about a puppy." Miguel drained his glass. "He told him he leaves the big decisions on artistic matters to his wife."

Vera and Nicko exchanged anxious looks, but added nothing.

At that moment, Imogen, Tim and Elspeth looked in and the party adjourned to review the Schwitters in the breakfast room, while the conference in the dining room continued. The picture having been carefully scrutinised, the talk moved on to the visual arts in general.

Nicko joined in a spirited exchange about Modernism and the Prince of Wales's views on the subject with Tim and Elspeth. Here there appeared to be a rift between the two, with Nicko hovering somewhere between them, but inclining, if anything, towards Tim's more conservative position.

Tim turned out to be a fan of the arch-classicist Quinlan Terry and a hearty loather of the works of Corbusier and his disciples, whilst Elspeth did not agree and put up a spirited defence of Foster's Gherkin at Canary Wharf - at which Tim threw up his hands in simulated horror. It struck

Nicko that the couple were able to differ radically about such matters without shedding any blood and he liked them the better for it.

The separate breakfast room conference finally broke up and they joined the rest, while Isaacs wandered into the sitting room, looking for his hostess, whom he addressed in his silkiest tone.

"A word in your ear, Vera, my dear," he alliterated. He drew her towards the door into the hall.

"The boy mustn't know," he told her. "It has got to be a surprise."

Vera said nothing, allowing him to continue.

"Father Christmas is bringing him a puppy," he went on. "Your husband has consented to it, but it must come from Father Christmas, don't you agree?"

"I hope Vitya's paying for it. Dogs are expensive."

"Nonsense. That's not how Father Christmas does things. He wouldn't hear of such a thing." He eyed her for a moment. "You do keep such customs, don't you?"

"In England we certainly mean to. Kolya will put up his stocking on Christmas Eve just as the other children do."

"I'm delighted to hear you say that. But I don't think we can put a month old puppy into a stocking, do you?"

"You are really much too kind!"

"But it has to be a surprise. I'll bring the little chap round myself on Christmas Eve once the boy's tucked up in his bed."

"And Vitya is happy?"

"Perfectly. Why should he not be? And what a lovely party, my dear. You're a wonderful cook. I adore your Russian food!"

"Tsina helped with it, but thank you! You're always welcome in our house."

He kissed her daintily on her cheek and slipped back into the dining room.

By now the evening was reaching a maudlin climax. Oleg Dobrinin had placed his arms round Viktor and Pavel's shoulders and together they had embarked on a rendition of 'The Song of Stenka Razin'. Alyosha was there too, rocking on his heels - quite a quantity of the bubbly he had been charged with had found its way down his own gullet - and conducting the choir. Imogen had joined them and was listening entranced to the doleful Russian sound - for Dobrinin, despite his unprepossessing appearance, and meagre physique sang in a surprisingly resonant bass.

The song completed with the Persian princess cast off by the Attoman to perish in the Volga, there followed a short round of applause from the others with fresh toasts, Alyosha having made a swift dash to the kitchen for a supply of chilled vodka.

A surprisingly witty speech - in both English and Russian - was made by Dobrinin and his glass was raised to Anglo-Russian 'drouzba'. A shorter piece followed from Pavel which included a gracious reference to Bailey's and the good work being done there by the Trubshaws to which Dick contrived a cheery riposte.

The last speech of all was made by Lord Isaacs of South Shields, the words flowing out of him in a steady stream of perfectly enunciated Standard Received English. Despite his left-inclined politics, there was nothing remotely Estuarine about the way he spoke - no contrived glottal stops, no proletarian posturing.

He referred nostalgically to days spent in Russia and the warmth of his friendships there, citing Turgenev and Chekhov. He then launched into a description of his favourite Russian film, 'The Ballad of a Soldier', which he had first seen as a teenager and had adored ever since. It was a simple tale of a young Russian soldier going home on leave from the Front during The Great Patriotic war and falling in love with a girl whom he meets on the train. But largely because of the good deeds he has undertaken on behalf of his comrades at the Front, he has only a few fleeting moments to spend with his mother before he has to return to the war from which he will never come back.

As Isaacs told the story, there was a tremor in his voice and for a second or so it seemed that he was about to weep.

"Vodka usually does that to him," whispered Miguel in Nicko's ear.

"He certainly a polished performer," pointed out Nicko. "You have to give him that."

There was a short derisory snort from Miguel, as the effusion of wistful praise for Mother Russia continued to flow from the lips of Lord Isaacs, some of it even uttered in Russian. The Russians present, most notably Dobrinin, appeared to be touched by what he was saying and the oligarch put a brotherly arm round the Government Minister's shoulder, while Viktor even started to look dewy-eyed.

Finally Isaacs returned to his opening theme of 'drouzba' - or 'friendship' - and calling the three youngsters forward- for they had been fetched from upstairs- for the ceremony- he declared that it was with them that the future lay, that they were the rock on which a long-lasting Anglo-Russian 'drouzba' would be set. He repeated the words in Russian, winding up with a toast in that language, which was followed by a short round of applause from his small audience, but a scarcely-suppressed groan from Miguel which surprised Nicko by the nakedness of his disloyalty.

With the conclusion of Isaacs' oration, it was time for the break-up of the party. The Khlebnikovs and the Trubshaws made their farewells. And as Tim and Elspeth were leaving, Nicko apologised for not having given more time to them, while confirming his next saloon bar meeting with the former.

As Nicko apologised, Tim squeezed his arm. "Not to worry," he said. "I could see which way the wind was blowing."

For a second Nicko did not know quite how to take it. "Anyway it was lovely meeting Elspeth," he came out with. "You and Tsina, seemed to be hitting it off," he added to her.

"Weren't they just," Tim said from the bottom of the steps. "Look after yourself, Old Boy. Feel free to confess all in the Cock and Hen."

Tim winked at him, in the same manner, almost, as Miguel.

Lord Isaacs left last, immediately after Dobrinin, who made an extravagant display of kissing Vera on both cheeks and addressing her as 'Verochka' to her considerable embarrassment. He landed a playful punch on 'Vitya' too, as he departed and whispered something in his ear, which caused the latter to nod and to grin. Isaacs, for his part, bowed and kissed the back of Vera's hand, like a beau of the ancien regime - which suited her better than the oligarch's slavering effusion. Miguel dipped his head and delivered his thanks to his host and hostess in elegant Spanish, then kissed Vera's hand in the same manner as his lord and master. But on the steps outside, he hugged Nicko and kissed his cheek, while a tight-lipped Lord Isaacs looked on.

Nicko felt something being slipped into the palm of his hand. When he looked, he saw that it was a printed card with a couple of telephone numbers on it.

CHAPTER FIFTEEN

A Private View

The following week Nicko spent his evenings at home. The phone rang several times: Vera to thank him once again for his help and then Viktor to tell him that he was about to make yet another trip across the Atlantic. Nicko mentioned the matter of the dog and his friend told him that it had indeed been concluded with Lord Isaacs, before being placed in the hands of Father Christmas- so it was very hush-hush. Kolya had to be kept completely in the dark.

Tim also rang to confirm their coming pub rendezvous, an event which was assuming an almost Masonic regularity. He dropped no further hints about the Mexican boy in their brief conversation, while the latter did not ring. Perhaps, Nicko reflected, the ball was being left in his court, though he felt hesitant about ringing either of the numbers on the card. But it was clear that a pass had been made at him, which he had not rejected. Nicko felt capable of playing Miguel's kind of a game up to a point at least, though he had a lot to lose if he allowed it to run too far, too fast. Violent physical passions were rather foreign to him in any case, so while he was flattered by Miguel's attention and had enjoyed his kisses, he was not going to fret if the boy did not press on too quickly.

As the school term was drawing to its close for the Christmas holidays, he dropped in on the following Saturday to see Vera. The house was full of flowers. Lord Isaacs had been sending her fresh blooms almost daily for a week since the party, with dainty billets doux written in French attached to them. Tsina answered the door and he found Vera in the kitchen. Alyosha was not in evidence, but she explained that Viktor had just returned from his latest trip to New York and that the pair of them had been discussing the dispatch and safe storage of pictures, as well as a suitable venue in which to display them to potential buyers. It seemed that Alyosha was not unfamiliar with locations in the West End where such an event might be staged, as well as being up to speed on the security aspect. The shape of Viktor's operation was becoming apparent to Nicko and the role that different personalities might be playing in it.

"Has he got Dobrinin a Rothko?" Nicko asked.

Vera shrugged. "Vitya told me nothing about it."

"And in the meantime you are expected to play the dutiful Mafia wife who turns her children out nicely, watches over their manners and never talks about business."

Vera stared at him. He was not normally quite so outspoken about her husband.

"After what happened in the summer, Vik's got a bloody nerve! Hell, he nearly got his own child killed! And now he invites that man, of all people, into his own home!"

"Stop it, Nikoshka. Don't imagine I don't think about that every hour of every day. But the quarrel in the summer was about property - about a Russian development at Tiva. At least I believe it was. Vik's out of all that now. Back to selling pictures, which is much safer. And Dobrinin's just another customer, who wants to buy one for his wife. And better to make peace than to go on fighting a war until someone's killed, isn't it?"

Tsina had left the kitchen and Nicko took the opportunity to hug Vera close and kiss her on her forehead.

"I'm keeping my fingers crossed for you, Verochka," he said. "For all of you. I pray that you're right."

For a moment neither of them spoke.

"Where's Vik now?" he eventually asked.

"Out with Alyosha. They'll be back soon, if you want to wait."

Nicko toyed with idea, but decided to leave it for the time being. He hoped things were taking a turn for the better: a genuine peace did seem to have been made with Oleg Dobrinin and Vik's return to art-dealing appeared to be going ahead smoothly, for the time being at least - except that knowing the way that it had operated previously, there could be no guarantee of it lasting. But hopefully it would be less dangerous than property developments in Montenegro.

* * * * *

All this he mulled over with Tim the following evening. Their conversation was taken up with the Russian expatriot scene, so that the part Miguel might be assuming in Nicko's life was left untouched, though Lord Isaacs' relationship with Russian oligarchs certainly was not.

Tim, needless to say, was fascinated by the whole espionage game and the possible penetration of the British Government itself. The part that might be being played by expatriot Russians who had received part of their education in the United Kingdom was something he raised also.

"Tell me more about Vik," he said.

"I'm not sure I can add much more to what I've told you already," Nicko replied. "I'm of Russian extraction myself and we met at public school as you already know. But Vik's Stalinist background is what intrigued me most about him. Here he was, getting a privileged British education, while at the same time being the grandson of one of Stalin's most powerful satraps- one who as far as I know never came a cropper as so many of them did. The family comes through the collapse of the Soviet Union with a fortune, though I know very little about any of its members, apart from Vik, who seems to have struck out on his own. His taste for western things, I suppose. But if you ask me if I think he's any kind of a spy, the idea's crazy, a crook maybe, but nothing more. They're all crooks. It goes with the turf, doesn't it?"

"Agents pop up in the most unlikely places," Tim said. "There was even one who was a master at my prep school." He nudged Nicko and winked. "And you're a kind of Russian- working in a prep school."

Nicko laughed.

"But we were quite certain that this guy was an MI6 agent who was being rested, which was perfectly feasible. He taught Latin, after all."

Nicko laughed. "Vik and I were great buddies," he said, "at school and afterwards. We got into all sorts of scrapes together and played up the Russian thing- Orloff and Nikishov. But the truth was he was a New Russian wide boy and I was a two generations away White Russian toff."

"And a snob."

"Of course I was a snob and I still am. Aren't you, Tim?"

Tim laughed and took a big pull at his glass.

"I haven't told you about the time Vik and I smashed a priceless Athenian red-figure krater, have I?"

"Lead on," Tim said pulling at his glass," but drink up first."

* * * * * *

It was in the following week, with the school breaking up for Christmas, when Viktor rang to invite Nicko over. There was something he wanted to show him.

"So you've got it here?" Nicko said. "That was quick work. Through a back door I suppose?"

"I don't know which one you're talking about." "Another of your dark secrets?"

Viktor chuckled.

"And you're quite sure that it's the real thing?"

"Kaneshna."

"But you want me to look at it?"

"Da."

"Da. Kaneshna. But I'm no authority on Rothko. I confess he's never interested me greatly, not being hooked on the American Abstract scene."

"Stuff that, Nick, I'd still like you to see it."

That was settled then. Nicko was to join his friend in Thurloe Square and they would go together to the place where the picture was being kept.

It was shortly after seven when he arrived and, after a brief word with Vera, he set off with Viktor and Alyosha in a taxi.

The latter seemed to be in charge, directing the driver to a side street off Sloane Square, where they stopped in front of a premises whose window was in darkness.

"This is all very cloak and dagger," observed Nicko.

The premises itself seemed to be deserted, though there was plenty of life in the street at that time of the evening. Alyosha produced a key and opened the door. There was no sound of an alarm counting off the seconds, nothing. The place might have been empty for months.

"Who does this belong to?" asked Nicko in a whisper.

Viktor shrugged. "God knows."

"You mean you don't even know and you're hiding a valuable painting here?"

Alyosha switched on a light and lead the way up a short flight of stairs to the first floor. On the landing, and the side away from the street, was a door and Nicko could see a light shining under it. Alyosha tapped on the door in what sounded like a pre-arranged code, then spoke softly in Russian. Nicko could not make out what he was saying, but, like the knock, it sounded pre-arranged.

"So someone is at home," Nicko said to Viktor.

The door opened and a head appeared round it, dark against the light inside the room. Its occupant beckoned the three visitors to come in.

It was a small room, a bit larger than a broom cupboard, and fitted out with an old gas cooker and a sink- the kind of place that might have been used for running up cups of coffee during working hours. A camp bed had been set up behind a Formica-topped table and standing on a chair, covered by what looked like an old curtain, was the thing that they had come to see.

"Tell me something, Vik," said Nicko. "Why does it have to be done this way? It's like one of those old spy thrillers where everything's dressed down and dingy. You know, the Smiley effect taking the place of Bond five-star glitz."

Alyosha smiled broadly while talking to the guard in rapid Russian.

"Is it to impress Dobrinin?" went on Nicko.

"I'm doing him a favour," Viktor said. "He's getting a bargain and the paperwork's all been looked after as well."

"I would have thought if anyone could afford to buy a painting at the going market rate it was Dobrinin," Nicko pointed out. "This looks pretty cheesy to me."

"Leopard's don't change their spots, do they? Remember that, you old cunt!" Viktor gave his chum a playful poke in the ribs.

"At least that's one you haven't forgotten."

"And, as you've said yourself more than once, it's our Russian way."

"Piss off," said Nicko in a low voice, returning the poke in his ribs.

Alyosha meanwhile had adjusted a table lamp so that its beam was spread evenly over the draped object. He stood to one side, a bit like a conjuror about to perform his master trick. Viktor nodded to him and he whipped away the drape with a flourish.

What Nicko saw certainly appeared to be the real thing, but you could never be quite sure with abstract pictures like this one at first glance. Of its kind it was an undeniably powerful picture. He guessed it to be about ninety inches by seventy and it consisted of a murky green rectangle, blurred at its edges, a narrow band of midnight blue separating it from a large white square, also with blurred edges that melted into a lilac ground.

"What's it called?" asked Nicko, having contemplated it for a minute.

"It doesn't have a name," Viktor said. "After all, it isn't a picture of anything in particular, is it? It's itself and nothing else. An object in its own right."

"Really, Vik, you're getting quite existential," quipped Nicko.

Viktor mouthed a four letter word at him.

"It's certainly a strong picture," conceded Nicko, "but I think I'd prefer a Schwitters. Are you sure Dobrinin is going to like it?"

"It's for his wife, don't forget- who's already seen a snapshot and given it a title."

"Rather missing the point, isn't she, in view of what you've just said?"

"She's named it "A Symphony in Green, Blue and White.""

"It doesn't look very symphonic to me, but then I suppose you can read into it what you want. I guess that's the idea- it's a kind of aid to meditation. Dare I ask how much he's paying for it?"

"You may, but I'm not going to tell you. And anyway it hasn't quite been settled yet. They still have to see it in the flesh."

"Is he coming here for it or are you taking it to the Great Khan in his saray?"

"He's coming here."

"I'm surprised he's taking the risk."

"There isn't any risk."

"After the shenanigans in Montenegro he mightn't quite see it that light - despite you two being best mates at the housewarming. The picture could be a bait."

"He'll bring his chums, while I'll have Alyosha here with a couple of his boys as well." He nodded in the direction of the guard, who, with a tattooed neck and shaved head, certainly looked the goods.

"Are you writing the script for a Russian version of 'The Godfather', by any chance? There was rather a good one about Russian Mafiosi I saw recently- I've forgotten the name of it."

"Piss off, Nick. Where's that famous Russian soul of yours?"

"It just sounds a wee bit over the top, that's all - as a way of selling a picture, I mean."

"But it's no ordinary picture."

"Hm. We might argue about that. What do you make of it, Alyosha? Is it your type of thing?"

The Russian smiled, shrugged his shoulders and said nothing.

The Rothko was shrouded once more and the guard lit a cigarette.

"I hope he doesn't set fire to it," Nicko said, "but then a few scorch marks might add a further resonance."

"You think it's crap, don't you?"

"I didn't say that, Vik - or at least not quite. And, anyway, what do you think of it? Anything at all? But if we're talking about Modernism, I prefer Schwitters."

"I'm talking about greenbacks."

"I know you are. When are you not?"

They laughed and exchanged their usual playful punches as they went downstairs.

* * * * * *

Back in Thurloe Square once more, Viktor was on his mobile and pacing the hall, while Nicko chatted to Vera and Kolya in the kitchen.

"Well," she said. "What did you think of it?"

"It's certainly a powerful picture in its way, but I'm not sure about it."

"Do you mean you don't like it?"

"You see, Verochka, I'm one of those fogeys who likes to see the hand of the craftsman in the work. In this case I'm not sure that I can."

"What does Vitya think?"

"You know Vik." Nicko pretended to count banknotes off in his palm.

"That's a stupid question, isn't it?" She glanced at her son, who was reading a comic and paying no attention to what was being said.

"I have to confess I'm a bit at sea with Abstract Expressionism. I like Schwitters better. There is a puckish quality in his work somehow. And that family thing too, I suppose."

Viktor came into the kitchen and rumpled his son's hair. The boy muttered a protest and went on reading his comic.

"Well?" Nicko asked.

"Well what?"

"Has the Great Khan granted you an audience yet?"

"All arranged. Tomorrow night," said Viktor. "He knows where to go."

Vera sighed and glanced at the ceiling.

"Anything the matter?" her husband asked her in Russian.

"I hope it will be all right, that's all," she replied in the same language.

"You don't sound very happy. What would you like me to do?"

Nicko understood the simple Russian.

He turned to the boy. "What's Father Christmas bringing you, Kolya?"

A scornful look crossed the boy's face. Patronising talk of that kind did not go down well with one of his age.

"Is it going to be like those wonderful Christmasses in Russia?" pursued Nicko, altering his tack. "But without the snow? And - who is it there? Father Frost?"

"I hope so," said the boy. We're going to decorate the tree on Christmas Eve and put the presents under it."

"That sounds great."

"Where will you be?" asked Vera.

"In the family nest - as usual, I suppose. With Mother, very quiet and dull. She's on her own now, of course."

"You must bring her here sometime," Vera said. "I'd like to meet her."

"Kaneshna," added Viktor. "It's been a long time since I saw her. We were still at school then."

Nicko left soon afterwards and made his way to the Underground station. The street was quiet, but he as he approached the station he heard rapid footsteps behind him. He looked back over his shoulder and saw a slight figure, bareheaded, but with his coat collar pulled up round his face, bearing down on him. He seemed to be the object of the person's pursuit.

"Hullo, Nicko," the pursuer said in a soft voice as he drew abreast.

"I was waiting for you to leave the house," the fellow went on.

"Good God, Miguel, for a moment I thought I was going to be mugged."

"You can call me 'Miggie' if you like. Most of my friends do." "You were waiting for me to leave? Where's Mark?"

"He's away on some Government business. So bugger him."

"Strong words, Miggie."

The other grinned and squeezed Nicko's shoulder. "You don't like me saying things like that?"

"You're a naughty boy, Miggie."

The Mexican boy laughed or rather giggled.

"Have you had a quarrel?" went on Nicko.

"We're always having them. I get sick of his fucking politics. Where are you going now?" "Home - to my flat." "Can I come with you?"

"If you want to," said Nicko. It seemed so easy, the most natural thing in the world for him to say.

They squeezed each other's hands as they went down into the Underground station together....

CHAPTER SIXTEEN

Father Christmas Calls and a Family Chore

Christmas Eve had arrived and Nicko decamped to Sunningdale the day before to join his mother. He went a little sooner than usual as it was to be her first Christmas without his father.

Nicko had seen little of his sister while he was growing up. Nearly eight years separated them. Not long after she had graduated from Cambridge, she had married David, who was starting out in the Foreign Office. She had met him in his final year in King's. So, in Nicko's last years at school, at the time he was making friends with Viktor, she had virtually disappeared from his life. While his father had tried to be even-handed between his offspring, his mother, though taking her son's part against him on a number of occasions, clearly saw the household of her diplomatic son-in-law as a congenial retreat, especially after the grandchildren had started to arrive. And this time, too, as soon as Christmas was over, she would be off to Rome for the New Year.

But Nicko felt no compunction about slipping back into Town on the afternoon of Christmas Eve to spend time with his Russian friends. He wanted to be there to help welcome the puppy that Lord Isaacs would be bringing for his godson and to witness its introduction to the house- a secret process, of course, to be kept from Kolya.

Isaacs had rung to say that he would be around about teatime and a plot had been hatched to distract Kolya while the pup was being smuggled into the house and placed in Alyosha and Tsina's basement flat, where hopefully any canine whimpers would not reach upstairs. Tsina was happy to play surrogate mother to the little fellow so recently taken from his own mother's teat.

Vera was to make sure that her son was safely parked in front of the television when Lord Isaacs arrived. Instead of entering through the front door, by the breakfast room, he would creep down to the basement by the outside steps, bearing his precious burden, where Tsina would admit him. Having delivered his charge, he was then to come upstairs to join the Nikishovs for a festive drink, leaving Father Christmas to complete the business.

Nicko had volunteered to play his part, by helping to distract the boy during the critical moments should it be necessary, but Viktor expressed caution: the matter should not be overplayed, thus arousing Kolya's suspicions. It had to be kept as low key as possible and if the lad expressed any hopes of getting a puppy for Christmas, their collective response must be to sound non-committal.

After all this had been settled, with Kolya parked snugly in the breakfast room, and while they were awaiting the coming of the Government Minister, Viktor took his friend into the dining room.

"It's all done," he said. "How do you say in English? All done and dusted?"

"Yes Vik. I assume you're talking about the picture. And that the Great Khan is satisfied and has paid you a fair price for it?"

\"In crisp new dollar bills - every fucking cent." "Real ones I hope?"

"Piss off Nick. Of course they're real."

"And it all went smoothly? No one got twitchy?" "Nyet."

"It was a good party then? Drinks all round in the broom cupboard?"

"Not this time, but we were good chums." "No unhappy memories of Montenegro?"

"Viktor laughed scornfully. "We're all grown up."

"There was someone else who very nearly didn't get that far. But it never happened. So now there should be plenty in the kitty for Christmas."

"It's a pity you won't be with us." "Alas, duty calls. Mother."

"You could always bring her here."

Nicko looked at his friend. "I hardly think so," he said. "At least not this time."

"What about the Feast of Epiphany? The Orthodox Christmas? She might enjoy that."

"I'll think about it," Nicko said. "It's a kind offer, but I think she'll be in Italy then."

With Kolya tucked safely in the breakfast room in front of the television, enjoying a slice of Christmas cake and a glass of Coca-Cola, Vera came out of the kitchen and whispered in her husband's ear. He nodded and looked at his watch. Together they went to the end of the passage beyond the kitchen, where the stairs lead down to the basement.

Nick followed as they descended and Viktor knocked on Alyosha and Tsina's door.

It was opened by Tsina. No, Lord Isaacs had not arrived yet, but they were expecting him at any minute. Nicko noticed the dog basket and a rubber bone under the kitchen table, where Alyosha was sitting and enjoying a cigarette.

"I hope he isn't late," said Vera anxiously.

"He has a chauffeur to drive him home if he's working," Nicko pointed out, "and he's a big enough noise in the Government, so he ought to be able to escape more or less when it suits him."

As if in answer to his words, there came a light tap on the outside door, followed by the lean features of Lord Isaacs peering round it. Instantly his lips spread into a broad smile under the ski-jump nose, while a hand brushed back the hank of dark hair that had flopped over his forehead.

"Merry Christmas, everybody!" he purred.

He entered the room, bearing no puppy. But, coming immediately after him, was Miggie cradling a little furry bundle in his arms, with a bright green and red ribbon tied in a bow round its neck.

"Ho! Ho! Ho!" joked Isaacs.

"Merry Christmas," chirped Miggie, who immediately kissed Vera on the cheek, to be followed by Lord Isaacs. Viktor took the dog from the Mexican boy, who winked at Nicko and poked him in the ribs.

"Does he need anything to eat or drink?" asked Vera

"He's just had his supper," Isaacs told her.

Alyosha meanwhile called the group to the table, where a bottle of vodka and glasses were waiting. Alyosha pretended to pour some of the vodka into the dog's drinking bowl, which caused Lord Isaacs to emit a squeal of laughter.

Vera pressed a warning finger to her lips, in case the sounds of merriment should reach the boy upstairs. It was better to go up at once, leaving Tsina in charge of the new resident in the basement.

The men quickly downed their vodkas and the puppy endeared himself to Viktor, by nuzzling into the palm of his hand and licking it. He was then passed round the others, until he ended up in Tsina's arms, where she cradled him like the child that he was. Lord Isaacs looked on, his face fixed in a benign seasonal smile.

Tsina offered the dog a biscuit- which was readily accepted- and had her cheek licked in thanks. She then put him in his basket with the rubber bone, but the little rascal was out immediately, sniffing round everbody's feet.

Vera led the visitors upstairs, leaving Tsina and Alyosha with the newcomer. They trooped into the sitting room, which had been provided with a tray of drinks in readiness. Kolya was then summoned to join the company from the television in the breakfast room, which he abandoned reluctantly.

A large Christmas tree, which he had helped to decorate, filled the window space and there were already a number of parcels beneath it.

"Merry Christmas, Kolya!" piped Miggie.

It was repeated by Lord Isaacs who, in his silkiest tone, added, "And what's Father Christmas going to bring you tonight, young man?"

A scornful look crossed the boy's face. "I don't believe in him!" he retorted, and, turning his back, stamped his foot.

"Kolochka! How dare you!" his mother scolded him. "You must never do a thing like that again! And turning you back on people is very rude. Say you are sorry to Lord Isaacs!"

The boy mumbled a grudging apology and Lord Isaacs chuckled lightly as a token of its acceptance. It was not the season for bad grace, especially for a practised politician, after all.

"Well, anyway, what would you like for Christmas, even if it doesn't come from Lapland?" he purred.

"I want a dog like yours."

The politician's face lit at once in a crafty smile. "I might be able to help you there," he said. "But there is something you have to do first. Do you know what I mean when I say you have to swallow your pride?"

The boy shook his head.

"Well, you said just now that you didn't believe in Father Christmas…"
"I don't. Or Father Frost."

Lord Isaacs sighed. "But you want a dog, you say? Well. There's only way you will get one and that's to write Father Christmas a nice letter. And if you leave it where he can find it, I'm sure he'll give you what you want, but we haven't got much time. It is Christmas Eve, after all."

The boy looked at the others with a confused expression on his face.

"That's a very good idea," his mother urged him. "You must do exactly what Lord Isaacs tells you, Kolochka!"

"And I can help you write your letter," said Miggie. "I'm good at writing nice letters."

193

The boy saw that there was no choice but to fall in with the childish game that he was being caught up in, if there was to be any chance of getting the thing he wanted. He could see that he was being treated like an infant, but had sufficient acumen to bite the bullet.

"Where can we write our letter?" asked Miggie.

"In the kitchen," Vera told him. "Go Kolochka! There's paper on the shelf - you know where it is. Now, who would like a drink?"

Viktor positioned himself behind the drinks and the nibbles and started to dispense. It was a cheery party, joined fifteen minutes later by Miggie and a flushed, but more upbeat Kolya, brandishing the epistle.

"Well done, son," said his father in a patronising tone.

"As it's already Christmas Eve," Lord Isaacs pointed out. "It might be better if I take the letter myself to make quite sure that Father Christmas gets it in time. After all it would be a shame if he came without a puppy, wouldn't it?"

Kolya's eyes wandered ceilingwards, but he managed to put on a presentable smile.

Viktor, though he did raise the matter, was aglow with his recent business success, leaving it to Lord Isaacs to amuse the company with some rancid anecdotes about his political colleagues. His malice, delivered as it was in carefully measured doses, was enthralling. Kolya had returned to the breakfast room, so was not privy to it and, Nicko could not help noticing that Miggie had retreated to the far end of the room with a large vodka and a bored expression on his face.

When the Government Minister shifted to the subject of his stay on the Dobrinin yacht, Nicko was all ears, but at that point Viktor, and indeed with the support of his wife, steered the talk back into less potentially choppy waters. There was to be no rocking of that particular boat.

That Mark Isaacs was not a man to cross - so much was plain. Nicko could not help admiring his brio and, needless to say, his eye for a young man, which was something that couldn't be denied him, much as he disliked his politics. It was said that, despite having only recently been created a life peer, and without holding any of its leading portfolios, Lord Isaacs was the power behind the Administration. Serpentine though the man was, Nicko felt rather flattered to be in his orbit.

Isaacs glanced at the clock on the mantelpiece. "My goodness, is it that time already? We must be off, mustn't we, Miggie?"

The Mexican boy climbed to his feet and gave Nicko's hand a squeeze as he went past him.

"God, I do get sick of his crap," he whispered in his ear.

In the hall, Vera summoned Kolya from the breakfast room to say goodbye to their guests.

Isaacs looked at the envelope in his hand, which had been dutifully addressed to 'Father Christmas, Lapland'. "What pretty handwriting!" he exclaimed. "I'm sure Father Christmas will be pleased to see that." He ruffled the boy's hair and Kolya produced an expression between a wince and a smile, but as Miggie went by the two of them exchanged playful punches.

"I must go too," Nicko said, when the door had closed. "Mother Dear will be getting very grumpy."

But five minutes later, when he was in the street a figure stepped out the shadows. This time there was no doubt who it was and it came as no surprise.

"Nicko," Miggie said, "when can we…?" He smacked a kiss on his cheek.

"Steady on." Nicko looked about him.

"It's all right. He's back at home. When can we…?"

"You mean when can you come again?"

"Of course. You want me to, don't you?"

"Kaneshna."

The Mexican looked puzzled.

"Of course," said Nicko in English. "Should I say it in Spanish? I'm afraid I don't know how. But it'll have to be after the Christmas holiday and whenever you're allowed out."

"That shouldn't be too difficult. He's off to a conference in Basle soon after New Year."

"Give me a buzz," Nicko pressed his hand and kissed his cheek. "And you can tell me more of your own fascinating life story, Miggie. You hardly got started the last time. Born - where was it? In a little town in Yucatan, wasn't it? Which makes you a Maya? Then a student in the Big Apple? Eventually ending up in bed with Baron Isaacs of South Shields in the Royal Borough of Chelsea! It could be a great story - when we have filled in the missing bits."

"I hope not 'ending up'," said Miggie. "It's not going to end with him, however big a shit he gets to be in your Government! And that's not going to last much longer either. He'll probably be out by the end of next year!"

"But like the proverbial cat, he'll land on his feet."

195

"He will if they let him."

"And who can stop him? Can you? You're the most likely one, but would you want to do a thing like that? You mustn't be ungrateful, Miggie."

The Mexican boy grinned and inserted a finger into the front of Nicko's trousers.

A door opened further along the street.

"Miggie? Are you there?" Lord Isaacs called out.

Miggie gave a brief snort of exasperation, while the Government Minister came down into street.

"Ah! There you are!" he said "I thought you were never coming home." He sounded annoyed.

"Motherfucker," Miggie muttered under his breath.

"Don't be naughty," Nicko told him. "You must do as you're told or Daddy will be very cross."

Miggie swung an imaginary cane though the air a couple of times.

"He doesn't beat you, does he?"

Miggie grinned.

"And you let him do that?"

But before he could reply, Isaacs had advanced down the pavement, somewhat agitated, but still able to give Nicko an ingratiating smile.

"After New Year," whispered Miggie. "Kaneshna."

As Isaacs drew level the Mexican boy turned to meet him.

"On my way," he announced airily.

The Government Minister took him by the arm and walked him firmly back to his house. As he went Miggie swung his free arm, miming the swish of a cane and turned at the same time to grin at Nicko over his shoulder.

My God, thought Nicko, what would the Red Tops do with that? The Grey Eminence of the Cabinet keeping a whipping boy, one he likes to beat?

He had left his scarf in the house so he went back and Vera opened the door to him.

"So you're going to stay with us for Christmas after all, Nikoshka?" she said.

"I forgot my scarf."

"Oh, I thought you'd changed your mind."

"I've just been chatting to Miggie. The relationship is interesting - with Isaacs, I mean."

Vera gave a short laugh. "Is it?"

"Of course most of it's public knowledge. Isaacs has a chum who works for the British Council and arranges student exchanges, that sort of thing and he fixed him up with Miggie - that's how people tell it, anyway - but what they get up to - that could be dynamite."

"Nikoshka, I don't want to know. Not now anyway."

"Well, I must love you and leave you." He took her in his arms and kissed her, long and hard.

She eased her way from his embrace at length, tenderly, but firmly.

"Your scarf," she said, "where did you leave it?"

"Either in the kitchen or in the breakfast room. Or is it in Alyosha's flat?"

She retreated into the house, while he waited in the porch. A couple of minutes later Kolya appeared bearing the scarf.

"Your scarf, Uncle Nicko."

"Thanks, Kolya. I'm sure you'll have a wonderful time and that it's going to be fine about the dog."

"I hope so. It's the only reason I wrote that stupid letter. But it wasn't really me who wrote it. Miggie told me what to say. He's good at that sort of thing."

"A Merry Christmas to you, Kolya. I'll see you very shortly. And my love to your Mama and Papa." He gave the boy a formal kiss in the middle of his forehead.

Going quickly down the steps, he set off to the station. The street was deserted now, no Miggie lurking in the shadows this time. No doubt he was doing a schoolboy penance for crossing his master, but then Nicko thought of the kind of schoolboy penance that he was about to undergo himself for the next two days in Sunningdale.

* * * * * *

When Nicko got back to his mother in Sunningdale it was late. He found her still up, and felt rather piqued that she should have waited up for him, as if he was still a teenager. That, of course, was the root of the problem: in his mother's eyes Nicko had never grown up, and she was anxious to see him settled in a conventional fashion. What had passed between him and Miggie in Finchley would have aroused her total incomprehension and abhorrence. So Mrs Orloff went on hoping that the right girl would come along soon, and stiffen her son's backbone. She was like her own mother.

"Merry Christmas, Ma," said Nicko, as he entered her small sitting room.

"We're not quite there yet," she answered severely, glancing at the small travelling clock on the chimneypiece. "But nearly. You're late. Where have you been all this time? Seeing those Bolshevik friends of yours, I suppose."

Though of solid English stock herself, Margaret Orloff had taken on board most of her late husband's White Russian attitudes. And it went without saying that she was a snob of a particularly English kind as well, with a hearty disdain for those whom she considered to be parvenus. New Russians, starting to make their way at the close of the Soviet era, fell into this category.

"If you're talking about the Nikishovs, yes Ma."

"Do people of that sort bother about Christmas?"

"Of course they do. Very much so. Ours, and no doubt their own as well, when that comes round."

"Well that's a relief to know. I suppose they get disgustingly drunk."

Nicko laughed. "I've never seen them like that, but it's possible a couple of them might. Vera and the boy certainly won't. He's fitted into Bailey's perfectly, by the way, the very model of an English schoolboy. They're all getting very excited. They've got him a puppy which they're trying to keep a secret until Christmas morning."

"You make them sound almost human."

"Really, Ma, you're bloody impossible."

"Were there many people, at that do the other night, or whenever it was?" enquired his mother in a more emollient tone.

"Not many. The dreaded Lord Isaacs was there. As I told you, he's a near neighbour and it's his dog that sired the puppy."

"I've only ever seen the man on television and I think 'reptile' is the best word to describe him. Why do you have to mix with such people?"

"He's better in the flesh," said her son. "Oily, certainly, but pleasantly aromatic at the same time, I can see how he rubs along with people."

"I hope he's not rubbing along with you."

Nicko shook his head and laughed. He could have said 'no, he isn't, but his boyfriend is.' It would have really put the cat among the pigeons, but it was a good thought all the same - confounding both his mother and

Lord Isaacs at the same time. Instead he reached across to the decanter on the on the shelf beside him and poured himself a glass of port. "Would you like one too, Ma?"

She shook her head and the talk grew desultory as they discussed Nicko's sister and her family in Italy, before turning to Nicko's job as a prep schoolmaster. Mrs Orloff made it plain that she thought it unworthy and preferred what he had been doing before, though quite what had gone on between Viktor, Freddie Ryedale and himself in the Russian market remained a closed book to her. She wistfully imagined her son serving up his expertise, with lashings of charm, on the Antiques Roadshow one day. And then, inevitably, she got round to the topic of the right girl - which was especially tiresome as they had rehearsed it earlier in the day and Nicko felt that there was nothing more to be added. He cut it off by draining his glass and saying that he was ready for an early night, although it was not yet eleven o'clock.

"You ought to go too, Ma," he advised her. "Tomorrow will probably be rather a long day."

When Nicko got to his bedroom, he found a stocking stuffed with presents already laid across the foot of the bed. They were all carefully wrapped in Christmas paper, but convention had it that he was not to open them until the morning. There really was something to be said for finding himself a wife and escaping from this kind of thing. He tossed the stocking with its contents on one side, undressed and went through his routine of twenty press-ups before climbing into bed with a book. Tomorrow was not something he was looking forward to: breakfast, then the opening of presents under the tree with appropriate exclamations of surprised pleasure; church, followed by a full Christmas lunch at the nearby Prince Consort Hotel, which did a good seasonal trade out of the likes of Mrs Orloff, who preferred not to cook for themselves. Then it was back to the house to feed the Siamese cat, a light tea, which of course included Christmas cake, followed by some television. By that time, however, the pressure might be easing and Nicko able to settle down with a decent single malt - something which he had enjoyed when his father was alive, at least.

And that was exactly how it went.

* * * * * *

On Boxing Day Nicko did the right thing by staying for lunch, then giving his mother a dutiful kiss, he headed back into town, a free man once more.

A Tale of Two Russians

But instead of going straight to Finchley, he went to Chelsea. He wondered how they had got on, especially he wanted to see how Kolya was making out with his puppy. For example, what was he going to call it? And then his thoughts turned to Miguel. What sort of a Christmas had he just had with Lord Isaacs? He imagined it been something quite cloying, where he was expected to act out the part of the child to the Government Minister's grown-up one. It was only a guess, of course, but the more he picked up about the Government Minister's proclivities, the more extravagant his speculations were becoming.

When he arrived in Thurloe Square and rang the bell, he was met by an excited Kolya, with an equally excited puppy yapping at his heels. The two young creatures were already firmly bonded.

"So you got your puppy after all, Kolya?" his godfather said, "though it wasn't really a surprise, was it?"

"Not really. I had been making such a fuss about it, hadn't I?"

"That's true, Kolya. You were driving your mother and father crazy."

Coming into the house, Nicko opened his night case and took a package from it, which he handed to the boy.

"I should really have put this under the tree with the other things," he explained, "but I thought we'd get Christmas Day out of the way first."

The boy tore open the package, to reveal a handsome leather dog's collar. He hugged his godfather round his knees and poured out his thanks.

"There's a plate on it for you to put his name on, along with your address and telephone number," Nicko told him. "You must do it as soon as possible. It's very important. He has got a name, I suppose?"

"He's called Stenka - after the Cossack hero. He's a Russian dog, after all."

"Doesn't that sound a bit like 'stinker' which, as you know, means something smelly in English?"

But the boy stood his ground, the dog was Stenka. "It was Alyosha's idea."

Nicko picked the puppy up and had his face licked.

"You know about housetraining a puppy?" he asked.

I've cleaned up five puddles this morning," Kolya informed him proudly, "but I took him outside in time for his poo."

"He'll need plenty of walks," Nicko said. "Are Papa and Mama at home?"

Vera came out of the kitchen where she had been listening to their conversation.

"I'm glad you remembered to say 'thank you' for your present," she told the boy as she took the collar from him and looked at it. "This is lovely, Nikoshka," she said.

You must get the dog's name address and telephone number on it as soon as possible. There's a place for it."

"Run upstairs and tell your father Uncle Nicko's arrived," she ordered the boy. "Stenka can go with you."

Nicko could not help noticing that mother and son spoke to each other all the time in English now.

"You had a good Christmas? And Vik's happy?"

Vera gave one of her exasperated sighs. "He was hardly ever off the telephone all day. He never uses his e-mails. It's always the telephone- even on Christmas Day - it's so annoying."

"Apart from that it went well? Kolya really loves his dog."

"I shouldn't complain. It went fine – quiet - by ourselves, Alyosha and Tsina and the dog as well of course, who was loved by everybody."

"Stenka."

"Stenka. I heard what you said to Kolochka. But he likes the name."

"It's a doggy-sounding one at any rate and it's Russian."

"Oh Nikoshka, thank you for your lovely present, by the way, which you left under the tree. I'm like a child, forgetting my manners!" She took him in her arms and kissed him.

"I see you've got it on. That's a big enough 'thank you'."

It was an antique cameo brooch, with a profile of the Goddess Athena that Nicko had picked it in a dealer's shop in Harrogate a couple of years earlier, when he had been working with Freddie Ryedale and had held onto for such an occasion.

"And you must open your presents," said Vera. "But we'll wait 'til we're all together. It'll be like having another Christmas."

"All for me? I hardly deserve it."

"Of course you do, Nikoshka." She placed a finger firmly on his lips to cut off any further protests.

Viktor meanwhile had come downstairs and, looking into the sitting room, nodded at Nicko. Leaving mother and son re-arranging things under the tree, he steered his friend into the kitchen. Nicko could see that he was fidgety.

"Merry Christmas, Vik," said Nicko. "I hope work isn't taking the place of pleasure."

"I think we've found a Kandinsky."

"Good God. A real one?"

"Babko seems pretty sure. The provenance adds up, but it's still going to need careful handling."

"Can you trust that man, Vik? Remember the game you were playing yourself back in Novgorod."

"Babko? Yes, I think so. I can smell a rat when I need to. Yes?"

"Yes Vik, but you know as well as I do that authentication is the key to everything. Your provenance has to be watertight."

Viktor grinned. "What's that other English expression? Don't teach you grandmother how to suck eggs?"

"Spot on Vik!"

"So now - what's it to be? I've got a load of Stoly in the freezer. We can use some of that before Father Christmas arrives. He's coming back, you know. A special one-off visit for our very own Uncle Nicko!"

They downed their vodkas in the kitchen with their customary toast. But Nicko felt uneasy about what Viktor had said about the alleged Kandinsky. And exactly who was this Babko? And how did he manage to lay his hands on works by the likes of Rothko and Kandinsky and launch them into the international market, apparently without having to fork out astronomical sums for them in the first place? It was hardly the same as stumbling across an old watercolour in an English provincial saleroom, the sort of thing Freddie Ryedale might have happened upon and missed. And it was the paradox of Viktor, that while he had proved a not unskilled practitioner in the art of deception himself, there was a reckless gambling streak in him when he seemed to throw all caution to the winds.

Meanwhile Alyosha and Tsina arrived and the second Christmas got underway in the sitting room. It had been darkened and was lit only by a pair of table lamps and the fairy lights on the tree. Nicko's presents had been well chosen, almost certainly by Vera. They included a couple of beautifully painted lacquer boxes - a winter scene with sleigh racing across a snowy landscape and a summer one of a view across the open steppe. Nicko fell in love with them at once. From Kolya also came something Russian: a small set of matrioshka dolls, representing famous characters in Russian history which included Ivan the Terrible and Joseph Stalin. Viktor supplied a bottle of the very best Russian vodka.

Stenka barked and revelled in attention, before depositing a large puddle in the middle of the Turkey rug, to the delighted squeals of his young master, who was promptly dispatched by his mother to fetch the means of cleaning it up. So everyone was blissfully happy until the time came for Nicko to leave.

"One thing I forgot to tell you," Vera said to him as he stood in the porch. "We had a call from Ludmilla and she was asking after you. She hopes to come to London soon, probably in the Spring. I thought you might like to know."

CHAPTER SEVENTEEN

Creative Aspirations and a Thickening Plot

It was curious, Nicko reflected, how he had begun to write Ludmilla out of the plot that was running through his mind. After the summer's adventure in Montenegro, she should have been there still, but even then she had seemed to be on the margin of events, while the real action had involved others. Of course most of the time she had been lost in a book- her beloved Patricia Highsmith. So what was bringing her to London now? Vera had told him that she was planning to resume her literary studies, but could say no more than that. Nicko speculated that it might be something to do with the crime novel and maybe the event in Cetinje had whetted her appetite for that very thing.

But in the meantime he had to put his mind to more immediate matters. The new school term was beginning in ten days' time and the prospect of blowing a whistle on a chilly football field was not an appetising one. He had tried to wriggle out of taking games, but had not been entirely successful, and, in any case, being a relatively new member of staff, he had felt obliged to show willing. He could just about handle a game of football, but was hopeless when it came to rugger - which he had not played since leaving school.

Much nearer to his heart, he was thinking of starting an art history course which had Dick- and especially Imogen's - blessing. It would include visits to the leading London galleries, so while Viktor speculated in Rothkos and Kandinskys, Nicko would be revealing to kids the great masterpieces of European art. He felt that it was more wholesome than supplying Oleg Dobrinin and his kind with abstract backdrops to show off their womenfolk.

So for three days he trudged round the National Gallery, the Tate and the British Museum. He was a regular visitor to these places anyway, but now something vocational was entering into it. He liked the idea of passing his enthusiasms on to others and there were children at hand to enable him to do it. Several of them he could see were ripe for such a venture, coming, as they did, from the sort of homes where such things were valued. So he began to draw up an inventory of works that might fire the curiosity of eleven and twelve year olds.

Subject matter and treatment were crucial, he felt: things which a child's imagination might readily latch onto. The Pre-Raphaelites and their medievalism was a good place to start. He recalled his own childhood when he had poured over encyclopedias in which some of their works had been used to illustrate the text, and he had been haunted by them ever since. But he was equally determined to do the whole canon of European art justice, stopping just short of the more extreme manifestations of Modernism, which in his eyes were more likely to cut off an emerging childish interest than to foster it.

Apart from his customary meeting with Tim, he saw none of his friends over the New Year and the days immediately after. Instead, he immersed himself in a world of pictures- a place where he felt at home. Only Vera rang, a couple of times, and he went to bed early with a mug of Horlicks and a novel. In a way he liked this dead time of year best of all, when the world was still asleep, before the arrival of Spring.

And when he switched off his light and settled down to sleep, he thought how nice it would be to write a book about Art for children; that one day might become a classic. Nicko felt uneasy in the world of Cyberspace, while a book was something real that you could hold in your hands. It was tangible, where you could feel the texture of its pages and turn them backwards or forwards at will, with none of the technical hazards and capriciousness of electronic gadgetry. He would float his idea with Tim at their next meeting....

Next morning it was the British Museum again, where classical sculpture and Assyrian bas-reliefs could be made interesting: the latter mainly because of their subject matter - the representations of war and hunting and the explicit manner in which they were handled. Not that he would overlook the museum amenities already provided for children of course. He would check them out and perhaps include a brief critique of them for other users.

It was while he was studying a Roman copy of a figure of a Greek athlete, that he felt a finger being passed down the back of his neck. Without turning round, he knew who it was.

"I thought it was you, Miggie, but where have you left his Lordship?" he asked Miguel.

The Mexican boy grinned. "He's gone for his conference- and left with a hangover- which serves him right. You shouldn't try to pretend you're only eighteen when you're more than fifty." He looked around. "This place's great."

"Have you never been here before?"

Miguel shook his head.

Nicko laughed. "But how the hell did you know where to find me? Or is it just a coincidence?"

Miguel shrugged and grinned slyly by way of a reply, while they both eyed the figure of the naked athlete without speaking for a few seconds.

"I'm working on a book about Art for kids," Nicko explained, finally breaking their silence. He indicated the statue. "What do you think of him?"

Miguel caressed the form with his gaze. "Probably the same as you do, Nick. Oh, there's something I wanted to ask you. How does the Russian boy – Kolya - like his dog?"

"He loves him of course and giggles when he pees on the carpets- as you'd expect."

"That'll please Lord Mark. When he can spare the time from running the country to think about it."

"The power behind the throne, with a finger in all sorts of pies. You know what I mean?"

"Sure I do. And he knows everyone who matters. Mind you, I don't think many of them like him very much."

"But they pretend to."

"Yeah, and suck the shit out of his arse."

"That's certainly one way of putting it, Miggie. But tell me something else: why do you hang out with him? I mean, when he treats you like a small boy and you think he's such a turd?"

"The pay's not bad. Better than I'd be getting most places in town, I guess. And give him this, he has some pretty interesting friends- or people he calls friends."

"Name some of them."

"Well there's the Prime Minister of your country for a start. And your Queen too. I haven't been presented to her yet, mind you, but I have met some of the other Royals."

"Such as?"

"I can't tell you that. Not even you, Nick. Let's have a look at some more of these nice boys, shall we?" He started to examine another athlete.

"He's a kouros," Nicko explained.

"A kouros? Is that a Greek or Roman word?"

"A Greek word. It means an athletic young man - or youth."

"And are all these Greek boys?"

"Yes."

"God, it must have been great living in Greece!"

"They weren't all as good looking as these, mind you. There were plenty of ugly ones as well. We are only looking at the best."

They spent a good half hour together, with Miguel revealing his almost total ignorance of classical art, which gave Nicko the opportunity to hone up his own pedagogic skills. The Mexican boy's New World beauty, alongside some of the finest renderings of the young male body by the sculptors of European Antiquity, stirred Nicko into a kind of rapturous eloquence. Eventually, feeling somewhat drained by their experience, they retreated to the glass-covered main courtyard for a coffee.

It went without saying that Nicko's researches in the British Museum were concluded for the day. As a result of things that had gone before, they were already settling into what was the domestic routine of a shared life. Miguel slipped out to a nearby ethnic food market and brought home the ingredients to make a Mexican meal, washed down with Californian red wine, followed by Green Chartreuse and a Single Malt whisky, which they sipped, lying together on Nicko's handsome Cappadocian rug.

"Do you ever do this kind of thing with Mark?" asked Nicko.

"We don't lie on the floor, if that's what you mean. By the way, Nick, I prefer it when you talk about 'Lord Isaacs'- it suits him better."

"Lord Isaacs then."

"He touches very little alcohol at home. He mostly drinks juice."

"That does surprise me having seen him putting it away at the Nikishovs."

"Sure he did then - but at home he's different. How do I say? He's more like a monk."

"You're not serious, are you?" "Sure I am."

"But then," mused Nicko," monks have got up to some pretty dodgy things, haven't they? This stuff we've been drinking." He pointed to the half-empty bottle of Green Chartreuse standing in the hearth, "That's made by monks. And he may be playing another kind of game with you - you know, the stern novice-master keeping naughty Brother Miguel, the cheeky little novice, in check."

Miguel sat up. "Let's go to bed, Nick. It's more comfortable than lying here."

"Sure. We'll take our drinks with us. Lord Isaacs isn't looking." Before standing up, they locked their bodies together and exchanged a kiss.

* * * * * *

It was after eleven the next morning when Miguel eventually left in a taxi. Nicko had insisted on it. Isaacs was due back from his conference in Basle later in the day, and he wanted to feel that Miguel was safely home before he arrived. As he waved him off, he pondered on what had just passed between them. Miguel was still something of a mystery. How, for instance, had he just happened upon him in the British Museum, admiring a specimen of Greek male beauty? When asked about it, he had merely smiled back at him in an enigmatic way. The guiding hand of a higher power possibly? Or something more down to earth than that, like lowdown peasant guile?

Tomorrow it would be back to duty, but the distraction had been immensely worthwhile. The Mexican boy seemed able to give Nicko so much of what he wanted, lying with him under the sheet in his bedroom in Finchley. Anxieties about his own manhood and what was expected of him by his mother, for instance, had evaporated. Miguel had been everything, filling his thoughts when he closed his eyes as much as when he lay with them open, gazing into the sweet, boyish Mexican face.

But Lord Isaacs? He had to fit in somewhere, casting a dark, possibly diabolic, shadow. The man's political ruthless was public knowledge, usually taking the form of administering poison in a tasty sweetmeat. Some of his friends- or allies- were shady too, and in a number of cases probably murderous, Oleg Dobrinin being an example, so it might be a simple enough matter for him to swat off a tiresome gnat like Nickolas Orloff as a favour should he ever be called upon to do it.

Over his breakfast of grapefruit juice, toast and marmalade the following morning, Nicko was still musing on the business of the triangle that appeared to be developing between Miguel, a leading member of the Government and himself. The frank manner in which the Mexican boy had expressed himself on the subject of Lord Isaacs' more outré sexual tastes intrigued him and he thought that if he had been another kind of person, he might have been tempted into blackmail. But such an enormity was outside Nicko's league and he could no more exploit it than steal from a supermarket shelf. All the same, it gave him an agreeable sense of power to know that such a prominent public figure lay within his potential grasp, at least.

It was half past nine when Nicko stirred himself to return to the British Museum and carry on with the work that he had abandoned with the appearance of Miguel. But just as he was leaving his phone rang, as it invariably did when he was on the way out.

He could hear a barely audible female voice which seemed to be saying something in Russian and for a second he thought it might be Vera. But she would have spoken in English and certainly not in such a subdued conspiratorial tone.

"Who's speaking?" said Nicko rather impatiently in English, before repeating it in Russian.

There was a low chuckle. "Ludochka," replied the voice. "You haven't forgotten me so soon, have you?"

"No of course I haven't, but this is a great surprise!" Nicko tried to make it sound as if it was an agreeable one, but somehow the knowledge that it was Ludmilla did not raise his spirits, which were still on a high anyway following his success with Miguel, while, if anything, the Russian girl's call tended to lower them. "How could I possibly forget the girl who fell so madly in love with Ripley?" he added, hopefully trying to strike the right jocular note.

"I've given him a rest - for the time being," said Ludmilla. "I've read all the books." "But how can you possibly desert Ripley?" protested Nicko, continuing in his attempted jocular vein. "He's a very dangerous man to cross."

Ludmilla chuckled lightly again.

"Where are you ringing from?" he asked her.

"A friend's house."

"Anyone I know?"

"I don't think so."

"But you'll be seeing Vik and Vera, so you can give me your news there?"

"And you'll give me yours too, Nikoshka."

"'Bye then. See you soon."

She repeated it in Russian and replaced the receiver.

* * * * * *

That evening he decided to give Vera a ring, hoping that she might be able to fill him in a bit more on Ludmilla. When he spoke to her, he learned that Ludmilla was already in Thurloe Square and that they were having tea together.

"Would you like to have a word with her?" Vera enquired.

"It can wait. We spoke this morning."

"Come here on Saturday, Nikoshka. Or would Sunday be better? You and Kolochka could take Stenka for a walk."

"How is Stenka, by the way? Still making messes on the carpets?"

"He's fine," Vera said, "But," she added, dropping her voice. "He doesn't like Ludochka. When she arrived, he growled at her."

"Maybe she's not a doggy kind of person and he could smell that. They can, you know."

Vera laughed. "I'm not sure what you mean."

Curiously, Nicko did not think it odd that the dog should have growled at Ludmilla, while it had taken to Tsina straight away.

What do animals know - or at least sense- that we can't? he wondered.

In the meantime he thought that he would talk to Tim about Ludmilla. In Montenegro he had found her presence unsettling, while her arrival in London seemed to be adding an extra ingredient to the pot. Nicko enjoyed spiriting up such metaphors and trying them out on a friend.

He told Tim about Ludmilla and how detached she had appeared to him in Montenegro during the holiday, and how she had spent most of her time lost in a book.

"So?" said Tim. "Nothing particularly odd about that, surely?" What kind of a book?"

"Patricia Highsmith."

Tim laughed. "Well that sort of fits, doesn't it?"

"She was fascinated by Ripley. Whenever we talked, it was usually about him."

"Of course," said Tim. "She's a Russian, isn't she? The killer making his existential choice… Raskolnikov aspiring to Nietscheian heights….. that Dostoyevskian angst, all very Russian.."

"There's not much angst about Ripley," pointed out Nicko. "He just doesn't want to get caught, that's all- and nor does he. Russians are hooked on crime fiction anyway - especially the English variety. You should hear them banging on about Conan Doyle and Agatha Christie. They treat it as a serious genre."

"A bit nerdish, perhaps? Like our Tolkien cult?"

"Possibly. An awful lot of them are anoraks and maybe that's what's brought her here - to write her thesis on the English crime novel."

"But Highsmith was an American."

"She's read all of her stuff - so she could be moving on to fresh pastures - Hercule Poirot or even Miss Marple."

Tim laughed. "I'd rather like to meet this Ludmilla of yours. You must bring us together."

"I will see her on Sunday, when hopefully more will be revealed."

Tim took a long pull at his glass. "How's Miguel?" he asked. "Not walked out on Isaacs yet?"

"Not quite." Nicko hesitated. He was still not quite sure how much he could tell his friend about the Mexican boy. "Anyway we must get you and Ludmilla together. And Elspeth too, of course. She might find her of interest. I'm sure it can be arranged. I don't know where she's staying yet, but she'll have her friends."

Vera rang later when he got home to confirm that Ludmilla would be there on Sunday, but that Viktor was going to be away again.

"Crikey, where to this time?" Nicko asked her.

Vera vented one her sighs. "How do you say it? I lose track?"

"The States again?"

"Yes, the States again. But not New York. He said something about New Mexico. It wasn't clear."

That set Nicko thinking again of Miguel. "I'd like to go there one day," he remarked. "It's the one part of the US that I really want to see. I suppose he's chasing a Kandinsky?"

"God knows. But this Boris Babko - he must be a Ukrainian with a name like that - is the agent. I'm not sure he can be trusted, but Vitya has to judge that for himself."

"He's had enough experience," Nicko told her, attempting to sound reassuring. "He must have learned something from his scrapes."

Deep down he wondered if Vik would ever learn, but simply crash on until his luck finally dried up. He recalled what he had read about his friend's forebear - the Stalinist satrap in Kolyma. The gene seemed to have been passed to the grandchild: to live it up while the going was good, with not too much regard for consequences. The thought set Nicko pondering the matter of his own 'Russian soul'.

So in the time that remained until Sunday, he busied himself with his artistic survey and jotted down a few notes for a rough outline of the children's guide. He also dropped in to Bailey's for a word with Dick about the coming school term and to prepare a few lessons. In the meantime he heard nothing from Miguel and did not like to ring, not even on the boy's mobile. Lord Isaacs' shadow was a long one.

* * * * * *

Sunday arrived, Nicko having felt strangely impatient for it. Not that he had ever been drawn to Ludmilla in the short time that he had known her - but with her back in play the plot seemed to grow more interesting. Generally he was fond of its characters- the Nikishov trio at its centre in particular.

He arrived shortly before two, having announced his willingness to go for a walk with Kolya and the dog. He thought that a fairly extended one that took in Kensington Gardens via the Albert Memorial would be interesting and Stenka could be let off the leash to run on the grass. It was important, he told the boy, that a dog should be allowed to run freely and to know when to return to his master.

"How are you getting on with the housetraining, Kolya?" he asked as they set out. "Are you still cleaning up his poo?"

The boy grinned. "He's getting better. We take him into the road behind the house where people won't walk in it."

"You have to be very strict with dogs. They expect it."

"Sometimes when he pees on the floor Mama puts his nose in it."

"Good for her. We should do it with some people as well."

"The boy stared at him and grinned. "Which people?"

"Ha! That's my secret."

"You can tell me."

"No I can't. It wouldn't be my secret any more." He felt that he would have liked to rub Lord Isaacs' ski-jump nose in his own ordure, but he wasn't going to say that to Kolya. Bearing in mind where the dog had come from, he needed to sound positive with regard to his Lordship.

"What about Papa?"

"I wouldn't dream of such a thing. Your father's my oldest friend."

"Mama was cross with him the other day."

"Was she really? Why was that?"

"Because he's always going to America. She says he's never at home when he should be."

"Naughty Papa. But he's working hard to earn the money that feeds you and sends you to school. Now tell me something else, Kolya. What do you think about Ludmilla Mikailovna coming to see you? A bit of a surprise, don't you think?"

The boy shrugged his shoulders and scowled. "Not really. I sort of knew that she would turn up one day." He gave the dog's lead a tug and walked on a short way ahead.

"Aren't you pleased?"

"Why should I be? She wasn't very nice to me."

Nicko left it there and they enjoyed a perfect afternoon in the Gardens, which were ideal for Stenka to run loose in. Already he understood that he must not get too far away from his master, even when one of his own species might be trying to lure him into a canine game. It was late in the afternoon, with a sinking sun and lengthening shadows, when they got back to Thurloe Square

As they went in they could hear the sound of a conversation going on in Russian in the sitting room. Kolya went straight to the kitchen with the dog while Nicko put his head round the sitting room door.

Ludmilla leaped to her feet. "Nikoshka!" she exclaimed and ran to hug him in a tight embrace.

"It's great to see you," said Nicko, even though he wasn't sure that he really meant it.

"And you," she replied. "You're looking so well. Does the teaching still suit you?"

He eased himself gently from her embrace. "For the time being it does, but the money's not good. It's a great little school, though, run on old-fashioned lines, traditional teaching methods, a proper school uniform and bright kids. Kolya's one of them."

"So I hear and he's doing very well."

Nicko nodded. "He's getting more like an English boy every day. But he mustn't forget that he's a Russian one too."

He glanced at Vera, who smiled and shrugged her shoulders.

"What do you think, Verochka?" Ludmilla asked her. "Do you want him to be an English boy?"

"He must try to be both," put in Nicko.

There was another non-committal shrug from the boy's mother.

"Where is he by the way?" asked Ludmilla.

"In the kitchen feeding his dog."

"I don't think the dog likes me very much. It growled when we met earlier."

"Stenka's a Russian too. There may be significant dialectical differences between you."

Vera got up and went to the door. "Kolochka," she called, "come and say hullo to our guest."

Kolya emerged from the kitchen, holding the puppy against his chest. "Hullo, Ludmilla," he said rather stiffly.

As soon as he set eyes on her, the puppy in his arms growled at her.

"You see?" Ludmilla exclaimed. "That dog doesn't like me. Perhaps I have the wrong kind of smell."

"Nonsense, Ludochka," Vera said.

"Well, Ludochka," said Nicko swiftly changing tack. "Tell me all about it!"

"About what?"

"Your work. What else?"

Vera rose and left the room with her son.

"The English crime novel from the middle of the nineteenth century to the present day," Ludmilla declared.

"Crikey. I might have guessed. It's a big enough subject. Is it to be a dissertation for a doctorate?" Ludmilla nodded.

"Are you sure you're not biting off more than you can chew?"

Just for a second she looked puzzled by the expression. "I don't think so," she said.

"What about poor old Ripley?" went on Nicko. "He used to be a friend of yours. Is he cast out?" "What about him?"

"Well, a psychological examination of his childhood and how it made him into the man he became, sounds if it might be a good topic for a dissertation," suggested Nicko.

"The crime story since Agatha Christie," Ludmilla said. "That's my principle subject, but I have to begin in the nineteenth century."

"So bye-bye Patricia Highsmith?"

"Not quite."

Kolya meanwhile returned, bearing a plate of sandwiches and a sponge cake, followed by his mother with the rest of the tea things.

"This is a very English meal," observed Nicko, "like the ones I used to know."

Ludmilla explained her dissertation further. The final section was to centre on the post-Marxist Russian crime story and its roots in the English tradition. Nicko could not but be impressed by the scale of her ambition and to ask her about the means at her disposal to see it through.

She was working at the University Department of English, she explained, and had access to the British Library. Funding appeared to be no problem: it was sourced in Russia though she was vague on its precise details. Meanwhile she was living with a friend from Moscow, who was connected with Amnesty International in some capacity. It was all just a little mysterious and consistent with the Ludmilla Mikhailovna that Nicko remembered.

"At least you won't be far from Baker Street, Ludochka," he pointed out,

Rather cheekily she stuck out her tongue at him.

"What's happened to the Montenegran Royal Family?" he enquired. "Have they gone the same way as Ripley?"

"They have not been forgotten, but I must do one thing at a time."

"I'm very relieved to hear it."

They chatted generally about their lives in London, though Nicko could not help noticing that the name of Oleg Dobrinin was never raised. Vera, he noticed too, was a little reluctant to say exactly what her husband was up to, beyond stating that he was back in the art market, which brought Nicko into play and his current means of earning a living, as well as Kolya- who waxed enthusiastic about his new school- especially about the chance it gave him to play football. Nicko, however, did not raise the subject of his proposed children's guide, but wondered which would see the light of day first; his book, or Ludmilla's about the Montenegran Royal Family.

It all seemed pretty relaxed, but at the same time Nicko felt relieved that Ludmilla had shown no sign of wanting to settle with the Nikishovs in their spacious house. Perhaps Stenka had put paid to that. Finally, she looked at her watch and exclaimed at the time.

"I must leave you at once," she said. "I have someone to speak to about my thesis. What is he called? My supervisor?"

"On a Sunday?" queried Nicko,

"It's more of a social call really," she explained. "But a necessary one."

"I'll see you to the station."

"No you won't. You'll stay and talk to Verochka," she told him. "I'm perfectly able to find my own way." She pressed his hand as she spoke.

She got up and kissed Vera perfunctorily on the cheek, but did not do the same for Kolya. As he shut the front door, Nicko saw her stop on the pavement, glance back the way she had just come and start rummaging inside her bag.

"The same old Ludochka," Nicko observed to Vera. "As self-contained as ever."

"I wonder who her friend is. She told us nothing about her," said Vera.

"Better with her than with you here. Stenka's got her measure, I reckon."

"You don't like her, do you, Nikoshka?"

"I'm not sure what I think about her. But like the proverbial cat she always manages to land on her feet."

"She seems to have plenty of friends."

"In the right places too. And with money."

"I don't know about you, Nikoshka, but I think I'm ready for a drink?"

Once in the kitchen, Vera opened the freezer and took out a bottle of vodka. She handed it to Nicko with a small cut glass tumbler which he filled to the rim. For herself you took a mini-bottle of white wine from the fridge and a plate of smoked mackerel fillets.

"Nasdorovia!" declared Nicko raising his glass.

Vera returned the toast and sipped hers.

Nicko stayed for supper and talked about school with Kolya and the friends he was making. Apart from Evgeni there was one English boy in particular- Andrew Pickard. Nicko approved: he was a bright, cheerful boy with a developing sense of humour. His father was something in the foreign office and had even done a spell in Moscow back in the Yeltsin era. Though Andrew knew nothing of Russia himself, he drew on his parents' experience to feed a burgeoning imagination. Nicko liked him not only for his charm, but for his obvious appetite for his own subject. He was an ideal companion for Nikishov. Whatever scrapes Viktor got into in the future, it was essential in Nicko's eyes that his son should complete his English education. Bailey's was giving him the right start.

So Nicko was pleased with what he was hearing, his satisfaction reinforced, needless to say, by further glasses of Viktor's vodka. As the boy went upstairs for his bath, he found himself starting to doze, with thoughts of his recent encounter with Ludmilla merging into others of Miguel.

When Vera came back downstairs, he stirred and made an effort to sound intelligible.

"Kolya's making some very good friends," he told her. "The Pickard boy is a great chap. His father's a diplomat."

Vera eyed him with critical sympathy. "You've drunk too much, Nikoshka. You can't go home like that."

"I'm all right. And if I have, it's your fault."

"You will stay here tonight. That's an order, Nikoshka. Prikaz."

"How's Lord Isaacs, by the way?" he asked inconsequentially. "Have you had any more news of him? I haven't seen him on television lately."

"I've no idea. I haven't seen him since Christmas. But really, Nikoshka, you're a naughty boy, so you're going to bed here."

She was right of course and he did not argue. After a light supper, when he ate very little, she took him upstairs, undressed him and helped him into her own bed. After which, she looked in on Kolya and went down to put the dog out for a few minutes at the back of the house.

Nicko meanwhile snuggled down under the duvet and went to sleep. When he woke his head was clear. That was the great thing about vodka: you could sleep it off and feel no unpleasant after effects. The bed light was on and Vera was sitting up beside him, reading a book.

"Feeling better?" she asked.

"I'm fine."

Vera put aside her book and stroked the bridge of his nose.

"Do you do that to Vik?"

"Sometimes, but he's always in such a hurry." She snuggled close to him. "You never seem to be in a hurry, Nikoshka. It's one of the things I like best about you."

He gave her a long kiss on the middle of her forehead.

"You're a little boy, really no different from Kolochka. But I've said that to you so many times before."

"And I'm still not sure how I'm meant to take it. Are you telling me that I haven't grown up yet?"

"No, Nikoshka. You've grown up, but you're still a little boy at the same time. It's hard to explain."

He looked bemused and she pecked his cheek, at the same time sliding a hand under the duvet, seeking out his manhood. Nicko realised that he was naked and, lying on his back, he allowed her go to work. Her manner of kneading his member was very satisfying: he closed his eyes, and conjured up a dark face with almond eyes.

217

Did Vera have the slightest inkling about Miguel? It hardly mattered if she did. The two of them were melding into one another so perfectly.......

Finally they drew apart with little grunts of satisfaction and, rolling to different sides of the bed, fell asleep.

In the morning Vera was up first. Nicko checked his watch and started to climb out hastily too, being afraid that Kolya might erupt into his mother's bedroom and find him where his father was meant to be, but she pushed him back again.

"Stay where you are and keep quiet," she ordered him. "I'll see to Kolochka. He's probably still asleep."

She tiptoed onto the landing and returned. "Fast asleep," she said. "Running about with the dog has made him tired."

So Nicko lay contemplating the ceiling, while she slipped into the bathroom and ran a shower. He was still lying there, in lazy contentment, when she went out to wake up her son.

Twenty minutes later she was calling up to him to come down for breakfast.

Kolya was not the least bit put out by his presence at the breakfast table. Indeed he appeared to take it for granted now that his godfather was one of the household's fixtures. He rattled on about the dog, who was sitting gazing up at him with an expectant look on his small face, Stealthily he tried to slip him a piece of sausage from his plate.

"Stop that Kolochka, at once!" snapped his mother. "You must never do that! Dogs are not the same as people. You must feed them only once a day and never at the table. Am I not right, Uncle Nicko?"

"Quite right." Nicko went on to stress how dogs were only happy if they were lean and fit. "I don't like lapdogs," he said and then explained what that term meant. "When are you expecting Vik back?" he asked Vera.

"When he comes. He'll probably ring me when he's leaving. He usually does."

"Is he still chasing the Kandinsky?" "I think so."

"And that crook Dobrinin is pleased with his Rothko?"

"He should be considering how much he must have paid for it."

"Did Vik not tell you?"

"We never talk about those things any more. Speaking for myself, I would be happy not to see that man ever again." As she spoke she glanced out of the window into the garden with a nervous frown on her face.

The events of the summer were at the top of Nicko's mind too.

"It's going to be interesting with Ludochka in town," he came out with at length.

"Why should it be?" said Vera in a flat tone of voice.

"She's such a dark horse."

Vera did not reply.

Kolya asked to be excused and left the room, while the others continued to sit in silence. Finally Nicko got up and kissed Vera on the back of her neck.

"You'll call again soon, won't you Nikoshka? And never mind about Vitya," she said.

"Of course I will."

As he wandered back to the Underground, he noticed a figure ahead him that he recognised. The rolling 'gunslinger' gait told him immediately. He wondered if he ought to try to catch Miguel up, but decided not to. For some reason he felt awkward about having to explain why he was leaving the home of his Russian friends so early in the morning. It was a strange hang-up, but a real one nevertheless.

But it made no difference because he ran into him at the ticket office anyway and Miguel asked him no questions, but went straight into a conspiratorial mode instead.

"My friend, the Prince of Darkness had a visitor last night," he whispered confidentially.

"Oh? What's unusual about that?" "It was a woman."

"That is unusual," Nicko said. "But he is a political beast, after all."

"A Russian woman."

"Now that might be more interesting. What time was she there?"

"Sometime between half past six and seven."

"Do you remember her name?"

Of course. We have met once before."

"Was it Ludmilla Mikhailvona by any chance?"

"What a clever boy you are."

"And you met last summer at Tiva? On the Dobrinin pleasure cruise? Did she have anything interesting to say then?"

"Not to me she didn't. She talked to the Prince of Darkness, while I was sent out of the cabin- on an errand." "They were alone together?"

Miguel nodded.

"Well you can bet your bottom dollar that there was one thing they didn't get up to on their own."

"And I suppose she and the Dobrinins were chums?"

"Naturally. There was a lot of talk in Russian, but I saw them together just once - when we all met for drinks. Ludmilla Whatshername only drank juice."

"So you can't tell me anything interesting that passed between them?" Nicko gave Miguel a tap on his nose. "Sorry, Nick. I don't speak Russian."

"I'll forgive you this time. Where are you off to now?"

"Into town- to spend my pocket money."

"Try not to spend it all at once. Oh and how long did your Russian visitor stay last night?"

"About three quarters of an hour, She said she had another appointment."

They descended to the northbound platform and took the next train as far as Piccadilly, where they parted, Miguel down Regent's Street and Nicko towards the National Gallery. As he walked down the Haymarket, his thoughts swung between Vera and Miguel and how smoothly it seemed to be working - for the time being, at least. It was an odd situation, with its possible pitfalls, but he was determined not to lose his foothold. Meanwhile he had to put his mind to the guide book. He mustn't lose sight of that.

CHAPTER EIGHTEEN

And Thicker Still …

Three days later and after the new school term had begun, Nicko had a call from Viktor which came hard on the heels of one from Miguel. He had just returned from the States and had a problem.

"What kind of problem?" asked Nicko.

Viktor dropped his voice. "I'd rather not talk about it on the phone, if you don't mind. I could e-mail it to you if you liked."

"No, don't bother with that."

Viktor released a heavy sigh. "Can you get across?"

"Not before Saturday- in a couple of days' time. Will that do?"

He had just fixed Friday night with Miguel, since his Lordship was off to Rome that morning.

Viktor discharged another big sigh.

"You sound done in. I promise I'll make it on Saturday morning, if you can hold out that long. But there's nothing you can tell me right now?"

"Saturday it is then. Thanks old boy." He put the receiver down.

He's back in the shit, Nicko told himself, and it could be serious if it involves Dobrinin again. Why did that bastard have to roll up here so soon after what happened in Montenegro? He thought of Vera and her son. She had set her heart on starting a new life and now not only was Kolya speaking English fluently, but he had settled happily into his new school. Now it was bloody Vik, screwing things up with his mad ideas, dragging his nearest and dearest down into his stinking hole with him.

The next evening, putting his marking to one side, he went into the West End for his regular natter over malt whiskies with Tim, whom he now trusted as a safe repository of his confidences.

"Vik's back in the shit," Nicko informed him. "The usual Russian kind."

Tim laughed lightly. "That doesn't surprise me. It seems to me that's where likes to be best - snug inside a Russian privy."

"It's the others I worry about," Nicko said. "Verochka and young Kolya - especially after what happened last summer. Dobrinin was behind that and then what happens? The bugger rolls up in London, hard on the heels of the others and lo, Vik's back doing business with him - just months after he tried to kill his child and he even invites him into his own home! You saw Dobrinin at Christmas. Butter wouldn't have melted in his mouth! Vik thinks that as long as he's not actually treading on the big man's toes he'll be safe!"

"He's a gambler- a Russian who enjoys his own kind of roulette."

"He likes to think he's a gambler certainly. But I've got a hunch that something's gone sour over that picture he flogged to Dobrinin - the Rothko. I'm only guessing. Vik was great when it came to faking pictures - or getting other people to fake them. He had an excellent chap in Novgorod and between them they made a pile in the Russian market. Peshkov was in the top league - a fine painter in his own right, I reckon. But the truth is, Tim, Vik has got no eye himself. He could be taken for a ride just as easily as any of his punters."

"And in the meantime he's back selling fakes?"

"I'm not sure if he knows that he is. He may actually believe that he's selling the genuine article this time. Again I'm only guessing. But passing a fake off on Dobrinin would be utter madness, especially if he's got some means of checking its provenance."

"If Vik's eye is as lousy as you say it is, why does it have to be pictures?"

"I suppose he's decided that it's safer than holiday homes in Montenegro. He thought he was onto a big hit that time, until he crossed Dobrinin and came a cropper. As far as the oligarch was concerned, it was probably a matter of squashing a bothersome fly - a bit like Stalin sorting out one of his political opponents, real or imagined."

Tim laughed. "Of course we can't be sure of any of this- at least not until you've spoken to Vik."

"He thinks his phone's being hacked. He may be right, of course."

Tim released a guffaw. "Of course he thinks his phone's being hacked! What self-respecting or aspiring oligarch doesn't? My tongue feels like the Gobi Desert, by the way, and I rather think it's your turn, old boy."

* * * * * *

Nicko was back in Thurloe Square by eleven on Saturday morning. It was Alyosha who came to the door with an anxious-looking Vera behind him. They went straight into the kitchen, while Alyosha drew the bolt on the front door, in addition to turning the key.

Nicko sat down and noted Vera's grim expression.

"Oh my God," he said. "As bad as that, is it?"

"Oh my God," echoed Vera, with a look of despair look in her eye.

"Where's Vik?"

"Upstairs in the study."

"And Kolya?"

"In the playroom - upstairs."

"And Tsina? Downstairs?"

"Da."

"Can you tell me anything? Or shall I leave it to Vik?"

"I'll tell you something and he can tell you the rest."

"It's about one of those bloody paintings, isn't it? That thing he sold to Dobrinin?"

"You've guessed it."

"It wasn't very difficult."

Vera shook her head.

"Is it what I think it is?"

"He's been tricked, you mean?" She nodded.

For a second Nicko smiled inwardly. Dear old Vik! Hoist on his own petard and not for the first time either! I bet he doesn't know that expression, so I'd better explain it to him.

"I suppose the bloody Rothko is a forgery and he didn't spot it. Mind you, that stuff is easy enough to fake and it serves Oleg Dobrinin damned well right if he thinks it's the sort of thing to hang on his walls!"

Vera was silent and he took her hand.

"I could see it coming. It simply had to happen. But who's faked it and who's blown it? Or did Dobrinin check it out for himself?"

Vera pushed the inside page from a New York newspaper across to him. She pointed to a single column with a photograph of a middle-aged balding man. The piece was titled: 'Art scam. Dealer arrested.' It did not say very much, but that the man's name was Boris Babko and that he had been arrested for allegedly marketing faked paintings by various modern masters, including Mark Rothko. A leading Art Historian's conclusions on a number of the works in question was quoted in the piece.

Nicko sighed. "It would have to a bloody Rothko, wouldn't it? Is it the same one, I wonder? Not that it matters. Did Vik really not see what this guy Babko was getting up to?"

"You'll have to ask him that. It has also been on the television news over there."

"Then the cat is right out of the bag." Explain that one to Vik as well, he told himself. "Our oligarch friend will demand his pound of flesh. And how, if he knows he's been made to look an idiot!"

"Please Nikoshka! don't say that! It's driving me crazy!"

"Of course we don't know that Dobrinin's picture isn't genuine. But there's another possibility. If it isn't and Vik knew all along, might he not have been getting his own back for what happened in Montenegro?"

"I've no idea, Nikoshka. None at all! But the man must know by now and… and… it's Kolochka that I'm scared about!" She leaned forward onto the table and buried her face in her arms.

He came round the table and hugged her. When he looked up he saw Kolya standing looking at them with a puzzled expression on his face.

"I'll go up and have a word with Vik," he said, standing up.

As he left he ruffled the boy's hair in a way that was meant to be reassuring and was rewarded with a smile. He thought of making a chirpy remark about school, but couldn't think of one and went on up to the study at the top of the stairs on the first floor.

Viktor was there. The curtains were half drawn and he was sitting in a small armchair to one side of the window.

"My old Russian friend!" he announced in a hopeless attempt at jocularity. "Has Verochka explained it to you?"

"Most of it, but I'd guessed already. It just had to be a fucking Rothko, hadn't it? You already know what I think of Abstract Expressionism. You'd have been better off sticking to Shishkin."

Viktor essayed a grin. "Piss off, Nick!"

"I won't bang on about it, but what the hell were you doing trusting this Babko bloke? Unless you and he stitched it up together- which on balance seems the more likely."

Viktor looked steadily at his friend, but did not speak.

"Did you think knocking off a Rothko looked easy? After all you weren't exactly trying to do a Rembrandt, were you?"

"It's what they all seem to want and they don't ask too many questions. You know what my people- yours too- are like, Nick. And anyway we still don't know for certain if this one is a fake or not."

"And Dobrinin of all people! What's he going to think? That it's a quiet bit of score settling? Selling him a fake, while convincing him at the same time that you are a good boy now, keeping off his turf and even inviting him into your own home?"

Viktor grinned, but said nothing.

"You're a fucking reckless idiot, Vik, and I don't give a shit what you do to yourself. It's your family I think about."

"If anything happens to me, you'll look after them, won't you, Nick? I know that you love them as much as I do." Viktor pressed his hand and his jaw wobbled.

"Christ, Vik, have you forgotten Cetinje? Who were they taking pot shots at then? Your own son in a pedal car!"

Viktor said nothing for a minute. "You're right Nick. I've been an idiot."

"That's putting it mildly. But enough said. What next? Dobrinin will probably know by now that he's been landed with a fake. I guess he might not mind too much, just as long as the rest of the world doesn't find out, but as soon as it does, he'll be shown up for what he really is- a vulgar Russian oligarch."

Viktor frowned thoughtfully and peeked through the curtains into the garden outside.

"You can't live this way for ever, Vik." Nicko went on, "peeking round the curtains, waiting for someone to take a pot shot at you."

"That's something I'll have to work out with Alyosha."

"I just hope you're right. That's what you're paying him for, isn't it? But anyway, is there something I can do in the meantime? Anything you need? I trust Verochka will keep you topped up with vodka."

"Kaneshna. She's a good Russian wife."

"And you're a good Russian husband?"

Viktor seized his friend's hand and squeezed it hard. "You'd make a much better one! With your Russian soul, Nick, really you would! I mean that!"

Nicko shook his head and looked him straight in the eye. "Don't say things like that, Vik. Really you mustn't. Never repeat it. You've got to pull through this mess, change your ways and cherish your family. You're one of the luckiest men alive, if you only fucking knew it!"

The two friends embraced each other and Nicko went back downstairs. In the kitchen Vera had been joined by Tsina. He sat down heavily at the table.

"He's sitting up there… waiting to be shot. I didn't ask him, but I suppose he does come downstairs?"

"He comes down for his meals and spends time with Alyosha and Tsina in their flat."

"But does Dobrinin even know? I mean that Vik has sold him a fake?"

"He has to know," said Tsina. "All the people Alyosha talks to know."

"Look, Verochka. It's you and the malchik we have to think of. We don't want a repetition of last summer. You have to get Kolya to school and back each day."

She turned to Tsina.

"Alyosha's been thinking about that and is working something out." Tsina said.

"I suppose he knows what he's doing and just how nasty people like Dobrinin can be." Nicko paused before going on. "It's the familiar story. He looks nothing at all, a runt of a man, but he's got a mountain of money and an army of oprichniks to beckon up as well. And yet…. he's probably just as scared as Vik about what could happen to him at any time. It's as if Josef Stalin never died. Everyone looking over his shoulder all the time, expecting the blow to land, but not sure when or where it's coming from."

Tsina smiled and lit a cigarette. She blew a big cloud of smoke into the air. "That's how they say it was," she said. "I was too young to know of course, even in Gorbachev's time. But all those hours spent at the kitchen table… asking ourselves who we were and what made us different from other people… all those big questions Russians keep asking themselves and can never answer…" She blew out another cloud.

"All so true," Nicko put in. "But before we get too Chekhovian we must think what we're going to do."

They sat in silence for a moment.

"Maybe," Nicko resumed, "I could ask Dick Trubshaw to arrange for Kolya to sleep at school during the week and to come home at weekends."

Vera frowned unhappily.

"It's just a possibility and he may not be very keen of course. It might set a kind of precedent and the boy still has to get out to play games."

"And at the weekends, he would be at home?" Vera said.

"I think that's where Alyosha might come in," pointed out Nicko, "and of course he might have a better idea. He's the professional after all."

"I'll fetch him," said Tsina.

She left to collect her husband.

Vera squeezed Nicko's hand. "I have such a dreadful feeling," she said.

"Don't," Nicko tried to reassure her. "At least this time you're clear about who the enemy is and have more people to protect you. Shall we fetch Vik?"

It felt odd to Nicko, talking like this. He was quite unused to sounding so assertive. Was it the old aristocratic principle that was meant to have been killed off by the Revolution surfacing once more? For all his pushiness and bravura, it was a quality that Viktor as a New Russian lacked. He could drive a hard bargain, and fire up a banya, but somehow lacked the instinct for command of a true aristocrat. Nicko was inclined to think so anyway and Vera appeared to go along with him, child-lover that she held him to be, notwithstanding.

He arrived back in the kitchen with Viktor at the same moment as Alyosha and Tsina. Kolya meanwhile was safely parked in front of the television in the breakfast room, so a nod from Viktor to Alyosha produced a bottle of vodka and frosted glasses out of the freezer and the party assumed the aspect of a council of war.

Tsina rejected the offer of a vodka, but Vera broke her habit and accepted one. No words were spoken as Viktor charged the glasses and handed them round. Then he folded his hands and looked round at the others like a chairman ready to open proceedings.

Until the vodka eventually brought on a degree of incoherence, things ran smoothly enough, with Viktor ostensibly in the chair. The security of the household and its day to day business were discussed first: how the house itself was to be secured against unwelcome visitors; the matter of coming and going for shopping and supplies, and of getting the boy safely to and from school, without attracting attention. Even the question of exercising the dog had to be considered. Viktor's personal position involved a brief, though passionate discussion: should he remain in the family nest or decamp to reduce the risk to the others? Despite Alyosha pointing out the added danger of him remaining at home and it becoming known to his enemies, he felt that his place was with his own. He could not live with himself, he declared, if he deserted them, despite the risk he posed by remaining.

Nicko meanwhile cast his mind back to the party before Christmas, where he had observed a surprising intimacy growing up between Viktor and the oligarch, which was a bit like Stalin roistering with his cronies and then arranging to have them arrested. His thoughts turned to Lord Isaacs and his friendship with Dobrinin. Where would he be, if his yachting chum turned vicious, virtually on his own doorstep? It might mean a few tricky questions for the Government. And Miguel? Was he not a part of it too, with a role to play, perhaps, in an unfolding drama? It sounded a little farfetched, but not inconceivable.

It was Alyosha who addressed the immediate security issue: the matter of the family's movements outside their home. The boy would be taken to and from school by himself in a taxi, though it might be a problem if too regular a pattern was noticed by anyone watching the house. And taxis, after all, could be ambushed. It was necessary, therefore, to get hold of a firm which could provide security with discretion. Alyosha assured them that he knew the right man: a fellow Russian whose integrity he could guarantee absolutely. He had talked to Viktor about him before. This man could also supply many of Vera's daily needs and transport her husband whenever he needed to leave the house. It was hoped, anyway, that the crisis might be defused before too long. Alyosha felt fairly confident of that, though he did not spell out his reasons. Nicko thought of Isaacs again. What pressure might he be able and willing to bring to bear on the oligarch? He had, after all, given young Kolya a generous present. Perhaps Miguel might even be the means of testing that particular water.

* * * * * *

Lord Isaacs was in Rome for a conference, which enabled Miguel to join Nicko for a couple of nights. On the second one, they went into town together, took in a film in Shaftesbury Avenue and moved on to a Spanish restaurant that the Mexican boy knew. He assured Nicko that he had never once been there with the Government Minister. Nicko talked to him frankly about his Russian friend and the mess he had got himself into. So where did things really stand between the oligarch and the Government Minister?

Miguel shrugged. "He doesn't talk to me about him, but I know he's thinking of joining him on the yacht again in the summer. International trade." He winked at Nicko.

"It has to be, doesn't it? Christ you and I could make a mint out of this if we wanted to, couldn't we, Miggie?"

Miguel frowned, rather uneasily.

"Only joking, of course. But seriously, my friend has landed himself in the shit and needs someone to help get him out of it again. After all, his Lordship was pretty good about the puppy so maybe he could square things with his sailing companion too."

"Is that necessary?" said Miguel. "Surely all your friend has to do is to give Dobrinin his money back and say he's sorry, and that he had made a genuine mistake."

"It sounds reasonable, but there's probably more in it than the money. I don't think the actual sum means a great deal to Dobrinin. There are likely to be all sorts of other things tangled up with it. Pride, the need for revenge, and to put down an upstart, before he gets too big for his boots. Russians, you mustn't forget, Miggie, have a long tradition of Mongol cruelty behind them. I'm a bit of a Russian too, Miggie, and I can sense it."

Miguel laughed. "Fuck it, Nick, you're English! As English as it's possible to be!"

Nicko smiled. "But seriously, Miggie, could not your patron- or master or partner or whatever you call him- put in a word with Dobrinin? As far as the money goes, Vik could settle it right away. I'm pretty confident of that."

"Sure I'll try him, but I have to catch him at the right moment. Life's a bit of a rollercoaster with his Lordship, as I think you know." "Your bum certainly looked a bit bruised last night."

Miguel grinned. "He only used his slipper on me this time. It hurts less than the cane."

"Christ, the Media will have a field day!"

They went back to Finchley for a final fling, before the return of the stern master from Rome.

* * * * * *

Nicko was waiting on Bailey's front steps for the taxi to arrive with Kolya shortly before nine o'clock. Alyosha and the boy's mother had both come with him and they quickly entered the school, where Nicko diverted his godson towards his class, while Vera went into Dick Trubshaw's study. Alyosha in the meantime loitered in the porch.

Nicko caught Vera as she came out of the study.

"All well?"

She nodded. "So far."

"And Vik?"

"At home by himself, with the dog."

"Kolya seems fine. How much does he know?"

"We haven't told him about the picture, if that's what you mean."

"I had a word with Isaacs' young friend, Miguel, and he thinks the Great Man might be able to ease things with Dobrinin. It's worth a try."

"Can you come tonight?"

"Can I make it Wednesday?"

Vera nodded her assent and joined Alyosha who was waiting to take her shopping in Knightsbridge.

Dick Trubshaw was hardly over the Moon about the part his school might be playing in a Russian vendetta, but loth to let go of the link. His Russian clientele, after all, valued the very things about British life that he did himself, more so indeed, than many of his compatriots. Their determination to assimilate was worth encouraging.

Nicko apologised for what he might have brought on him and his school, but pointed out that no one knew quite how the oligarch was likely to react. He might simply shrug the matter off as long as he got his money back, or equally he might not. It was going to take some time to unfold. Nicko also raised the baleful name of Lord Isaacs of South Shields and how he might possibly have a key role to play.

Isaacs was hardly Dick's favourite politician, but he did not press that point. He was anxious only that his school should not be dragged into the slough of Russian score settling. But with fabulously rich Russians arriving in London every day, he could not afford to be too fastidious.

Kolya of course was aware that something big was afoot involving his father in particular and was not slow to talk about it with his classmates. Most of the children knew what was meant by the term 'New Russian', as they had heard it being bandied about in their own families, and now such beings were starting to appear in their midst, Evgeni Khlebnikov being the first, and more recently Nikolai Nikishov. In a curious hangover from the Cold War, the boys talked about them as spies. It was a harmless piece of schoolboy joshing, of course, and Evgeni told Kolya to see it that way. In fact Kolya was starting to enjoy the attention it generated, particularly when one of his classmates called him 'a spook'. It seemed to excite an awed respect in the other eight year olds, which was flattering.

Nicko informed his mother that her son was enjoying the element of notoriety as far as it was understood by the young children. She was not pleased and wanted to crush the idea completely. Partly it was a matter of safety, but more so because those were the very things that she had wanted to escape from in the family's new life.

Viktor meanwhile was on the phone all the time. He had little time for texting, but used his mobile exclusively. He agreed with Nicko that an approach to Dobrinin would probably have to be made, through a middleman, but he wasn't going to grovel, a concept he expressed to his old friend in vividly scatological terms. But nothing had been heard from the oligarch so far, one way or the other. It was assumed that he had been apprised of the facts regarding his purchase and was biding his time, a ploy which was itself a form of riposte. Keeping his foe on tenterhooks was an agreeable sort of revenge to be going on with. But then, of course, no one really knew. The water would have to be tested and perhaps Lord Isaacs was the best placed to do that.

Viktor agreed in principle, but hesitated, not knowing how thick his Lordship really was with Dobrinin.

"I'm not quite sure about Isaacs," he said. "He had some pretty dodgy friends in Brussels. That's where he got together with Oleg Pavlovich, after all."

"He was on board the yacht when we were in Montenegro. But of course it doesn't mean that he was party to any of the dirty work," pointed out Nicko.

"And he's been bloody decent about the dog," admitted Viktor.

"Puppies and boys are both in his line, I guess. Look Vik, that boyfriend of his might nudge him our way. I could have a word in his ear."

"The Mexican boyfriend?"

"The same. His Lordship must have all sorts of skeletons rattling around in his cupboard and I expect Miguel knows about quite a few of them."

"Go ahead," said Viktor, "but don't twist his Lordship's arm too hard. His sort have a nasty way of slipping free and biting back."

"There speaks the voice of experience."

"Piss off." "And you too."

"If Isaacs pulls it off I can make it good with him," said Viktor.

"You mean you can offload another dodgy Rothko onto him, or would he rather have a Kandinsky?"

231

Viktor chuckled, a little like his old self.

"I think he'd rather be Prime Minister," observed Nicko. "That's what he'd really like, though it would mean shedding the title and becoming humble Mr Isaacs again. But he could always revert to being Baron Isaacs of South Shields when it's all over, if it matters a lot to him. Mind you, Miguel just has to spill a few beans to bring his whole house crashing down."

"And you reckon that there are beans to spill?"

"Of course there are. A big bagful. I'm sure about that."

"Ah, Nikoshka, you're no longer the malchik with the big Russian soul that I once thought you were! Count Nikolai Orloff - how should I say? Has come of age at last?"

"Fuck off, Vik. Our job is to keep you alive, isn't it? Not to see an ice pick driven into your cranium."

"You flatter me."

"I don't mean to."

So it was settled. Nicko should ask Miguel to put out a feeler in the direction of Lord Isaacs, with a view to his Lordship bringing his influence to bear on Oleg Dobrinin in order to get Viktor off the hook. That he had already discussed it with the Mexican Boy, Nicko did not let on. His blossoming relationship in that quarter was something that he wanted to keep to himself.

* * * * * *

Home once more, Nicko could not resist fixing a meeting with Tim ahead of their regular one. He wanted to put him in the picture, though he knew that he would need to be cautious about the number of people he told. That done, he rang Miguel, who did not reply, so he left a message on his mobile. He was careful to avoid using Isaacs' landline.

It was nearly midnight when Miguel returned his call.

"Hullo Sweetiepie," cooed Nicko back at him in a faux mawkish manner. "The other night was bliss! I can hardly wait for the next! But this is just to tell you that I've spoken to Vik and he would like to draw your lord and master into the plot to make it right with Dobrinin, if he can. He thinks it's worth a shot. So, darling, can you raise the matter with the Mighty One and then maybe Vik can get in touch himself?"

"Another cruise is being arranged for the summer."

"Where to this time?"

"He said something about the Caribbean. Or it could be Corfu again."

"The first's almost your neck of the woods. Or I should say jungle? I suppose you'll be going?" "A bit early to say."

"And who knows? Isaacs might even be Prime Minister by then."

A snigger came from the Mexican boy.

"Don't be silly, Miggie. I'm being serious. And serious about Vik, too. He's got himself into the shit well and truly, but as his old school buddy I have to help him out of it again."

"I'll have a word with the Mighty One. He owes me a few favours."

"By the state of your bum he certainly does. But there could be something in it for him as well, of course. What kind of pictures does he like?"

"He calls himself a Modernist."

"Does he indeed? That figures. Well, Vik might be able to oblige him there."

They chuckled together at the prospect.

So far so good, just as long as the oligarch was not seeking rapid revenge for an affront done to his self-esteem. Nicko went to bed reasonably content with the part he was playing in the affair. Chewing it over with Tim would be agreeable too.

* * * * * *

Shortly before leaving to meet his friend the phone rang. It was Ludmilla. Nicko was instantly on his guard.

"Hullo, Nikoshka," she said. "I suppose you've heard?"

"Heard what?"

She chuckled. "Come on, Nikoshka! Of course you have!"

"O.K. then, what can you tell me? About Dobrinin, I mean."

"Why should I be able to tell you anything about him?"

"Well, for a start, do you know him? Have you ever met him?"

"I met him once. When he was giving away prizes at my university."

Nicko refrained from making the obvious riposte, but steered instead onto neutral ground. "Is he interested in Literature as well as Fine Art, then?"

"I suppose he thinks he should be. As well as football. But really, Nikoshka, Vitya was being very foolish if he thought he could sell him a fake picture."

"It might not have been deliberate, but a genuine mistake. And anyway we're still not sure that it is a fake."

Ludmilla laughed, rather disagreeably, Nicko thought.

"Vik's got a poor eye," Nicko went on. "He easily could have made a mistake. But is there anything you can tell me about Dobrinin? Does he even know? And if he does, how's he taking it?"

"I know no more than you do, Nikoshka. I spoke to Verochka and she's worried - as you'd expect her to be. All I say to you, Nikoshka, is be careful. Vitya has to look after himself in the end."

"It's not just Vitya I'm thinking of."

"Ah."

"What's that supposed to mean?"

"Just be careful, that's all. You've already seen the kind of things Russians do to each other and you've read our history."

"It's mine too, don't forget. That's why I'm here."

"Be careful. That's all I'm saying to you. When will you next see the Nikishovs?"

"I don't know yet. I'll have to give Verochka a ring. But I see the boy every day at school. He's enjoying it, by the way."

"What? School or the business of Dobrinin's picture?"

"Both."

"And after what nearly happened in the summer!"

"I don't think he's put the two things together. Anyway, Ludochka, I have to fly. There's a friend waiting to see me."

"But take care of yourself, Nikoshka. I really mean that."

"You too, Ludochka. Oh, I nearly forgot to ask. How's Ripley?"

Ludmilla laughed but didn't answer his question.

* * * * * *

Tim was sitting in their usual corner in the Cock and Hen with a number of broadsheet papers spread out in front of him. They lay open at the relevant inside pages. Nicko had already seen some of them. They told of the arrest of one Boris Babko, an art dealer in New York, who was Ukrainian by birth and alleged to be the author of a large-scale scam which involved selling bogus modern paintings to Russian oligarchs and other super-rich folk, none of whom were actually named, but there was the usual spread about their lavish life styles, their highhanded methods of doing business and settling scores. One paper featured the assassination of Leon Trotsky, including also a reference to the Litvinenko affair. The piece speculated on the lengths to which oligarchs might be prepared to go, as well as the part being played by the FSA. The material on Babko seemed to have come straight from the New York press and there was no mention of Viktor or any others who might be linked with him. A list of artists whose works were likely to have been forged was provided however, included the names of Rothko and Kandinsky.

Tim, needless to say, was revelling in it - just as Nicko knew he would be. After all, he was acquainted with several of the possible parties to this particular scandal.

"My problem is this," Nicko told him. "I can't really understand why anyone should want a bloody Rothko in the first place. Does that sound terribly philistine?"

"You mean you'd rather have a Landseer or a Lord Leighton?"

"O.K. I'm an arch-reactionary, a tweed-clad fogey, but you have to admit that both of those would be a bit harder to knock up than an abstract expressionist. Dobrinin is like most of his kind, a slave to fashion- no different from your average footballer and his WAG partner."

And so it went on, the pair of them downing more whiskies than they usually did and never letting go of the topic. Then the thought of Ludmilla suddenly floated into Nicko's mind and their telephone conversation earlier that evening.

"Did I ever talk to you about Ludmilla Mikhailovna?" Nicko said.

"The one who was in Montenegro with you - who was always buried in a book?"

"Well, she rang this evening, just before I came out. She's here in England."

"Another one. The plot does indeed thicken."

"She was devouring Patricia Highsmith in Montenegro and now she's doing a thesis on guess what? English crime fiction. As you know, Russians are fixated on the stuff. Anyway she rang to talk about the Dobrinin business, which Vera apparently told her about, and warned me to be very careful - in effect to distance myself from it. It sounded like a shot of a kind over my bows."

"A Russian femme fatale? My God, the plot really does thicken. The clichés are piling up."

"Ludmilla's hardly a femme fatale. But she told me that she had met

Dobrinin once- at some sort of a prize-giving in her university. But I know for a fact she met him again at Tiva - not that she said anything about it to anyone else at the time."

"Did she win a prize?"

"She didn't tell me that. But at least she's seen him at close quarters - as you have too, of course."

Tim smiled, flattered to be associated, however marginally, with a scandal that might be breaking in the broadsheets.

"But I still don't quite know what she might have been up to in Montenegro. You know, with the Big Man offshore with Isaacs on board and Vik having to be slapped down for attempting to steal a march on him in the Tiva property market. It's pregnant with possibilities."

"As the Bishop may once have told the Actress," said Tim. "Or was it the other way round?"

On the way home Nicko continued to reflect on the business. Tim was relishing it - as he seemed to be himself. Even young Kolya was gaining an indirect kind of kudos at school from it. All of which was not as it should be, when there was possibly so much at stake, innocent lives for instance. What had Stalin said? Once a man's dead, he ceases to be a problem. He'd pulled that one off with Trotsky, who, nevertheless, deserved what he got in Nicko's book.

CHAPTER NINETEEN

Cloaks and Daggers and an Unexpected Encounter

For nearly a week Nicko allowed the matter to lie fallow. He rang Vera once and got no reply from her or anyone else. But her son was in school the next morning, delivered by Alyosha, with whom Nicko had a whispered word and nothing appeared to be amiss. No more word was heard from Ludmilla either.

But the lack of movement was unsettling. After all, if a blow was going to fall it would probably be when they had been lulled into a sense of security and were letting their guards down. Nicko resolved to call on the Nikishovs at the weekend. He also decided to give Miguel a ring in the hope of fixing something for Sunday.

When he arrived in the early evening on Saturday the door was opened by Alyosha.

"All well, Alyosha?" he enquired as he crossed the threshold.

The Russian nodded.

"Is Vik at home?"

Alyosha pointed towards the staircase.

Before going up to see his friend, Nicko thought that he had better have a word with Vera, so he went into the kitchen where he found Kolya sitting at the table doing his weekend homework.

"Nice to see you working so hard, Kolya," he told the boy. "I'll tell Mr Trubshaw." What a pompous old fart I sound, he told himself. "Where's your Mama?"

"Upstairs, talking to Papa."

"I won't disturb you any longer, Kolya. I'll just pop up and have a word. Everyone well?"

The boy nodded.

Nicko went up and knocked lightly on the study door. "Hullo?" he called softly, feeling somehow that the situation required a muted tone.

Vera opened the door and behind her Nicko could see Viktor talking on his mobile.

"May I come in?"

"Of course." Vera took his hand and pressed it warmly.

Nicko raised his eyebrows in an unspoken gesture of enquiry, while Viktor continued with his call. He was speaking in Russian.

"I'm glad you've come, Nikoshka," Vera whispered.

"I hadn't heard from you for a few days, so I thought it was time to look in. Kolya's hard at work doing his weekend prep, I see."

"He loves his school," she said "and I'm so grateful. Whatever happens we mustn't stop that."

"Well he's certainly doing well and making friends fast. They're all great Chelsea fans."

Vera said, squeezing his hand once more.

Viktor in the meantime had finished his conversation.

"My apologies, Old Boy," he said in a manner meant to sound breezy. "Business never stops."

"Well? What's new?" asked Nicko, going straight to the point.

"Not much. Things seem to be quiet. It might mean anything."

Nicko waited for him to continue.

"What of Dobrinin?" he asked at length.

"Apparently he's left town."

"If he's up to anything, it's better not to be too close to the action. He doesn't want to get splashed with the blood, does he?"

Vera sighed. "Do you need to say things like that, Nikoshka? There's no end to this, is there?"

"So we're taking no chances," Viktor said.

"I'm glad to hear that."

"In the meantime I need some fresh air and to stretch my legs." Viktor stood up.

"Where are you going? Is it safe?"

Vera discharged another exasperated sigh. "When school has finished we must get away somewhere. This cannot continue."

"I leave it to Alyosha," Viktor explained. "He guides my steps. It's a nighttime business, never at the same time and we vary our route. He's found a couple of nice spots for a quiet drink. I leave it to him."

"And you're off right now?"

Viktor nodded. "Would you like to come with us? Or would you rather stay here and talk to Verochka?" He cast an arch look at Nicko as he said it.

Nicko hesitated and glanced at Vera, who looked non-committal.

"This is the summer all over again," he said.

"I hope not," Viktor tried to reassure him. "I can't be absolutely certain that Dobrinin even knows yet that he's been landed with a dud Rothko- if it is a dud. And if he does, he might have bigger things on his mind right now. The price of nickel, for instance. Who knows?"

"You go with him, Nikoshka," Vera ordered him," and make sure that he doesn't do anything stupid. We can talk another time."

"Done," said Nicko. "I suppose Alyosha is giving the orders?"

"Up to a point," his friend replied, "but he knows who's the boss."

"Are we off straight away?"

Viktor looked at his watch. "Kaneshna." He pecked his wife on the cheek and whispered a Russian endearment into her ear.

They went downstairs, where Viktor had a word with Alyosha, who was waiting in the hall. Then he went into the cloakroom and re-emerged in a heavy overcoat and a broad-brimmed felt hat. The effect struck Nicko as theatrical.

"Your disguise?" he said. "You look like something out of an old black and white movie."

Viktor seemed flattered by the connection.

"Don't be late," Vera called down the stairs, repeating it in Russian for good measure.

To avoid an obvious appearance at the top of the steps, they went down into the basement and slipped up to the street that way.

"Sometimes we use the back door," Viktor explained. "There must be no set pattern. And now, of course, there are three people leaving the house instead of the usual two."

"Does Verochka ever come with you?"

"It's not allowed."

"That's what I like to hear," replied Nicko. "The smack of firm government." "Piss off."

"You too," responded Nicko.

It was chilly outside. Nicko pulled up his collar and thrust his hands deep into his coat pockets.

They set off in the direction of Knightsbridge. There weren't many people about, despite it not being late. Alyosha was watchful, but not conspicuously so. Scanning the street, he muttered instructions about when and where to cross the road or to take a turning, but did not hurry the pace. Viktor in the meantime kept up a lively banter with his old chum. They resorted, as they usually did, to their schooldays, mimicking the voices of the more eccentric masters.

Then as they turned the corner into Pelham Street, Alyosha glanced back. As soon as they had made the turn, he grabbed Viktor's arm and pulled him into an unlit mews. He put a finger to his lips while Nicko felt his Montenegran experience returning to him.

They pressed on down the mews, keeping in its deepest shadow, and halted at the far end. Where they had just entered Nicko now could see a stationary figure, outlined against the street lights. It appeared to be holding back. Then it moved across to the other side of the entrance and returned slowly to the middle where it paused once more. Whoever he was seemed unsure of which way to go, but then made up his mind and set off down the mews in the direction the others had just taken. Alyosha drew his companions deeper into the shadow.

"Shit!" muttered Viktor. "Shsssh!"

But for some reason the man who appeared to be following them did not press on. Though it was dark, Nicko could make out that Alyosha was holding something in his right hand which hadn't been there before. Perhaps the other had sensed something of the kind and was taking the cautious option. At any rate after a short pause during which he lit a cigarette- an old-fashioned filmic touch like Viktor's hat, Nicko could not help thinking- the man walked slowly back towards the lighted mews entrance and set off in the direction that the others had intended taking.

"Where's the bugger going to now?" said Viktor.

"Wait here," ordered Alyosha, repeating it in Russian.

He moved softly and swiftly back the way they had come and, stopping just short of the mews entrance, he stood close to the wall and looked down the street where the man had gone.

It seemed an age while he was up there, making no attempt to contact his companions, but finally he summoned them with a wave, and walked a short way back to meet them.

"We will cross the street," Alyosha said and, looking about him, led the way over, taking hold of Viktor's elbow at the same time.

Nicko could not help making a comparison between the lighted London streets and their human traffic with the apparently empty Billiardo in Cetinje, where the foe had seemed to lurk unseen. Viktor had been badly scared then, but now was almost cocky. Assuming a nonchalant manner, he shook his elbow free from Alyosha's grip and launched into a very passable rendering of the plummy tones of Hindmarsh, a master who had taught both Nicko and himself mathematics at Stanford.

Nicko responded in kind until Alyosha pulled them up once more.

"I know a different place where we might go which will be safe," he told them. "But please make less noise."

Somewhat chastened, the rowdy pals fell silent.

Cutting and weaving, Alyosha led them into Knightsbridge. Nicko was impressed by the Russian's knowledge of the byways of London's West End- which, needless to say, was better than his own. He congratulated him and was rewarded with a broad Slavic grin.

"When we go home, we'll take a taxi," Alyosha said. "It'll be less trouble."

Soon they arrived outside a small public house, called 'The Falstaff' in the area behind Harrods. Like most West End pubs at this time in the evening, it was doing a brisk business and Alyosha cast a rapid eye over its clientele as they went in, then nodded his satisfaction to the others.

The two Russians squeezed onto a banquette, Nicko insisting on buying their drinks. He went up to the bar, where he froze in his tracks.

At its far end of the bar, perched on a stool and leaning back against the wall, was Miguel. He did not appear to be drinking wine or beer, but something stronger that seemed to be working its effect. Christ, thought Nicko, why does he have to choose this of all places in the whole bloody capital?

It would be better to pretend that he hadn't seen him and to slip away with his drinks. Viktor and Alyosha would both have recalled him from the party in Thurloe Square, but drawing a presumably well-oiled Miguel into their conversation would be dangerous. And anyway was he alone? If he had company, what kind was it? Luckily the spot where they were settled was out of the sightline of anyone at his end of the bar, so hopefully he would remain unaware of their presence.

But something else troubled Nicko: the Spanish boy's companion, assuming that he had one and wasn't drinking alone. A surge of jealousy flared up inside him and Nicko felt sorely tempted to confront the boy then and there and to challenge the man sitting next to him. For somebody was clearly was keeping him company, exchanging the occasional word with him as he balanced precariously against the wall on his stool. Nicko could only see the back of the man's head: a thatch of greyish-blond hair spilling over the turned-up collar of a dark blue coat. It wasn't Mark Isaacs, and it meant nothing, until he saw the man's hand wander across to his companion's knee and to squeeze it.

Miguel, who had his eyes closed, opened them and his features lit up in a big smile.

"What were you saying to me just now?" Nicko heard him saying.

The man leaned towards him and whispered something, which drew from the Mexican boy a flirtatious tinkle. Then he took his hand and Miguel made no attempt to withdraw it.

Nicko slipped away, back to his companions, ablaze with jealousy, though he had still not seen his rival's face. Judging from behind, he appeared to be an older man, possibly older even than Mark Isaacs, so perhaps in one sense he did not have a serious rival in love. After all, Nicko was conscious of his own still-youthful charms and however well-heeled this suitor might be, he could hardly compete in the Theban stakes.

Alyosha stood up to take the drinks from him and he sat down on a chair, facing the other two on the banquette opposite. That way his face could not be seen by anyone at the bar and the next expedition in that direction would be performed by one of the others anyway.

"We must keep our voices down," Nicko warned the others. "No noisy Russian toasts."

Viktor raised his glass and touched Nicko's. "Fuck off," he said in a whisper.

"You too," returned Nicko in his ear. "Cheers Alyosha, nasdorovia!"

The Russian raised his glass and nodded amiably.

Viktor looked hard into his friend's face. "Is something biting you? You've got that look on your face."

"No, nothing in particular. It's just that we have to be so bloody careful, that's all - especially after our little adventure on the way here. I'm sure Alyosha would agree."

The occasion was too tense for much show of liveliness. Nicko turned a couple of times to look in the direction of the bar, but was unable to see Miguel, though he could still see his companion's back. When Alyosha arrived at the bar to get fresh drinks, the man turned to glance at him over his shoulder and Nicko saw that he was indeed an older man, a wealthy City punter, no doubt. Miguel gave no sign of recognising the Russian whom he had of course met in the Nikishov house.

Viktor insisted on standing a final round, Nicko urging him to make it a short one. He watched him approach the bar, his heart in his mouth. To his considerable relief, there were no exclamations of recognition on the part of either Viktor or the Mexican boy. But when his friend returned he clearly had news to impart.

"Guess who I've just seen," he announced.

Nicko raised his eyebrows in faux enquiry.

"Someone we both know," went on Viktor.

"Don't keep me in suspense."

"Isaacs' young friend. His pretty boy. There's another bloke with him. He looks a bit older than Isaacs."

"Better to let sleeping dogs lie."

For a moment Viktor looked puzzled.

"I don't have to explain that one to you, Vik, surely? Do I?" Viktor mouthed the f-word back at his chum.

"A taxi, I think," said Alyosha, taking out his mobile and pressing in a number. He spoke in English, but signed off in his own language. "The taxi will be here in ten minutes," he announced. "We must be ready when it comes."

In exactly ten minutes the driver put his head round the street door and caught Alyosha's eye. They clearly knew each other. Alyosha marshalled his party out of the pub, Nicko not daring to look back, in the hope that he would go unnoticed by Miguel. But it wasn't to be.

"Nick!"

Viktor stared at him, "Guess who seems to know you," he said.

"Shit," muttered Nicko.

"Like that is it?"

Nicko turned back in the direction of the bar, while Alyosha shunted Viktor out into the street.

As he approached the bar, Nicko assumed a surprised expression.

"Well, well, well, it is a small world!" he exclaimed. "Fancy bumping into you in here, of all places!"

It sounded hollow.

"Come and say hello to Pete."

The other man nodded coldly in Nicko's direction, not enamoured of the prospect. Well at least I can put him out of his misery, thought Nicko. "I'm afraid not," he called back. "I have to fly!"

He blew Miguel a fleeting kiss, which Pete didn't see, and mouthed the words, "I'll give you a ring!"

"I can't hear you!" called back Miguel.

This time Nicko spoke the words out loud, earning himself a glare from Pete. Defiantly he blew a second kiss to the Mexican boy, and set off after the others.

He piled into the back of the waiting vehicle, which set off immediately.

"So Isaacs' young friend remembers you?" Viktor said.

"It would seem so." Nicko wanted to remain discreet, but was enjoying a sense of triumph at the discomfort that he had just caused Pete. Miguel had certainly made no attempt to hide from him, grinning in reply to his airborne kiss.

"I wonder where his keeper is tonight?" went on Viktor.

"Probably in a dark corner somewhere, plotting a transaction with your tormentor. Maybe Dobrinin's trying to offload a dodgy Rothko onto him. And while they're at it, the boy's been allowed off the leash."

And by an odd coincidence when they got back to Thurloe Square and found Vera watching the television news, who should pop up on it, but Lord Isaacs of South Shields. He was signing a trade agreement with an Arab head of state - a dictator who had in his time been a thorn in the flesh of the United Kingdom. The package included a clause about the possible exchange of prisoners from each other's custody- which in effect meant the United Kingdom surrendering convicted terrorists in return for oil. Looking at the Minister's smile as he shook the tyrant's hand at the closure of the deal, Nicko recognised the Mark Isaacs who had slipped into the Nikishovs' basement, bearing a new puppy. It was a little more difficult, perhaps, to envisage him applying a swishy bamboo to a naughty Mexican boy's bottom.

"Well, well!" exclaimed Nicko. "Not haggling with Oleg Dobrinin over the price of a Rothko after all, but with an Arab potentate over a barrel of oil. Maybe the Rothko's thrown in."

Viktor chuckled, while Vera frowned. So far they had not mentioned the incident in the mews to her.

It was Alyosha, however, who felt it was incumbent upon him to do so.

"Are you really sure about it?" said Vera at the conclusion of his account.

Alyosha shrugged. "Not completely, but we must keep them guessing."

"Which is easier said than done," pointed out Vera. "We have to take Kolochka to school and to bring him home again, don't forget."

"Perhaps I should disappear," suggested Viktor.

"And then they'll flush you out by kidnapping your wife and child," said Nicko.

Vera shuddered. "Don't say things like that."

"Can you not reach an agreement with Dobrinin by offering his money back and tell him that you were duped the same as he was?" Nicko said. "I could even act as your middleman if you liked. He might fancy dealing with a real Orloff," he added with a smile.

"Don't be too sure of that," Viktor pointed out. "In Russia there are plenty of others with the same sort of name - think of all those Lebedevs and Medvedevs."

"But seriously Vik, I mean it. I'll help in any way I can."

His friend took his hand and pressed it.

"And another thought," went on Nicko. "His Lordship of South Shields, should we not approach him? He and Oleg are shipmates, after all."

They chewed over various possibilities without coming to any conclusion, though an approach to Dobrinin via a middle man seemed the most sensible.

Nicko was now beginning to grasp the pigheaded intransigence of Russians in such matters, when the urge to settle a score or to avenge a slight seemed to outweigh any attempt to reach a sensible settlement. Why rub Vik out, after all, if he was prepared to settle amicably? But then, he reflected, what did they actually know of the oligarch's intentions anyway? Or if, indeed, he had any? There was a Stalinist miasma of fearful uncertainty about the business, and it was still possible that the Big Man would not even bother to strike at all. Or he might bide his time, taking his revenge cold later, when it suited him better.

Alyosha insisted on ordering a taxi to take him home when the time came to depart at nearly midnight. Alone in the taxi, it crossed his mind that Tim might be the best one to discuss the approach of a middleman to the oligarch with.

Once back home, he decided not to ring Miguel to confirm the following evening and to contact Tim in the morning, who, no doubt, would enjoy the cloak and dagger moment in the mews. Indeed, that's where Nicko felt that Tim might play a useful part: he enjoyed this sort of thing, as was plain from his reaction to the description of the Montenegran shenanigans.

Also, like Nicko, he was a sufficient snob to be fascinated by the New Russians' efforts to worm their way into a class they perceived to be more sophisticated than their own. Nicko's own roots had, of course, interested him as well. The penniless Orloffs already had class when they fled the Revolution and set about rebuilding their fortunes. The rollercoaster of History and its ironies appealed to Tim, and Nicko felt able to play on it, partly, he admitted, because it gave himself a romantic aura. So Tim might take a part too in this play about Old and New Russians.

When he spoke to Tim in the morning, Nicko deliberately withheld the details of what had happened the previous evening. Of course he could not be one hundred percent sure that there had been anything to Alyosha's suspicions at all, but they seemed plausible, especially as the Russian was a professional who appeared to know what he was about. It was going to make a good story, so Nicko dropped a few hints by way of a sweetener on the phone, referring back to Cetinje in a cryptic kind of way.

Then Nicko decided that it was time to give Miguel a ring. He thought it was unlikely that Isaacs would be back from his North African trip so soon, but he still could not be sure. It didn't really matter, though, because the Mexican boy usually had his mobile at the ready wherever he happened to be. But this time it was switched off and the possibility of Pete crossed Nicko's mind. He would try again later.

Then, minutes later, it was Nicko's turn to receive a call. It was Ludmilla.

"Hullo, Ludochka. How are things?"

"It's getting worse, Nikoshka. It's in all the newspapers."

"I know it is. But Dobrinin. Any news of him? He's supposed to be out of town. Where could he be? He's got a place in Provence, I believe, and a bolt hole somewhere else in this country. So if he's not at home, where the hell is he? I don't suppose it could be Dubai, could it? Or Moscow even?"

"I've no idea about that and I don't think it matters, Nikoshka. But I might be able to help." "Tell me more."

"Not now. We must meet. Tonight?"

"I'm afraid I can't make tonight. Later in the week maybe."

"I will ring you again."

"You do that Ludochka. Please." He replaced the receiver.

It was difficult to place Ludmilla in relation to the Nikishovs and indeed to the oligarch himself, though there was quite clearly a lot more there than was meeting the eye. Her tone as always was cryptic, while she seemed to hover on the sidelines, as if she was weighing up the action. Was she merely collecting copy for something she was intending to write one day? A crime story, possibly? But with her, could it run deeper and indeed darker than that? And of course might not the two things be linked? When I write all this down one day, Nicko told himself, I'm sure her role will turn out to have been a significant one.

Miguel still wasn't answering when Nicko tried him again, so he settled instead to meet Tim, who predictably enjoyed the description of the figure silhouetted against the street lights at the entrance to the mews, so redolent of 'The Third Man'. The cliché of lighting the cigarette capped it for him.

"He has got to be your man," he told Nicko. "Letting you know that he's right there, on top of you, and there's no wriggling free. And he'll know the watering hole you visited too and about your taxi ride home."

"Alyosha knows how to play that kind of game as well, don't forget."

Tim chuckled. "That's what it comes down to, doesn't it? They're all mixed up in it together, playing a grand game of cat and mouse. It's the element of revenge that might give it its tragic piquancy, if you like."

"While the innocent get struck down."

Tim laughed again. "We could get all Darwinist and existential about it. But I think the same thing might have been said of medieval warfare- you know- its aristocratic sporting aspect and the need to satisfy honour etcetera. And if we push it back even further, we might talk about hierarchies and alpha male dominance in the upper primates."

But Nicko's mind was running on what his friend had said about the spook's apparent omniscience, which sounded all too likely. It was all very well treating it as a game with its own rules and honour code, but there might well be innocent victims. Vera and Kolya immediately sprang to mind and indeed any unfortunate bystander who just happened to get caught in the crossfire. Viktor had chosen to play the game, after all, but his family had been given no choice. And the rules of this one drew no clear lines by excluding the innocent pawns who might be removed from the board in the process of checkmating him.

"I've been thinking, Tim," said Nicko. "Since you have a pretty fair idea of what all this is about, from a cultural or historical perspective, I mean, how would you like to take a small part in the play?"

"Me? I've never been an actor."

"I can't believe that. It needn't involve any risk."

Tim stared at his friend and laughed outright. "I should bloody well hope not! I've no desire to get myself killed in the crossfire of a turf war between Russian hoodlums!"

"It wouldn't come to that."

"Then what would it come to?"

"You've met Dobrinin. At Vik's party."

"Yes and a pretty miserable-looking shit he struck me as too, but then you'd expect that, wouldn't you?"

"Would you be prepared to talk to him?" "Christ, what do you take me for?"

"A very urbane West End property agent with the gift of the gab, who's used to rubbing shoulders with the higher echelons of British Society, as well as with New Russian oiks."

Tim took a pull at his glass and shrugged his shoulders.

"Well?"

"Well what?"

"Do you fancy the idea? A small, yet significant part in the play? You've got experience of handling Russians, after all. You must have some idea by now of what makes the average oligarch tick."

"And you reckon that Dobrinin is the average oligarch?"

"I don't see it otherwise."

"So I go spouting a lot of guff in a posh voice and talk him out of hounding his compatriot into an early grave? Is that what you're telling me?"

"In a nutshell. Tell him that Vik will give him full restitution for the dud painting, with an apology for making such a crass error, but one which was made in good faith nevertheless."

"You're a bloody idiot, Nick, but I think I could give it a whirl- if you or someone else set it up for me. It goes without saying I'll need to buy myself a bulletproof vest, and I won't be accepting any cups of tea and certainly no vodka."

"That shouldn't be a problem, but we'll have to think carefully and put out feelers in the right places."

"Easier said than done."

"Maybe. But there's one possibility: that Russian girl I told you about, the one who's, studying English literature here right now. Remember she's already met Dobrinin."

"Ludmilla? Can she be trusted?"

Nicko laughed. "I'm not entirely sure, but she's called me up, wanting to talk about the picture. She's been reading the papers and offered to help. I couldn't see her because I'm seeing you now, but she said she'd call back."

"So in the meantime we wait on tenterhooks to hear again from your Russian Mata Hari? So what do you need me for?"

"To lend tone to what might otherwise be a vulgar brawl- as the subaltern said when asked to explain the role of cavalry in modern warfare. I don't mean that entirely facetiously, Tim. Your presence at any discussions might flatter the khan and help to move things along. It would raise their tone and remove some of the rough edges. A civilised accommodation might be more easily reached that way."

Tim chuckled. "Well keep me posted, won't you? But in the meantime let's change the subject. I'm sick of talking about bloody Russians. How's the opus magnum coming along? Any fresh ideas? It's more important than a fucking Rothko."

Scooping up their glasses, Tim took them away for a re-fill.

CHAPTER TWENTY

Diverging Developments

Nicko heard nothing from anyone for several days. In the meantime he had to knuckle down and think about school work. Dick Trubshaw was trying to talk him into producing a summer term play, which, if the weather was fine, was traditionally performed in the shrubbery at the back of the school. He fancied the idea, as he felt that his own pedagogical interests lay in the Arts rather than in Sport. He felt, too, that with the real-life drama being acted out by his Russian friends, he probably needed one of the make-believe kind to keep his life in some sort of balance. So soon he was toying with the idea of writing a play of his own and considering the children for parts in it.

Ludmilla had not called back- which did not strike him as particularly odd, knowing what he did of her. Nor had he spoken again to Tim about his possible diplomatic role. The idea that two dramas, on separate planes of reality, should run side by side tickled his imagination. Might they penetrate and sustain one another?

Looking back to his own school days, Nicko recalled his love of Chaucer. He had read the Prologue to the Canterbury Tales under an inspirational master, who had even got his class to compose their own couplets in Middle English. But of the Tales, themselves, it was the one told by the Pardoner which had left the strongest impression on him with the neatness of its plot and its strong moral theme. It was short and sharp and could easily be turned into the kind of one act play - of perhaps forty-five minutes duration - that children might appreciate and perform.

Moreover the Pardoner himself, with his sackful of Papal indulgences and fake relics, was a weirdly fascinating character in his own right- the quintessential snake oil salesman, as old as Mankind, but with modern parallels. Nicko seized on the idea and, as the Muse went to work, it rapidly eclipsed everything else. He decided to write it as a play inside another play: a group of pilgrims would meet at the Tabard Inn on their way to the shrine of St Thomas at Canterbury- Chaucer's own format- but this would have to be a smaller party than in the original, while preserving some of its stereotypes like the Miller, the Knight and possibly the Wife of Bath. They would taunt the wretched Pardoner about his extravagant claims, while he would demonstrate his eloquence by telling them a tale of great power, which Nicko decided should end in a climactic dance macabre.

As he thought about it, everything else was put on hold. The children's guide to the art treasures of the capital, for instance, would have to wait. And for a couple of evenings, as he sketched the play's outline, he failed even to ring Vera.

Then ten days after his last meeting with Tim, as he was about to roll into bed, Ludmilla rang, bringing him down to earth with a bump.

"Nikoshka?"

"Ludochka?" For a moment he did not want to think about Viktor's messy gangster politics. "We must meet."

"Must we? Have you something new to tell me?"

"Sure. But how do you say it in English? From the horse's mouth."

"Which horse are we talking about?"

"The big one. Oleg."

"You mean Dobrinin?"

"Da. Kaneshna."

"You've spoken to him?"

"Da. Yes, Nikoshka."

"That was clever of you."

"It's a long story and now I am tired. I'll tell you when we meet."

Nicko could hear the sound of a stifled yawn.

"Well, well," he said, "Since we're talking about horses, Ludochka, you're certainly a dark one."

She laughed lightly.

"Tell me another thing, Ludochka, just as a matter of interest. You said 'Oleg' just now. Is that what you call him to his face?"

The laugh was repeated. "He's Oleg Pavlovich. When can we see each other?"

"I'm busy until the weekend. How about Saturday? In the morning, here? About tennish?"

"Ten o'clock in your house - or flat?"

"Do you think you can find it?"

"Sure, if you give me the address."

Nicko gave it to her and put down the receiver, and 'The Pardoner's Tale' aside for a few moments.

Oleg? What was going on there? And as usually happened when he was thinking about Ludmilla, his thoughts flew back to Montenegro where some of the performers in the real-life play had already been acting their parts and were now either onstage or waiting in the wings for their next entries. Even Mark Isaacs had been there: on board Dobrinin's yacht in Tiva harbour and with him Miguel. What had the oligarch made of the pair of them shipboard together? And there was Mrs Dobrinin- the most recent one. It was allegedly on her behalf that the fateful Rothko had been acquired. Did she have a significant part to play, beyond being an ornament of the Great Man's ego? 'The Pardoner's Tale' was one of greed and folly. Was the Russian one so very different?

Nicko began to entertain ambitious thoughts about the artistic possibilities of it all and then, as was his wont, started to have cold feet about the extravagant claims he was making for himself. Does anyone really give a damn what I think about Life and the World? Seriously, they couldn't give a shit. But, late as it was, he decided to have a word with Tim. He would need to update him on Ludmilla and he might sound him out about his own excursion into the dramatic genre as well.

Tim was already in bed and judging by some background muttering sharing it with someone else, probably Elspeth. He was not in a talking mood, even a little abrupt, but they agreed to put his own possible approach to the oligarch on hold until they had heard from Ludmilla. Briefly Nicko touched on his own dramatic endeavour and Tim expressed a polite interest, but put off further discussion until their next meeting.

"We'll discuss it when we're sick of Russians," he said. "You never know, I might even have a few ideas."

When Friday came, Nicko decided to take the bull by the horns and went straight from school to Thurloe Square. His conscience was starting to prick him, though Kolya had assured him that all was well at home.

Arriving at the house and ringing the bell, he was scrutinised by Alyosha through the spyhole set above the knocker. His identity confirmed, he was let into the house through a space only wide enough to admit him.

In the hall he was met by Kolya who had got home from school shortly before. The boy had shed his blazer and his stockings were near his ankles.

His striped school tie was hanging outside his jumper, its knot awry, and a grubby handkerchief was dangling from a pocket of his shorts.

"You look as if you've just been pulled through a hedge backwards," his godfather told him. "You remind me of Just William. Do you know who he is yet?"

The boy shook his head.

"Then it's time you did. Perhaps I should give you one the books for your birthday. But you can find them in the school library. Is Mama at home? And Papa?"

"They're both in the kitchen. We've got a visitor. A special one. Do you remember Lord Isaacs- the man who gave me Stenka?"

"Has Lord Isaacs come by himself? He didn't bring a friend with him, by any chance?" "By himself."

The boy led the way into the kitchen, where they found the Government Minister on his hands and knees coaxing the puppy from beneath the table with a biscuit. Viktor was on the floor beside him, but as Nicko entered they both stood up.

"Don't stop for me," he protested. "How do you think he's coming on? Stenka, I mean. Is Kolya doing a good job?"

"An excellent one," answered Lord Isaacs in his most ingratiating tone.

In his mind's eye Nicko had an image of his Lordship addressing the Upper House as it might be glimpsed on television, for it to be followed immediately by one of him applying a cane to the Mexican Boy's bottom, his features set in a grimace of righteous determination…

Meanwhile he continued to gush about the dog, while Viktor suggested a drink.

"It's a little early for me," Isaacs said.

"You'll have a cup of tea then?" suggested Vera. "That would agree with me very well."

They sat at the kitchen table, while Vera made the tea. She put a plate of sweet biscuits before them, which Isaacs immediately started feeding to the dog.

"He'll get spoiled that way," Viktor warned him.

"A small treat once in a while," replied the politician smoothly. "He's been such a good boy and has earned one. And I'm quite sure that Kolya here will see that he doesn't get spoiled. One meal a day and a good walk. Is he getting his daily exercise?"

253

The others glanced at each awkwardly. How much did he need to know?

"We try to give him a walk every day," Vera assured him. "If we can't manage it ourselves, Alyosha or Tsina are very kind."

"I'm sure he likes a jolly good run in the park," Isaacs said.

"I sometimes take him to the park," put in Kolya.

"I'm very pleased to hear it." The Government Minister stroked the boy's hair gently.

A brief silence followed, which was broken by Nicko.

"You know something?" he said.

The others looked at him for elucidation.

"This scene - here with us, now. It reminds me of Russia."

Viktor discharged a snort, mixed with a sigh. "Here we go."

"I mean with us… sitting at the kitchen table like this and drinking tea. We only need to start a soulful discussion of the kind that's supposed to take place in a Russian kitchen…

"Like in a play by Chekhov? Except they don't happen in kitchens," suggested Isaacs.

"Someone has got to start baring his soul," ventured Viktor. "And it needs to be a Russian soul," he added, giving Nicko a mocking glance.

"Not in front of the children," warned Isaacs. "We should stick to dogs and other animals."

It was starting to sound strained and Nicko felt relieved when, after another ten or so minutes, the Government Minister glanced at the kitchen clock.

"Good gracious!" he exclaimed. "Is that really the time?"

It stood at a quarter to six.

"I must fly at once or I'll get into terrible trouble!" The Government Minister fluttered a hand and rose to his feet.

The others rose too.

"Please don't stand up for me," Isaacs protested. "I'm sure your man can see me out. I'm delighted that Stenka is doing so well. It's quite made my day! Young Kolya here is the perfect master!"

He put an affectionate arm round the boy who suddenly looked startled.

"And thank you so much for such a lovely tea," he gushed, as he set off in the direction of Alyosha at the front door.

Kolya was rubbing the seat of his shorts. "He pinched my bottom," he said.

Viktor looked at Nicko and grinned, while Vera frowned.

"Well, well," Nicko said. "What are we to make of that? Not just Kolya's bottom, I mean." He gave the boy a playful punch.

"Lord Isaacs has much charm, there is no doubt about it," Vera said.

"He was very nice to Stenka," added the boy. "But why did he pinch my bottom?"

No one was willing to answer the question.

"He's a friend of Oleg Dobrinin," Viktor reminded them.

"Did you manage to…?" Nicko paused with a sidelong glance at Viktor.

"No," his friend replied. "Not this time. But, put it this way, the door remains open." He put a cautionary finger to his lips and nodded in the direction of his son who was picking the puppy up from the floor.

"Time for your bath, Kolochka. You're very dirty," his mother said.

"You won't forget to put Stenka out?" he replied. "He's not making nearly so many puddles now."

"Of course I won't. Now, upstairs at once."

The boy made a token show of dragging his heels, but did as he was told.

"Isaacs blotted his copy book a bit that time, didn't he? I mean pinching the boy's bottom," Nicko said.

Viktor shrugged. "It was hardly very serious. At least we know where he's coming from."

"There was a master at my prep school who liked pinching my bottom," said Nicko, "and it wasn't the end of the world. But these days you can't be too careful. Health and safety drives Dick crazy. It used to be much easier."

"Anyway we need to keep Isaacs sweet, even if he did pinch my son's bottom," Viktor said.

"Something I was going to tell you," went on Nicko. "Ludochka rang. I said I'd see her tomorrow. That's one of things I came to tell you."

Vera frowned and bit her lower lip.

"How's the history of the Montenegran royal family getting on?" asked Viktor.

"She said nothing about that. She's busy frying other fish. Her thesis on the English crime novel - which is more up her street somehow."

Viktor shrugged. Literature did not mean a great deal to him.

They were silent for a moment. The mention of Ludmilla, for some

255

reason, had a sobering effect and neither of the old school chums could think of anything sufficiently facetious to say.

* * * * * *

Back at home Nicko toyed with the idea of ringing Miguel, but decided to leave it for the time being. Instead he took his paperback copy of 'The Canterbury Tales' down from the shelf to look at 'The Pardoner's Tale' and to consider ways of adapting it. Almost immediately it began to fall into place. For instance, the three riotous young men in Chaucer's tale bore no names, so Nicko christened them Tom, Dick and Harry, which gave them some of the universal quality of an Everyman. As he sketched his outline, his mind turned to casting the children he knew for particular parts and found that it helped drive the creative process by fleshing it out with real people. The characters sprang quickly to life and began to speak inside his head.

He roughed out the first scene, which was to serve as one arm of the bracket containing the Tale itself. Four pilgrims, an Innkeeper and a serving wench made up the cast for this part and he jotted down snatches of dialogue which enabled the characters to introduce themselves and to start revealing their personalities… a knight, a miller, a wife of Bath - to give a girl a part - and of course the Pardoner himself. The innkeeper needed to have his say too… and the serving wench…

Eventually sleep got the better of him and he went to bed, having postponed a pile of marking until the next day.

The following morning he was marking essays at the dining room table at nine o' clock, but it was nearly eleven when the doorbell's ring announced Ludmilla's arrival. The delay did not surprise him and she made no attempt to apologise for it.

Instead she gave him a generous peck on the cheek.

Nicko could not help noticing the eye shadow and the whiff of perfume, things that he had not previously associated with Ludmilla, who, if anything, had been inclined to frumpiness. She was wearing an expensive cashmere jumper under her coat and a gold bracelet'

"Life looks as if it's being kind to you, Ludochka," Nicko pointed out.

She smiled and said nothing.

"I've set out on a literary quest of my own," he said. "But we won't talk about that just yet, because you have something else to say to me. Coffee?"

"Thank you."

He helped her off with her coat and she sat in his small armchair.

"I'm afraid I've only got the instant kind," he apologised as he arrived with a tray.

"That'll be fine," she replied. She poured a large dollop of milk into the mug and clicked a couple of her own sweeteners in with it.

"I should keep some of those," Nicko said. "So Ludochka, what news?"

She took a cigarette from a packet in her bag and lit it. "I'm sorry. I should have asked you first. It's very rude of me. Do you share this terrible habit? I don't remember you doing it in Montenegro." She offered the packet.

"I don't smoke myself, but I'm perfectly happy if you do. I'd rather that than a mobile phone."

"Thank you. I'll try to remember that." There was a pause while she blew a big smoke ring. "Oleg, Oleg Dobrinin," she began.

"I suppose that's where we must start."

"How much do you know about him?"

"Not all that much really. The bit Vik's told me and what I've read in the papers. I know he owns half the mineral resources of Siberia- or seems to anyway- and has just acquired one of the most expensive properties on the London market. And that he cruises the high seas in a luxury yacht." He looked hard at her as he added this. "And he he's got some powerful friends, in our Government, such as Lord Isaacs of South Shields. Oh and like most of the oligarch tribe he's said to have blood on his hands - as you'd expect. It's even been suggested that he might be interested in Art, especially the modern kind- or maybe it's his wife who is."

"You're wrong about the last. There's no Mrs Dobrinin."

Nicko said nothing so she went on.

"There have been girlfriends, but he married none of them. "

"I understood that a Mrs Dobrinin residing here in London rather fancied the works of Mark Rothko." Ludmilla shook her head.

"So? These girlfriends, what kind are they?"

Ludmilla lowered her voice despite there being no particular need to. "They - how do you say it in English? provide him with different services. Not a thing most wives can be expected to do. And it's not only girls…"

"You mean our oligarch friend might even be gay? That certainly fits in with Isaacs."

Ludmilla shrugged. "He's like a Turkish sultan."

"He certainly doesn't look like one. But tell me, Ludochka, how do you know all this?"

She blew another smoke ring and eyed him steadily. "I know Oleg. Really quite well."

"It doesn't surprise me, Ludochka, to hear you tell me that. And of course there's more to it than a university, prize-giving ceremony, isn't there? Should I be surprised?"

"Perhaps you should a little, because you seem to be such an innocent boy who's never grown up."

"Thank you for that! I've been told it enough times already- by another Russian as it happens."

"Sorry, Nikoshka, I didn't mean to hurt you."

"Let it go."

She leaned over and placed a repentant kiss on his cheek.

"Thank you for that too. Now, to get back to our oligarch chum, Oleg Pavlovich Dobrinin. He's a man with Ottoman appetites, O.K., but what's he actually after? I'm talking about this affair with Vik and I assume that he is putting the squeeze on him in some form or other - Alyosha seems pretty convinced that he is - watching the house and so on. But so far he's made no obvious moves - though he must know by now that he's been cheated over the painting. And of course there was Montenegro… Cetinje. So what's he up to? Just giving Vik a fright or really wanting to hurt him?"

"It's a long story and I'm sure Vitya has no idea of it. It's a family matter going back a couple of generations."

"You're telling me that there's some kind of an ancient score to be settled?"

"Yes, with an interesting historical side to it." She eyed him with a self-satisfied smile, pleased at the curiosity she was arousing, and plunged the end of her cigarette into the dregs of her coffee cup. "Of course you know something about the Nikishovs? Who they were and the part they played in the Soviet Union?"

"Vik's told me quite a bit. Grandfather was service nobility under Tsar Josef - if I can call him that - and a very big cheese in the Gulag administration. Comrade Nikishov…Absolute Master in the Kolyma gold fields, and no mere oprichnik either. Somehow he managed to escape the despot's bullet - which was an achievement in itself. Or was it luck? Either way, Vik's quite proud of him."

"And there's the irony, Nikoshka, the Dobrinins were nothing at all in Stalin's time. Quite the opposite."

"You're saying that while Ivan Nikishov was lording it as a Bolshevik boyar, the Dobrinins were serfs?"

"More than that, Nikoshka, they were Nikishov's serfs. That is Oleg's grandfather and his great uncle were. The family had been exiled to Siberia- as kulaks, I believe- and the two brothers were later arrested and found themselves mining gold for Nikishov. Grandfather Dobrinin died in Kolyma and it was his son, Pavel, who started to build the family's fortunes towards the end of Brezhnev's time. And then, when the Soviet Union finally collapsed it was Pavel's own son, Oleg - how do you say it in English? who was ready to make the killing."

"Not from gold of course, but nickel?"

"Da. From nickel."

"But why after all this time does he need to take it out on Vik for what his grandfather may have done to his family? Surely after all the things that have gone on in the last century he can put it behind him, can't he? Bloody Russian history never lets up, does it? And I don't suppose Oleg ever knew his own grandfather anyway- the one who died in Kolyma, I mean."

Ludmilla lit another cigarette. "It's not just that his grandfather died there," she said, "but the way he did it. You remember there were two of them- Grandfather Dobrinin and his brother?"

She paused and looked hard at Nicko.

"Well?"

"This something Vitya won't have told you, because he almost certainly doesn't know." She paused again. "The Dobrinin brothers were twins- the identical kind, I understand, and somehow they had remained together in the Gulag, even working in the same gang. Maybe someone hadn't the heart to separate them."

"Oleg's grandfather dies, so what happened to his brother?"

"He survived and was released in the thaw after Stalin's death."

"I suppose he was lucky."

"I'm afraid you can't say that."

"Why not?"

"He killed himself."

"Why did he do that?"

"It was to do with his twin brother's death."

Nicko said nothing, leaving her to tell him.

"He was shot by his twin - on the orders of Nikishov."

"My God, can that be true?"

Ludmilla nodded. "I don't know all the details. There was a mutiny of some kind, among the prisoners, and Nikishov decided to make an example. He took every tenth man from among the mutineers and executed him in front of the others. But the prisoners themselves were made to act as their own executioners. And it amused someone - Nikishov himself apparently - to add - how do you say? an extra refinement? By making one twin shoot the other. The twin who killed his brother was spared, needless to say."

And it was Vik's grandfather who ordered this?"

Ludmilla nodded.

"So how do you know about it?"

"Because the twin who executed his own brother and survived was my own grandfather."

"My God. And Dobrinin knows all this as well?"

"Kaneshna."

"Do you see him here in London?"

She nodded. "I saw him yesterday- after he'd got back from Russia."

"So you're related?" She nodded again.

She drew heavily on her cigarette and he looked at her steadily- or at least as steadily as he knew how. They were silent as he took it in.

"Tell me, Ludochka, last summer…when you were working with Vik and Vera… you knew who his grandfather was?"

"Kaneshna."

She smiled and nodded. "Of course."

"A bit of a coincidence, wasn't it? I mean running into Vik and Vera like that in Montenegro?"

"Not really. Oleg had his eye on Viktor Nikishov for some time. The holiday home development in Montenegro. That annoyed him. Vitya's interference gave him the excuse to…"

"…kill two birds with one stone? To avenge his grandfather at the same time as removing a rival, or an irritant at least, because Vik was notreally a big player?"

She looked at him, but said nothing.

Suddenly Nicko felt riled. It was a horrifying story that she had just told him, but the bullet in Cetinje had very nearly killed the boy. "Did you help to arrange that business in Cetinje when Kolya was nearly killed?"

For a second she seemed taken aback by his vehemence. "No one was trying to kill Kolya," she said.

"It didn't look like that at the time- not to me, at any rate. And here in London, Vik and Oleg seemed to have buried the hatchet? You know that expression?"

"I think so."

"Oleg even visits Vik in his new home and then buys a painting from him."

"Which is a fake."

"It may be, but sold in good faith."

"Are you quite sure about that?"

"Of course I am. I think I know Vik well enough."

"I believe he's sold fakes before. All those Shishkins."

Nicko had no immediate comeback to that. "I don't know," he said without conviction, "but in this situation he would hardly try to pass a fake off on Dobrinin of all people, would he? Vik isn't a complete idiot."

Ludmilla shrugged and did not reply.

"So then," resumed Nicko "what next? In view of everything- especially that Gulag horror story- how do we find a way out? "

"Despite it all, Oleg's a businessman," said Ludmilla, "and he talks to other businessmen in ways that they understand. And about things they want."

"Except with Viktor Nikishov?"

"It may be necessary to find someone who can speak for him. How do say? A middleman?"

"You are reading my own thoughts."

"You're a clever boy, Nikoshka. Do you know anyone?" There was a trace of mockery in her voice.

"There's an estate agent, here in London- the one Vik dealt with- a pretty upmarket sort of guy. He and Dobrinin have already met."

"He sells houses? Big ones? In fashionable parts of the city?"

"The kind of places that Russians want."

"I'd like to meet this friend of yours. Oleg is interested in buying houses- not just for himself to live in."

"Now tell me something else, Ludochka. Whose side are you on in all of this? Do you really want to save Vik's skin? You're not out to settle old scores too, are you?"

"They belong to history, our history, which is a tragic one, and I've never met any of the people who did these terrible things. And now it would be better to talk business, wouldn't it? We can't re-write the past." She smiled. "But I think I can help you, if you'll let me try."

"You reckon you can soften Oleg up?"

"He wouldn't like to hear you using terms like that."

"I apologise. What I really meant is - to exercise a little family influence."

"I need to meet this estate agent friend of yours." She looked at her watch. "Now, as you English say, Nikoshka, I must fly!" She gave him a printed card. "My mobile number. Speak to your friend, then ring me."

They both stood up and she hugged him close and kissed him, but it was not the same as being kissed by Verochka.

Nicko was shaken by what he had been told. That Vik's grandfather had wielded great power under Stalin he knew already, and it both fascinated him and told him something about his friend, but the sheer sadistic enormity of what he had just heard was another thing altogether. It was just about the sickest thing that he could have imagined. Indeed, Nicko asked himself that if he was in Dobrinin's position would he not want to take revenge on the perpetrator's heirs? And yet how could it be remotely fair to inflict pain and misery on Viktor and his family, who were so far removed from the time and place of the atrocity? Nicko remembered a television interview that he had once seen with the son of Martin Bormann, Hitler's aide. The first thing that had struck him was how much better looking, more refined even, the son was than the father. The latter had married a handsome woman and the son had inherited her looks rather than his father's. The younger Borman, it appeared, as a form of atonement for the crimes of his parent, had worked as a Christian missionary, but one thing he had insisted on. "I cannot help being the son of Martin Bormann," he explained. "Nothing that I do can change that."

In the meantime Nicko thought it was time to have another stab at his play. And, despite of having so much else to think about all of a sudden, the thing began to run. He slotted a group of twelve year olds into parts for the Knight, the Miller and the Pardoner before he had even written a line for them and went on to apportion other parts too, including the boy who was to play the part of Death and to lead the rioters, Tom, Dick and Harry, off in a dance macabre.

He was making a tentative start on the opening dialogue, when the phone rang.

"Shit!" he exclaimed, toying with the idea of not answering it, as was his way sometimes. But with the dramatic revelations he had just heard, he felt duty bound to do so. He rushed across the room to take the call before it stopped ringing.

It was Mother, full of talk about Italy. His own family did not mean very much to Nicko and of course he suspected his mother of having already written him off, so talking to her for any length of time was a chore. But he listened dutifully to an account of the grandchildren's foibles, interjecting the occasional remark that he felt might pass for a sign of interest.

The upshot was that he consented to go to see his mother for lunch the following Sunday and, having been bound to that, he felt no compunction about closing down the conversation. He went to work once more on the opening scene of his play where the pilgrims assembled at the Tabard Inn. But, when he was devising a jocular welcome on the part of Mine Host, the phone rang once more.

The temptation not to answer it this time was strong indeed: but his conscience prevailed. At least it was unlikely to be his mother. It was Tim.

Rather testily he informed him of what he was attempting to do, if only he and the Muse might be left by themselves to work together. Tim was not unsympathetic and Nicko immediately regretted his petulance. He apologised and before Tim could state his own business, he launched into a rather breathless and abbreviated account of what Ludmilla had just told him. When Tim tried to probe him further, he suggested that they got together that same evening to air it properly.

"What I was about to suggest anyway," said Tim. "I think I might be able to help. But I need to know all the sordid details first."

So for the rest of the morning Nicko was left to work on his play and when he stopped it was nearly two o'clock. He congratulated himself on his powers of concentration. The meeting of the Pilgrims at the Tabard had been sketched in, while the Pardoner was about to open his sackful of fake relics and to face the scorn of his companions. The Miller had already given vent to his drunken coarseness, arousing the disapproval of the priggish knight who was aware of the presence of ladies. The Papal indulgences, promising the remission of sins, were to follow, but the concept would need to be made clear to a juvenile audience. Nicko put it aside for another day.

His thoughts turned back to Ludmilla's grim tale and he wondered if it could really have been as she had described it. After all, was not Ludmilla herself a potential weaver of fictions, possibly of an extravagant nature? And that idea of one twin being forced to execute the other hadn't he come across it elsewhere? Possibly in a short story he had once read? It was important to bring Ludmilla and Tim together as soon as possible.

He went out to buy himself a sandwich for his lunch, and when he got back he checked his answer phone which was his normal procedure. There was a single message waiting for him: from Miguel. The Mexican Boy whispered into his phone as though he did not want somebody in his vicinity to hear what he was saying. Not that he said much, but asked Nicko to ring him in the evening, rather inconveniently at the time he would be meeting Tim. However Nicko felt that it would be easy enough to slip off to the gents and talk to him on his mobile. He was very much aware of the Mexican Boy's state of bondage and how important the timing of calls must be to him.

* * * * * *

Tim, it went without saying, was fascinated by Ludmilla's story and the subsequent fortunes of the Nikishovs and Dobrinins.

"There's a novel there, surely- if it isn't too farfetched," he said.

"Perhaps she's working on it already," said Nicko.

"That business of one twin being forced to shoot the other. It rings a fairly loud bell. A short story I once read - set in a German concentration camp. But I'm buggered if I can remember the author's name."

"It's funny you should say that. It struck me in exactly the same way. I know the story you talking about, but nothing of its author."

"Wasn't there something about a photograph? German soldiers and camp guards liked to take snaps of their crimes and the tale's denouement hinged on that?"

"So Ludochka might have done a little plagiarising," observed Nicko. "But I'd like you to meet her all the same. Whatever may have happened between Nikishovs and Dobrinins, she says that she and Oleg are cousins and she seems to be privy to some of his schemes. He's interested in buying more property here in the U.K. by the way."

Tim raised an eyebrow. "You do surprise me! What stinking rich Russian isn't?"

"It could be a way in," suggested Nicko. "I mean if you and she were to talk things over - the state of the market and so on - it might be a way of taking the heat off Vik."

Tim gave a little snort. "So I'm being landed right in it too, am I? It's lucky I don't take sugar in my tea."

"Just have a word with Ludochka. I can fix it for you and, you never know with Dobrinin- he might even be able to open a few doors."

Tim laughed outright and took a large pull at his tumbler.

Nicko took a quick glance at his glass. "In the meantime nature calls. I'll be back in half a tick."

Miguel answered the call which he dispatched from one of the lavatory cubicles.

"I'm sorry about the other night," Miguel said. "There was nothing I could do about it."

"Does another person know about it?" asked Nicko.

"It's him I want to talk to you about."

"What about him?"

"I'm through with him. Finito."

"Good God, do you mean it?"

"Of course I mean it."

"Well I suppose your bum's had about all it can take. Have you told him yet?"

"Not yet. He's in the North and won't be back for two more days."

"So where will you go now, Miggie?"

There was a pause.

"Miggie? Are you still there?"

"Sure. That's something I wanted to ask you."

Nicko knew what was coming and said nothing.

"Nick?"

"I'm listening."

"I'd like to move in with you. It won't be for very long."

My God, Nicko thought, there's nothing I'd like better, as long as he keeps out of sight when necessary, that's all. For some reason he was thinking about Ludmilla. And what about Lord Isaacs? It wouldn't take him long to work out where the boy had fled to and he might prove dangerous. But then, Nicko reflected, I know a thing or two about Lord Isaacs that he won't want the world to get hold of.

"O.K. Miggie, if you reckon it's safe and it's not for too long. I'm a busy man these days." He was thinking of 'The Pardoner's Tale'. "Can you get over at about eight tomorrow evening?"

"Muchas gratsias, Nick."

The line went dead and Nicko flushed the lavatory before returning to his friend.

"So I can assume you're happy about meeting Ludochka?" he said to him as he resumed his seat.

"It seems I don't have much choice, do I?" said Tim. "The plot is thickening all the time- to coin a cliché. Now tell me about your play."

CHAPTER TWENTY-ONE

A Play Within a Play

Miguel arrived the following evening shortly before eight in a taxi. He a large hold- all bag and a small rucksack- nothing more. As he entered the flat he fell on Nicko's shoulder, giggling nervously.

"Does Isaacs still not know?" Nicko asked him

"I didn't leave a message for him, if that's what you mean," the boy said. "I fed the dog and left."

"When does he get home?" "Probably tomorrow morning."

"So you're in the clear for tonight. He might ring."

"My phone's switched off. I'm bloody hungry, Nick."

"Is this all your luggage?"

"All."

"We'll eat at home tonight. Just beans and a fried egg. And a bottle of cheap plonk. O.K. with you?"

"I'll do the cooking if you like. If you get the stuff I can do a Latino dish."

"That sounds good, but I'll do the honours tonight. Then I have a bit of work to do. Marking books for school and my play."

"Your play?"

Nicko proceeded to explain who Geoffrey Chaucer was. Miguel after all his years growing up in the United States was perfectly at home in the English language, but largely ignorant of its higher cultural manifestations. He could name a few North American writers, such as Mark Twain, and he had heard of William Shakespeare. Nicko could not help reflecting that if his young friend had been a Russian of the same age, he might have found himself being put him on the spot regarding Scott and Thackeray, while being discoursed to at length on the works of Conan Doyle and Agatha Christie…

So Nicko explained patiently who Chaucer was and the kind of things that he wrote. He then went on to describe a pardoner. The holy relics bit Miguel could grasp from own his Mexican roots.

"But why do you want to turn this stuff into a play?" he demanded to know.

Nicko did his best to explain, justifying himself by treating it as a bridge into higher literature which would help his pupils later in their school careers.

"Won't they be bored?"

Nicko felt riled. "You have a bit to learn about English kids, Miggie, at least the kind I teach. And Russians ones too," he answered tartly.

Miguel shrugged, unconvinced, but did not think it worth pursuing.

"One thing, Miggie," said Nicko, "you haven't told me yet. Who was that friend of yours, the guy you were talking to in the pub the other night?"

"Are you cross with me?"

"No, not cross. Just curious, that's all."

"He wasn't a friend. I'd never met him in my life before. He just came across to me and started talking. I knew what he wanted, of course. It happens all the time in that place."

"You go there by yourself?" The Mexican boy nodded.

"You have to be careful in London pubs, a nice-looking lad like you all by himself," said Nicko.

"You should try the ones in New York."

Nicko carried the luggage up to the little room at the back which served as a spare room.

"I'm afraid a bit pokey," he explained. "It wouldn't suit Lord Isaacs."

"Fuck Lord Isaacs."

"You've said that before."

It was beginning to sound like joshing with Vik.

When they were finally sitting down to their simple supper in the tiny kitchen, Nicko quizzed Miguel about the dreaded Isaacs and what he was thinking of doing now that he had escaped his clutches.

"Frankly, Miggie, I think you're doing the right thing. How you put up with all that spanking for so long is a mystery to me, unless…" He looked at him and raised an enquiring eyebrow.

"Unless I liked it too, you mean?"

"Well, did you?"

The boy shrugged. "He paid me enough for it. I have to give him that."

"And there were the holidays as well, I suppose? Cruising the High

Seas with Mr Dobrinin."

"Sure. They were worth a few extra stripes." "So what next, Miggie?"

The boy shrugged again. "Maybe it's time to be heading back to the States."

"Is there anything there for you? Your family? I suppose you've still got one. You've never really said anything to me about them."

"Sure I've got a family- a kind of a one, anyway."

"Where are they now?"

"In different places. A brother in Dallas; a step one in New York; my Mom, she's in Baltimore- or at least I think she is. She was when I last heard anything, living with a guy I've never met. Oh and then there's my sister, Dolores, she's back south of the border- Mexico City- gone back to her roots, I guess. If there're any left to go back to,"

"So what are you going to do now?"

Miguel looked him with a puckish grin on his face.

"Eat up," Nicko ordered him abruptly. "We'll forget about work tonight and go to bed early instead. I've got a bottle of brandy we can take with us."

The Mexican Boy leaned on his shoulder and kissed him. "I love you, Nick," he whispered. "Christ I do!"

Miguel's skills, well-honed in the Big Apple and the British metropolis, made up for Nicko's own lack of expertise, and the boy already knew how to get him going, rather the way that Vera did. For one so young, he was remarkably adroit at timing a partner's climax.

At seven o'clock Nicko leaped out of bed. "Christ, I'll be late!" he exclaimed.

The Mexican Boy was still more than half asleep, mumbling something in the last act of his dream.

"Stay where you are," Nicko told him. "I'll be back about six. Help yourself from the fridge."

It was a rush getting to work and he was five minutes late for his first class, where one of the boys commented on his jaded look.

"A rough night, sir?" said the sharp twelve-year-old.

Nicko responded grumpily and several of the class exchanged what they felt to be knowing glances.

He was home again soon after six and found Miguel stretched voluptuously on the sofa watching the Twenty-four Hour News.

"You look tired, Nick. Would you like a cup of tea?" he said, lowering his feet to the floor.

"Thanks. Is that something you did for Isaacs?" "Fuck him."

"As you keep saying, fuck him, Miggie. Did anyone ring? I forgot to tell you not to answer the phone. Better that they should think no one's in."

"I'm afraid I did answer it. About a quarter of an hour ago. It was a woman, who said she'd call back later. She didn't say who she was."

"I think I can guess. Maybe I should ring her."

"She didn't sound English."

"It was Ludochka. A very dear Russian devushka."

The boy frowned. "A friend of yours?"

"Only a business one, Miggie. Nothing for you to wet yourself about. Now piss off to the kitchen and make some tea."

He tapped him on his bottom lightly as he left and the Mexican Boy turned and grinned back at him.

Half an hour later Ludmilla rang. Nicko signalled the boy out of the room and he obeyed.

"Saturday morning," she said. "Have you spoken to your friend yet?"

"I have and I think he'll play. But he's no fool, Ludochka. There has to be something in it for him as well. Nor does he want to be landed in the shit if anything goes wrong."

There was a pause while Ludmilla pondered the idiom.

"I'm talking about Russian shit, Ludochka - which is a particularly unpleasant kind."

She laughed. "Kaneshna. I know you are."

"I'll have another word with him. Maybe he can come over on Saturday and meet you then."

"O.K., Nikoshka. Oh and who's your young American friend, by the way? He sounds nice."

"A friend of a friend. He's just passing through."

"Will I meet him?"

"Probably not."

"A pity. I liked his voice."

"Saturday then." Nicko put the phone down. Then he dialled Tim's number, but got no reply. "O.K. Miggie, I've finished," he called.

"Do you fancy going out for drink? Miguel asked. "You must know some of the places round here."

"Not tonight. I'm knackered. But you go if you like. There's a place across the road- The Blue Boar- I sometimes drop in there."

A Play Within a Play

The boy looked hesitant.

"What's the matter? Have you got no money?"

"A little. Mark owed me some - my allowance he called it - so I helped myself from the kitchen drawer when I left."

"You mean you nicked it?"

"He owed it to me and anyway it's less than he owed."

"Naughty boy, Miggie" said Nicko with mock severity. "How many would he have given you for doing a thing like that?"

"Fuck Lord Isaacs."

"As you never stop saying." Nicko took his wallet from his pocket and handed him a ten pound note. "Now run along. I want an hour or two to play with my play. And after that when you're back, and I hope not too pissed, we'll have a bite to eat and maybe open a bottle."

Lightly tapping the boy's bottom, he eased him out. Then he sat down and started to sketch a dialogue between Mine Host and the Mistress of the Tabard, as they awaited the arrival of the pilgrims. A potboy- a good part for a small boy in his first play- rushed in to announce the arrival of the cavalcade. The pilgrims followed, bursting upon Mine Host who gave each and all a hearty welcome. Only the Pardoner was missing, but came slinking in behind the others, bearing his sack. It was, of course, important to establish his ambivalence from the start. Chaucer described him as a eunuch - obviously Nicko had to leave that detail out - while his role as a loner needed to be made clear. His recent romp with Miguel crossed Nicko's mind as he conjured with the character and he smiled to himself.

He was so engrossed that he did not hear Miguel come softly back into the flat, until he placed a hand on his shoulder. The Pardoner had made his entry and the joshing was about to begin. Nicko jumped.

"Christ, you gave a fright!"

Miguel leaned over to see what was on his laptop screen.

"Does it make any sense to you?" Nicko asked him.

The boy shrugged and Nicko set about filing what he had just been writing.

"Are you pissed?" he enquired.

"A little. I met a very cool boy."

Nicko frowned. "Not too cool, I hope?"

"He wasn't as cool as you, Nick," Miguel assured him. "Nothing to worry about."

"Well that's a weight off my mind. News time, I think."

He switched on the television and they were confronted by Lord Isaacs.

"You can't get away from him, wherever you go," complained Miguel, thrusting his tongue out at the screen.

His Lordship was being interviewed on Teesside, where he had been discussing the imminent closure of a pharmaceutical plant. In his silky fashion, he was hedging his and the Government's position. Listening to him, Nicko had a suspicion that he was secretly sympathetic to the management's point of view, but with his party being on the Left he was having to adopt an emollient tone towards the union involved. The region's votes were of course crucial, if the Government was to have any hope of winning the forthcoming General Election.

"You have to take your hat off to him," Nicko pointed out. "Butter wouldn't melt in his mouth."

Miguel only made an impatient clucking noise.

But beneath the Minister's emollient tone, Nicko sensed something darker. What it might be he could not guess, but he recalled his gift of a puppy to young Kolya and the manner in which he had pinched the boy's bottom. He watched him now as he smiled ingratiatingly, his mouth opening wide under the ski-jump nose, his lantern jaw thrust forward and the hank of thick dark hair tumbling engagingly across his brow. Occasionally he brushed it aside and pursed his lips as he listened with a show of close attention to the words of his interlocutor.

"He's a real pro. You have to give him that," observed Nicko.

"Fuck him."

Nicko sighed. "If you hate him so much, why did you stay with him for so long?"

"I think I've told you."

"Well he certainly isn't wielding his stick tonight. Mind, watching him now, there are moments when I can see him doing it. And I didn't tell you that he pinched young Kolya's bottom."

"You don't have to. Switch the motherfucker off."

Nicko did as he was bidden. "Did you switch your phone off?"

Miguel nodded. "Sure. We won't be hearing any more from him tonight at any rate," he said.

Nicko went to the drinks cupboard and took out a bottle of Claret, which was swiftly drained and by the time they were squeezed together in Nicko's bed they were both feeling so drowsy, that the previous night's raptures could not be repeated. Nicko had, in any case, to get up in time for work. It didn't do to be late for it two days running.

Miguel meanwhile settled in, keeping his phone firmly switched off. Isaacs had presumably returned from the North by now, but so far nothing had been heard from him.

"Have you ever walked out on him like this before?" Nicko asked Miguel.

"Sometimes, but I usually made some excuse and told him I was going. I don't think he always believed me."

"Can I believe you now?"

"You're not Mark Isaacs."

"And I'm afraid I can open no doors for you." "I don't expect you to."

* * * * * *

Lord Isaacs appeared on television once more at the end of the week, this time addressing a party conference in Liverpool. He appeared to be unchallenged and in full control.

"Probably the most powerful man in the Government," Nicko observed.

"But for how much longer?"

They looked at each other and laughed gleefully.

* * * * * *

In the meantime Nicko had confirmed his appointment with Ludmilla and passed word on to Tim who promised to be there.

"I'm going to be busy this morning," he informed Miguel on Saturday. "Cloak and dagger stuff involving Russians, so you can take yourself off for the day, but make sure Isaacs doesn't find you, that's all. No doubt he's got his spooks out looking for you by now. Are you all right for cash?"

"I think I'll manage," said the boy.

Nicko nodded and looked him squarely in the face. "Be very careful, that's all."

The boy smiled, and hugging Nicko, kissed him on the back of his neck as he left.

Tim arrived punctually, as was his wont, but Ludmilla as was hers turned up nearly half an hour late.

"I suppose you're used to this kind of thing?" Nicko said to Tim as the time dragged on.

"All the time. Sometimes they never show up at all."

"Who are the worst?"

"It's hard to say really. It's between the Russians and the Arabs."

Finally Ludmilla did appear, breathless and apologetic, saying something about her supervisor requesting a piece of work that was overdue.

"How's Oleg?" enquired Nicko.

"I haven't seen him, I've been too busy," she explained. "But he's back from Moscow."

"What? Too busy to see Oleg? You can't mean it surely?"

She did not know if her leg was being pulled or not, so she said nothing, toying with her amber bead necklace for a few seconds, before taking a packet of cigarettes from her bag, which she offered to the others who declined.

"Do you mind if I do?"

"Go ahead," Nicko said.

She lit up, still waiting for one of the others to speak.

"Oh, I nearly forgot. This is Tim."

Tim leaned over and took her hand. "Ochen priatni," he said

"Very good," she replied. "You speak Russian?"

Tim laughed. "Not at all, but I speak to Russians- which is the next best thing."

"And speaking of Russians," interjected Nicko. "We have to get Vik off his hook somehow. Whatever sins his forebears may have committed, they're history by now, Russian history. And one thing I feel pretty sure of: Vik has never been told the story of the Dobrinin twins."

"It's like something out of a folk tale," Tim said.

Ludmilla glanced at him sharply. "It's interesting you should make that comparison."

"I suppose it really did happen?" remarked Nicko. "It sounds almost too gruesome to be true."

"Don't you believe it?" said Ludmilla.

"Only that both Tim and I have both read the same short story somewhere with the same theme. The identical twin of the Dobrinin version, you might even say."

"Very droll," put in Tim.

"But in the story the execution of one twin by the other happens in a German concentration camp," Nicko explained.

Ludmilla gave a shrug. "That doesn't surprise me. It probably happened in any number of places, or things like it. The Germans were sadists- look at all the photographs they took of their war crimes. What's the word for it? War tourism?"

"Well, assuming that the story is true, it still doesn't make Vik guilty of anything," Nicko said.

"The concept of guilt by association can have no place in the modern world," added Tim portentously. "Except perhaps in the Italian South."

"And in Russia too, it might appear," Nicko said. "So," he continued, "if it's got nothing to do with what is alleged to have happened in the camp in Kolyma in Stalin's time, what other reasons might Oleg Dobrinin have for wanting to harm Vik? His attempt to muscle in on his racket in Montenegro? Or could it be an attempt to pass off a fake painting on him? Done in good faith, I have to say."

"There was something more," Ludmilla said.

The others stared at her.

"The oath."

"What kind of oath? You never said anything about an oath," Nick pointed out.

Ludmilla took a long and hard pull at her cigarette and discharged a cloud, which Tim fanned away.

"According to Oleg," she went on, "the twin who shot his brother swore it to him before discharging the bullet into his neck that he would avenge him, should he survive. So he claimed anyway. There was of course a second pistol pressed against his own neck at the same time."

"Can all this really be true?" Tim said. "It sounds more like a gangster movie the more you tell of it," Tim said.

"Oaths are supposed to mean a lot to Russian maffiosi," explained Nicko. "They treat them in a very Masonic sort of way. Loyalty is not something to be questioned."

"But can we be sure that Dobrinin didn't come up with all this much later on - he or someone else connected with him? After all, the man's a gangster who's presumably collected his own share of scalps in his time. If he took off his shirt you'd probably see he's got tattoos as well." Tim shook his head and laughed.

"I've told you what he has said," pointed out Ludmilla, choosing to

275

overlook his description of a man who was her relative. "So where do we go next?" asked Nicko.

Ludmilla looked hard at Tim.

"Why are you looking at me?" he said.

"You're an estate agent, aren't you? Quite an important one, they tell me, with the key to the door."

"Not a bad metaphor in its day, but a little passé by now, I fear."

"Look Tim, it boils down quite simply to this: our oligarch chum is interested in the London property market and he'd like to do business. He probably wouldn't be averse to an arrangement that suited both parties, one of whom might be your good self," said Nicko.

"And one which leaves me under a pile of Russian ordure when it comes unstuck?"

"That won't happen if we do it in the right way," explained Ludmilla.

"If the oath binding Dobrinin to pursue to the death even the grandchild of the man responsible for his great-uncle's murder can be set aside for the sake of a piece of business, what happens to me when it falls through?" Tim objected.

"You're not a Russian," said Ludmilla. "That's the difference, a big one, and besides…"

"…there'll be a nice little sweetener for me? A second home in St Petersburg, maybe? as well as a converted izba in Suzdal? Now I'd rather fancy that!"

"You must decide for yourself about things of that sort, while at the same time making sure that Vitya is safe."

"That's what really matters, Tim," Nicko said. "I don't want to get mawkish, but I'd do everything in my power to make sure of that, not just for Vik's own sake, but for his family's as well."

"Of course, your brother Russian." Tim laughed lightly.

They looked at each other without speaking for a few seconds.

"All right," said Tim at length. "When can you take me to meet your chief, Ludmilla? I suppose I'll have to leave my weapon at the door."

Nicko seized his hand and shook it warmly.

"Can we have some coffee now, Nikoshka?" demanded Ludmilla.

"My apologies," Nicko said. "I forgot." He left the room to repair the omission.

The main business settled, the talk over the coffee shifted to Russian literature. Ludmilla was impressed with the sheer quantity of it that Tim had imbibed, though, of course, in translation. In fact the pair of them seemed to be hitting it off so well that Nicko began to feel left out.

"I'll give Vik a ring," he announced, getting to his feet.

Vera answered, so he explained the situation to her.

"Your friend? He won't be in any danger?" she asked anxiously.

"I doubt it. Tim knows how to look after himself. He's getting on fine with Ludochka by the way. They're talking about books and putting me to shame. I left them deep into Lermontov."

"He still must be very careful." There was a strong hint of reservation in her voice.

"Look Verochka, I'll try to get over tomorrow evening. Vik and I can talk matters over then. About six?"

"Da, Nikoshka."

"It will give me an excuse to escape from Mother. I promised to have lunch with the dragon on Sunday."

"You shouldn't talk about your own mother in that way, Nikoshka! It's very naughty of you!"

"You haven't met her."

"At six you will come and maybe you can help Kolochka with his homework. He has to write an essay describing a sunset."

"I'm sure he can do that perfectly well by himself. And anyway, if I helped him it would be cheating. But now, if you don't mind, I must go back to the symposium on Lermontov. Dobre dan."

He returned to the small sitting room where he found his two visitors still talking hard.

"Settled anything yet?" he enquired breezily.

"There's nothing to settle," replied Tim. "It's so refreshing to have it straight from the horse's mouth, that's all."

* * * * * *

It was almost midday when they decided to go into town for a light lunch, followed by a stroll in Kensington Gardens. Nicko was not concerned about Miguel. He had given him a spare key and already he knew how to make himself at home. Nicko was not going to let his arrival affect the other areas of his life.

The Gardens were breezy and rather chilly, but for Nicko London's green spaces were one of the best things about it. Tim was glad to come along too and to provide a description of the Albert Memorial for Ludmilla, about which he prided himself on being something of an authority. It reciprocated their dissertation on Russian literature and he offered to give her a tour of London's architecture and monuments as well. The idea was swiftly taken up.

"Don't forget it, Tim," she commanded him. "I should like nothing better."

They had a very late lunch at the Pilsudski in South Kensington, over which they lingered, toasting one another extensively, a tipsy Ludmilla, taking her vodka in a mannish fashion and intoning the usual Russian oration about 'drouzba'. Tim seemed unruffled by the prospect of the diplomatic role lying ahead of him, while Nicko brooded on the prospect of Sunday lunch with his mother.

But it could be worse, he tried to reassure himself, just as long as I can keep it to once a month only.

* * * * * *

The next day Nicko took the train to Sunningdale from Waterloo and walked up to his mother's house from the station.

I can see the appeal of living in such a place, he admitted to himself, as he walked up the leafy street.

His mother had just returned from Church. Lunch was keeping warm on a hotplate in the dining room: a small joint of beef, which Nicko hoped would not be overcooked.

"Drinks, Ma?" he asked breezily as he went to the cupboard.

"I think I'm ready for a sherry." G and Ts were for the evening only.

Nicko poured the sherries and joined her in the conservatory that looked out across the lawn. Winter was a good time to sit there: it was warm and they were surrounded by the semi-tropical plants that Mrs Orloff favoured, so one had the sense of being in a quite different climatic zone. As part of the ritual, he congratulated her on the choice and condition of her plants. It was something he could say with a reasonable degree of sincerity. Mrs Orloff was a keen gardener with a pretty good eye, he had to concede that, at least. Nicko occasionally told her that if she hadn't missed her vocation she might have been another Gertrude Jekyll.

"I'm afraid the war put a lid on things of that sort," she would complain, "except for growing vegetables, of course. But if I'd grown up when you did it might have been different."

It annoyed Nicko the way she turned round an intended compliment to take a pot shot at him, implying that he had frittered the opportunities in life that she herself might have taken if only she had had the chance.

Better, he reflected, not to flatter her by comparing her with celebrated gardeners such as Gertrude Jekyll, but simply to express his admiration and to ask a few sensible questions.

This Nicko proceeded to do, in a dutiful, formulaic fashion which probably did not take his mother in.

"Well what about you, Nicko? Still happy teaching little boys?" she said, abruptly bringing the horticultural theme to an end. "There are little girls too, Ma."

She gave a little snort. "They're all mixed up these days. And the pay's bloody awful, isn't it? Aren't you looking for something better?"

However hard he tried to circumnavigate the theme, he invariably got sucked into it in the end.

"I keep my eyes open," he told her.

"You need to do a bit more than that. Show some oomph."

He sighed. "Jobs in the Art Market are not exactly plentiful at the moment, Ma. They don't grow on trees."

"I'm sure if you tried hard enough you'd find something. You must know a few of the right people, surely?"

"As I keep trying to tell you, Ma, it's not a good time, a very bad one as a matter of fact."

"It's never a good time. That excuse doesn't wash with me."

"Really, Ma, this is meant to be a pleasant occasion, isn't it? Can't we talk about something else? Are you thinking of another cruise?"

"How are those Russian friends of yours?" she said, brushing aside his question. "The Communist ones?"

"They're not Communists, Ma. Why do I have to keep telling you that? Anything but, as a matter of fact. Viktor was at school with me."

"Wasn't it his father- or was it his grandfather? who was something big under Stalin?"

But that doesn't make Vik a Communist, Ma. He's what's usually called a New Russian." He sighed. "I thought I'd made that clear by now."

"New or old, they are all tarred with the same brush after what they did in 1917. They need to have their Tsar back again."

"Stalin was a sort of Tsar- a terrible one, like Ivan. But we won't go through all that again, Ma, if you don't mind. I think it's time to eat, don't you?"

They went through to the dining room, Nicko going via the kitchen to collect a bottle of wine from the fridge. He poured his mother a glass and fetched the joint over to the table to carve it.

For a few moments things proceeded in silence, apart from Nicko complimenting his mother on the meat being sufficiently rare.

"Give me some more news, Nicko," she demanded at length.

"What kind of news, Ma?"

"About yourself, you silly boy."

"I think I've told you everything," he replied, making little attempt to keep the exasperation out of his voice.

"When are you bringing her to meet me? That's the news I'm waiting for."

"Who are you talking about, Ma?" For some reason an image of Ludmilla flashed through his mind, followed immediately by one of Miguel.

"Your latest flame," she persisted. "I assume that a young man like you has got a flame and that you're just being coy about her."

Nicko knew perfectly well that she assumed nothing of the kind and had adopted this cumbersome approach as a way of telling him that it was high time he was hitched up and producing a crop of grandchildren. He toyed with the idea of telling her straight to her face what had passed between himself and Miguel. But it was just an idle, mischievous thought. And there was a practical, mercenary element to his caution: Mrs Orloff was well off and hopefully something would come his way one day, instead of all going to her grandchildren and the shelter for stray dogs or whatever else was her particular charitable fad.

"All in good time, Ma," he answered stiffly. "As soon as Miss Right arrives, you'll be the first to hear, never fear."

"If she ever does."

"Oh for God's sake, just drop it, can't you?" he flashed back. I've a bloody good mind to throw the truth right in your face, you witch! he said to himself, but you may have half-guessed it already. That's the reason you can never leave the thing alone!

Silence hung heavily over the repast, until Nicko felt obliged to break the deadlock. But he wasn't going to apologise to her for what he had just said. He was a grown man, after all, not a small boy. There, of course, lay the root of the problem.

"Have you got any ideas for this year's cruise?" he finally came up with.

She mumbled something inaudible, going through her usual ritual of appearing hurt.

"I've heard there are some very good ones going to the Baltic," her son went on.

"Are there really?" she muttered. "I think I'd prefer somewhere warmer."

"There are those marvellous Hanseatic cities," said Nicko, "places like Tallin. And I believe Helsinki is well worth a visit too. And finally you wind up in St Petersburg. One of the great jewels of European civilisation!" God, he thought, am I really saying all this?

"It was a much better place in your great-grandfather's time," Mrs Orloff pointed out in a dull tone of voice. 'Being hurt' was inclined to be a protracted affair.

"Probably it was," said Nicko. "But it's on its way back to being a great city again. There's a huge amount of restoration work going on."

"Is there really?" Silence.

"If you'd like somewhere warmer, Ma, why not try the Adriatic?" suggested her son. "Something, say, that takes you from Istria in the North as far down as Albania. I was pretty impressed with what I saw of Montenegro last summer, in spite of all the recent development. Kotor's a great place.... And there's Split too... which is in Croatia... There's Diocletian's Palace...."

He had not told her about the incident in Cetinje. It would have confirmed her worst suspicions about the Russians who came after the Revolution. It struck Nicko as strange how she clung to such notions so tenaciously three or more generations after that event, especially as she had not a drop of Russian blood in her own veins.

Pudding followed, during which Nicko dropped the topic of cruises and enquired dutifully about his sibling's young family instead. She warmed to it somewhat and he feigned interest in their petty foibles the way he usually did. He was threatened with photographs while they took their coffee.

"Are we having it in the drawing room?" he asked, "or shall I take it through to the conservatory? It might be nicer there. We can admire the plants at the same time. And talking of which, before I go I'd like to have a proper look at the garden, if I may. I know it's the wrong season but...."

"Nicko?"

"Yes, Ma?"

"You're talking too much. The way you did when you were little."

Hadn't Vera and even Ludmilla been telling him something like that - that he was just a little boy?

He stood up to go into the kitchen. "Coffee will be served in the conservatory," he announced stiffly, "and then I must be away!"

"Must you? Am I as boring as all that? You've hardly been here for five minutes." It had felt more like five years.

"I'll look at those photographs before I go," he said, before going to set the percolator. "And take a peek at the garden."

A few minutes later he returned with a tray and, without a word, poured the coffee.

Meanwhile his mother had laid out the photographs of his nephew and niece on the table between them. He duly exclaimed at the advances they appeared to have made since he had last seen pictures of them, expressed opinions on possible family likenesses, and listened valiantly as Mrs Orloff dilated still further on their little ways. She concluded with a eulogy of her daughter's diplomat, husband, David, and the glittering prospects that lay before him, which certainly included an embassy. All of which served to underline her disappointment with the son, sitting before her.

Nicko fingered a nearby Hosta.

"I do love these things," he said.

"Do you really? Or are you just saying it to please me?"

He uttered sharp sigh of frustration. "I simply can't win, can I?"

"I love the Hostas especially," his mother said, ignoring his retort. "And I'm glad that you've noticed them."

Conversation trickled on for another quarter of an hour, each party trying not to say the thing that might provoke a lasting rift.

But finally Nicko made a show of looking at his watch and exclaiming about the time. "Good heavens! Is it as late as that? I really must fly! I'll have to leave the garden 'til another day."

"Off to see your flame, are you?" his mother asked with a large dose of malice.

He ignored it, but at the same time he was not going to provide her with an alternative account of his immediate intentions. His mother did not rise from her chair when he got up and gave her a perfunctory peck on the cheek.

"Don't move," he ordered her. "I'll see myself out. Thank you so much for a lovely lunch."

"Do you really think that? Or are you just trying to say the right thing?" "Really, Ma, you're completely impossible!" He uttered it in what he hoped sounded a jokey tone, despite her peevish response to his platitude.

"When do I see you again?" "I'll give you a ring."

"Don't leave it so long this time."

"I won't," he lied. "'Bye. Don't forget to send my love on to bellissima Italia," he called back from the passage. "And think about that cruise. I strongly recommend the Adriatic."

With a sense of emancipation, Nicko made his way to the station to catch the next train back to Waterloo. On the way down he had bought a Sunday paper and had shed the bulk of it before going to his mother's- he only wanted the main news pages, the book and arts reviews and the television listings- and now he settled into it as he was carried back to London. Opening the centre spread, he was confronted by Lord Isaacs just returned from his recent expedition to the North-East of England. In an uncanny kind of way the man seemed to be following him. A general election could only be a matter of months away and the Government looked to be on its last legs, which put the futures of Lord Isaacs and his friends on the line. The article discussed the possible alternative careers for a man, who, after all, was still only in his mid-fifties. Maybe another posting in Europe - from which he might return to restore the fortunes of the Government at a later time seemed an outside possibility.

But Nicko, as he read the piece, could not help thinking about his Lordship's return to Thurloe Square to find that the Mexican Boy had deserted him, without telling him where he was going. What frantic thoughts might be racing through His Lordship's mind? And in view of the sort of things he had got up to with his young catamite, Lord Isaacs' future might be more problematic than was generally appreciated. And as for Miguel, what did his immediate future hold? Would Isaacs put two and two together perhaps and try to track him down him through Nicko himself? in the hope, maybe, that he might point him in the right direction?

But Nicko's immediate concern was with those other denizens of Thurloe Square and what he might find there.

Alyosha answered the door in the usual manner, having checked the caller through the spy hole first.

"All well Alyosha?" It was becoming the routine opening line to be spoken on his arrival.

The man nodded and Kolya arrived in the hall.

"Mama and Papa at home?"

"In the kitchen." "How's Stenka?" "He's fine."

"Have you finished your homework? Mama told me about your essay, describing a sunset. I did that once and won a prize for it- but I was a couple of years older than you when I wrote it."

The boy nodded. "Lord Isaacs has just been. He left a few minutes ago."

"What did he want?"

"To see how Stenka was getting on. He asked if you were at home."

"Well I'm not. Is that all he wanted?"

The boy shrugged and Vera came out of the kitchen. She put her arms round Nicko's waist and hugged him tight.

"It's so wonderful to see you, Nikoshka!" she declared. "Somehow it always seems such a long time. How was your mother?"

"Don't get me started," he replied. "I've had a bellyful."

"A bellyful?"

"More than enough. But more important, how's Vik?"

"Come and talk to him."

Viktor meanwhile had sidled into the hall where he had observed his wife greeting his friend.

"I hear Isaacs has just been," Nicko said. "I hope he didn't pinch any bottoms this time."

Viktor eyed his son who was hovering at the breakfast room door. "I've heard no complaints."

"Did he say why he was here?"

"He said that he was looking in on the dog- to see how the training was coming on." Viktor grinned knowingly at his friend. "I hope he's not grooming my son," he added softly.

"Miguel's walked out on him and landed on my doorstep."

Viktor frowned. "For God's sake, be careful Nick. I trust the Great Man doesn't know that. He might be dangerous."

"The boy moves on as soon as he's fixed something up. He's talking about going back to the States. But if you think his Lordship is dangerous, just look at what Miguel has got on him. He could sink him once and for all without doing himself any harm. And make a pretty penny out of it at the same time- that goes without saying."

"All the same, Nick, get rid of him as soon as you can." He eyed his friend anxiously.

"Don't worry. I'll keep myself out of the shit." "You must. One of us in it is quite enough."

Nicko went over to the breakfast room and stuck his head round the door. "Where's Stenka?" he asked. "I trust he has earned a star for being a nice clean dog."

"He's hasn't done a poo inside the house for a whole week now," declared Kolya proudly. "He's been a very good dog." He patted the animal, lying on the sofa beside him.

"Lord Isaacs must have been pleased." "He was."

"I'm glad to hear it."

Nicko returned to the boy's parents, where he immediately launched into an account of the conference with Tim and Ludmilla. He omitted nothing, including, of course, an account of the alleged atrocity in the camp in Kolyma - Ludmilla Mikhailovna's relationship to the Dobrinins. He spoke soberly and the others listened without interrupting. Beyond shaking his head and emitting an occasional short sigh, Viktor showed no emotion.

"That's Mother Russia for you," he said when Nicko had concluded. "Eating her own children."

"I've come across the same idea before," Nicko replied. "In a story I read once. It was set in a Nazi concentration camp, where one twin was forced to execute the other. But be that as it may, Tim and Ludochka seem quite happy to hatch something between them that could get you off the oligarch's hook. They were hitting it off pretty well, by the way."

Neither Viktor nor Vera said anything. They appeared to be still digesting the grim tale that had preceded the optimistic forecast.

"Did you know anything at all about that business in the camp?" Nicko felt compelled to ask. "Could it ever have happened?"

Viktor shrugged. "God knows. I never heard of it if it did. But then it's not the sort of thing a family might want to talk about."

Vera leaned across and took his hand.

"Time for a little refreshment, I think," Viktor said, getting to his feet. I think you've earned something after your storytelling, Nick."

285

"Especially after what I had to go through at lunchtime."

Vera frowned. "You're very hard on your mother, Nikoshka."

Viktor placed some smoked salmon and a few small blinys on the table and poured the vodka into three frosted glasses. Then he raised one.

"To bloody fucking Mother Russia!" he declared savagely.

"Must you speak like that?" protested his wife.

"To a safe deliverance and a happy future," supplied Nicko.

"That's better," Vera said.

"You're not drinking, Verochka," complained her husband.

"No I'm not. " She set about positioning the slices of smoked salmon on the blinys and squeezing a little lemon juice over them.

Viktor recharged Nicko's and his own glass.

"Go easy," said his friend. "We have to discuss matters further."

"Savtra," declared Viktor. "Tomorrow. This takes me back... back to the very beginning..."

"You mean when we smashed Uncle Frank's krater?"

"Kaneshna! That was the greatest one of all- at the beginning! And we're not finished yet! No by God! Nasdorovia!" He tossed back the contents of his glass.

"Vitya, please!" his wife pleaded.

"I'll drink just one more time," announced Nicko. "Not only to the successful outcome of their mission, but to Tim and Ludochka's partnership!"

"What are you saying, Nikoshka?" asked Vera,

"I think they like each other - Tim and Ludochka."

"But hasn't Tim already got a girlfriend? That nice girl he brought here?"

Nicko shrugged his shoulders. It seemed a shame if Elspeth should be on the way out, but it was still early days yet. Viktor meanwhile proclaimed a thunderous toast, raised his brimming glass, clashed it with Nicko's and spilled most of its contents onto the table. Vera snatched up the bottle and returned it to the fridge.

"That's enough," she said.

Nicko did not stay long. He would not let Vera cook for him and he realised that with Viktor in his present state there would only be more drinking. Vera rang through to Alyosha in the basement and he ordered a taxi to take him home.

Nicko, meanwhile, went across to the breakfast room where he found Kolya watching television with the dog still beside him on the sofa.

"He's looking great, Kolya," he told him. "You must be feeding him on the right things and if he gets his exercise every day he'll have all a dog needs."

"Most days he gets a run in the garden and we take him to the park a couple of times a week," said the boy.

"Tomorrow we'll be starting on King Henry VIII," Nicko informed him. "You'll like that, A bit like your Ivan Grozny- loads of executions."

"It sounds great."

When the taxi arrived and Alyosha let him out, Nicko suggested that it would do his friend the power of good if he could escape the house by a similar means once in a while. He would be happy to join them on their exeditions and the coming weekend would suit him perfectly. As he left the house Vera followed him onto the steps.

"Thank you, Nikoshka," she said, kissing him tenderly on the bridge of his nose in the way that he liked.

On the way home Nicko's thoughts went back to Miguel and how things had turned out with Lord Isaacs. When he got there, he found the flat empty. Lifting the receiver of his landline telephone he found no messages. He put some baked beans in the microwave and toasted a slice of bread. Then, pouring himself a glass of white wine, he settled down to read the review section of his Sunday paper. A glass of whisky followed with an arts programme on BBC Four. He half-watched it, drowsy with his alcoholic intake, and it was after eleven o'clock when he could make out the sound of a key scratching in the Yale lock on the outside door.

At last, he thought. He felt relieved, because a vague sense of unease about the whereabouts of Miguel had been mounting inside him.

The Mexican Boy finally succeeded in opening the door and came through to Nicko.

"Where the hell have you been?" the latter said sharply. "I was getting worried."

The boy, who was dishevelled, managed to look contrite.

"Were you?" he replied. "I'm sorry about that. I met some nice guys, that's all."

"I'm quite sure you met some nice guys. What would Lord Isaacs have to say about that?"

"Fuck him."

"I expect it would be a case of 'naughty boy, bend over and touch your toes.'"

"Fuck him."

"As you never stop telling me. But he might have a bit of a point, mightn't he? Have you heard anything from him?"

The boy shook his head.

"There are no messages on the phone either and he hasn't got my e-mail address, but I don't suppose that'll stop him if he's desperate. Have you had anything to eat, by the way?"

"Sure. We had pizzas."

"You and the 'nice guys'?"

"Me and the 'nice guys'"

"Just be careful, Miggie- but I expect you know that by now." He felt a stab of jealousy.

"Sure I do. What makes you think I don't?"

"Because you're so young." Patronising old fart, Nicko told himself.

"How was your mother?"

"Bloody awful as usual."

"I would never say a thing like that about my mother."

"Because she isn't mine, that's why. Now piss off and have a shower before you get into bed. You stink."

The boy slunk off, with a cheeky smirk on his face.

For a few moments Nicko enjoyed a sense of relief that he had returned to him safely, but talking to him in the manner he had just done, he could see how the boy's relationship with Lord Isaacs might have taken the form it had. He tried to suppress the thought that in his own case matters could ever move in that particular direction.

When he went through to his bedroom he found Miguel fast asleep and snoring gently. He took his clothes off and climbed in beside him, easing his sleeping companion across the bed to make room for himself. The boy mumbled, without waking, so Nicko kissed him on the forehead - rather as he might have done with Vera. He gazed at him affectionately for a minute before switching off the light.

Miguel stirred occasionally and shifted his position, but did not wake. He snored lightly and muttered from time to time in his sleep in what sounded like Spanish. Once he threw out an arm, which fell across his companion's face. That almost roused him and he muttered what seemed like a sleepy apology. Nicko took the opportunity to lean over to where he could make out his head on the pillow and kissed him- on his lips this time. The boy did not resist, but uttered a brief sigh, languidly accepting the tribute.

Finally Nicko fell asleep himself and it was only when he heard the

Mexican Boy stirring that he glanced at the bedside clock and saw how late it was. He had failed to set the alarm.

"Christ, I'll never get there on time!" he cried, jumping out of bed. "I'm terribly late," he told his companion. "You must get your own breakfast."

Meanwhile he raced into the bathroom, cutting shaving from his ablutions, and within fifteen minutes he was setting off down the stairs.

"Don't run away," he ordered Miguel as he left. "And watch out for Isaacs!"

"Fuck him!" Miguel called back down the stairwell, a little too loudly for comfort.

Nicko arrived ten minutes late for his first class, but as it was not something he made a habit of, no one complained. His employer took a gentlemanly approach to such matters, one which was reciprocated by his staff, who, after all, were working for a pittance, to enjoy the civilised conditions in a school like Bailey's. At the end of the eleven o'clock break time assembly Nicko managed to get hold of Kolya.

"Everything all right at home?" he asked him

"Yes, thank you sir," the lad replied, drawing the line correctly between home and school.

"Today we start on Henry VIII," Nicko reminded him.

"Yes sir. We're all looking forward to your lesson."

Standing in front of him now, with his tousled hair, in his green blazer and grey flannel shorts, it was hard to see Kolya as a child of the Steppe or of the Taiga- the great grandson of Stalin's overlord of the Kolyma gulag - a man capable of murdering his prisoners with nonchalant sadism.

* * * * * *

That evening Nicko rang Tim. He and Ludmilla had not been letting the grass grow under their feet. Dobrinin had consented to meeting Tim in his office at Murton and Bainbridge, accompanied by Ludmilla of course. There was no insistence by the oligarch on the meeting being held on his own turf, apparently. Ludmilla, it appeared, had fixed everything. Though Tim as yet had no clear idea of what the Russian might be looking for, he was making a few shrewd guesses. Where Viktor was concerned, Ludmilla's advice was simple: 'Let the kettle boil first'. Whatever wider settlement was reached, Tim would have to clear it with his own firm, but was reasonably confident that no major conflict of interest should arise.

All of this Tim rattled off to Nicko in an oddly charged voice.

"And how's Ludochka?" Nicko asked him when he paused to draw breath.

There was a rich chuckle and the sound of a heavily-planted kiss on the mouthpiece of Tim's phone.

"Moya devushka!" Tim said, resuming the phone before adding a kiss of his own.

"That hasn't taken you long."

"We're planning a trip to Petersburg at the beginning a summer."

"Already? Can I come too?"

"Ha! Ha! Very droll."

"Well, never mind. But can you still make it on Thursday? That's our evening, in case you might forget."

"I think so. With any luck I should have something positive to report."

"Anyway Tim I'm pleased it's all going so well."

Elspeth's dropped right out of the plot, Nicko reflected, which is sad in its way, because she had genuine literary interests- something which mattered to Tim. But then she was just a bit player, whom he had never got to know himself, sensing a touch of resentment, even, on her part at the way he and Tim had become such fast friends. Meanwhile Tim and Ludmilla coming together promised an unexpected and interesting turn in the plot of the bigger of the two plays….

CHAPTER TWENTY-TWO

More of the Same

With Vik's matter up and running, Nicko returned to the smaller of the two plays and soon lost himself in it. He drafted the entire opening scene in the Tabard Inn with the company, such as it was, gathered around the table: four seated pilgrims, with Mine Host in attendance, a maidservant and a potboy (a possible part for Kolya? Vera would no doubt be pleased to see him perform, however menial his role). He was satisfied at the way his characters were springing to life: the Knight with his priggishness; the Miller's coarseness (a good slapstick creation); the large helping of sauce provided by the Wife of Bath and the creepiness of the Pardoner himself. Each seemed well rounded and Nicko was happy with what he was achieving. After a couple of evenings, he was ready to bring on Tom, Dick and Harry….

Meanwhile Miguel came and went, showing no inclination to move on. Not a word had come from his once lord and master, who popped up again in a news bulletin, discussing the timing of the General Election, due in four or five months' time. He seemed to be perfectly in control, but, reflected Nicko, if only others knew the things that I know about him…

Miguel watched him without saying a word, merely sticking out his tongue at the screen from time to time while the great man talked on in his silkiest tones. He went out each evening, but was back by eleven and Nicko never asked him what he had been up to.

Yet despite the Mexican Boy's appearing to settle in, Nicko felt reluctant to press him on the matter. He knew that the issue would have to be resolved before very long, but for the moment he just let it run.

On the Wednesday they went to bed early and the performance of Miguel's first night of residence in the flat was repeated. Nicko felt so completely in tune with him and realised that ending his stay was not going to be easy. But Thursday came and his regular meeting with Tim.

He had not spoken to him since their last telephone conversation and was eager to find out what he had come up with.

Tim was already in their familiar corner with a glass of whisky waiting at the ready for his friend. He welcomed him with a broad smile and a note of elation in his voice.

Ludmilla was an obvious cause and Nicko could not help drawing a comparison with his own relationship with Miguel.

"So," he said. "Progress on all fronts?"

"I guess so." Tim raised his glass. "Cheers."

"Which are you going to tell me about first?"

"Dobrinin is coming to my office at the beginning of next week. Ludochka is bringing him."

"Well, well, you haven't been letting the grass grow under your feet, have you? And has he got the full picture? Not the Rothko, I mean, but that any arrangement that you and he might come to is contingent on- how do I put this? on him calling off his dogs and leaving Vik alone?"

Tim shrugged his shoulders. "I'm sure he understands that, but as Ludochka says he likes to take his time. How do I say? To clear his throat and keep us all guessing for a little bit longer. But she thinks he's coming round. He knows all about the Rothko scam, needless to say, but implied that financial compensation might be on the cards. It's in her hands right now."

"And next. How are things between the two of you? You don't have to answer that if you don't want to."

"The trip to Petersburg is already booked."

"What do I say? Should I offer you my congratulations?"

"If you want to."

"There's just one other thing and perhaps it isn't for me to raise it. Elspeth."

"What about her?"

"How's she taken it?"

"She hasn't had to. She was already taking herself off. I have had to explain nothing to her. The space was waiting to be filled. It was too easy, really."

"Well that's all pretty tidy, isn't it?"

"Drink up and fetch me another."

Nicko came back with fresh glasses and immediately raised his own. "To poor old Vik," he announced. "I'm really bloody grateful to you Tim, for all you're doing, but I won't rest easy until I know he's high and dry."

"To Vik," declared Tim. "I'll fight for him tooth and nail!" he added grandiloquently, if somewhat satirically.

Ludmilla filled their talk for the remaining time. Despite having sounded a positive note, in Nicko's mind there still lurked a flickering unease from the days in Montenegro and that was before he had heard the horror story of Kolyma. He could not help wondering what price Dobrinin might exact in the long run, even if the prospect of a deal with Tim was his immediate concern. But he didn't want to spoil his friend's newfound pleasure and, anyway, he told himself, who am I, of all people, to judge others in matters of this nature?

At home once more, he updated Vera, urging caution. She had nothing to report herself; no unusual sightings, the school run was going smoothly and also the dog walks in Kensington Gardens. Stenka had even relieved himself at the foot of Peter Pan's statue, which for some reason Nicko did not find particularly funny.

Miguel did not come in until after midnight. His dozy aspect told his host what he had been up to. He was cross with him and the boy stamped off in a sulk to the spare room.

Nicko was upset, reflecting how perfectly things had seemed to go the previous night, while at the same time reproaching himself for feeling the way he did. He needed to shed the boy at the first convenient moment, above all before Isaacs managed to track him down, which he assumed he would try to do.

But nothing came from that quarter, not even the most tentative feeler, and Nicko began to wonder how much Miguel had really meant to the artful politician after all. Yet if half of what the Mexican Boy had said about him was true, he had to be a worried man. The prospect of a big-time sex scandal hitting the Government with a looming General Election was not something to be shrugged off.

When Nicko arrived at Thurloe Square on Saturday afternoon, he met Alyosha and Kolya setting out from the front door with Stenka.

"Do you want to come with us, Uncle Nicko?" said the boy, addressing him in his out-of-school mode.

"Would you like me to?"

"Kaneshna. What do you say, Alyosha?"

The Russian shrugged to say that he was easy either way.

"Let me have a word with your mother first."

"She's with Papa in the kitchen."

Nicko went in and stuck his head round the door.

"I'm joining the expedition to the Gardens," he announced. "We'll talk as soon as I get back."

Viktor was looking a trifle edgy, his friend thought. The strain on him was telling, though the prospect of him being released from his predicament was beginning to look promising. Yet it could still go horribly wrong. This Nicko judged in a glance before setting off to the Gardens.

Back in the street, Alyosha had already loaded the boy and the dog into a taxi and Nicko climbed on board.

It was immediately apparent that that, as on the previous occasion, Alyosha and the driver were friends and had a standing arrangement.

They entered the Gardens by the Albert Memorial- an item earmarked by Nicko for his proposed, but temporarily postponed, children's guide to the art and architecture of London. In the meantime he decided to give Kolya the benefit of his research such as it was. He explained who Queen Victoria and Prince Albert were, managing to bring the Russian royal family into it also, and then told of Albert's untimely death, which had left the Queen distraught. He told him about Albert's interest in Industry and the Arts, and what the sculptures featuring the British Empire round the Memorial's base represented.

The boy listened, interested in what he was being told, but Nicko had already learned enough in his brief teaching career not to overload his pupils. That was plenty for now. It time to advance into the grassy plain and let Stenka run free. Kolya raced ahead, the dog scampering beside him, and released him well away from the path.

Barking furiously, the dog tore across the grass with Kolya in hot pursuit. Alyosha called to him not to get too far ahead and Nicko repeated it. But they lost sight of both boy and dog beyond an avenue of trees, bare though they still were of their leaves. Nicko and the Russian set off swiftly in the same direction. They could hear the faint sound of a dog barking, but as there were others about they couldn't be sure that it was Stenka.

"Kolya!" yelled his godfather.

A boy's voice could be faintly heard calling the dog's name.

"Bloody little fool!" cried Nicko, running in the direction of the sound.

Alyosha set off like a professional sprinter, easily outrunning his companion. Now Nicko could hear nothing, the boy's shout and the dog's barking seemed to have ceased. He was alone on the expanse of grass for Alyosha had vanished behind the line of trees, but he ran on and arrived at what appeared to be a kind of shrubbery where two paths met and there he saw Alyosha casting about, unsure of where to look.

It was the dog's growl that told them both what they needed to know. It came from behind the bushes, away from the path.

"Be a good boy, I'm not going to hurt you."

They could hear a man's voice, quite well-spoken, that could have been addressing either a child or a dog. And rounding a shrubbery they came upon Kolya, Stenka and a stranger who was squatting on his hams and apparently talking to the dog, who was growling magnificently for one so young. Alyosha stepped over to the little group and the man got quickly to his feet.

"A nice-looking animal," he said, nodding to Alyosha and Nicko before setting off along the path.

Immediately Alyosha began to berate Kolya in Russian. The boy looked chastened as the words went home, while the dog licked his hand sympathetically.

"Surely your mother must have told you never to talk to strangers," added Nicko. "They might do something terrible to you!" "Like what?" said the boy sulkily.

"They might try to kill you."

Alyosha repeated it in Russian for good measure.

"He wasn't going to kill me. He wanted to look at Stenka, that's all. He was a nice man who liked dogs." There was a defiant look in the boy's eye.

Nicko shook his head." You've got a lot to learn still, Kolya. You must never talk to strangers like that. Of course they sound nice and say nice things about your dog. That's the way they make friends and when they've done that they might hurt you."

"Hurt me? You said he wanted to kill me just now."

"It comes to the same thing. Believe me, Kolya, there are people like that and they hang around in parks to meet children just like you. You must promise me and Alyosha never to run off like that again."

"I was only following Stenka."

"Promise me Kolya! Or you'll be in trouble!"

The boy mumbled a promise and the party retreated the way it had come.

"I think we might stop off somewhere for a coke and an ice, don't you?" Nicko suggested, in an effort to revive the dampened good spirits. "But just one last thing, Kolya. Never take sweets from a stranger, from anyone you don't know. He probably wants to hurt you and that's the only reason he's being nice."

The boy said nothing, but just looked back at him with a puzzled frown, so Alyosha hastily switched the subject to Chelsea's chances of winning the Premier League which sparked a spirited exchange between them in a mixture of English and Russian. Nicko, who wasn't remotely interested in football, left them to it.

They walked as far as the Serpentine where they found a café open and Nicko stood the party ice-creams while the dog received a chocolate biscuit. Nothing more was said about dog lovers in the Gardens or strangers bearing bags of sweets, but Nicko managed to steer the talk away from football towards History. Apart from anything, he was eager to try out on Kolya some of the themes that he was hoping to develop in his children's guide. He talked about the Tower of London and told him that he was considering taking a school party there one day soon. Inevitably they got round to executions and the boy was hooked for the next half an hour, while Alyosha threw in the occasional very pertinent question about English history, at the same time making some shrewd comparisons with his own country.

The way Kolya seemed to be lapping it all up, a small boy's morbid curiosity notwithstanding, gratified Nicko. For instance, the child seemed to sense the pathos of sixteen year old Lady Jane Grey facing execution.

"When you're old enough you must study History at university," he told him.

"What did you study, Uncle Nicko?"

That drew them into the realm of Art History and talk of future visits to the National Gallery and the British Museum.

"You must learn all about the Greeks and the Romans," Nicko said.

Alyosha looked at his watch. "Time to go home, I guess.

They went back to the Albert Memorial, where they found a taxi that took them back to Thurloe Square.

Vera wanted to know all about the walk and while the boy was still present and munching a sandwich, Nicko gave her an edited account. Alyosha in the meantime had returned to Tsina in the basement.

Viktor came downstairs while they were chatting and, having dispatched his son to the breakfast room to watch television, took the inevitable bottle of vodka out of the fridge. There was the customary impatient sigh from Vera, but she added nothing. He placed the chilled glasses and filled them to their brims.

Nicko gave a full report of what Tim had told him, but warned him not to expect the all clear to sound too soon. A lot hung on the kind of deal that Dobrinin might do with Tim's firm. This needed to be good enough from his point of view to wipe out any residual notions of revenge. The settlement had to be sufficiently watertight to put an end to the cat-and-mouse games once and for all. Dobrinin would emerge marginally richer than ever- and more powerful as far as his foreign holdings were concerned, while Viktor would be free to fly his own kites, providing he kept off the oligarch's turf. Dobrinin, of course, would be fully recompensed for his dud Rothko, a matter that would involve Viktor personally, and Tim, it went without saying, would see a healthy cut too.

That was the way it looked, the best for everyone, and all the actors for the moment at least seemed to be following the script. They talked about Ludmilla's part in it and Nicko described the London estate agent's sudden infatuation with her, which aroused vodka-driven mirth in his host, while Vera looked anxious. Nicko felt that he was being a little unfair to Tim, but it was the usual case of the schoolboy silliness that took over in the company of his old chum.

Vera withdrew from the ribaldry. She looked at Nicko with stern disapproval as she went out, as if he was the one who should have known better and be restraining her husband. Russian husbands might behave the way Vitya was doing now, while English ones, especially of Nicko's class, were expected to do better. But then he was such a child- more like Kolochka really. She went and joined the boy in front of the television.

In spite of his display of irritation, she turned the sound down and asked him about his walk in the Gardens. He responded by recounting what he could remember of Uncle Nicko telling him about Prince Albert and Queen Victoria and about his promise of a visit to the Tower, which inevitably drew him on to the sombre spectacles that had once gone on there.

"Did Stenka enjoy his walk?" she enquired of the dog snoring on the rug.

That led on to the boy telling her about the friendly stranger who liked dogs and what Nicko and Alyosha had said to him. He felt rather bewildered and rather put out by it.

"They were quite right, Kolochka," his mother admonished him.

"Haven't I said the same thing to you, myself?"

"I can't remember," replied the boy. "How can they hurt you? He was just being nice."

"The world is full of cruel people Kolochka, many of whom you would never expect to do the bad things they do."

"What kind of bad things? Apart from killing you, I mean?"

"They might do that - and other things as well, but we won't talk about them just now." She restored the volume to the television. On this occasion the conversation had been carried on in Russian.

The talk in the kitchen meanwhile had declined in its usual fashion into imitations of eccentric schoolmasters and silly Rabelaisian noises. "Will you stay for supper, Nikoshka?" Vera enquired of Nicko as she came back in.

"If that's all right."

"Of course it's all right. By the way, Kolochka told me about the adventure with the stranger in the Gardens."

As she spoke Vera picked up the vodka bottle and, noting that it was empty, put it with the other kitchen waste.

Nicko emerged partially from the cloud that was beginning to envelope him.

"I was going to tell you about that," he said in a rather slurry voice.

"Not now. You're too drunk."

"No you're not, Nick," put in her husband. "Fire away. I'm listening. I like adventure stories."

Nicko, blurred as his thought process was, gave a rudimentary account of the meeting, which did not add anything to what her son had already told her. Vera said that he had done right. It was, after all, the kind of risk children ran all the time in public places and nothing more sinister than that.

"I think it may simply have been a case of a dirty old man in the park," Nicko concluded. "I don't think Oleg Dobrinin had anything to do with it and in any case the guy may have been perfectly innocent, a genuine dog lover. We didn't have time to find out. By the way, Alyosha seems to have got his taxis pretty well worked out."

"That's what we have him for," Vera said. Her husband gave an ostentatious yawn.

"No more for either of you tonight," she told them firmly.

Nicko yawned too and closed his eyes, while Viktor, who had drunk more than his friend, was already leaning on the table with his head resting on his arm.

After they had eaten, Nicko rolled into the bed in the spare room and slept soundly until almost six the next morning. On the table beside him he found a paperback copy of 'Crime and Punishment' in English. He hadn't looked at it since his university days and he flitted though it for a short while, reading the odd paragraph here and there. It was still a gripping read, after so long and, glancing back at the title page, he saw that it was the translation that he had originally read.

Then the door flew open and Kolya in his pyjamas threw himself on the bed. His godfather was irritated by this sudden invasion and pushed the boy away.

"Can't you see I'm reading, Kolya?" he pointed out.

"What are reading?" asked the boy in a mildly rebuffed tone.

"'Crime and Punishment' A book by one of Russia's greatest writers - Dostoyevski. Have you heard of him?"

"I've heard Mama talk about him. Is it written in Russian?"

"The original is, but this a translation, in English. I'm afraid my Russian isn't as good as yours."

"What's it about? Is it an exciting story?"

"In a kind of a way. It's about a man who commits a murder."

"So it's scary?"

"You could say that, but not scary scary."

The boy looked baffled and Nicko felt that his explanation had not been wholly adequate. For the moment he was not in a didactic frame of mind.

"Are your father and mother up yet?" he asked him.

"Not yet. I always wake up before they do."

"So I've noticed."

The boy nestled under the eiderdown.

"Am I allowed to read my book or not?" enquired Nicko.

"I'm not stopping you." The boy closed his eyes and pretended to go to sleep.

"Thank you Kolya. That's very nice of you. One day you'll be able to read in both English and Russian - which is more than I can do."

When he ventured downstairs at eight o'clock he found Vera in her dressing gown. Viktor was still in bed.

"Did you sleep well, Nikoshka?"

"Like a log."

"I hope Kolochka didn't disturb you. He wakes up so early."

"I had a visit at about half past six and he was introduced to the delights of Dostoyevski in an English translation."

"Oh dear." Vera laughed lightly and, coming behind him where he was sitting at the table, put her arms round his neck, and kissed him on the forehead. "How do you like your egg? I should know by now, but I've forgotten."

"If it's boiled, I like it runny."

Vera obliged and did him two pieces of toast as well.

"What time does Vik usually get up?" Nicko asked.

"Usually about nine. Alyosha comes in after the school run during the week and they make arrangements for the day."

"Anything planned for today?"

"A trip somewhere. Have you got any good ideas?"

"I'll have a think," Nicko said. He knew, of course, that he needed to get home to sort out Miguel. The shadow of Lord Isaacs loomed, despite nothing having been heard from him so far. Perhaps he was far too busy planning an election, but he surely must be anxious to know where his catamite had fled to. And anyway Nicko wanted to get back to writing his play. "I didn't tell you, Verochka," he said. "I'm writing a play."

"Are you really, Nikoshka? That's exciting. What kind of a play?"

"One for children to act. Do you know anything about Geoffrey Chaucer?" Vera listened as he explained. Meanwhile her son appeared, still in his pyjamas and placed himself at the table.

"Go upstairs and get dressed at once!" his mother ordered him sternly.

"There could even be a small part for Kolya in it," Nicko told her.

"You mustn't spoil him. He must learn to take his turn like the others," she said.

"Don't be too hard on him. Life can't be all that easy for him at the moment with a dad being chased by the Mafia."

"But he still needs discipline. He could easily be like… like…" she left it in the air.

"May I have a look at the Schwitters?" he asked on a sudden impulse.

"It's in the sitting room. The trouble is we hardly ever use the sitting room. 'Sitting room'- that's the right way to say it in English, isn't it?"

"Perfectly, Verochka. You're doing very well and so is your son. He'll grow up to be the perfect English gentleman - and Russian one too, of course."

She hugged him. "Come and have a look."

Vera had chosen well: a heavy, deeply-recessed frame in a pale shade of green which drew the eye into the picture perfectly, while picking up the tones of the artist's brushstrokes.

"I have a few problems with Modernism generally," Nicko admitted, "but not with Schwitters."

The fragments of newsprint and what looked like wrapping paper to which the artist had added his brushwork reached beyond mere representation. The picture needed no title. It stood for itself, an object in its own right. And yet it was humble, modest and unassuming. All this passed through Nicko's mind as he tried to assemble the words to describe his feelings about it. Abstract art, almost as much as the conceptual kind, sometimes involved unconvincing intellectual acrobatics where sincerity and clear understanding were lost. It was a bit like wine-tasting, Nicko decided.

"You chose well," he told Vera. "It's exactly the right frame for it. It draws you into the picture."

"But into what?"

"Into itself. That's sufficient, isn't it? Into its own space, its own universe."

"It's a beautiful picture, but I can't say I know why."

"Perhaps you shouldn't try to."

"Anyway, Nikoshka, thank you for helping me to find it."

She hugged him and kissed him, firmly on the lips this time. They held it for several seconds, until Vera drew gently away. Nicko was reluctant to let her go. He had never felt that way with any other girl or woman.

"I suppose I'd better look in on Vik - if he's awake," he said.

"Tell him to get out of bed and come downstairs for his breakfast. I'm not carrying it up to him- and nor are you."

Nicko found him sitting up in bed listening to his mobile, occasionally interjecting a few words of Russian into the incoming flow. He signalled to Nicko to sit down, but his friend remained standing.

Finally the conversation was completed.

"A message from Verochka," Nicko told him. "You are to get up at once and go downstairs if you want any breakfast. She's not bringing it up to you and I have had orders that I'm not to do so either."

"Piss off, Nick. Who's side are you meant to be on?"

"Not yours at any rate. Who were you talking to just now?"

"A guy in New York. Why?"

"A bit of an odd time of day to be talking to guys in New York, isn't it?"

"He's an odd kind of a bloke."

"I suppose if he's a friend of yours, he couldn't be anything else, could he?"

"Like you."

"Piss off."

They looked at one another without speaking.

"Quite like old times- last night I mean," Viktor came out with at length. "But I had a bloody peculiar dream afterwards. You were marrying Verochka. I was your best man and Kolochka was a page. It looked like a Russian wedding - at least I think it was."

"Christ."

"But it was fine. We were all very chuffed about it." "It sounds creepy, Vik."

"Why should it? We were all having a great time. If I remember correctly, you kept getting the giggles."

"I hope it doesn't mean anything."

Viktor laughed, while Nicko's thoughts flew back to Novgorod.

"I must push off now," Nicko said at length. "Is there anything I can do?"

"Nothing, old boy, it's just great to see you, that's all. Keep popping in. Alyosha runs all my errands for me."

"And remember Verochka is not bringing you your breakfast in bed."

"Piss off!" Viktor blew him a kiss and closed his eyes.

* * * * * *

Back in Finchley, Nicko found the flat empty. The bed in which Miguel had spent the night had been made up. The kitchen was in good order too: no dirty dishes, no breadcrumbs anywhere. The few belongings that the Mexican Boy had arrived with had gone, Nicko looked around for a message of any kind. He checked his computer and even the telephone, but found nothing. There was an air of finality about the good order that the place had been left in. There nothing hasty about Miguel's departure. It had been methodical and thorough.

But why was there no message? The little sod could have left something, couldn't he? If only to say 'thank you'. But then of course he might be coming back.

It seemed unlikely. And while he was not exactly grief-stricken, Nicko felt a pang of regret. He had enjoyed his nights with the Mexican Boy. He wondered if Lord Isaacs – Mark - somehow he always felt reluctant to use his given name - had tracked down the errant catamite. It was a possibility, though on balance Nicko felt that the boy had struck camp on his own initiative and was keeping a step ahead of his former master. He thought about his resources. Presumably he had a bank account of some kind.

But it was time to get back to his play. Now he set about the play inside the play: the Pardoner's tale itself. It flowed so easily that he felt no need to consult Chaucer's text. Tom, Dick and Harry: they were simple enough to draw- three young roisterers without a care in the world: arrogant, cocksure, callous, especially when it came to baiting the old man sitting on a stile with his back to them, who turned out to be their Nemesis. In the meantime he tells them that what they are now he once was and what he is now they will be… an observation that provokes derisive jeers. It ran as easily as if it was tripping off the Pardoner's own tongue.

Nicko worked right into the evening. The telephone did not ring once. Everything else was forgotten and when he stopped at last, he preened himself on his own powers of concentration.

* * * * * *

It was back to work next day, and he was home in time for the Six o'clock News, where it was the third item that caught his interest, as it was bound to. Lord Isaacs had pulled out of an important meeting with one of the country's leading motor car manufacturers at short notice. There was the predictable grouse from someone in the company, which an Opposition spokesman was exploiting. But there was no clear message from the Minister's own office, except to say that he was incapacitated, though not seriously, and that he was expected to be back at his desk in a day or two's time…

Nicko decided to give Tim a ring. At first there was no reply and he was about to replace the receiver when Tim answered. He sounded brusque, but changed his tone as soon as he realised who it was.

Tim had company, as was plain by the sound of dishes being cleared in the room behind him. Nicko did not enquire.

Anything to report?" he asked him.

"It's fixed for tomorrow- after lunch. At our office."

"No hiccoughs?"

"Nothing so far. Just Ludochka, the Great Man and myself. A smooth run, touch wood."

"I'm doing just that," Nicko said. "By the way, you didn't see the News just now?"

"I'm afraid not."

"Isaacs featured. Apparently he's indisposed. He missed an important trade meeting."

"Does that matter?"

"Not really, except that his boy, Miguel, has just walked out on him. He showed up here before going to earth somewhere, place unknown, unless Isaacs has snatched him back. He's got a mountain of dirt on his Lordship, which could sink him once and for all, not to mention the Government."

"Well, well, the plot is thickening into a positive sludge, isn't it?" "You'll keep me posted about tomorrow's meeting, won't you?" "Of course I will."

"And in the meantime my love, for what that's worth, to Ludochka." Nicko heard his message being passed on to someone in the room. "Laqua noche," he said. "Oh, and how's your Russian coming on?"

"I'm making inroads."

"In time for Petersburg?"

"Kaneshna."

"Even I know how to say that."

Nicko was satisfied the way things were moving, while he was pleased, too, with his own literary performance. He would say no more to Vera until he had heard the result of the conference.

Which he did the following evening. Tim rang through to tell him that it had taken place and that Oleg Dobrinin had been very expansive with lots of talk about 'drouzba'.

"So what has been agreed?" Nicko asked.

"Nothing's finally wrapped up yet," Tim told him, "but it's pointing in the right direction. Each party knows exactly where it stands and no one has got any illusions. It's down to the fine tuning now and working over the small print. My people, of course, will have to clear the property angle and there mustn't be any loopholes. No hostages to fortune. But it seems to be there in principle and with the right outcome for Vik. The

Rothko cock-up doesn't look like being a serious obstacle. In fact Oleg sounded mildly interested in doing something on those lines himself- a sort of sideline or hobby. Vik had better watch out he doesn't get his toes walked on."

"So when will the treaty be signed? I know what Russians can be like."

"Pretty soon. Probably in the next week or two. Ludochka is happy about it, anyway."

"Can I pass it on to Vik and Verochka?"

"Sure. But just ask them to be a little bit patient, that's all. They're Russians, so they should understand."

"Thanks for everything Tim. The Muse has been very indulgent, by the way, and the play's rattling along. Tomorrow evening? The usual?"

"Kaneshna. How could it be otherwise?"

"I'm relieved to hear it." Nicko replaced the receiver.

* * * * * *

When they met in the snuggery the following night, Tim was full of Ludmilla and her literary hopes. Cupid's shaft was soused in a shared enthusiasm for such matters which boded well, Nicko felt, for the days that lay ahead. Elspeth might never have been. He wondered what Tim was earning - it would be no mean sum, considering the firm he was working for, which was at the top of the game. It was a different universe to the one inhabited by an assistant schoolmaster. And if the settlement with Dobrinin proved successful, what kind of a figure might it be then? Ludmilla must, of course, have been very aware of all this and that mercenary consideration struck the only discordant note in an otherwise harmonious run of events,

Nicko steered the talk through the Montenegran royal family- a theme that Ludmilla seemed to be toying with alongside her thesis on the English crime novel- and onto his own play.

"Would Ludochka care to have a look at it?" he enquired. "It would be interesting to have a Russian perspective."

"I'm sure she would," Tim assured him.

Nicko glanced around their little snuggery, which was almost full with the usual mixed crowd. At a table immediately opposite them two men were chatting like themselves, each with a pint of beer in front of him. They talked softly, almost putting their heads together as they spoke, and from time to time cast rapid glances round the bar. Nicko had noticed them coming in behind him when he arrived. Now, when they saw Nicko looking across in their direction, they fell silent and simultaneously raised their glasses to their lips.

That set Nicko's mind running on a fresh track, but one with which he was already starting to get familiar.

"Those two blokes over there," he whispered to Tim. "Don't stare. I wonder if I'm getting paranoid, but I think they're trailing me."

"What gives you that idea? They look like two guys doing the same thing as us."

"There's a sort of deja-vu. I feel I've been there before. You can ask Ludochka about that."

"They don't look Russian to me."

The two men had resumed their conversation, but their voices were too soft to be able to pick up what language they were speaking. They drained their glasses at the same time and one of them stood up.

"Fancy one more?" he said in perfectly plain estuarine English.

"That could be Tony Blair, doing his man-of-the-people act," pointed out Tim.

"They're certainly not Russians. It may sound farfetched, but I think I could hazard a guess." "Lead on McDuff."

"I may be completely wrong of course, but they might be looking for a Mexican lost boy."

"And hoping that you will lead them to him?"

"It's certainly plausible. The same again?"

"Kaneshna. I won't say no."

Nicko went to the bar. As he approached it the man who had been renewing the beers brushed past him. He almost spilled the contents of one the glasses he was carrying gingerly.

"Sorry mate," he said.

"No harm done," replied Nicko.

Both parties settled back once more. Nicko, however, felted tempted to plant a tantalizing clue into his discourse for the others to overhear and then to watch their reaction.

"So Isaacs failed to show up for his meeting in West Bromwich," he said to Tim in a distinct but not too loud voice. "I suppose he was too busy plotting his next political assassination. You didn't catch the News?"

"I'm afraid not," answered Tim. "But why should something so trivial make the Six o'clock News, I wonder? The bugger seems to have a hell of a stranglehold on the Media's attention. Especially the Beeb's - they're always sucking the ordure out of his bumhole. Birds of a feather, maybe."

He spoke distinctly having twigged his friend's game.

"He's as slippery as an eel," Nicko added, more loudly this time.

"A cat that always manages to land on its feet?" suggested Tim. "But you must take your hat off to the guy. He's a survivor. Look at the way he's wormed his way back into the Government after coming unstuck in that passport fiddle. It should have finished him once and for all- but he was only sent to stand in the corner in Brussels for a time and await the call- which of course came."

"How about a stoat? Or a weasel?"

As Nicko had correctly surmised the party opposite had ceased their talk and were sipping their beers thoughtfully, trying to give the impression that they were not eavesdropping.

Then Nicko suddenly raised his glass and looked across at them. "Cheers!" he said. "To our mutual friend, Lord Isaacs of South Shields!"

For a second the two men looked rattled, but quickly recovered. "Lord Isaacs then. But I'm damned if I can see what you want to drink to that bugger for," one of them said. "Pardon the language."

There was a cheery laugh all round, which in Tim's case rose to a guffaw.

Then the other man who had not spoken, raised his glass to the Leader of the Opposition, referring to him as 'our next Prime Minister'. This was followed by another round of manufactured mirth.

"How about Her Majesty?" offered Tim.

They settled for her too, chortled a little about it, until one of the detectives, if that is what they indeed were, glanced at his watch.

"Time to be hitting the road," he announced. "Enjoy yourselves lads!"

Both men got up and left the snuggery.

"Routed," declared Nicko gleefully. "It was pretty plain when they followed me in what they were up to. Someone was hanging about in the street when I left home, but I can't swear that it was either of these two. His Lordship must be passing a few breeze blocks.

"Is he dangerous?"

"It depends on who you are, I suppose. But I'm only guessing. I don't think he's actually murdered anyone yet- but then you never quite know, do you? Some of the company he keeps certainly has."

The street outside was almost deserted, but Nicko looked around to check if they still had company.

"All clear," he said. "Not that it matters."

They walked to the Underground station together where they went their separate ways.

"My love to Ludochka," Nicko called after his friend. "And don't forget to tell her about my play, I'd like her opinion. And of course you'll keep me up to the mark on our oligarch chum."

"Kaneshna," Tim called back. "And take care. We've had enough cloaks and daggers for one night."

CHAPTER TWENTY-THREE

Two Writers at Work

Nothing more was heard from Tim in the next few days and Nicko decided to leave the ball in his court. There was no way he could hasten matters and when he saw the Nikishovs at the weekend, both husband and wife understood.

Viktor had left home a couple of times during the week, each occasion in a taxi, when he had visited a safe pub in the northern part of town with Alyosha. He appeared to be conducting business of some kind with New York, when Nicko arrived and felt free to enquire what it was.

"Who are you talking to?" he demanded to know as he entered the room. The conversation was being conducted at speed in Russian.

Viktor signalled to him to be silent until he had finished, at the same time pointing to an opened bottle of vodka on the writing table beside him. Nicko filled himself a glass and sipped it, as he waited for the verbal torrent to die down. He could pick out snatches here and there, and even noted the dreaded name of 'Rothko' cropping up a number of times.

At last Viktor put the phone down. It seemed that he was wasting no time during his incarceration and there was no doubt that he had considerable business assets to manage. The Nikishovs had never reached the dizzy heights of Dobrinin, but the foundations of their fortune had been carefully laid in Soviet days and the time that had followed. But listening to him now, there seemed to be something frantic about the manner in which Viktor was conducting his affairs. The volubility, the sheer outpouring of words, did not suggest a man in full control. And this harking back to Rothko? Did it mean he was getting shot of the thing once and for all? Or was he hatching fresh schemes? And in fairness to him, Nicko recalled, there was a time when, as far as the international art market was concerned, his friend did indeed seem to have the wind in his sails.

"What about Rothko?" Nicko asked him. "You're surely not planning another sting like the last, are you?"

309

Viktor chuckled. "Piss off. But we didn't do so badly with those Shishkins, did we?"

"Selling into London isn't quite so easy, but I daresay there are a few fish from the Mother Country who might still rise to your bait, though Dobrinin isn't one of them."

"I'm not looking at London. And who says I'm dealing in fakes, anyway?"

"You've got form."

Viktor laughed and reached for the vodka bottle. He recharged his friend's glass and filled one for himself.

"It's a bit warm, I'm afraid. I need to keep a fridge up here."
"Nasdorovia!" Nicko said, draining his glass.

They discussed Tim's meeting with the oligarch and agreed on the need to remain cautious, despite the former's optimistic tone. After all, a man like Dobrinin had not got where he had without keeping lots of tricks up his sleeve and squashing just one more tiresome bug would be no big deal.

But when Nicko described the burgeoning relationship between Tim and Ludmilla, Viktor shook his head.

"Does the guy have a bloody clue what's he's letting himself in for?" he said. "He may be good at selling houses in the best market on the planet, but has he got a fucking clue when it comes to women? Especially a Russian one like Ludochka?"

Nicko felt that he had a fair point, for Tim had indeed sounded a bit like a besotted greenhorn.

"Meanwhile we must let it play itself out," he said. "There's not much else we can do about it, is there? If Tim thinks he's in love and Ludochka that she's landing herself a fat trout, well good luck to them, as long as it lets you off the hook."

"Maybe you're right, but I've never been quite sure that I've been on a hook anyway. That's what makes it so difficult, you never quite know and when you think there's nothing in it at all and that you may be imaging things, then…" He drew a finger across his throat. "That's Russian business for you."

They talked no more about it and went downstairs to see Vera. The breakfast room door was ajar and they peeped round it. The television wasn't on and Kolya was busy writing at the table. Nicko crept up behind him and peered over his shoulder.

"What's this about?" he asked the boy.

"It's my English prep - for the weekend. "

"What are you writing about this time?"

"About taking Stenka for a walk in the Gardens."

"Can I read it - when it's finished?"

The boy did not reply, but went on with his task, while Nicko joined his parents in the kitchen.

"I see your son's hard at work," he told them. "His English seems to be coming on well, by the way. His form teacher says glowing things about him, that he's a natural and so on. He said he's writing about taking Stenka for a walk in the Gardens. I'd be interested to know what he writes about - dog-lovers who leap out of bushes and surprise small boys, for instance?"

"Maybe I should look at it," Vera said.

"I'm sure it'll be all right."

Vera handed him a cup of tea, Russian-style without milk and with a slice of lemon. There was a large bowl of strawberry jam on the table. Each dipped a teaspoon into it to take a mouthful from time to time. Nicko repeated what he had learned of the Dobrinin situation again for Vera's benefit.

"The only thing that nags me slightly," he said, "is the revenge element - for what was alleged to have happened in the Kolyma camp. Is it likely to run? We don't want your son to be burdened with ancestral guilt, do we?"

Viktor shrugged his shoulders. "Hell, Dobrinin's a Russian businessman isn't he? He built his fortune in the nickel wars, east of the Urals- which were a bloody enough business, so is he really going to care very much about what happened to his grandfather- who he didn't even know anyway- back in Stalin's time?"

"Let's hope not."

Nicko was just about to leave when Kolya arrived in the kitchen with the completed essay.

"You want me to read it?" his godfather said. The boy nodded.

Nicko scanned the three pages of text in the exercise book, which was written in a large rounded hand. The sentences were short and to the point. It began with a description of a ride in a taxi with someone he referred to as his uncle, Alyosha and the dog. The Gardens were cold and sunny, and Stenka had a great run on the grass, but he was a young dog who was inclined to be naughty and get too far way. Kolya described chasing him and leaving his companions behind. And when he reached Stenka he found a man giving him a biscuit. The man told him how much he liked dogs and asked this one's name. He said he liked the name 'Stenka' but thought it was a bit funny because it sounded like 'stinker', which means someone who makes a bad smell! That was all he had time to say, because the others caught up and he went away quickly.

"You didn't tell us about the biscuit," pointed out Nicko. "Have you just made it up?"

"No it was true."

"It makes a good story, Kolya, but all the same you have to be very careful of strangers who give your dog biscuits in the Gardens, Nick added.

The boy looked bemused, the way he had done at the time of the incident, so his godfather changed tack and commended him on his style and the accuracy of his grammar and spelling - which indeed were pretty good for one who been such a short time in the country. For instance, Nicko noted that his use of the definite article was perfectly correct- something that Slavic speakers, who did not use it in their own languages, often had difficulty with.

"This looks pretty good, Kolya. Mrs Lambert will be pleased."

"Thank you, sir."

Nicko wasn't quite sure if the boy was taking the micky out of him or not.

"There's no need to call me 'sir' when you're at home. It's only for school where all the other kids have to do it. I keep telling you that."

"No sir," replied the boy with a cheeky grin.

"Remember your manners, Kolochka," his mother admonished him.

"It's time someone took a stick to you," said his father.

"Tell me when you're next taking Stenka for a walk in the Gardens," Nicko said. "I might come with you."

"Yes sir."

Nicko gave the boy's ear a friendly tweak, at the same time as he kissed his mother on the forehead and before mouthing the f-word at his father.

* * * * * *

At home it was back to the play once more, which kept him busy for the rest of the weekend. By Sunday evening it was drafted, awaiting the process of revision. Nicko, who had dabbled in storytelling before, liked this stage of the operation after the heavy lifting had been done. Not that there had been much heavy lifting in this case. It was a short play for children, meant to last probably forty-five minutes in performance at the most.

It seemed so much easier on a laptop: adding and subtracting words; eliminating adjectives and adverbs where possible, while trying to find the nouns and verbs that stood up without their support - the relative ease, indeed, of running revision. And he marvelled how the likes of Dickens and Trollope had achieved the things they had, having to dip a quill pen all the time into an inkwell and scratch away with it... and the sheer volume of their output...Dickens dashing off his material to meet his deadlines, while at the same time editing a magazine and Trollope, assiduously setting about his daily stint before devoting the rest of his working day to the Post Office... Something to mull over with Tim and Ludmilla perhaps. But just thinking of her made him uneasy in the light of what he had learned of her relationship with Oleg Dobrinin and the alleged atrocity in the Kolyma camp. Tim was going to have to tread carefully and Nicko pondered ways of cautioning him.

Meanwhile he heard nothing from Miguel. Nicko presumed he had gone to earth safely somewhere. He had a feeling that the Mexican Boy knew more people than he had let on about. While he might have provided the Government Minister with the gratification that he craved, he probably had not been kept on such a short lead that he could not slip out and enjoy the occasional, albeit fleeting, liaison. Nicko just hoped that he would not slide now into a druggy criminality and, thinking it over, he concluded that the best thing he could do would be to head back across the water.

But the boy had a full magazine to fire off at his former keeper. The temptation to do so must be great, with a likelihood of a big windfall. That Isaacs was rattled was evident to Nicko by the tail he had apparently put on himself in the hope of leading him to the lost catamite. He had little doubt what the two in the pub had been up to, as their reaction to being confronted, albeit obliquely, had made plain: they had been momentarily winded, but were sufficiently professional to swiftly regain their composure. There was little point, though, in losing sleep over

Miguel. He had been a good bedfellow while it lasted, but that was as far as it needed to go.

Tim rang him on Wednesday, soon after he got home. He spoke quietly, deliberately keeping any excitement out of his voice, while declaring himself 'cautiously optimistic'. Dobrinin had not kept him hanging about and there had been no attempt on the oligarch's part to throw his weight around in a high handed show of power. His manner had been almost meek, which reminded Nicko of the air of insignificance, even of dullness, that he had projected at the Thurloe Square party. Indeed, he had left most of the talking to Ludmilla, who had represented his interest in way which Tim confessed he had found a trifle odd, considering his own developing intimacy with the Russian girl, though she had tried to reassure him with the occasional furtive wink.

All this Tim described to Nicko, while making the oligarch's position clear as he understood it. He was eager to gain a foothold in the London property market and was prepared to reach a generous settlement on terms which Tim could take back to his colleagues.

"And what about Vik in all of this? He's part of your equation surely?" interjected Nicko.

"Of course he is. But put it this way, the handling of that was more oblique."

"Which means? Isn't that the main point? To get Vik, and more importantly his family, out of harm's way?"

"That part of the discussion went on largely in Russian, though I was provided with a translation."

"I hope it was an accurate one."

"I think the position is clear. First, Dobrinin is prepared to accept a fair recompense for the dud picture, while assuming that it was a genuine mistake on Vik's part, and he's perfectly happy to put their relationship on a normal working footing, as long as they avoid treading on one another's toes."

"And the Gulag business?"

"He shrugged it off, or at least appeared to. They may have talked it over in Russian, without me understanding, but as he put it to me- in English this time- it was an episode in their country's past, and no more than that- a part of history that was dead and should not be allowed to affect the living. "

All in all Nicko felt satisfied with what had been achieved so far.

"Have you arranged another meeting?" he asked.

"Probably in a couple of weeks' time. Ludochka said that she'd keep me posted."

"And Vik? Presumably the heat's coming off and he's a free man once more?"

"Better to err on the side of caution for another fortnight. You never quite know with all these Russian heavies prowling about town right now. There might be the odd loose cannon among them. It should all be made clear in a couple of weeks."

Nicko had to settle for that and thanked Tim warmly for his efforts, while he kept clear of asking him for any details of the commercial deal that he might be hatching with the oligarch.

He phoned his news through to Viktor, who sounded pleased, and went over to Thurloe Square at the weekend to talk it through further. Nicko was impressed with his old friend's patience. He seemed to be keeping his spirits up and developing a fresh line of business at the same time.

"Oh by the way," Viktor told him. "Kolochka got a star for that essay he wrote about the dog."

"Mary Lambert thinks the world of him. As far as she's concerned the sun shines out of his arse." "As bad as that, is it?"

"Mind, don't tell him I said that. At least, not in those words."

"He mustn't get spoiled and turn into a teacher's pet. A dose of the cane from time to time wouldn't do him any harm, but I don't suppose you are allowed to do that anymore."

"Sadly not. Being allowed to beat the boys used to be compensation for a schoolmaster's lousy pay. But that sort of thing's been left to Mark Isaacs and his kind. No doubt he'd oblige you, if that's what you want. There's a vacancy there, now that his boyfriend's jumped ship."

"And what news of him?"

"Nothing so far. I expect he's lying low, waiting for his moment to pounce."

"Say this for Isaacs, he was bloody good about the dog."

"True," conceded Nicko, "but with the Prince of Darkness it could hardly have been completely innocent, could it?"

"And I'd like to know what he and Oleg Pavlovich really got up together during his time in Brussels."

"That's not hard to guess. As trade minister there he would have had plenty of doors to open for him or at least leave discreetly ajar. But Miguel can really dump him in the shit. Not only him, but the entire Government. Isaacs is the power behind the throne, after all, and if he goes down, the rest go down with him. But then they might be doing it anyway."

They chatted in this vein and sipped vodka, until Vera arrived. She had been shopping with Kolya and Alyosha.

Having listened to Nicko's account of Tim's efforts, she asked him to pass on their heartfelt thanks.

"Mind you," he reminded her. "We're not completely out of the woods yet, but it's looking pretty good. I don't know any of the details, but Oleg and Tim each look like landing a big fish."

"And Ludochka?"

"The joker in the pack- as we say in English. As a member of the Dobrinin clan, there's got to be something for her. She seems to have got her hooks into Tim- for the time being at least. I don't know how long it'll last. We'll just have to let it run, until we're quite sure Vik's in the clear."

Vera shook her head. "That woman could still destroy us all."

"That's a bit dire, isn't it? She's got an agenda of her own - that's pretty obvious - not the same one as her cousin, but of a more cerebral kind. Then I'm only guessing."

"Aren't we all?"

As he was leaving Nicko stuck his head into the breakfast room and spoke to Kolya.

"I hear Mrs Lambert was pleased with your essay," he said. "Yes sir."

"I've already told you not to call me 'sir' at home, Kolya. How many times to I have to keep repeating it?"

"Papa says I need to be caned."

"Did he tell you that? Maybe he's right, but, I'm afraid we don't do that kind of thing in English schools anymore. Perhaps he might do it himself. Anyway, well done on the essay. I'd like to have another look at it sometime. And how's the real star of the story, Stenka, by the way?"

"Alyosha's just taken him out for his pee."

"Good for Alyosha. I don't know where you'd be without him. See you on Monday morning, Kolya." "Yes sir."

As Nicko went into the street, where it was beginning to get dark, he nearly bumped into another pedestrian on the pavement who immediately quickened his pace and walked rapidly up the street.

With his head down, he was carrying a briefcase under his arm, and his hands thrust deep inside his coat pockets, he appeared to have come from the Underground station. Lord Isaacs was clearly in no mood to be waylaid. As they passed, he noticed Nicko and hesitated for a second, as if he wanted to speak to him, but then seemed to think better of it and went straight into his own house. Nicko felt tempted to raise the matter of the private detectives with him - he was still preening himself on the ease with which he had rumbled them, while feeling flattered at the same time that he should have merited such attention. As he saw the Cabinet Minister passing through his front door, he wondered what was dominating his thoughts- high matters of state or the whereabouts of his missing catamite and the blow that he might soon deliver. Or was he hurrying home to take his dog out? After all, he was a dog lover and without Miguel it would be by itself in the house.

Nicko set off in the opposite direction and for some reason he wondered what his mother might make of Mark Isaacs. She would abhor his politics- there could be no doubt about that- but what of the other things he got up to? On the face of it, if they did not simply bewilder her, they would disgust her profoundly and yet… in some shadowy ill-defined way, there seemed to be something that the two of them had in common… At home again, it was back to the drawing board and burnishing 'The Pardoner's Tale'. For two whole hours he sat, enjoying the pleasure of revision- the stage where a work starts to take on its public persona. How would it strike other people? With a play of course it needed to work at two levels: firstly it had to impress the person who was asked to read it and then it had do what it was primarily intended to do, be performed. Nicko felt confident about the latter, but what about the former? If it worked as a piece of action, then surely the first criterion should also be filled, but nevertheless what would Tim think of it? And Ludochka?

It was while he was speculating on these lines, that the telephone rang. It was Miguel.

"Where the hell are you ringing from?" demanded Nicko.

"I'm at the airport. At Heathrow."

"Where are you going? New York?"

"Yup."

"Isaacs has got the wind up. He's even had a couple of guys tailing me."

The Mexican boy cackled gleefully.

"So, what now?"

"I dunno. But you've been good to me, Nick, really good to me. I won't forget it."

"Nor me. It's been great."

"I just wanted to say thanks and if there's ever anything I can do - but Hell, I don't need to give you all that shit!"

"That's O.K., Miggie. You know where to find me. And you've got my e-mail address. Oh and one other thing - does Isaacs know yet that you've left him for good?"

"I've said nothing to him."

"Shouldn't you do that at least? Just to set his mind at rest?"

Miguel laughed again, a trifle unpleasantly, Nicko felt. "Mark Isaacs will hear from me soon enough. But if you like, you can tell him that we've spoken to each other. Anyway, Nick dear, bless you and remember what I've said: I won't forget you! I never shall!"

The sound of a kiss being planted on a phone's mouthpiece reached Nicko before it went dead.

Nicko put the affair of Miguel and Isaacs to the back of his mind. If the Mexican Boy simply melted into the American landscape from whence he had come, the Government Minister would have got off very lightly, considering the story that could be told. And it tickled Nicko that he was himself also privy, in part at least, to the knowledge of the man's degrading proclivities, though he lacked the hard evidence for them that Miguel possessed.

He decided not to pester Tim until he had had time to talk to Dobrinin again, but he was anxious for him to look over his play which he printed out. And Ludochka too. She, no doubt, would appreciate its moral theme- most of all, perhaps, the scene in which Death dragged the three young rioters off in a Dance Macabre. He wondered how her researches into the English crime novel were progressing and if a medieval topic might have been a more fruitful one.

* * * * * *

Two weeks since their last conversation, Nicko got in touch with Tim. They had not spoken to each other in that time.

"I was just about to ring you," Tim told him.

"Something to tell me?"

"I think so, but not in writing yet. On my side the Firm is cautiously, but positively interested and our friend for his part appears willing to open a few doors."

"We'll end up a Russian colony at this rate," said Nicko. "But better that than a bloody caliphate."

Tim laughed. "Too true, but aren't they trying to be a bit more English than the English themselves? Grouse moors, Royal Ascot, and the leading public schools? I forgive them for all of that."

"Like the Orloffs when they first got off the boat?" added Nicko. "Sure. Their hearts are where they ought to be. But you say nothing's written down yet, so where does it leave Vik?"

"It seems to be no problem. Dobrinin, shrugs his shoulders, spreads his hands - a bit like an Italian, if you ask me - and just says 'kaneshna' when I ask for guarantees."

"And Ludochka?"

What was meant to be a languid sigh reached Nicko's ear.

"Still as bad as that, is it?"

"Still as bad as that. But, seriously, Nick, she believes that it can all be packaged neatly and the ghosts properly laid."

"Look Tim, it's about time you brought her over here - to risk my cuisine and to look at my play - we can even take parts. I'd really like your opinion and of course Ludochka's as well. Oh and one other thing, Miguel's flown back to New York. He phoned me from Heathrow on his way out. So we should be seeing no more of Isaacs' chums. Though I confess I found their attention rather flattering."

* * * * * *

The play reading happened a week later in Nicko's flat. Tim arrived with Ludmilla, bearing a statement in both English and Russian- the text of a treaty, formally declaring an end to the hostilities between Viktor Ilyich Nikishov and Oleg Pavlovich Dobrinin.

"Does this really mean anything?" Nicko asked. "Has it any legal basis whatsoever?"

Ludmilla shrugged. "Vitya will understand it," she said. "Oleg has pledged his word to accept its terms and - how do you say it? to call off his dogs.

"Shall I tell Vik straight away?"

"We need to have a signing ceremony," said Tim, "a meeting of the two parties on neutral ground. Nothing can be rushed. A slip in the protocol might have awkward consequences. Some of these guys may still have twitchy trigger fingers."

"And you personally?" Nicko asked him.

"In the bag or very nearly so."

Nicko eyed Ludmilla. "You as well, Ludochka?"

"Kaneshna." She squeezed Tim's hand.

"So everyone's got a present - except me! It's drinks all round then," Nicko declared. "And after that, you should be ready to brave my spaghetti Bolognaise. And afterwards - if you're still feeling up to it - you can review my play. Your opinion is especially necessary, Ludochka."

He rose to pour the drinks.

It was a cheerful meal, washed down with a generous supply of Chianti, and Ludmilla dilated at length on St Petersburg, where she and Tim were shortly bound. Nicko, of course, remembered it from his gap year, assisting Viktor on his launch into business. He recalled it, with a kind of a sentimental Tsarist wistfulness, which Ludmilla listened to indulgently. Finally he served a very decent port with a ripe Camembert, before announcing the first of a series of obligatory toasts.

"To Viktor Ilyich Nikishov and his family!" he declared.

Oleg Dobrinin was drunk to next and then a more coy offering was made to the present company. Finally Tim toasted Nicko, by which time the decanter was empty.

Nicko then brought the coffee into the sitting room and poured brandies for Tim and himself, Ludmilla declining.

"I have to think clearly about your play," she told him. "Will you read it to us? Or do we each take a part?"

"I'm afraid I've only got the one copy, so I'd better read it - if you can bear that," he said.

"Kaneshna," said Tim. "I'd prefer it that way."

"You're using that word too much," Ludmilla admonished him. "I'll have to teach you to speak Russian properly."

"Kaneshna,"

Ludmilla struck him with a cushion.

Nicko then explained the play's source in 'The Canterbury Tales' and found that the Russian girl was already familiar with them, though she had never read any Middle English. She even knew what a pardoner was. He then threw himself into it with gusto, providing his characters with the accents and tone that he felt matched them best. Occasionally he broke off to explain the play's setting more clearly, but mostly he proceeded uninterrupted. Ludmilla nodded and occasionally looked as if she was about to say something, but checked herself until he had finished, when she gave a polite round of applause, which Tim joined in. Nicko, playing the part of impresario, responded with a polite bow.

Ludmilla asked him then about the children who would be performing the play and, while complimenting him on his skillful adaptation, wondered, perhaps, if the theme might be a little too grim for ones of such tender years - a comment Nicko found a trifle odd, considering her predilection for Ripley.

"I was thinking of Death, leading off Tom, Dick and Harry in that dance," she pointed out. "It's quite frightening."

"But kids like to be frightened," said Tim. "I mean there's got to be a witch or a devil or a spook of some kind in it somewhere. Like your famous Russian witch."

"You mean Baba Yaga? What you say is perfectly true," conceded Ludmilla. "It's a fundamental element of a fairy story. And in your case, Nikoshka, you underline the moral of the tale with your dance of Death- a powerful medieval symbol, which I like."

They chatted on in a similar vein, Nicko with the warm feeling that his friends had liked what he had written and were not going through the motions of trying to spare his feelings. In due course the talk reverted to Oleg Dobrinin and the lifting of the threat to Viktor. Tim assured Nicko once more that he would be in touch as soon as the pact was sealed and Ludmilla urged him against giving the Nikishovs full clearance until that was done.

Nicko went to bed a satisfied man - satisfied with the sign of real progress in the matter of his old friend, but more so, perhaps, because of the positive reaction to his play.

CHAPTER TWENTY-FOUR

Peace in Our Time

It was when he was rummaging in the wall-cupboard in the spare room following Miguel's departure that Nicko came across something that had been niggling him. On one of the shelves was a pile of dusty paperbacks which he had forgotten, and among them was one in particular, a collection of short stories with the title of 'The Tulip Garden and Other Stories', which rang a bell. He could not remember how he had come by it, possibly he had picked it up from a basket outside a secondhand bookshop. Certainly the author was no one he had ever heard of before. The title story, he recalled, was a dark tale with a Turkish theme, set in Istanbul, but it was the third one in the collection which really nudged his memory. It was called 'Two Pictures' and a quick glance reminded him what it was about: one twin being forced to execute the other in a Nazi concentration camp, a situation replicated by the event alleged to have taken place in Kolyma….

A few days later Tim called back with the news that Nicko had been waiting for. Viktor was ready to sign up to the deal and a meeting was set with Dobrinin in a restaurant that was mutually acceptable. Nicko rang the Nikishovs and spoke to Vera.

She was cautious. "I hope that no one is playing tricks," she said.

The pact, to which her husband had assented, she agreed, appeared watertight, but she was insistent that Alyosha should accompany her husband to the meeting with Dobrinin and that Tim also be present, a condition that she had already urged.

Nicko stressed these points to Tim, who said that there should be no problem, and that Ludmilla should also be present. Already he had booked a table- in the basement dining room at the Pilsudski where they could talk freely.

"Bloody Russians," mused Tim. "I hope they appreciate all this. Sorry, I shouldn't be saying that to you."

He was intrigued by what Nicko told him of the coincidence between the short story he had just uncovered and the atrocity in Kolyma. It's identical twin, Nicko reminded him.

"I don't know if it takes us any further forward," he mused, "but it certainly gives food for thought."

When Nicko rang back to the Nikishovs, he spoke this time to Viktor who sounded more sanguine than his wife. He effused 'drouzba' and reconciliation, as well as the need to expunge any recollection of wrongs that had occurred in the Stalinist past.

"You will all have to be clean," Nicko reminded him. "Dobrinin, Alyosha, and yourself, of course. Ludochka and Alyosha will need to see to that."

Viktor sounded almost euphoric. Nicko suspected that he had been hitting the vodka and wondered if the oligarch was treating the matter in a similar fashion. Somehow it seemed less likely.

Things moved swiftly from there, the well-oiled wheels turning smoothly.

The meeting was set for the coming Friday, as soon as the oligarch had returned from a short overseas trip. Alyosha and Ludmilla in the meantime got together and settled the security discreetly with the restaurant's manager, who appeared to be taking the matter in his stride. Nicko of course was not going to be present, and, apart from Tim, the chief broker, it was to be an all-Russian party. He asked his friend about Dobrinin's shock troops and was assured that they would be kept clear of the scene itself. Ludmilla had it in hand and Alyosha seemed satisfied.

Peace appeared to be firmly on the agenda. Late on Friday Nicko rang through to Vik to ask him how it had all gone. Vera answered the call.

"How did it go?" he enquired.

"Vitya says it was fine and Oleg wouldn't stop hugging and kissing him." She gave a contemptuous sigh. "Russians."

"So everything's settled? Finally? Once and for all? Peace in our time?" He immediately regretted that particular phrase.

"Da. God willing."

"And nothing was said about the Kolyma affair?"

"It was mentioned only once. But Oleg and Vitya hugged one another and each vowed that there would be no more of it. They all wept and drank too much vodka. I hope Kolochka won't grow up to be like that."

Nicko thought of Kolya in his school blazer and grey flannel shorts and the image hardly matched that particular picture.

"Oh and one other thing," Vera went on. "Oleg Dobrinin's invited us to join him on his yacht this summer. But that might be going a little too far. Apparently Mark Isaacs is expected to be there. They are picking him up in Corfu, where he's got a friend, who has a villa."

"Oleg seems to have arranged things nicely with Tim."

"I know nothing about that, but Tim must be getting something from it."

"Bless you, Verochka. I don't suppose Vik's in a fit state to talk to me right now and anyway I think I trust your account more."

"That's sweet of you, Nikoshka, but you are being a little bit naughty."

"I'll drop by tomorrow, if I may."

"Of course you may. Bless you, Nikoshka!"

* * * * * *

When Nicko arrived in Thurloe Square the next day, he was embraced by Vera and then by her husband, who flourished a piece of paper under his nose.

"Peace in our time?" said Nicko, regretting once more the repetition of that unfortunate phrase.

"I believe so."

"Droozba?"

"That's a bit far. But we've been asked to join him on the yacht."

"With Isaacs?"

"Quite possibly."

"It would be interesting to see how he gets on without his catamite." Nicko thought of Kolya, but didn't say anything.

"Dobrinin was interested to hear about the dog, by the way. He talked about getting one for himself. He fancies a fellow Siberian."

"And Ludochka? She seems to have played a big enough part. It's funny we don't hear anything about the one we should be calling Mrs Dobrinin."

Viktor laughed. "We've talked about that before. But let's go out for a drink, shall we? We needn't take Alyosha this time."

"Are you quite sure it's safe?"

"Kaneshna. I think the man needs a break, don't you?"

"What's going to happen to him now?"

"He stays with us - he and Tsina - as long as they want to. I pay him well enough, don't I?"

"Piss off, Vik, what do I know about that?"

"Don't be late," Vera called after them. "And be careful."

It was like old times with Viktor dilating on his latest schemes. In his recent confinement he had not been idle, but in regular contact with New York and something was on the boil.

"Babko's out of the frame," said Viktor. "There're probably going to be criminal charges, not brought by Dobrinin, but other dissatisfied customers."

"Yet he sounded like the right sort of guy to be knocking off Rothkos - a fellow Ukrainian."

"But don't worry about me, Nick. I've learned my lesson."

"What about the Kandinsky? Fallen through as well?"

Viktor shrugged his shoulders, without replying.

"So no more silly buggers?"

Viktor looked at him thoughtfully. "What do you know about the Constructivists?"

"Not a great deal. They're not really my cup of tea."

"A bird has whispered in my ear - yes?"

"Yes, Vik."

"Whispered in my ear that that a cache of their work has recently come on the market- specimens of their poster art mostly, I believe, stuff from the early Soviet period, before Uncle Joe forced everyone into his Socialist Realist straightjacket. Apparently it belonged to a Jewish collector- according to my informant."

"The heir to Babko?"

"The collector's the interesting part. It'll make you laugh. His name's Isaacs."

"The very same?"

"The stuff's only just come up - in the last week. It kind of fits."

"Isaacs is a common enough Jewish name."

"But interesting all the same, don't you think?"

"He could have offered it straight to Dobrinin, and cut out the middleman. If it is him, that is."

"Perhaps he'll find the kind of sucker who'll pay ten times more for it over there than Dobrinin would. Remember he's burnt his fingers once." Viktor smiled ruefully.

"Keep right out of it, Vik. That's my advice. You were better at handling Shishkins - they were intelligible at least, this modern stuff is much more dangerous."

"What is your English expression? Nothing ventured, nothing gained?"

"Yes Vik. Except that in your case the ventures are liable to blow up in your face! You're a bit like a Soviet coalmine."

"Drink up, you cunt, the night's still young."

"All the same," mused Nick, "the thought of Isaacs flogging off his collection of Soviet art, if he's got one, tickles me. If it is him… and I wouldn't mind some Constructivist posters myself, not that I share any of their politics…"

They descended into their usual relative incoherence, with Viktor launching into his fantasies of the future which now included a bolt hole in the Caribbean. Apparently he had even raised that possibility with his mysterious new contact in New York. Nicko steered the talk- as far as he was able to- home again, to Kolya and the progress he was making at school.

"He's turning out to be everything Verochka wants him to be," he explained. "A perfect English boy. It would be great if he went from Bailey's to his Dad's old school and then to one of our leading universities."

"Like his godfather, you mean?"

Viktor's voice was sleepy and slurred, so Nicko ordered up a taxi to run them home. In spite of the treaty that had been signed with Oleg Dobrinin, he still didn't want to linger for too long in a public place with Viktor in an inebriated state.

Vera met them with a mildly disapproving air as they piled into the house, with her husband gabbling in English and Russian and much too loudly. He was back on the topic of the Caribbean bolt hole. Nicko looked at Vera with a shrug, while Stenka came bounded out of the kitchen to sniff their shoes.

"Have you eaten?" enquired Vera.

"Just a bag of crisps," said Nicko.

She insisted on serving up fried eggs on toast and would not allow Nicko to go home in his present state.

"Don't worry about a toothbrush," she told him. "I have a spare one. And tomorrow is Sunday. You can sleep for as long as you like. You're not going to your mother's, are you?"

"Nyet."

"Well that's fine then. So after lunch you can go with Kolya and Stenka to the Gardens."

In a heavy-handed, drunken fashion, Nicko clicked his heels together and saluted, while Viktor, who was the worse for wear of the two, subjected his wife to a prolonged kiss on the cheek, followed by a mumbled Russian endearment in her ear, before stumbling off to bed.

Vera looked at Nicko and sighed. "I hope it's not going to go on like this."

"He was letting his hair down," he explained. "Demob happy, as they used to say of British soldiers when they were discharged from their military service. It's the first day of the school holidays." In his befuddled way he felt that he had better stop mixing his metaphors.

"What did you talk about?"

"The usual Vik things. New business ideas- he wants to stay in the art market."

"Having been nearly killed there, but I suppose it's safer than houses. We don't want any more of that Montenegran nonsense, do we? Leave that to Oleg Dobrinin. We've got enough money anyway. The only problem is, does Vitya know enough about art?" She squeezed his hand.

He returned the squeeze. "Where's Kolya? Tucked up in bed?"

"Kaneshna."

He drew his chair from his side of the table and joined her on hers, placing an arm round her shoulder. For a fleeting second, Miguel's face flashed before him, but Vera's fair Slavic features swiftly replaced the mestizzo's darker one. Without more ado, he pressed his lips to hers, which sent a tremor rippling down into his loins. They broke, then repeated it, after which Vera drew back.

"We're both being very naughty, Nikoshka, with Vitya upstairs," she said. "But I do love you!"

He mumbled incoherently and tried to kiss her one more time.

She stood up. "It's bedtime, my boy," she told him firmly. "I'll fetch you a pair of Vitya's pyjamas and leave them in the spare bedroom."

Nicko meekly did as he was told. It was enough adventure for one night and he was feeling very sleepy.

In the morning it was Kolya who roused him as usual. He arrived bearing a mug of tea, with the dog bounding after him. Stenka leaped onto the bed and started licking Nicko's face, while the boy made no attempt to draw him off.

"He loves you," he said.

"He's going to spill my tea."

Only then did Kolya drag the dog off the bed.

"Is your Papa up?" asked Nicko.

"Yes. He's got a headache,"

"I'm not surprised."

Alyosha and Tsina were in the kitchen when Nicko went down. Both were in a cheerful mood. Viktor, despite his headache, had been pressing them to stay on because he still had a use for them, he insisted, and they were clearly pleased.

Quite the milord or grand seigneur, thought Nicko, wondering whether his grandfather, the Lord of Kolyma, had ever patronised his underlings in like style.

Anyway it seemed that Alyosha and Tsina were also going to have a place in the new order following the Dobrinin/Nikishov Pact and Nicko felt pleased for them- as Vera clearly was.

She gave Nicko his breakfast and poured him a large mug of black coffee. A few minutes later, Alyosha and Tsina departed and he took himself to the newsagent near the Underground station to buy himself a paper.

Viktor was a little under the weather and despite having just worked his charm on his fellow Russians, not particularly communicative. He said nothing more about the Caribbean bolt hole, which had been filling his mind the previous night, and nothing about Lord Isaacs and the rumoured hoard of Constructivist artwork. But after a leisurely lunch, he declared his intention of joining the party going to the Gardens. Vera decided to come along as well to make it a real family outing.

* * * * * *

It turned into a carefree occasion under a benign sun. The boy chased his dog madly on the grass, joined from time to time by his father and Nicko, while Vera looked on contentedly. She squeezed Nicko's hand when they were left alone together for a moment and they exchanged looks that needed no words.

It was ice-creams in the café by the Serpentine, stood by Nicko, who afterwards tore himself reluctantly away to make the journey back to Finchley.

But as soon as he was there, he was mulling over his play and reading the parts to himself as he thought they should sound. Despite the positive comments he had received from his friends, he knew that he had to distance himself from his own creation and try to look at it critically.

At the same time he sought to picture the individual children who might play the parts and wondered what the medieval tone he had attempted to retain in his text would sound like when delivered in piping treble voices. Yes, he decided that he had been faithful to his source while bearing in mind the circumstances of his rendering of it before a modern, and largely juvenile, audience. Of course it still had to be submitted to Dick Trubshaw for his approval, but he foresaw no difficulty there. Dick liked his staff to come forward with bright ideas and not wait to be prodded. He had little time for a part-time approach to teaching in his school, that reduced it to a way of supplementing a housekeeping budget or paying for a summer holiday. Nicko jotted down a provisional cast list - children mostly between eleven and thirteen, the ceiling age for the school - but there were a few small parts younger ones as well. Kolya, for instance, might be squeezed in as the potboy, delivering tankards and clearing away dirty plates under the eye of the Goodwife. Verochka, no doubt, would enjoy seeing her boy clad in medieval fustian.

In bed he re-read 'Two Pictures', a story by that obscure author, in a cheaply put together paperback with a hint of self-publication about it. The parallel was uncanny, but surely coincidental. After all, it was not difficult to come up with something so exquisitely sadistic if the opportunity presented itself. Nikishov wouldn't have been the first....

* * * * * *

And now things fell quietly into place. As Spring advanced, affairs in Thurloe Square seemed to have settled into a tranquil equilibrium, while Alyosha justified his retention in Viktor's employ by keeping an eye open for any dark clouds that might yet appear on the horizon. Tim and Ludmilla duly went off to St Petersburg for their holiday and came back husband and wife! Nicko had not been warned in advance that it was on the cards, but was not altogether surprised, though he wondered at the same time if it was built to last.

Not a word was heard from Oleg Dobrinin, while Tim expressed himself well satisfied with the agreement that had been reached between his own firm and the oligarch, alongside the treaty signed between the two Russians in the Pilsudski restaurant. Nicko did not press him for more details. Meanwhile a General Election was due to take place in the summer- the last possible time- which the Government was predicted to lose, at the same time placing a question mark over the future of Lord Isaacs of South Shields. Nicko had heard nothing more from Miguel, now supposedly back in New York, whence Viktor had made a couple more business trips, accompanied on one occasion by Alyosha. He was full of projects involving the art market and there was further talk of the cache of Constructivist posters that was alleged to be coming up for sale. Dick Trubshaw, in the meantime, gave Nicko's play the green light and it was slotted in for the last week of the summer term.

A good six weeks before the performance date, Nicko drew up his cast list. He had no shortage of volunteers, quite the reverse in fact. Though he had seen none of the children act before, he already had a fairly good idea of who could do what. One problem was finding enough girls' parts, so he asked Mary Lambert to train up a little dance troupe to represent the idea of Spring - the time when medieval people traditionally set off on pilgrimages, as Chaucer spelled out in his Prologue to 'The Canterbury Tales'. He also thought of getting a boy to recite the poet's own words from the Prologue to proclaim that fact. He even toyed with the idea of giving the part to Kolya, but decided that medieval English verse might be putting a little too much strain on one, who, though making rapid strides with the modern kind, was still a relative newcomer to it. Kolya would serve as a humble potboy, with a bossy eleven year old called Dorothy Bradley playing the Mistress of the Tabard to keep him in line.

Dick approved the cast list and went ahead with sending out the invitations to parents and other friends of the school. The local M.P. was invited, while Nicko even ventured the name of Lord Isaacs and Dick did not demur. The music teacher, Steve Henderson, set about putting a soundtrack together, dipping into his own collection of troubadour songs and at the same time looking for something more disturbing for the Dance Macabre.

Nicko was touched by all the enthusiasm that was being heaped on his project. There appeared to be no sour grapes, as was so often the case when someone took an initiative of this kind, and the parents of the children who were taking part in the rehearsals were only too willing to pick them up later from school than they normally did. One mother, who had worked in the theatre, even offered to take on the wardrobe, while Vera came forward, to offer her sewing skills.

Nicko had never produced a play in his life before, though he had acted in a few during his own schooldays. He needed to feel his way and he thought perhaps of involving Tim and even his wife, to view some of the later rehearsals and suggested ways of sprucing it up. But for the weeks that it took, little else occupied his mind: Viktor's affairs; the looming General Election with its consequences for Lord Isaacs; Oleg Dobrinin… all were eclipsed by Bailey's production of 'The Pardoner's Tale'.

And Kolya too, small though his part was, shared in the excitement. So, while it was a nerve-wracking time- producing a play with young children was like walking a tightrope - it was a happy and fulfilling one too for Nicko.

* * * * * *

Shortly before it was due to come off, the date of the General Election was announced for a day in three weeks' time- a fortnight after the final performance. Lord Isaacs was in charge of his party's campaign strategy- as indeed had been the case ever since his return to Westminster from Brussels.

The decision had been made to perform the play in a large downstairs space - two classrooms that could be joined into one for school concerts. It was to be performed in the round with the audience arranged on three sides of the acting space.

The first performance was to be in front of the school, while the outside guests were invited for the following day, a Saturday. A few prompts and a brief show of stage fright on the part of bossy Dorothy Bradley, of all people, when she had to give the potboy a dressing down for being tardy with the ale, were dismissed as first night hiccups and forgiven. The Primavera ballet devised by Mary Lambert was deemed a minor triumph. She had taken the Dance Macabre in hand as well, and with Steve Henderson's score, the result was suitably scary. Though Tim and Ludmilla had been unable to attend any of the rehearsals, Nicko felt confident about the work's reception on the all-important Saturday. Imogen Trubshaw pronounced herself impressed, a view endorsed by her husband, who usually left judgements of an artistic nature to his wife.

The General Election campaign was in full swing and was already bad news for the Government. But with just one week to go, Lord Isaacs still managed to slip into Bailey's to watch the play. It was hardly his territory politically speaking, but he sounded in good heart and unburdened by any personal or political cares. Indeed, he seemed at home in the company of well-heeled Bailey parents.

"Very decent of you to make the time to come," said Dick. "You must be a very busy man right now."

"All work and no play makes Jack a dull boy," replied the politician airily. "We have to keep some sense of proportion in our lives, don't we?"

Among the other guests he spotted the recently sitting M.P. for the constituency and a dead cert for re-election. He immediately buttonholed him and the two of them withdrew to a corner of the room, where they held a conversation, punctuated by loud chuckles.

Nicko, in the meantime, was in a state of nerves the like of which he had not known before, but steadied himself by instilling confidence into his young actors, who seemed a good deal more relaxed about it than he was. Soon they were kitted out in their fustian and enjoying having their make-up applied by Eleanor Finch, their art teacher.

"All right tonight?" Nicko asked Dorothy who had fluffed her lines at the start of yesterday's performance. "You're going to be fine and be sure to give that idle potboy a good roasting!"

"I'll do my best, sir."

"No mercy, mind."

"None, sir."

After a brief general pep talk, in which the producer told his cast how impressed the headmaster had been with yesterday's performance, and a reminder not to gabble their lines, but above all to enjoy themselves, Nicko took his place in the front row of seats, with his prompter's script on his lap. Tim and Ludmilla sat immediately behind him, while Vera was at his side, having slipped up from the tiring room. Viktor was in New York.

Ludmilla leaned forward. "Good luck," she said.

"You must never say that," her husband corrected her. "You should say break a leg."

She frowned. "What do you mean 'break a leg'?"

"It's a way of wishing you luck without tempting fate," Nicko explained over his shoulder. He observed Isaacs sitting in the back row behind him, still in earnest conversation with the Opposition candidate, a man, moreover, who had a good chance a post in the new Government should his party win the Election.

332

And it all went swimmingly well. The low light in the curtained room conveyed the mood of the play perfectly; Steve Henderson's soundtrack ran like clockwork, while the brief recitation of the poet's own lines and the Primavera ballet performance set it in motion on entirely the right note. The children performed with a confidence that surprised even their producer. Dorothy Bradley as the Goodwife was as good as her word and smartly cuffed the potboy when he tipped the contents of a tankard down the Miller's back. Kolya winced, but took it in good part. Nicko glanced sideways at Vera, who smiled and nodded her approval at her son's chastisement.

And the creepy Pardoner, brushing off the jibes of his fellow pilgrims and, trying to flog his wares, duly launched into the tale of the three young rioters, Tom, Dick and Harry: their first unknowing encounter with Death, sitting on a stile with his back to them, then coming across the hoard of gold… and their outburst of glee… the meeting of Harry with the sinister apothecary who sells him the poison, with which he spikes the wine he has gone to buy while the other two guard the heap of gold and plot to knife him on his return, so that they can share the spoils between two instead of three…the murder of Harry and the death throes of the others when they drink the spiked wine…then the arrival of Death to lead his carrion off in a dance…

As he drew them away and the fearsome throbbing rhythm of the Dance Macabre died away, there was a round of applause and a shout of 'bravo!' from Ludmilla who then leaned forward and patted the author/producer on his back.

Despite his considerable narrative power, the wretched Pardoner suffers further putdowns from his fellow pilgrims- except for the Miller who has slumped face down onto the table in a drunken stupor, and is snoring loudly. The actor who spoke the prologue finally steps forward to end proceedings before the lights dim….

Vera turned and kissed Nicko on the cheek, while the cast lined up to take its bow. Nicko, glowing with triumph, was shunted forward to join the company. From where he stood, he could see Mark Isaacs clapping loudly and calling for an encore. Then Dick Trubshaw stepped forward and made a brief, jokey, but warm speech of thanks.

"Well done Kolya," Nicko whispered to the youngster next to him. "Your Papa would be very proud of you. I know you mother is."

The boy looked up at him and grinned. "Thank you, sir."

As the cast started to mill about with their proud kinsfolk, Nicko found Mark Isaacs beside him, gripping his hand. There was even a tear in the politician's eye and a catch in his throat.

"That was utterly… utterly… exquisite!" he exclaimed. "Utterly moving!" He hugged Nicko warmly, while an image flickered through the latter's mind at the same time of Miguel, bending down meekly to be chastised by the stern Cabinet Minister…

"I really don't know how you do it! …I really don't!" Isaacs effused. "It makes me think what a waste of time my life in politics has been!" He turned to Kolya who was standing beside his godfather. "My word, you did well, Kolya," he said. "You didn't have a great deal to say, but you did it beautifully!" He stroked the boy's hair. "And that costume suits you perfectly."

"Thank you, sir."

The politician chuckled and stroked the boy's hair a second time.

As he gushed about the play, Nicko felt that he was trying to tell him something more. It was curious that at such a critical moment in a General Election campaign, the Government's chief strategist felt able to slip off to watch a school play in a place so distant from his own political turf. But then it crossed Nicko's mind that it was in just such a place that he probably felt most at home. Lord Isaacs of South Shields bows out of politics following his party's defeat to begin life afresh… as a schoolmaster….

Nicko left him in the company of Dick Trubshaw, while he did the rounds of the parents and basked in their appreciation for what he had got their children to achieve. The praise rained down and Vera came and joined him, putting her arm round his waist, while drawing her son close on her other side.

"This is wonderful, Nikoshka," she said in a low voice. "Just what I dreamed of for Kolochka! You really belong to us now!"

Nicko gave her hand a big squeeze and kissed her cheek. "It's a pity Vik wasn't here to see it," he said. "But next time we'll give Kolya a bigger part and he can come and watch that."

Vera made one of her cynical snorts, before peeling off to have a word with Tim and Ludmilla.

Refreshments were being laid on in what had been just been a theatre and Nicko glanced round to see where Mark Isaacs had got to. The Parliamentary candidate was still present, busy working the room - at ease among his own - whilst the Government Minister was nowhere to be seen.

CHAPTER TWENTY-FIVE

The Balloon Bursts …

It was on the Sunday before polling day when the news broke that would drive the final nail into the Government's coffin.

The paper carrying the item on its front page was not his normal Sunday diet, but it caught Nicko's eye on the newsagent's rack and, glancing at it, he was unsurprised by what he saw. He could not resist pointing it out to the newsagent.

"I could see this coming," he declared portentously. "I've known something about it for several weeks now and was just waiting for it to break!"

The man tried to sound only very mildly impressed. "These politicians," he remarked. "They're all the same, aren't they?"

As he looked at the picture of Mark Isaacs and read the first lines of the report, Nicko flattered himself with a sense of personal importance, for being privy to the facts of a national scandal before it broke. He might even add his own halfpennyworth, if he felt so inclined, and would no doubt make a good deal more than that out of it, but instantly he rejected the thought. Cashing in on another man's misfortune, however much he had brought it upon himself, was something he found hard to do.

The feature filled the entire front page and a double spread in the middle of the paper as well. There were a number of photographs of Isaacs, and these could only have had one source: the Mexican Boy had spilled the beans at last, with an all-too-explicit account of the man's proclivities. It was terrific stuff. The paper seemed quite sure of its ground and contained no rebuttal by Isaacs or anyone else on his behalf. Miguel had gone to town, pulling out all the stops. The feature in the central pages provided a detailed description of the kind of chastisement that had been metered out by the Government Minister, including a mock-up reconstruction of a traditional school beating, with the culprit spread over the arm of a chair and a mortar-boarded, gowned figure lining up a cane on his backside.

Naturally Nicko wondered how much Miguel was being paid for it.

The paper would be making a mint for itself, needless to say. After all, he had bought a copy of it himself, something he would never normally have done. As soon as he got home he rang Tim.

"I don't suppose you've seen this morning's 'Sunday Echo'?" he asked his friend.

Tim, who sounded sleepy despite the relatively late hour, assured him he hadn't and it wasn't his kind of a paper anyway.

"I should go out and get a copy before it's sold out, if I were you. It's right across the front page and the middle ones as well."

Nicko could hear Tim whispering to someone beside him and the faint rustling of sheets. When he spoke to him again, Tim sounded more wide awake.

"So the balloon has burst and Isaacs is hurtling to his doom?"

"It looks like it."

"Miguel's spilled the beans then?"

"Mexican ones." As he uttered it Nicko realised it was a pathetic joke. "I could give you the gory details, but you'll probably prefer to read them for yourself. They're pretty explicit. And anyway, it should be on the Twenty-Four Hour News by now, as well as coming up in the political chat shows."

"Well that puts the Election in the bag, doesn't it?"

"It was pretty well in there already. But I'd like to know what's next for Isaacs. I can't help feeling a bit sorry for him."

"Piss off, Nick, Nick, you're loving it."

"Yes, I suppose I am. But Christ, what a thing to have to live with."

"He was walking a tightrope all the time and must have considered the possibility of a fall, surely?" "True, but all the same…"

"How about coming over here for a spot of lunch? Ludochka's been preparing one of her Russian stews and her salads are blissful."

"If that's O.K.? About oneish?"

The Twenty-Four Hour News was the next thing, which might include a statement from the Minister himself or a Government spokesman…

A story like this one, breaking just days before a General Election, was bound to top the bill- despite the disposition of the main broadcasting channels to side with Isaacs and his Leftist politics. And it was there: his Lordship being glimpsed fleetingly as he was driven off at speed, while a junior party spokesman made a game attempt to put the matter on hold.

But the embarrassment was complete and even the opposition parties refrained from outright crowing, which somehow seemed cruelly indecent, since the thing spoke loudly enough for itself. The studio commentators repeated what their commonsense had already told them: that the Election was lost for the Government and that this was the defining moment, the visible manifestation of its death throes, that last nail being driven into the coffin lid. It went on and on. Clusters of reporters, TV crews and press photographers were seen packing the pavement outside the house in Thurloe Square, which was protected by a strong police unit. Nicko felt tempted to give Vera a ring to get her reaction, but decided to leave it 'til later. The Prime Minister was glimpsed in his own constituency, but was too busy to comment. He knew anyway that the writing was on the wall for him and his government, but like a cornered bull, he was putting his head down to charge and to receive the final death thrust. When challenged about Isaacs, he tossed a remark over his shoulder as he walked briskly into his constituency office, that there were bigger issues to worry about, and that it was probably got up by a rattled Opposition anyway. Then the door slammed shut behind him.

But where was it going to leave Mark Isaacs and his relationship with Oleg Dobrinin? wondered Nicko. And how much more manure had Miguel still to unload? Only the photograph of Isaacs together with the Mexican Boy - which had already been published in the Echo - appeared on the screen. It would be surprising if there was not fresh ordure moving down the pipeline.

Meanwhile the media was gorging on what it already had. Nicko having enjoyed Ludmilla's stew and salad - Tim was right - her salads were terrific - they sat and watched the news together. By four o'clock still no word had been heard from Isaacs himself, or even of his whereabouts. The media crush in Thurloe Square was getting bigger by the hour, while the only Government statement came from a junior spokeswoman, who reiterated the Prime Minister's passing remark that it was probably got up by 'a rattled Opposition'- that phrase had stuck- though her party

'liked to think' that its leader was playing no direct part in it, but all the same it just went to show 'the depths of his naivety' and his 'unsuitability' when it came to handling serious 'affairs of state'…. the Sunday Echo was notorious for its political bias and 'all-too-ready to play its part in discrediting a senior member of the Government, especially this one, so close to a general election….'

The Twenty-four Hour News had tagged onto its late evening bulletin a feature about the gay scene in its various manifestations - in particular the 'naughty schoolboy' theme. A leading psychiatrist was produced to offer his opinions about the nature of such fixations and how they might arise. Mark Isaac's name was not mentioned, of course, but those of other bygone personalities were. The topic - so endlessly titillating - seemed to have displaced the election's other issues. After all, this was what the voters liked best, Nicko could not help thinking.

He left off calling Vera until the morning and rang her shortly before going to work, but it was Alyosha who answered the phone.

Mother and son were both at home, he explained, and he was about to set off to school with the boy. It would mean braving the throng on the pavement outside. As Viktor was still away, he fetched Vera and put her on.

She confirmed what the television had already told him about the state of affairs in the square and she did not seem particularly fazed by Miguel's revelations. Indeed she even teased Nicko gently about the so-called 'English vice'.

"It's Vik who wants his son to be beaten at school," he reminded her, "not me. But we don't do it anymore. You have to go to Singapore if it's what you want. Of course we don't know what happened to Mark Isaacs when he was a child, do we? No doubt someone will tell us one day."

"We mustn't let Kolya find out too much," Vera said. "But I expect he'll be asked questions at school."

"And most of the others will know something about it anyway," pointed out Nicko. "They're metropolitan kids, after all. So where's Vik off to this time?"

"He's in Moscow."

"Back in an old hunting ground. Doing what?"

"Selling pictures - or least I think he is."

"Real ones or fakes?"

"I've got no idea. I've stopped thinking about it."

"I suppose he knows what he's up to."

Vera laughed. "I'm still thinking about your play and so is Kolochka," she went on. "You must make him do it again and give him a bigger part next time. When are you coming over?"

"I must do penance in Sunningdale on Sunday. But if I can escape soon enough, I might be with you in the evening. I hope the police will allow me into the square."

"Hopefully it will have died down by then."

"I fear not. These things can last for months. We enjoy them too much."

"You're enjoying this one, aren't you Nikoshka? You're very naughty."

"Sunday then."

"Da."

They kissed their respective mouthpieces.

* * * * * *

The Government's election strategy appeared to be in tatters. The cat was out of the bag and it was too late in the day to slap down an injunction. Isaacs himself had disappeared from the television screens, but dominated the news channels. He had been sighted once, arriving in Thurloe Square in the back of a police car, and being propelled through his front door by four hefty constables in HIV jackets. When he had made his escape was a mystery, probably through the back of the house under the cover of darkness, which was his natural element. The Opposition was subdued even; not want to look as if it was milking the issue- or so it appeared- while nobody seemed interested in serious political questions anymore. The world, meanwhile, was holding its breath, waiting for further revelations, hopefully before any injunctions could be laid, and indeed the attitude of the media in general was one of publish and be damned. It was fascinating, Nicko felt, how Mark Isaacs had become embedded in the public imagination, like few other politicians. And yet amid all the sniggers, there was a hint of pity for the man. No one seemed very surprised by the nature of the revelations; they were entertained rather than outraged. The coming Sunday was eagerly awaited, while the mysterious catamite had not yet been run to earth. One thing was clear: the Echo was confident of the accuracy of what it was being told.

Nicko's Saturday morning was taken up with a school trip to the National Gallery. Once the play was over, his interest had reverted to his children's guide to London's treasures. It went well. He had deliberately selected pictures of a classical nature, ones that told a story or ones that revealed the English countryside as it used to be, and the children bombarded him with questions. It went so well that it strengthened his resolve to push ahead with the book. In his mind's eye he already could see it on the shelves of the Gallery bookshop.

On Sunday there were the papers, including 'The Echo', to be read. The other papers had caught up with the story and were building on the previous week's speculations, while the next installment of Miguel's revelations provided further material, but did not break fresh ground with additional twists. A description of a schoolroom set up on the top floor of the house in Thurloe Square amplified the caning theme of the previous week. The victim had been kitted out as a schoolboy for these sessions and the master had apparently been concerned about his personal neatness, with matters such as the state of his fingernails…

There was naturally speculation about what was yet to come and the suggestion that the whole thing might even be a hoax. The Echo, anticipating the latter speculation by its rivals, promised, that when the moment was ripe, it would draw back the curtain to reveal the identity of their informant. Then let Lord Isaacs pile on his injunctions and try to deny it.

But in fairness to the peer, he had so far attempted nothing of the kind. He had maintained a total silence and had only been glimpsed on that single occasion. His work for re-electing the Government was, of course, at a standstill, and one paper even hinted that he might be dead.

Nicko dragged himself reluctantly down to Sunningdale, taking several of the papers with him. He wondered what his mother would be making of it. After all, she could hardly have missed it and he had told her of his acquaintance with the man through his Russian friends. So he was hardly surprised when she launched into the topic before he was even through the door.

"Some pretty unsavoury sort of company you've been keeping, Nicholas," she said.

Nicko was not sure whether this was a genuine admonishment or a ponderous attempt at humour. His mother's wit was not exactly rapier-like. He put up his hands in a gesture of surrender. "Not guilty, Ma. I've been party to none of the shenanigans, I can assure you of that. I'm innocent, as pure as driven snow."

It was a good thing, he realised, that he had never mentioned Miguel to her, sensing as he did her suspicions about his own proclivities.

Mrs Orloff inevitably saw the matter in its political light, as reinforcing her profound suspicions of any party that described itself as left wing.

"Morality simply doesn't exist for them," she declared. "Anything goes, as long as it isn't normal, decent family life."

Nicko had a slight problem when she came out with statements of that kind. Of conservative inclination himself, he believed in traditional things like the nuclear family, while still enjoying the liberating air of Bohemia- or the company, at least, of some of its denizens. Such people were better not in government, it went without saying, and he was cheering on the Opposition in the forthcoming election, but nevertheless he took a certain pleasure in the radical chic of the likes of Lord Isaacs.

Anyway for the duration of Sunday lunch, he left his mother to make the running as she usually did, while tossing in the occasional token show of interest in what she had to tell him about his siblings' affairs.

Mrs Orloff engaged in her usual insinuations that her son was not doing himself justice by footling about in a preparatory school, which seemed such a waste of all the money that had been poured into his education. He told her about his play and how well it had been received, but she showed scant interest, making only a dismissive reference to a nativity play that she had once been forced to take part in as a child. He decided not to mention his proposed guide book to the artistic heritage of London.

Instead he emphasised what he called 'the love of the subject' as a reason for teaching the young, something that transcended mere moneymaking - the satisfaction in handing on to others the things that you yourself love… how much he deplored the jargonised, dumbed-down, social engineering that passed for education in so many schools today and the ignorant, politically-motivated teachers who were its appointed custodians… and how it riled him to hear schoolchildren referred to as 'students' instead of 'pupils'…

But the idea of loving your subject- and communicating that love for its own sake- was something that Mrs Orloff in her snobbish obtuseness refused to grasp.

"But when are you going to start making a bit of money?" was her riposte. "It's all very well talking in this high-minded way, but in the end you have got to make it pay - especially if you're starting a family."

His mother had arrived at the place that she always did and Nicko made no attempt to argue with her, but brought the conversation back to the General Election, which sufficed until it was time to make his escape, when the closing ritual of being told that his visits to Sunningdale were too infrequent took place. She was shortly to embark on a cruise - on the lines of one he had suggested to her earlier in the year - so, as he departed, he complimented her on her choice and added a feeble joke about her finding a dream partner, which brought down upon himself the retort that he should have anticipated.

"It's about time you found yourself a partner, young man, dream or otherwise."

Nicko merely offered up a sigh, kissed the unrelenting brow and made his escape with a chirpy 'bon voyage!'

There was still a media scrummage on the pavement in Thurloe Square, but he wove a path through it, managing, even, to expend a morsel of sympathy on the folk who had to earn their keep in such a demeaning fashion. Tugging at other people's coat tails, paparazzi-style, was not Nicko's way and he was usually disdainful of the people who made their living by it.

Alyosha let him in. He and Kolya had been back from the Gardens for about half an hour. They had taken a taxi home and had been mobbed by the horde in the square, hoping to find a missing Government minister on board. Alas, it only contained three Russians, one of whom was a dog.

Vera was fed up with it. "Why can't Lord Isaacs appear and end it?" she complained. "Then he can run away and hide."

Nicko said that it was not as simple as that. "Somebody must know where he is. Maybe Oleg Dobrinin does. And how's Vik?"

"He phoned last night. He said things have gone well for him."

"Really?"

"You don't sound as if you believe it."

"Dear old Vik. You need to have it in writing."

Vera uttered her usual weary sigh. "I despair."

"You must never do that, Verochka. Promise me you won't."

She stroked his cheek. "Dear, Nikoshka," she purred.

Her son meanwhile had appeared and caught her in the act.

"Have you washed your hands yet?" she asked him sharply.

"Yes, Mama."

"Show me then."

The boy obediently presented her with his hands. His glance passed from her to Nicko as he did so.

"All well, Kolya?" asked Nicko in a bright voice.

"Yes thank you, sir."

"How many times do I have to keep telling you not to call me that when you're at home?"

"Sorry sir, I forgot - I mean Uncle Nicko." A grin crossed the boy's face.

"That's more like it."

"You can go and watch the television now - if you want to," his mother told him.

"I'll go and let you and Uncle Nicko have your chat," the boy said.

"Cheeky boy," said Vera as soon as he was gone.

"He's no fool. How could a son of yours - and Vik too- be a fool?"

"He's a cheeky boy. I hope he isn't like that at school."

"Not a bit of it. His manners are an example to the others."

"I don't believe that, Nikoshka."

"Ask the Trubshaws and Mary Lambert. There's a parents' meeting coming up, by the way. If you don't believe me, you can ask them then."

After several minutes their hands reached out to each other by their usual unspoken agreement across the table. Vera's voice fell away to a soft purr and Nicko's also grew more tender, although the substance of their talk did not change. It was mostly about plans for the future - Nicko's in particular: the projected guidebook and his hopes of writing another play to follow up his recent success.

Vera listened to him and urged him to push ahead with both schemes.

"My mother tells me that I should be earning a lot more money than I am, and as long as I'm not, I'm wasting my life."

Vera shook her head and did not speak.

"Lunch was ghastly as usual," Nicko went on. "I can see the way it's going to go and it always does. But there were no surprises, so I didn't get worked up."

"Poor Nikoshka. It's so sad to hear you talking like that about your own mother." She squeezed his hand, while there was a note of reproof in her voice.

"I try not to quarrel with her," he went on, "but it's the repeated insinuations that rile me most. I can see them coming and hold my tongue. But it isn't easy, I can tell you."

He fell silent and Vera stroked his cheek, before getting up to prepare Kolya's supper.

"I think your mother might like Vitya - if they had a chance to meet," Vera said. "He makes a lot of money, after all."

343

"I'm afraid I have to differ. She's as English as they come, but her husband, as you know, was descended from a White Russian, while Vik's family were Reds and big ones at that. In spite of his English public school education, I don't think she can get her mind round that. He's tarred with the Bolshevik brush, the murder of the Tsar and his family and all the things that followed on from it."

"But that's all history now, terrible history yes, but it's gone! And Vitya knows how to make money." She waved her hand to indicate the splendour of their surroundings. She leaned over him again and squeezed his shoulders. "Poor Nikoshka! You're still so young and your mother is so impatient!"

"Mine's worse than most. I'm sure yours was never like her."

"But being married with a young child has its problems too, Nikoshka, even if your husband does make lots of money. And, as you can see for yourself, being married to Vitya isn't easy- especially when he has made so many enemies. You know what we Russians are like, Nikoshka. It isn't easy."

"But he's safe now, isn't he? He and Dobrinin have signed their treaty. You're all safe now."

"But does that change anything? We Russians don't seem to change, whoever's in charge of our country! I want it to be different for Kolochka!"

"He's doing his best, Verochka, turning into what you want him to be- an English schoolboy."

Vera sighed. "He was so good in your play, Nikoshka, even though he just had a small part to play".

"That's only the beginning," Nicko said.

"I wonder what Vitya would have thought if he'd been here? Did he like that kind of thing when he was at school?"

"I don't think he was interested."

"I don't suppose he was. Art is something you buy and sell. That's your New Russian for you."

"Don't be too hard on them. There are plenty of English people too who're like that. We have our share of philistines."

"I hope Kolochka won't grow up to be a philistine." She shrugged and shook her head. "You're staying for supper, aren't you, Nikoshka? It won't be much, but help yourself to vodka from the fridge."

At that moment Alyosha arrived with Tsina and Nicko poured two vodkas.

Tsina made a fuss of the dog, which had been curled up in his basket, before going to Vera at the sink and starting a girlie conversation in their own language. Sitting down beside Nicko, Alyosha put an affectionate arm round his shoulder.

Nicko asked him about his security arrangements following the settlement with Oleg Dobrinin and it was clear that Alyosha was not letting his guard down. The family could move about more freely now, but it was vital that the boy, in particular, did not wander off on his own. Nicko recalled the dog lover in the Gardens, but Alyosha was alluding to a crime syndicate centred on a certain Russian restaurant in the West End. It seemed a more complicated business than one of Oleg Dobrinin defending his own turf, or settling a personal score over a dud painting.

Which set Nicko thinking of Isaacs again and he asked the Russian what he made of it all. Alyosha reached out for the bottle of vodka and recharged both of their glasses. He tossed back his own and his expression became conspiratorial.

"He's in it too," he said.

"What do you mean? A member of the restaurant mob?"

Alyosha shrugged. "He's probably not a member of anything."

"We know that he's got his fingers in all sorts of pies- as we say in English," said Nicko.

Alyosha laughed. "And Russian ones too. He's got Russian friends. You've met one of them."

"People he can trust?"

Alyosha shrugged. "He'll come back again- in spite of that scandal about the boy. In a different place and at a different time." Alyosha recharged his own glass. "You're not drinking," he told Nicko, before launching into a grouse about the circus camped on the pavement outside his window- the noise it was making and the lights which shone into his flat, despite his efforts to exclude them.

"Nasdorovia!" he announced, downing another vodka.

Nicko was feeling tipsy and their speculation about Lord Isaacs' future lapsed. Alyosha, meanwhile, tried to break into the Russian conversation at the sink, but the two women did not want to listen to him, and took themselves off to the living room.

"To Vitya!" he announced, having charged his own and Nicko's glasses.

Nicko did not reply.

"Vitya!" Alyosha repeated almost defiantly.

Hesitantly Nicko raised his glass and took a sip.

"To Vitya!" Alyosha said for a third time. "But he's going to die!"

"Aren't we all?"

"But Vitya sooner than the rest of us. I know it." He mumbled something in Russian.

"How do you know it?"

Nicko wondered at first if he had received some intelligence through the Russian grapevine, but that was followed by a sinking feeling that they were about to descend into the realm of conspiracies and extravagant speculations about life and the true nature of the Universe, the themes drunk Russians were all too ready to embark upon. And not just drunk ones either: he recalled talking to bright educated woman he had once met who had informed him in all seriousness that Moscow was the healthiest place to live in the entire country because it had been built in a circle.

"I had a dream," declared Alyosha portentously, "about Vitya."

"I dream about people I know all the time," offered Nicko defensively. "I've even dreamt about you, Alyosha. But it was a perfectly innocent dream, I hasten to add."

"Shall I tell you my dream?"

"I'd rather you didn't Alyosha, if you don't mind- if it's going to be upsetting. I don't want to hear your nightmares."

"I dreamed that Vitya was dead and that Verochka had married another man."

"I sometimes dream things of that sort. You don't have to tell me any more."

Alyosha shook his head, like a great shaggy dog shedding the remnants of sleep. "Nyet!"

"Let's not argue about it," Nicko glanced at his watch. "Verochka will want to get back into her kitchen soon."

For a minute his companion was silent, but when Nicko attempted to stand up, he put out a hand and pressed him back into his place.

"Verochka will be very happy," the Russian declared.

"I'm glad to hear that, at least," Nicko said. Then, on an impulse, he filled their glasses with the last of the vodka in the bottle. "To Vitya!" he announced grandly, "and a long life to him!"

Alyosha mumbled the name 'Vitya', adding something inaudible in his mother tongue.

"Now it's time to let Verochka have her kitchen back," Nicko stood up. He felt surprisingly steady on his feet, despite the amount he had just been drinking. "There are many things we must talk about, Alyosha, you and I, when we have the time," he said. "I'm sure that you have some very interesting things to say about life in other parts of the Universe, for example."

"Spasibo," the Russian replied, missing the irony of Nicko's remark. "Yes, there is much for us to talk about." He took his hand and pressing it, touched it with his forehead in a brief bow. It was a deferential, almost servile, gesture. "Tsina!" he called.

Vera came back into the kitchen. "Tsina's just left," she informed them, eying Alyosha with misgiving. "What have you been talking about?" she asked Nicko.

"Not very much. About the meaning of our place in the Universe, that's all. But we hardly got started. The alcohol took a hold of us too soon." He was not going to tell her about Alyosha's dream.

Nicko saw Alyosha to top of the basement stairs and made sure that he negotiated them safely. Then he ate with Kolya and his mother at the kitchen table. The boy chatted away to his godfather, who could not help noticing that neither mother nor child had anything to say regarding the absent member of the family. It set him thinking of Alyosha's portentous remarks, but he put the thought to one side. Mostly they discussed the recent play and school, with Vera stressing to the boy what she expected from him in the future, which left Nicko wondering who this display of conscientious parenthood was intended for.

He steered the talk away from the classroom to the dismal topic of football, to draw the boy in. Kolya immediately took the bait and when the topic had had a good ten minutes' airing, his godfather veered back to the capital's historical sights and the promise of future expeditions to see them.

All in all it was an evening of contentment, in marked contrast to lunch at Sunningdale. Vik, meanwhile, never got a look in, which Nicko felt had a certain justice about it, but when Vera pressed him to stay the night, he declined. Monday and work were immanent.

At the door, before opening it and forcing a passage through the encamped mob, Vera drew him close and pressed her face against his shoulder.

"Darling Nikoshka!" she said, repeating it in Russian in what sounded suspiciously like a sob.

Nicko lifted her back gently, cupping her chin in his hand. He pressedhis lips to hers and their tongues met, sending that familiar charge racing through their bodies, which seemed as good as anything that had passed between himself and Miggie…. but unlike his experience with Miggie, there was a sense of a mother's protectiveness, which fused with the procreative impulse. And, as if to round off the effect, Vera drew back and tapped the bridge of his nose in her admonitory fashion.

"We're both being naughty again, Nikoshka," she said sternly.

Nick kissed her once more and she did not try to prevent him. "It's been a wonderful evening," he murmured, "even though Alyosha and I didn't reach any satisfactory conclusions about why we exist."

"It's best when there were just the three of us," she said, " by ourselves."

Then they opened the door onto what E M Forster had once described as the world of anger and of telegrams.

"Bless you Nikoshka!"

"You too, Verochka!"

She did not linger in the step, but swiftly closed the door. He could hear her calling to her son, before he set off down the square.

On the way he paused to ask a TV cameraman if there was any news of Lord Isaacs.

The man shrugged. "Buggered if I know."

"I suppose he could be anywhere. He's probably out of the country by now."

 "Do you know, the guy? Are those folks chums of his?" the man said pointing to the house Nicko had just left.

"I've met him once or twice- socially."

The man gave a loud guffaw and poked Nicko in the ribs. A few of the others gathered round them.

"This guy knows him- socially," the cameraman announced to chuckles all round.

"And the guy who's been spilling all the beans in New York: I've met him too," Nicko went on. "He's a Mexican, a boy in his late teens and he lived here with Isaacs until they split up a short while ago. But you must know all that anyway."

Meanwhile more wasps were being drawn to the jam pot and Nicko began to regret his impulse to talk, but was flattered, all the same, by the media attention. He saw danger ahead and, pushing his way through

THE BALLOON BURSTS ...

the throng, tried to flee in the direction of the Underground station. A television news reporter, whom he recognised from the screen, was hot on his heels and it flashed through his mind to stop and answer the man's questions, but at the same moment a taxi was inching its way through the square and, seizing his chance, he flagged it down. He leaped on board, asking to be taken to the Knightsbridge Underground station.

The driver was naturally curious about the scene he was witnessing in the square: a man apparently fleeing from the media scrum and landing hurriedly in the back of his cab. He, of course, knew what the circus was all about.

"Your name wouldn't be Isaacs, by any chance?" he quipped.

"Sorry to disappoint you, alas not," replied Nicko, "but as matter of fact I do know the guy - slightly."

"Only slightly?" The man sounded disappointed.

"It's very innocent, I'm afraid. Nothing to report," Nicko said. "I'm sorry about that."

"That's a pity. I shouldn't have bothered picking you up, should I? As a matter of fact I've driven him a couple of times. He had a young lad with him then. I suppose he's the one who's been talking to the papers. He was a dark lad, might have been an Indian."

"The Mexican kind, actually."

"Ah, do you know something the rest of us don't? You must do, surely." he slowed down, in no hurry to deliver his passenger to his destination.

"Take me on to the Green Park station," Nicko told him.

"So this Mexican lad sold his story to the Sunday Echo about life in the classroom under Lord Isaacs. I had a teacher who was like that. He used to wallop our backsides with a leather belt. They could do things like that to kids in those days. Not such a bad thing either. It kept us in line, at least, while we treated it as a bit of a badge of honour. You were nobody until you'd been walloped by Rogers. A bit more of that now wouldn't go amiss. Isaacs might have got a point there. But how come you know Lord Isaacs?"

Nicko laughed, "There was nothing of that kind between us. Some of his neighbours happen to be friends of mine, that's all. I've met him there - along with Miguel."

"Miguel? Is that the lad's name?"

"That's him. Now you know something the BBC doesn't. If I tell you more will you let me off my fare?"

349

"That depends on what you tell me."

Nicko told him a little bit about Miguel- what he himself had learned about his life in Mexico and the United States, but did not divulge anything of what had gone on between them. Eventually they arrived at Green Park.

"It's been good talking to you," the taxi driver said. ""I've learned a lot."

"I'm glad to hear it. That's my job. I teach." "I thought you might."

"But I'm not allowed to wallop the kids."

"More's the pity. I must get off home to switch the telly on. Miguel. I can remember that name."

"It's common enough - Spanish for Michael," pointed out Nicko.

The man waived his fare, in spite of Nicko trying to press something on him.

On the Ten O'clock News it was the leading item, taking precedence over an important speech by the Prime Minister in the North of England. A breathless commentator - the very one who had pursued Nicko into the taxi - was interviewing a member of his own camera crew who described meeting a man, emerging from one of the neighbouring houses - one where a Russian family was living… that added spice to the dish… and his brief account of a Mexican boy in his teens, now in New York … there was evening a tracking shot of Nicko's back as he set off down the street…

And a passable description of himself too, but attempts to elicit further information from the Nikishov house had proved a failure. If Alyosha had been too drunk to answer the door no one else was going to. As regards his Lordship himself, his whereabouts remained a mystery, though the money was now on him having slipped out of the country. Naming no names, a Russian connection was offered up as a possibility…. Then it was the turn of the Prime Minister's speech, followed by the Leader of the Opposition, boring on with kids in a playground - about football…

Not unexpectedly, the phone rang a minute or two later and it was no surprise to hear Tim's voice.

"I've just seen the News and guess what? But I expect you've seen it too. Someone's blown Miguel." There was a strong hint of insinuation in his voice.

"It was bound to happen sooner or later. I'm surprised it's taken so long."

"Was that you they were talking about just now? It sounded like a pretty good description of you."

"I fear it was."

"Got a wee bit carried away, did you?"

"Possibly. But it was coming anyway, so what difference does it make?"

"Ludochka's loving it. She says it's the perfect plot for a thriller."

"How is she by the way? Started writing her book yet?"

"Which one?"

"I don't know which one. Maybe you can tell me. The Montenegran royal family?"

"She hasn't said anything to me about it."

They arranged their usual pub rendezvous. Tim's marriage seemed to have made no difference.

CHAPTER TWENTY-SIX

Washed Up on an Ionian Shore

Election day loomed and still the fate of Lord Isaacs was up front in the news. Speculation about his disappearance had unleashed a comparison with the disappearance of Lord Lucan back in the Nineteen-Seventies. Had Lord Isaacs of South Shields fallen on his sword out of sight somewhere, vanishing, perhaps, for all time? To remain shrouded in a mystery fitted the man, Nicko felt, but as for falling on his sword, he was not quite so sure about that.

Viktor meanwhile got back from Russia, after a trip that had taken him to the far east of the country- even to his ancestral fiefdom of Kolyma. He was full of excited talk of the contacts he was managing to make - which sounded to Nicko like the usual bunch of new rich types in search of the right sort of props for their emergent lifestyles. In no time at all Viktor was off again, across the Atlantic this time, making up, it seemed, for the time during which his life expectancy had apparently been menaced by Oleg Dobrinin.

Tim, meanwhile, was keeping his own dealings with Dobrinin close to his chest. He informed Nicko that things were moving along perfectly smoothly, but added no more than that, and his friend did not press him. Ludmilla, no doubt, was playing her part.

Polling Day arrived at last. Nicko had been invited to spend the night at Tim's and to go to work from there the following morning- almost certainly after a sleepless night. Ludmilla was to prepare one of her traditional Russian dishes, with a salad, of course, while Tim laid on the champagne, anticipating a result that they could celebrate.

Nicko voted and went on to his friend's. Well-fed and primed with alcohol, they settled down to watch the first results coming in.

But before a word was spoken about the Election, there was other breaking news: Lord Isaacs' body had been washed up on the island of Levkas in the Ionian Sea. Already the media were descending on the small island and any comment about the polling that had just been completed was on hold.

Nicko's immediate reaction was to think that the cunning fox had intended it as a parting shaft aimed at the Prime Minister, with whom he was known to have had a less than genial relationship. We all go down in the ship together kind of thing… and, indeed, it was a line already being taken up by some of the commentators, who were steering the discussion back towards the Election.

The news was of course too late to have any effect on the polls which had just closed, but it seemed a symbolic marker for the fall of a government that had been in power for too long and was mired in sleaze.

After that it was difficult to concentrate on the Election results themselves, but as they started to roll in they were utterly predictable. The Government was about to be swept from power and the Opposition win by a landslide. No nonsense about hung Parliaments- which was a relief to Tim and Nicko.

Ludmilla, meanwhile, had sat with them to watch the results and had said nothing during the coverage of Lord Isaacs' death. She merely sighed and nodded, as if it was almost something that she had been expecting to happen all along. Her manner, if anything, was detached, as if she was looking down from Olympian heights at mere mortals sporting in the dust below.

She caught Nicko's eye. "Your politics are sometimes like ours," she said. "They end in death."

"You think he could have been murdered?"

She shrugged. "I've no idea. Possibly, but probably not. Suicide sounds the more likely."

Nicko recalled the media tycoon, Robert Maxwell, and how he had escaped public ignominy by casting himself into the waves.

Mark Isaacs had probably been on board a yacht, plying the Ionian Sea and it was not hard to guess whose.

"Where is Oleg, by the way?" Nicko asked Ludmilla. "He wouldn't be taking a Spring break in the Med. by any chance?"

She smiled. "Are you suggesting that he might have pushed Lord Isaacs into the sea?"

"Very unlikely, but he might have been sheltering a friend on the run. It would have suited Isaacs to take a cruise right now."

"Oleg sailed from Tiva two weeks ago. He likes to fly out in his private plane and to sail from there."

"And Isaacs takes a final dip in the Ionian Sea," mused Tim. "There could be worse places to do it than that. The water must be pleasantly warm at this time of year, and in sight of Sappho's Leap, what's more. At least it suggests that the man was literate."

* * * * *

In the meantime the Government went out and the Opposition came in, promising to address the Nation's economic woes. The Isaacs affair was just one symptom among a number pointing to the Government's downfall: the scandal was deemed to be characteristic of a terminally ill administration, a point that most of the commentators kept labouring. But the hunt was still on for Isaacs' betrayer. The Media were now armed with the name of a boy of Mexican origin- Miguel- who was probably living in the United States, but where exactly? Nick wondered what his taxi driver had received in return for the tasty morsel, that had he had accepted in place of a fare from South Kensington to Green Park. It had coincided very tidily with the discovery of the Minister's body.

Two days after the Election and Nicko was once more watching the dramatic events unfold with Tim and Ludmilla.

Oleg Dobrinin now came in for some press attention, though he was in no hurry to break off his cruise and to hurry back to England. There were said to be a number of guests on board the yacht, as well as his current, but reclusive, partner, and a pair of new players from Russia- two daughters in their mid-twenties from an earlier liaison. Ludmilla identified them as soon as still pictures of them appeared on the screen.

"That's Galina and Katya her sister," she informed the others, "by his first partner."

"And what about the most recent so-called Madame Dobrininova?" asked Nicko. "When do we get to see her?"

"The first so-called Madame Dobrininova was his secretary," Ludmilla explained. "It lasted for fifteen years before they separated. This one was a quite well known television actress."

"So why does she hide herself away? Her kind are hardly shrinking violets, are they? No one seems to have set eyes on her."

Ludmilla shrugged. "She gets everything she wants. And I don't suppose Lord Isaacs was the only one who needed to cover his tracks. Have I said that right?"

"It's fine. And Oleg protects her- in a manner of speaking? A pity for

Isaacs that he couldn't have done the same for him. But anyway, I doubt she has anything to hide, quite like he had. Still it's a bit of a case of the princess marrying the frog- Dobrinin, I mean. A football player might have suited her better."

"With a love nest in Dubai?" suggested Tim.

"I think she'd prefer to have the yacht," said Ludmilla. "There are times when she uses it without him."

"And what about the crew?" put in Tim.

"They're Montenegrans mostly. " Ludmilla glanced at Nicko. "You can guess the situation. Oleg's put down roots there."

"So the 'Anastasia'- that's its name, isn't it? is a floating bordello? Or at least on occasions," said Tim. "It sounds just about the right milieu for our recent ministerial chum. They probably provided plenty of his sort of fun - those Montenegran matelots, I mean."

Ludmilla went to bed, leaving the two men by themselves. She had been working all day and said she wanted an early night.

"Which was it today?" enquired Nicko. "The Montenegran royals or Agatha Christie?"

Tim shrugged. "I haven't a clue. It might be something quite different."

"And she never talks to her husband about what she's doing? Aren't you supposed to be privy to such things?"

"That's a private conversation between Ludochka and her laptop."

"And everything's tickety-boo with Oleg? When he's not cruising in the Ionian with disgraced British Government ministers, I mean?"

"Touch wood." Tim leaned forward and touched the coffee table.

"I won't press you, Tim, but you're happy, aren't you? I mean with Ludochka."

"Put it this way, neither of us is filing for a divorce quite yet."

Maybe it was that very English sort of reticence that had drawn Ludmilla to Tim- those vestiges of a stiff upper lip that had fallen so far from fashion at the time of Princess Diana's death. Tim did not thrust his feelings on the world. There was something pleasantly nineteen- fiftyish about him, which appealed to Nicko, who, despite the tension between himself and his mother, shared her distaste for emotional incontinence.

But Ludmilla still puzzled him- as she had done ever since he had first met her in Montenegro. The Dobrinin tie-up was significant, ominous even, but did those events in Kolyma amount to so very much after all this time? The animosity left in their wake must have largely burned itself out by now, leaving just one more chilling footnote to the rule of Josef Stalin. Of course fresh vendettas were arising in the New Russia all the time, but the time for pursuing ones from the Soviet Terror was surely gone. Ludmilla, with her academic bent, surely must be able to see that, and yet… Nicko still couldn't get her in focus, though Tim seemed happy enough with her for now at least. And then there was that mention of an oath…

* * * * * *

At Bailey's they were of course pleased with the result of the General Election, though Dick Trubshaw expressed his concern for the sad fate of Mark Isaacs to Nicko, while joking at the same time that he might have 'offered the bugger a job if he'd been prepared to wait just a bit longer.'

"The bugger had élan," he told Nicko. "You can't take that away from him, even if he called himself a socialist and would have liked to have forced us into a single currency. Any word of the boyfriend?"

"I've heard no more than anyone else."

"I don't suppose you have. There was a bloke emerging from the Nikishovs' house whom they said on the Ten O'clock News knew something. But he was off down the square like greased lightning, before anyone could pin him down and talk to him." He gave Nicko a shrewd glance. "How's Kolya's pup?"

"Getting bigger by the day- as you'd expect. Eating them out of house and demanding plenty of exercise."

"I wonder what's happening about Isaacs' dog now that he's lost his master?"

There had been no mention of a dog in any of the reports about Isaacs, so presumably it had not been left alone in the house.

The drama of a change of government went ahead, with some reference to a New Dawn, but nothing to match the heady expectations that had marked the birth of the previous administration. This time round there appeared to be some sense, at least, that Rome was not about to be built in a single day. Meanwhile the Isaacs scandal began to home in on Oleg Dobrinin and the part Russian oligarchs were playing in British life. An inquest on the dead minister was to be held in Greece, where naturally the owner of the yacht, on which Isaacs had been a guest, would be expected to answer some questions. But the 'Anastasia' took its time, making a leisurely run to the port of Igoumenitsa. Once it had docked, there was a scramble to interview the oligarch as he stepped ashore, looking as inscrutable as possible in a pair of wraparound sunglasses. His partner came with him- a woman in her later thirties, on the plump side and probably past her prime as a TV starlet. Naturally there was much press and television speculation about the vessel's passenger list - be they politicians, run-of-the-mill celebrities or whoever. And about Isaacs… how had he managed to make the run to Montenegro, while the scandal was breaking about him?

Dobrinin said very little, but made no attempt to keep the media at bay. His replies were perfunctory and perfectly civil. Along with the sunglasses- which he did not remove- a kind of low key inscrutability was his chosen mask. Yes, he would answer questions about the dead politician in the proper place and at the proper time, which was not right now. He had nothing to hide and the tragedy was perfectly explicable- as would be made clear. No, he knew nothing of the man's betrayer or of his present whereabouts. "Now would you mind? My wife and I are looking for something to eat…"

Ludmilla smiled and nodded approvingly as she watched his performance on the Twenty-Four Hour News Service. Tim and Nicko plied her with questions about the first soi-disant Madame Dobrininovna and the daughters resulting from that arrangement.

"It's rather dull, really," she informed them. "Oleg's hardly a physical catch, is he? And I don't suppose he ever was. Lisa's still in Russia and the two girls divide their time between them. There are no hard feelings, it seems. I think he made her a generous settlement."

"And the present incumbent?"

"No children and soon she'll be past it anyway. As you can see, she's putting on weight. She keeps out of sight when she's at home, but still likes a fling, which she gets on board the 'Anastasia'."

"The floating bordello," Tim said.

"Where Mark Isaacs could spank the occasional naughty cabin boy?" added Nicko.

Ludmilla looked at him. "Would you like an invitation, Nick? I'm sure we could arrange one for you."

Nicko chuckled awkwardly.

"And don't I qualify for one too" put in Tim. "I am your husband, after all, and I'm doing some very important business for the paramount chief."

"Kaneshna, my darling," Ludmilla planted a generous kiss on his cheek. "Of course you do."

Nicko turned to the topic of Viktor, whose affairs seemed to have been eclipsed by the drama of Lord Isaacs.

"He's hardly ever at home these days," he said, "now that he's a free man again. If he's not in Moscow or New York, he's in Tomsk."

"Selling pictures?" Ludmilla smiled and shook her head.

"I believe so. But I haven't seen anything he's bought since that so-called Rothko. Vera says nothing about it. But he usually rings her from wherever he is. He wants to know how the boy's getting on"

"And how is he getting on?" asked Tim.

"As well as could be hoped - turning into the English child that his mother wants him to be, but a pleasantly old-fashioned one - polite, and just a weeny bit cheeky. He's a natural charmer and manages to get the mix about right. And he's pretty bright too. Money's no problem, needless to say. Vik might be beginning to turn into a bit of an oligarch himself."

Ludmilla laughed and snuggled up close to her husband on the sofa.

"Would you like to be an oligarch?" she asked him.

"Me? I don't think I'd make the grade. I could never compete with you Russians. I don't know how to handle a handgun, for a start."

"We could teach you, or someone else could use it for you- if you paid him enough. And what about you, Nick?"

"In no way. My folks were Whites, not Soviet spivs."

Ludmilla happened to be unfamiliar with the term 'spiv', so he explained it to her, while she seemed a little taken aback by his vehemence.

"You despise us, don't you Nick? Is it for what happened to your family?"

"Of course I don't despise you."

"But your people managed to escape and start a new life. Others weren't so lucky."

"Yours were good communists, but that didn't save them."

"Kaneshna. Revolutions, how do you say? Eat up their own children."

"Yet some of you survived. You're here Ludochka - married to an Englishman and studying literature at one of our leading universities."

"Aren't I lucky?" she said a trifle cynically.

"It's a great turnaround," Nicko went on, "and good luck to you. The Revolution was a tragedy for the Russian people and indeed anyone else who was touched by it. I've no sympathy whatever for Bukharin and his chums, when I think of what they were prepared to do to other people for the sake of their Messianic drivel. Fanatical filth… the whole lot of them!"

"And you include the Nikishovs in that? Vitya's grandfather?"

"Yes I do- but not Vik."

"You'd spare him, then?"

"Of course I would. Future generations can't be lumbered with the sins for their forebears."

There was a moment's silence in which Ludmilla lit a cigarette and Tim went to the drinks cabinet.

"What's it to be?" he asked.

It was gins and tonics all round, which they sipped while half-watching the television, until Ludmilla lowered her feet to the floor and went out to prepare a plate of smoked salmon sandwiches.

For the moment at least they had nothing more to say to one another. Nicko wondered if his attack on the leading Bolsheviks might have given offence, but then he had heard Russians say the same thing, and more vehemently than he had just done, while, anyway, Ludmilla was pretty thick-skinned- despite- or possibly because of- the things that members of her family had endured in the not-so-far-distant past.

* * * * * *

When Nicko took himself to Thurloe Square on Saturday, it was empty. Lord Isaacs was lying at rest in a mortuary in Epiros, awaiting the verdict of a Greek coroner, so the media had struck camp. Nothing more was revealed about the man's proclivities and Miguel remained silent and his whereabouts a mystery. The papers and the TV channels started to give a fuller coverage to the prospects facing the incoming government.

Kolya bounded to the door with Stenka, when his godfather rang the bell.

"He's growing fast," Nicko told him. "He won't be a puppy for much longer. I don't suppose you know what happened to his dad?"

The boy shook his head.

"No one's said anything about finding a dog in the house. He must have found another home for him."

"I hope he hasn't been killed," said Kolya.

"We'd know if he left the body there," Nicko reassured him. "Maybe he's found a new home. Anyway Stenka looks fine. You're giving him plenty of exercise?"

"He has his walk every day. Alyosha or me take him out."

"Got an essay to write for your weekend prep?"

The boy nodded. "'Things I like doing.'"

"And what do you like doing?"

"Taking Stenka for a walk in the Gardens."

."You've already done that one. You must think of something different. Is Mama in?"

The boy nodded and Nicko went through to her. She gave him a beer from the fridge and expressed her relief that the media circus had at last moved off. Naturally she was following developments in the Isaacs affair and wondering about the whereabouts of Miguel and the part he might yet play. She and Nicko also discussed the fate of the dog, Stenka's sire.

"I hope he didn't kill him," Vera said. "We could have given him a home, if there was nowhere else. At least they're both boys."

"We kept father and daughter together in the same house once," Nicko said. "It was fine until we mistimed things. But the pups turned out O.K. Not to be recommended, though. Any word of Vik?"

"He's flown to New York- direct from Moscow."

"I suppose he's chasing something."

"He may be. He never tells me anything about his business, but asks after Kolochka all the time and how he's doing at school. He keeps repeating to me that boy needs to be beaten- but I don't think he really means it."

"They had stopped doing it before Vik ever came to school here, so he doesn't know what he's talking about."

Which brought them directly back to Lord Isaacs and what was likely to happen to his house.

"That could be something for Tim," Nicko suggested.

"And Oleg Pavlovich?"

"You might have Russian neighbours."

Vera frowned. "There are too many Russians living in London now. It soon won't be an English city anymore."

"Maybe it isn't already. And I suppose I'm a kind of a Russian too."

"As you always remind us, Nikoshka, but it's not true, even though you have a Russian-sounding name. You're English and I love you for it! And Kolochka will be English too- like you!" She spoke warmly, almost with passion. "You're as English as… as a red rose… and…and… William Shakespeare!"

He put an arm round her and kissed her. "You like our national bard? It's funny, but we've never really talked about him."

"I love the play 'Hamlet'" she declared.

"That's very Russian of you, Verochka. "Russians like to claim him as one of their own - all that existential angst. But have you read it in English? It's odd, isn't it? that we've never talked about it before?"

"Kaneshna. 'Hamlet' and 'Macbeth'." "That's my favourite."

"I want Kolochka to see his plays."

"He will, Verochka, but give him time. The school will see to that and no doubt where he goes to next will as well. Dick's pretty hot on introducing the kids to their own country's literature."

They sat holding hands and Vera rested her head on Nicko's shoulder, but did not speak for a few moments until they heard footsteps in the passage and Kolya appeared in search of a fruit yoghurt, which he helped himself to from the fridge,

"It's not suppertime," his mother told him sternly. "You shouldn't eat between meals."

The boy merely grinned and departed to the breakfast room with his yoghurt.

"I'm much too weak with him," said Vera, placing her head on Nicko's shoulder once more. "Perhaps, Vitya's right. But tell me something else, Nikoshka. Have you ever talked about Shakespeare to Ludochka?"

"No, I don't think I have. Why?"

"She must have read his plays,"

"I suppose she must have done- some of them, at least."

"She's… how do you say? A serious scholar?"

"I suppose she is and Hamlet's her kind of a character. Maybe I should ask her."

"You know, Nikoshka, perhaps I shouldn't say this to you, but I don't like Ludochka. I know a terrible thing was done to her family in Kolyma, but I still thought it was wrong when your friend married her."

It hardly surprised Nicko to hear her saying it. There was more to it than mere bitchiness.

"She's Oleg Pavlovich's friend and after what he tried to do to Vitya, can she ever be trusted? And why was she in such a hurry to marry your friend? "

"That surprised me too, I'll admit. No doubt the white nights of St Petersburg had their effect- though it was perhaps the wrong time of year for them. Tim's a romantic at heart and he loves Russian literature."

"She's seduced him. How do you say it? To open doors?"

"I'm not very keen either, Verochka. But he might tame her by giving her some of the things she wants. We must keep our fingers crossed."

Vera muttered something in Russian and they dropped the subject. The three of them had supper together in the kitchen as usual. The rest of the house was handsomely furnished by now, in a large part under Nicko's influence, but somehow the kitchen remained the focus of its life. In that sense, they might have been in a cramped little kruschevka on the outskirts of one of Russia's provincial cities. Indeed, Nicko felt that better use had been made of the apartment in Novgorod than was being done here in London, where he had the feeling of sheltering inside the keep of a fortress, which had not been the case in Russia. But then, he reflected, as he had done so often, that the kitchen was the true heart of Russia's cultural life. Great ideas did not need great settings. After all, Einstein's famous equation was jotted down on the back of a used envelope in a patents office.

After half an hour the phone rang. It was Viktor. A conversation went on between husband and wife in rapid Russian, which Nicko as usual could not follow completely. But it grew heated, amounting to a quarrel, which Vera suspended for a moment to dismiss Kolya from the room. He departed with a sulky expression and Nicko wondered if he should remove himself as well, but as he stood up to go, Vera waved back into his place. The heated exchange went on for another minute until she broke it off and handed the phone to Nicko.

"Vik? Where are you ringing from? New York? I couldn't follow a lot of what was being said, but Verochka was pretty pissed off about something….what have you been up to? You've sold a picture?... not a fake this time, I hope… What?...to a man in Vladivostok? Christ…Not another Rothko, please God… a what?... a de Kooning?... that sounds just as bad… Kolya?... he's doing fine… no, he hasn't been beaten yet… and he's not going to be either… when are you coming home? I couldn't help hearing it, Verochka's pretty cheesed off with you… but you'veheard all the latest stuff about Isaacs… his body being washed up on a Greek Island… hc was on Dobrinin's yacht… you know that?... The big question is, did he throw himself in or was he pushed? I wouldn't put it past one of your guys to do just that, but you know more about their ways than I do…We've had a change of government, but I'm not sure it's going to make much difference… early days yet… Cheers then, you old bugger! Nasdorovia!"

Vera was frowning at him as he returned the phone to her.

"I told him what I thought of him," she said. "Leaving his family all the time and then talking the way he does about his own child!"

Nicko sighed. "At least he rings up and shows some interest. He sounds like the same old Vik to me."

"I'm not so sure. That affair with Oleg Pavlovich has frightened him, I think."

"But, Verochka, you understand better than I do who the Nikishovs were. He's lucky to exist at all, I guess."

"That's the thing I want to escape from- as you know so well, Nikoshka. I don't want my son to grow up to be another criminal who gets killed. After all, it very nearly happened to him, just for being Vitya's son!"

He hugged her close. She was still tensed up from her quarrel with her husband and was on the brink of tears. Without a word Nicko went through to the dining room and poured two large whiskies at the drinks table.

"Swallow this," he ordered her.

As she lifted her glass he touched it with the edge of his own. "Nasdorovia!"

Vera mouthed his toast in reply and took a cautious sip from her glass. She winced slightly.

"Has Kolya finished his homework?"

"I don't know, but he stays in until he has."

From the direction of the breakfast room they could hear the sound of a powerful motor car engine being revved up.

"He watches too much television and now he wants a computer," she said.

"I'm afraid they all do. I hate the things myself. Children were happier when they could curl up with a book."

"Anyway it's time he was in bed. It's long past his bedtime." She got up and crossed the hall.

Nicko could hear a tetchy exchange going on between mother and son, but not in Russian.

As soon as Kolya had cleaned his teeth and was in bed, Nicko went up and read a chapter from 'The Hobbit' to him. Then his mother kissed him good night and switched off the light. Downstairs they wasted no time. Nicko recharged the glasses and they went through to the sitting room, turning on a single table lamp only. Not a word passed between them as they settled down on the sofa. They touched glasses and drank, Vera grimacing slightly.

"You don't like whisky? Would you rather have something else?" Nicko asked her.

He tried to get up, but she pulled him back down again. "Silly boy. It's not the drink I want."

He sank back into the cushions and she took his glass from his hand, placing it on the rug in front of them. "Silly boy," she repeated.

"Why am I a silly boy?" he demanded to know, at the same time relishing being talked to like that.

For an answer she pressed her lips against his own. Nicko surrendered by sinking deeper into the cushions under the pressure of her body. Her tongue tickled his and the familiar tremor ran through him. Then, galvanised into motion, he lifted her legs up onto the sofa so that she was lying directly over him. They stayed that way, locked in a tight embrace, their lips pressed together.

In the end, the need to breathe drew them apart while Nicko could feel the pressure of his penis against his pants. Vera put her hand into his trousers to confirm it for herself.

"Come up to bed," she said softly. We must be quiet in case Kolochka's still awake. But you know that by now."

Without a word Nicko scooped up his glass and followed her.

Vera stopped outside the boy's door and listened. Then, pushing it open without making a sound, she put her head into the room, before turning back to Nicko with a nod. Finally she shut the door, but not completely, allowing a sliver of light to reach inside from the landing.

Together they went into the main bedroom and undressed. Nicko had never done it with any other woman, but now he stripped off his clothes like a practised philanderer. He realised, it went without saying, that he was unlikely to do the same with anyone else, but Vera had opened that door to him by treating him as a grown-up child. The very term of endearment she used with him- Nikoshka- seemed to say as much.

So now they went to work quietly- in part because words were superfluous, but also because at the back of their minds was the boy asleep across the landing.

They left the bed light on and snuggled under the duvet. The room felt slightly chilly, which if anything increased the need for the warmth generated by their bodies. Once again they put their lips together and Nicko hooked a leg round one of Vera's, pressing his rigid penis against her stomach.

She shifted her position slightly. "Not so fast, Nikoshka," she whispered. "You have to be more patient." She tapped him lightly on the nose, in her token of admonishment.

With an inarticulate grunt, Nicko eased back and in that same instance an image of Miguel floated into his mind…

Then, just as before, it seemed to melt into Vera so that the two became indistinguishable… His penis throbbed and he knew he could hold back no longer.

"Verochka," he muttered. "I love you too much!"

"Kaneshna," she answered him in an oddly matter-of-fact tone, but drawing him closer to her at the same time.

Verochka - Miguel… Miguel - Verochka… it mattered not which, his member was calling the tune right now…

Afterwards they lay on their backs, mumbling petty endearments. Then, after about ten minutes, Vera sat up.

"Kolochka," she said.

"What about him?"

"He may have woken up."

"I can't hear anything." Nicko tried to pull her back down, but she thrust the cover aside and got out of bed. She crossed to the door and went out onto the landing.

She returned a minute later.

"Still in the Land of Nod?" Nicko said. "Yes. I think I know what that means."

"The Land of Nod? When I was little I had a nanny who used to tell me at bedtime; that I was off to the Land of Nod. It made it sound like going on an adventure."

"I'll remember to say it to Kolochka." She sat on the edge of the bed and released a heavy sigh. "Vitya never thinks of saying things like that to a child."

"Perhaps he's got more important things to think about. Things like making the money to pay his school fees, for instance- which includes my salary, by the way."

"I've no idea. He tells me so little and as soon as he comes home he's away again somewhere else. But he can't be spending all the time buying and selling pictures, can he? And what does he really know about them anyway? Look how he was tricked by that Babko."

"That's easily done."

"But he doesn't understand what art is, not like you, Nikoshka."

"Thank you, darling. You've told me that before. Now get back into bed again. It's chilly out here. I thought Russians liked their rooms baking hot. You're different."

"Perhaps I'm turning into an Englishwoman and prefer colder rooms."

"My mother always made a virtue of it. No central heating on or fires lit before the middle of October. She's not quite so bad now that she's getting old. And both my boarding schools were pretty Spartan. Lots of long runs or games of rugger on cold winter afternoons."

"It's done you no harm."

Though no sportsman, Nicko had to admit that it hadn't.

Vera climbed back into bed and snuggled up close to him.

"You did well this time, Nikoshka, but you still have to learn to be more patient."

"Try telling that to my cock."

"Your what?"

"My cock - my penis. It's a good old English word. Have you not heard it before?"

"Cock. You've taught me a word I didn't know, Nikoshka."

"And you've taught me plenty of things I didn't know." He leaned over her and kissed her.

"But you must be more patient, Nikoshka."

"Tell, me another thing, Verochka. How does Vik get on? I mean in this kind of way? Whatever else he's done, he's given you a fine boy."

"I don't want to talk about Vitya. Not now, if you don't mind." She turned over on her side, away from him.

They talked sporadically for a little while, until Nicko got out of bed and went downstairs. He returned a few minutes later with a tray of drinks and biscuits. As they sipped their G and Ts, Nicko could not help noticing how Vera seemed to be developing a taste for English drinks.

Then they snuggled down again, having drained their glasses and eaten the biscuits. Vera giggled softly and murmured to herself in Russian. He let her run on, trying from time to time answer her with some of the Russian phrases that he knew. But eventually they grew tired of it and fell into wordless love play. As he became aroused once more, Nicko tried to put into practise what she had told him about being patient and taking his time, but when an olive-skinned face with black almond eyes swam into his vision, that became impossible.

"You need more practise," she said to him "You're still in too much of a hurry." She tapped the bridge of his nose. "But, I love you for it, Nikoshka."

* * * * * *

With the morning, despite it being Sunday, Vera was up early- in anticipation of her son who was liable to arrive in her room and climb into bed beside her. Nicko tiptoed to the bathroom and was already downstairs fully clothed when he heard the sound of the boy's voice upstairs.

When Kolya came down as he did not seem the least surprised to find his godfather in the kitchen. That he should be stopping overnight now seemed perfectly natural.

Vera fussed about the homework that needed to be finished and, once it was done, if he asked his Uncle Nicko nicely, they might go together with Stenka to the Gardens. After his boiled egg and toast, the boy retreated to the morning room, now his established territory, to complete his task while Nicko slipped out to a newsagent for a couple of papers. Back home Vera chased him into the sitting room to read them by himself. She handled him in a mildly brusque way, a bit like the way she treated her son.

Oleg Dobrinin was on the front page of each. He had given the Greek coroner his version of events surrounding the death of Lord Isaacs-something that Nicko had not picked up the previous night, because he and Vera and not thought to watch the TV news. It was clearly a case of suicide, he stated, brought about by the revelations of his boy lover. The judgement that it was a symptom of the last Government's terminal decline were aired yet again.

And that seemed to be that. No one had yet run Miguel to earth, though his story had been perfectly timed to produce the maximum impact from the exposure of Lord Isaacs. Nicko wondered how much the Mexican Boy was getting from it. There were of course plenty more speculations in both papers about shenanigans on board the 'Anastasia', the louche lifestyles of its celebrity passengers and plenty more about Russian oligarchs and where they stood in relation to British society, which was becoming repetitive.

As good as gold, Kolya completed his homework promptly and presented it to Nicko to look through - something he felt a little chary about doing, as he felt that he was straying onto his colleagues' turf. He found that the boy had taken his advice in part at least and had included other things besides his dog. He had written really rather well about Kensington Gardens, mentioning Petar Pan, and then about Chelsea Football Club and going there with Alyosha. Nicko was impressed with the way the boy was learning to string English words together on paper and told him and his mother so.

So after a light lunch it was off to Kensington Gardens with Kolya and Stenka. It was a mild, sunny day and there were no encounters with suspicious dog-lovers this time. They raced about on the grass and re-visited Peter Pan where Nicko told the story of the boy who never grew up. Then it was home for tea, after which Nicko went back to Finchley, having passed a very satisfactory weekend.

He had been home less than half an hour when the phone rang. The voice he heard was quiet, speaking almost in a whisper, but he recognised it at once.

"Miggie," he said. "Where the hell are you ringing from this time?"

"The United States."

"That's a big place."

"It's great to talk to you Nick. Really it is, believe me."

"You're keeping your head down pretty well, aren't you? The whole world's looking for you- after all that shit that you've chucked at the fan."

"It had to end that way."

"Dobrinin told the Greek coroner that it was suicide and it looks as if he might agree."

"Sure it was suicide."

"And you, Miggie? Do you give a damn? Is that what you wanted? For him to top himself?"

There was a short rather impatient sigh.

"And what are you being paid for it, Miggie? Enough to keep you in comfort for the rest of your life I guess."

"You think I'm a cunt, don't you?"

"I do a bit, Miggie, but I still love you."

"Who was that Greek guy who flew too close to the Sun? "

"He was called Icarus."

"That's him. And he got his wings burnt off, didn't he? That's Mark Isaacs for you. If it hadn't been me, it would have been some other guy."

"You could be right there, Miggie."

"And you could have spilled the beans too, Nick. Thanks for not doing it."

"I guess you need the money more than I do."

"Look Nick, if there's anything I can do, just let me know. I'm really grateful to you- honest I am- you must know that. And I love you too."

"Piss off, Miggie. Don't get me wrong- I mean that in a nice kind of way. I'd love to see you again if you're ever back on this side of the pond."

"Christ, you're a pal Nick!"

The script was beginning to creak and there was something else on television that Nicko wanted to watch.

"Look, Miggie, give me another buzz after we've both had time to think things through a bit. Then you can tell me what your plans are. Bless you Miggie, and don't do anything I wouldn't do!"

"You're a pal Nick - a real pal!"

CHAPTER TWENTY-SEVEN

An Enigma Wrapped in a Riddle

Nicko heard nothing more from any of his friends until the end of the week. At school Mary Lambert was impressed with Kolya's weekend effort and told his godfather so.

"I hope you didn't write it for him," she joked.

Nicko assured her that he had played no part in it- which was a shade short of the truth, and passed on her accolade to the boy's mother, which confirmed to her that she was doing entirely the right thing for him: he was taking to his English preparatory school like a duck to water. But if only Vitya- who seemed to be spending most of time abroad- could show a bit more interest in their son, instead of pontificating in a general kind of way from a distance…

On Friday Tim rang with the news that Oleg Dobrinin was back in town.

"Things are moving," he said.

"In what direction?"

"The right one, I think. Ludochka is keeping in touch. She's already spoken with the Great Man."

"And any more on his Lordship?"

"Nothing, except to say that the Greek coroner will probably reach the right conclusion - namely that the man cast himself to the waves, rather than having to face out a big spanking scandal."

"Which will suit Dobrinin perfectly."

"There's little doubt of that. How about tomorrow night? The usual?"

"Da. Kaneshna. How's your Russian coming on, by the way?"

Tim laughed. "Oh by massive leaps and bounds - what else would you expect?"

* * * * * *

Kolya had been given a star by Mary Lambert for his essay and his half term report was glowing. Vera rang immediately to inform Nicko.

"And any word from Vik?"

"He left a message and says he might be back in London next week, but he isn't sure yet." She sighed. "Really, Nikoshka, I don't think I care."

"Don't say things like that, Verochka. He'll settle down again, now that Dobrinin's thugs are off his back."

"Maybe that's the way he prefers it."

"What? Waiting for a bullet and not knowing when or where it's coming from? I hardly think so. But let me know when he's back. I'll have a word with him."

"Kolochka wants to speak to you."

The boy was full of his good school report and his recent star. Rather cockily, he kept calling Nicko 'sir' until he was ordered as usual to stop.

* * * * * * *

When Nicko met Tim the following evening, he found him eager to talk about Ludmilla.

"She spoke to Oleg Pavlovich yesterday and there is to be a meeting- in his own home. I must say, I can hardly wait to see what the place's like."

"Probably full of kitsch. So it's nearly in the bag?"

"Ludochka seems to think it so."

"And how is her literary career?"

"I've no idea. She works most of the time in her faculty library and I never really get to see what she's up to."

"And she doesn't talk to you about it?"

Tim shook his head. "To be honest with you, Nick, she's a much darker horse than I ever imagined."

"I could have put you right on that one." "She goes off for long walks by herself." "That sounds pretty Russian to me."

"She doesn't pick fights, mind you. No hard words pass between us- but there are long periods when there are no words at all. She does the bedroom bit. There're no problems with that."

Tim gave himself a reassuring chuckle, but Nicko sensed an underlying unease.

"Is she bottling something up?" went on Tim. "Or building up to some kind of a creative outburst? I've no idea. It's the Dobrinin link that intrigues me and that business in the camp in Kolyma. She could write a great book about that, if she chose to. I might even give it a shot myself, if she doesn't and I could include Vik's slant on it as well. It's grim, but it's a cracking good yarn!"

Nicko realised that a reappraisal of his Russian wife was already starting in Tim's mind and that he might be having second thoughts about his precipitate rush into wedlock. His head might have been turned by reading too many Russian classics: Tolstoy, Turgenev and Dostoyevski being the most likely culprits.

They dropped the subject of Ludmilla to speculate yet again on the death of Lord Isaacs. Nicko decided not to mention his renewed contact with Miguel for the time being at least, which meant that neither of them could add very much to their earlier ruminations, so they turned to Vik and his hectic gadding about between Russia and the United States. Then Tim turned the light onto Nicko himself, who was rather taken aback by his friend's apparent penetration.

"I think you meet a need, Nick."

"Whose? Mine or Vik's?"

"Both."

Nicko left him to continue.

"It seems to me that Vik in his heart of hearts doesn't really like family life at all." "And me?"

"You're different and in a way the answer to his problem. He trusts you - loves you even - in the best Platonic sense, I hasten to add, as a kind of brother - one he can fall back on, when things go wrong. But at the same time I guess that he's a bandit at heart who knows that his luck is going to run out one day. And he isn't jealous- a mark in his favour- and not particularly sentimental."

"But what's in all that for me?"

Tim laughed. "I think you know perfectly well, Nick, but you want me to say it." "Naturally I do."

"Forgive me for putting it this way, but you're not exactly a Casanova, are you? Vera sees that, though I'm not privy to anything you say to one another. She can see that you're fond of the boy, who reciprocates your feelings, and that's the way she draws you out of yourself."

It was as if his friend had been a fly on the wall. How on earth had he managed to work that out? After all, he had never observed Nicko by himself in the Nikishov home.

"How the hell do you reach this conclusion?" demanded Nicko.

Tim smiled. "Reading between the lines… what passes between us in our meetings here… the drift of our chat… and a bit of inspired guesswork."

"You ought to be a bloody novelist."

His analysis matched Nicko's own to an uncanny extent, but he wondered whether Tim possessed the same degree of psychological penetration when it came to his own wife.

"You don't have to tell me if you don't want to," Tim said, dropping his voice to a confidential whisper. "She's the first, isn't she? The one who helped you to break your duck?"

"I think I can tell you that, Tim. Verochka's the first and it's working for me."

"And the last? The one and only?"

"We'll leave that pending, if you don't mind. At the moment I think so, but only time will tell. Swallow what's left in your glass, Tim. We've got time for one more before you return to the marital couch."

Tim smiled and drained his glass.

"Have you ever thought of writing a novel yourself, Tim?"

"It's crossed my mind occasionally. Maybe I will, one of these days."

"Don't leave it too long."

Nicko went to the bar and returned with their freshly charged glasses.

"To our Russian womenfolk!" he proclaimed. "Verochka and Ludochka!"

Tim raised his glass, with a reflective frown on his face, and silently joined the toast.

* * * * * *

It was an hour later and Nicko was in bed, about to sleep when Tim rang.

"Tim!" he exclaimed. "Anything the matter?"

"It's Ludochka. She went out and hasn't come home yet."

Nicko glanced at the clock by his bed which read five minutes after midnight. "It isn't all that late, Tim. Give her a bit more time."

"She's never stayed out as late as this before."

"I thought you said that she liked going for walks by herself."

"But not at this time of the night." "What do you want me to do, Tim?"

"I don't know, Nick, but I'm worried. She can probably look after herself- but as we were saying earlier, she's a dark horse."

"Are you suggesting that there might be somebody or something you haven't been told about?"

"I don't know, Nick. I simply don't know."

"Look, Tim, ring me as soon as she's got back. There's probably nothing in it. But if for any reason she's not back by the morning ring me first thing. Now try not to worry. She's no fool."

"Thanks. I'll try."

Nicko switched off the bed light. For a moment or two he puzzled over Ludmilla, but his thoughts drifted to Verochka… with a pinch of Mexican spice.

Shortly after seven the phone rang. As it was a Saturday morning Nicko was still in bed.

"Tim here."

His relaxed tone indicated to Nicko that nothing was amiss.

"Is she back?"

"Yes. I'm sorry I bothered you."

"And all well? Any reason given?"

"She's flaked out and in bed. It was about five o'clock when she rolled in."

"Rolled? And the worse for wear?"

"Probably, but I haven't had a chance to talk to her yet. She just wanted to sleep."

"As we have to remind ourselves, Ludochka's a dark horse. Drink or drugs?"

"Christ, I hope neither."

"And of course you haven't a clue whether she was with someone else or just on her own?"

"As I told you I haven't had a chance to talk to her. I'm just relieved she's back and felt that you ought to know. But she looked a bit of a mess. Her hair was all over the place."

"Tell me more, when you know more, Tim. But at least you've got her back- that's the main thing. I can guess what you've been feeling."

Nicko felt relief for his friend, yet uneasy about the course things appeared to be taking for him.

The Sunday papers included another beguiling detail in the Isaacs affair: apparently when the body was washed up on the Hellenic shore it was clad only in a silk dressing gown of oriental design. If Isaacs had dropped over the ship's rail, he had chosen the nighttime to do it, which was hardly an illuminating piece of information, yet the serpentine dragon pattern of the dressing gown was a fitting addition to the tale. Nicko wondered what the effect might have been if it had been a Mexican Aztec design, rather than a Chinese one. But either way, the disgraced government minister had staged his exit with panache.

For part of the day, Nicko marked kids' work - a chore he had to force himself to do, but by evening his curiosity had got the better of him and he rang Tim.

His friend answered the phone and updated him before he had even questioned him.

"She's drowsy still, but quite settled. I don't know whether to call a doctor or not. So far she's told me nothing."

"She must have taken something. A substance of some kind."

"Possibly, but she's perfectly calm- just sleepy."

"Are you sure you can manage? Is there anything you'd like me to do? I'm not sure what, but you tell me."

"I can't think of anything, Nick, but I'm out of my depth I have to admit. Ludochka's a mystery- I should have seen it sooner, I suppose. There are things about her I simply can't fathom."

"At least you've got her back in one piece. Just keep me posted. We'll have to play it by ear," he added, platitudinously.

Nicko rang Vera to inform her of what had just passed with Ludmilla. She did not sound surprised and assumed immediately that the girl had been dosing herself with some proscribed substance. She was scornful of Tim for allowing himself to be so readily snared. Nicko was less harshly judgemental, but inclined to agree with her. It seemed so odd that Tim could operate effectively in the cut and thrust of one of the world's leading property markets and yet display such naivety regarding his marriage. Surely he ought to have seen where Ludmilla might be coming from, especially with his experience of dealing with Russians of the new kind? Nicko told Vera that he would be keeping in touch with Tim about developments.

"I'm sorry, Nikoshka, but I never trusted her. And then learning what we know now…"

Nicko said that he was suspending judgement for the time being and turned to the question of Viktor.

"No more news," Vera told him, "but he will ring me as soon as he's arrived. Kolochka's stopped asking about his father- which means something, I think."

"I'll have a word with him when he gets back," said Nicko. "I'm sorry I didn't get over to you today. I had to spend half the day marking bloody books."

"Kolochka's?"

"Not this time."

"That's good, I'm pleased to hear it. But all my love, Nikoshka. I'll tell you when Vitya comes."

* * * * * *

It was the middle of the week when he heard from Tim again. He sounded rather subdued, as if he was afraid of being overheard by someone in the next room, so Nicko suggested that he come round. They could even knock up a meal together and share a bottle of wine.

"Is it all right to leave Ludochka?" he asked

"Of course. She seems as right as rain now. That was one thing I wanted to tell you, but…" he dropped his voice, "it's not quite as simple as that."

"Say no more now, Tim." Nicko ordered him. "Drop in tomorrow at about seven. We'll talk about it then."

* * * * * *

Tim arrived precisely on the hour, as if he had been impatient to be there. Nicko uncorked the wine and made an offering for his friend to taste. Tim went through the ritual of sluicing it around his mouth and pronouncing it very acceptable, but Nicko took a sip and pulled a wry face.

"No way!" he exclaimed.

"It seems all right to me," pointed out Tim.

"You can't mean it!"

"Of course I mean it. It's perfectly drinkable. You won't get me to tell you otherwise."

Nicko laughed and topped up their glasses. "I wouldn't really have a clue if it wasn't."

Tim got straight down to business.

"Ludochka's all right again. No serious affects from whatever it was, but frankly Nick, I'm still concerned about her."

"Go on."

"When she's at home she spends all her time writing and she's started locking herself in the lavatory with her laptop."

"Maybe that's where she's at her most creative? Sitting on the throne."

"But somewhere where I can't see what she's doing. She tells me that it's the best place she knows for focusing her thoughts properly."

"Focusing them on what? English crime fiction or the King of Montenegro?"

Tim shrugged. "I think she keeps to crime at her faculty and everything else at home, but that's really a guess."

"Then it might be the King of Montenegro."

"Whatever it is, she doesn't have to lock herself in the bloody shitter to do it, does she?"

"Any chance of getting hold of the laptop?"

"She takes it with her to the faculty."

"She could be writing her autobiography and about you and Oleg Dobrinin for all we know- which might make a good story. All fixed for the next summit, by the way?"

"This coming Saturday. In the Great Khan's yurt. It might even be a chance to meet the alleged Madame Dobrininova."

"You must tell me all about it - and, mind you, no details spared. But there's nothing new about this New Russian thing. It's been going on- since when? Probably the seventeenth century - with the odd historical blip, like the Bolshevik Revolution. And now we're both caught up in it."

"You with your Russian name."

"And you with your Russian wife. A hawk, that's what Orloff means. The 'off' ending is like the 's' or the affix 'son' on an English surname, implying possession."

"Ludochka has explained all that to me. She tells me a number of interesting things, but clams up about others."

"Anyway Dobrinin is going to play ball?" "God willing."

"Thanks in good measure to your enigmatic Russian spouse, no doubt. Come on Tim, which one is she? Fetch up a female character from the depths of Russian literature. Which one is she?"

Tim shook his head. "I wouldn't know where to start."

"How about one of those Chekhovian women, who bang on about going to Moscow, but never do?"

Tim shook his head. "Ludochka's not like them. Definitely post-Chekhovian."

"And post-Soviet as well?"

Tim thought for a moment. "I'm not quite so sure about that, though I can hardly see her marching under a red banner in a May Day parade. And she's not exactly the astronaut type either. Nor can I see her operating a lathe or cutting coal, for that matter. But she might have written a definitive account of the Kiev-Rus state - a strictly Marxist interpretation, needless to say. A rising star in the Soviet academic firmament, despite a wobbly Siberian start. I'm talking about the era of de-Stalinisation, after the Terror. Anyway, Nick, that's enough of Ludochka. What about your own plans? Any more plays in the pipeline? The last one was a little jewel. So I plead with you not to hide your light under a bushel."

Nicko felt flattered. He was longing to discuss his artistic hopes with someone, but was afraid of appearing self-centred and knew how bored he got, listening to other people banging on about their own aspirations. He told Tim that he was already thinking of another short play on the lines of the previous one - maybe taken again from Chaucer- or possibly an adaptation of a morality play this time - and then, having said enough about that, he shifted to the children's guide to the art treasures of the capital.

Tim had liked the idea and now offered himself as a possible partner in the venture. Nicko was touched and seized his hand.

"Orloff and Mumford!" he declared. "They hang together pretty well, don't they? Like Gilbert and Sullivan or Gabbitas and Thring or… or Hillard and Botting or…or…or Fortnum and Mason!"

They burbled on, Nicko eager not to lose sight of his idea. He could already see how the 'Mumford' end of the partnership might handle the mundane aspects of the project, while the 'Orloff' one was left to enjoy the more creative ones.

For some time they got quite carried away and Tim appeared to forget his worries about his wife. They were like a pair of schoolboys, a state that Nicko, needless to say, fell into easily. Sunday afternoon was set for a first joint survey of the National Gallery. That its bookshop might already contain material rendering the scheme redundant did not trouble them.

The enterprise was firing up and they argued earnestly over which works were to take pride of place.

Suddenly Tim broke off.

"It's just crossed my mind," he said, "that Ludochka might have a few ideas about this as well."

Nicko frowned. Was this an attempt to hijack his great idea? Tim coming aboard in a supportive role was one thing, but to include his moody and unpredictable Russian spouse was another.

"Do you really think that would be such a good idea?" Nicko countered. "We want to keep things simple, surely?"

"It's just that I think it could be right up Ludochka's street and might keep her from brooding."

"This isn't therapy, Tim."

"Of course it isn't, but she might come up with some good ideas and if it helps to keep her on the rails at the same time…well, we could kill two birds with one stone."

"Do you honestly think that Ludochka's going to be interested in putting together a kids' guide to the museums and galleries of London?"

"I could try her."

Somehow the light seemed to be going out of Nicko's great idea. But they settled all the same on their own trip to the National Gallery- without the benefit of Mrs Mumford.

Tim glanced at his watch. "I must be getting back," he announced. "I need to pop into Waitrose on the way."

On his own, Nicko thought about his friend and his marriage to a Russian. It was full of pitfalls, he realised, but then something similar had occurred in his own family in the early years of the previous century and what exactly was going on now between himself and Verochka? He was an Orloff, Nicko reminded himself, and a kind of a Russian too.

* * * * * *

The two friends met on the steps of the National Gallery, as they had arranged. Nicko had arrived first and was contemplating the empty plinth in the square below and thinking negative thoughts about the talentless exhibitionism that it had recently given rise to, when Tim rolled up.

The latter was beaming.

"You look pretty chuffed," Nicko said. "Can I assume that yesterday's summit reached a satisfactory conclusion?"

"I thought of ringing you, but decided it better to look you straight in the eye."

"Tell me the glad tidings."

"All is well," declared Tim. "All done and dusted and I even met the alleged Madame Dobrininova as a kind of a bonus. First impressions suggest that she comes up to expectations."

"Of what? The footballer's wife or something else of that ilk?"

"You might say that, but more of her later."

"And Ludochka? No more rollercoaster changes of mood?"

"On the contrary. She came up trumps yesterday. Dobrinin was pretty deadpan throughout, positively Soviet as a matter of fact- he's a dreary little shit, let's be frank- but she worked him round to where he needed to be. I left it to her. Mind you, there might have been something of a show trial about it - a bit of scene-fixing before the event."

"So who's been brainwashing who?"

Tim laughed. "We're signed up. It only requires the nuptial knot to be tied, but that's a formality."

"So you're all very happy bunnies and two of you about to make a big killing."

"Kaneshna."

"And where's your ace negotiator now?"

"I left her in Shaftesbury Avenue. She wanted to see a film, about Russian mafia in London of all things."

"Talk about taking a busman's holiday- as one of my grandmothers was fond of saying."

"Time now for us to look at some pictures," Tim said. "Where do we begin?"

They entered the gallery and went up the stairs. Nicko had already drawn up a list, but assured his friend that he was open to other ideas.

"Let's do it chronologically," he suggested." We can begin with the Middle Ages and the Renaissance."

Tim concurred and they went into the Sainsbury Wing, where Nicko took his notes out of his pocket.

"Subject matter is important," he told Tim, "and if there's a story to tell."

"It helps them to read a picture, if they know their Bible," Tim pointed out.

"It can be a good game- searching for clues and making guesses. The aesthetics can be left 'til later."

So far there seemed to be a meeting of minds.

Nicko had listed Bellini's 'Agony in the Garden', 'Christ Mocked' by Hieronymus Bosch and, by way of contrast, "Venus and Mars' by Botticelli. Each contained a good story, as well as scope for comment on the handling of the subject and what the aim of the picture was.

Keep it simple, Nicko told himself. But already he realised that the quantity of material was overwhelming. Wherever he looked, there was something to arouse curiosity in the young minds that he was so eager to encourage. For instance, 'The Arnolfini Wedding' by Jan van Eyck opened up all sorts of possibilities about fashions in clothes and house furnishings in the fifteenth century. Nicko realised that his problem was going to be an abundance of material and that he would have to set himself very strict criteria for the selection he finally made. Tim would be a great help, as long as he kept the book's particular market in mind.

They argued, quietly, but insistently, each expressing his preferences for the kind of things that he felt might make the most direct inroad into an immature imagination.

"I suppose we ought to check with the bookshop first, before we get too carried away," said Tim. "We need to be sure that someone hasn't got there first."

Nicko knew he was right of course, but felt a certain trepidation about taking a step that might burst his bubble.

They checked the books on the children's shelves, where there was a reasonable quantity of material, but nothing quite of the kind that Nicko had in mind. His hopes were given a fillip, while at the same time he realised that he might be biting off a bit more than he could chew. Tim was going to be essential to the project.

Meanwhile Tim bought himself a companion guide to the Gallery and a fridge magnet of 'The Arnolfini Wedding'.

"I'm afraid I can't resist these things," he confessed.

They decided that it was enough for one day.

"What's happening about Ludochka?" asked Nicko, as they settled down with lagers in St Martin's Lane.

"I said I'd meet her in the Pilsudski at about seven," said Tim, "which of course is a regular haunt of yours. You could join us."

Nick accepted. Meanwhile they had time on their hands to dawdle over their drinks and air their views on what they'd achieved that afternoon, after which Nicko announced his intention of popping up to Foyles, before meeting Tim at the restaurant at seven.

He spent a happy half hour browsing in the bookshop, where he found a copy of Anthony Trollope's 'Orley Farm', something that he had been meaning to read for a while. Afterwards he strolled back down through Trafalgar Square to Whitehall, before turning up to Piccadilly Circus. It was mild and he was in no hurry, just enjoying the simple satisfaction of taking in the sights and sounds of the people about him. Anonymity was one of life's more rarified pleasures, he reflected. He had more than hour to kill before meeting Tim and Ludmilla, but he decided to go straight to the Pilsudski in South Kensington to enjoy a couple of vodkas on his own first. He toyed with the idea of dropping in on Vera down the road in Thurloe Square, but knew that tearing himself away in time would be difficult and dropped it. A couple of solitary and reflective vodkas would be the thing. He might even read the introduction to 'Orley Farm'.

He walked up to Green Park, before taking the underground the rest of the way to South Kensington, where he picked up a copy of the Evening Standard- now in the ownership of a Russian oligarch- as he left the station. In the restaurant he settled himself at a corner table by the window. He still had more than an hour to kill before the arrival of the others and he wondered, perhaps, if he ought to have postponed his vodka for a little while longer, but the double shot was served up to him with a pickled herring, so he spread his paper and started to read it.

There was no news that immediately grabbed his attention. Nothing about Lord Isaacs, for example, but there was a statement by the new Chancellor of the Exchequer, about the economic mess left by his predecessor and the need for drastic spending cuts. After a quarter of an hour as it was turning dark outside and although the lights were on in the restaurant, he raised his newspaper to catch the extra light. As he did so the street door opened and two people came in and went to a table at the far end.

It was a man and a woman. She was hidden from Nicko's view, while her companion remained standing as he removed his raincoat, before sitting down. The woman glanced at her watch, said something to him and he turned to order drinks from the waitress.

It was Oleg Dobrinin who was sitting opposite to Ludmilla.

Neither of them had seen Nicko at the far end of the restaurant, so he swivelled his bottom on the banquette and lifted his paper again to hide his face. They were too far away, however, for him to hear what they were saying and, indeed, they appeared to be taking care that no one should.

But that they should be meeting here of all places, so soon before the arrival of her husband struck Nicko as extraordinarily reckless. What if Tim turned up sooner than expected? And why meet Dobrinin in a place like the Pilsudski anyway? It struck Nicko that Ludmilla got some sort of a kick out of running things close.

Continuing to avert his face, but stealing brief glimpses from behind his paper, Nicko sipped his vodka. He was reluctant to order a re-charge for fear of revealing his presence, while at the same time it tickled him to be spying on a Russian oligarch in a Polish restaurant from behind a newspaper, which was owned by another Russian oligarch, who had once been an officer in the KGB!

The two Russians leaned across the table towards each other, until their heads were almost touching. They could have been siblings- it seemed that kind of intimacy. Meanwhile, the waitress arrived with a glass of vodka and an orange juice.

Behind his paper Nicko raised his glass and mouthed the word 'nasdorovia!', as the oligarch lifted his to touch Ludmilla's orange juice, before throwing it back in one.

Ludmilla appeared to be doing most of the talking, while Dobrinin nodded from time to time, in apparent agreement with what she was saying to him. Then, finally Ludmilla glanced again at her watch, and leaned across to her companion to whisper in his ear. He immediately stood up and put on his raincoat, pulling the collar up at the same time. As he approached the cash desk by the door with his bill slip, Nicko cowered behind his paper. But just as Dobrinin was leaving, he stopped suddenly and, glancing back, his eye caught Nicko's. There was a flicker of recognition on the oligarch's face, but Nicko looked down at his paper again, as if giving it his close attention. Then the man was outside, moving in the direction of the Underground station. Nicko felt the cold draught from the open door.

He looked down the room in Ludmilla's direction. She had still not noticed him, but was lazily sipping her orange juice. Then she opened her bag, took out a small notebook and pen and started to write, pausing only to ask the waitress to remove Dobrinin's empty glass.

Nicko took the risk now of ordering a fresh vodka. And thus it remained until the arrival of Tim fifteen minutes later, just after seven. It was only then that Ludmilla looked up and caught sight of Nicko at his table near the window.

What began as a smile of greeting for her husband standing in the doorway, turned to a puzzled frown at the sight of his friend, already ensconced in the restaurant with a vodka and plate of pickled herring before him. Nicko waved at her in a breezy manner.

After exchanging a few words with Tim, explaining that he had missed seeing his wife until now, he wandered over to join the others, where he sat on the banquette beside Ludmilla, while Tim took the place which Dobrinin had just vacated.

"I didn't see you there. Have you been here long?" Ludmilla challenged him.

"Just long enough to swallow a couple of vodkas," replied Nicko.

She scowled, but said nothing.

Tim, sensing the tension, chipped in. "I invited Nick to join us," he explained. "I hope you don't mind, dear."

"No, of course I don't. We know each other well enough, don't we?"

If he had not been observing her a few minutes earlier, Nicko might have missed the note of menace in her voice.

"Was it a good film, darling?" enquired Tim.

"Not bad. At least they used real Russians in it, who spoke with the right Siberian accent."

"That's as it should be." Tim glanced awkwardly at Nicko.

"Well? Shall we have something to eat?" suggested Nicko. "I've already started with pickled herring."

"A good idea," said his friend. "I could eat a horse right now, but how about some drinks first? I know you've already started, but that's no excuse." He gave a forced little laugh.

"Let them be on me," announced Nicko. "What's it to be?"

"G and Ts all round?" said Tim.

Ludmilla nodded. "And you?" she said. "Tell me about your afternoon."

Tim launched into an account of the visit to the National Gallery, with Nicko providing the occasional interjection, and Ludmilla nodded, appearing to give their words thoughtful consideration.

Occasionally, while her husband was speaking, she glanced at Nicko sitting beside her, as if they somehow were sharing something unknown to him and Nicko's returning glances made it clear that they were.

Once she pursed her lips and frowned at him, when she felt that something he had just said about the National Galley might have led them to the topic of the current fine art market and the role certain Russian oligarchs were playing in it. Sensing that the name of Oleg Dobrinin was near the surface of Nicko's mind, she wanted to prevent it being spoken.

But between them they managed to confine their talk to the subject of national collections in general and Ludmilla was able to air her impressive knowledge of the Hermitage, which the others of course were also reasonably familiar with. They even got mildly heated over certain modernists and the way they had been treated in the Soviet era.

Oleg Dobrinin had been excluded from their wide-ranging survey by Ludmilla's judicious steering, until Tim who by now was well wined, brought him up.

"I must say," he declared, "I was interested to see what Oleg Pavlovich had on his walls. I'm afraid nothing called out to me, but least it didn't appear to be footballer's tat, despite the things that have been said about Tatiana Yurievna." He chuckled at his feeble pun.

Ludmilla frowned caution at Nicko by pursing of her lips, to warn him off taking up the comment, but willfully, it seemed to her, he ignored her signal.

"Vik could probably give them a hand, despite blotting his copybook with a dud Rothko," he said. "He could probably tell them where their investments might increase or at least hold their value."

"It's funny, I had a feeling I saw him on my way here - Oleg, I mean," put in Tim, "but I was probably mistaken - he hardly shows up in a crowd." Ludmilla turned to Nicko and fixed him with another cautionary frown.

"He may be one of the richest men in London, but he's still free to walk its streets, isn't he?" she pointed out. "And of course it's much easier if no one knows who you are."

"True," replied her husband, "and I couldn't even be sure that it was him- which I presume is the way he wants it."

"Wouldn't you?" she said.

"I'm quite sure I would, darling."

A token display of affection followed, in which Tim clasped his wife's hand, while she contrived to wink simultaneously at Nicko over the top of his head.

Food was ordered, beginning with fish starters, then they moved on to the hunter's stew - which on this occasion Nicko felt was a bit too heavy and rich. He wasn't mad about Polish cuisine anyway. They washed it down with a plain, but pleasant, Hungarian red wine and decided to do without the desert, but ordered large brandies with their coffee. By now the talk was sporadic and evasive. Ludmilla's unease was palpable to Nicko.

She steered the talk away towards literature, thus managing to keep it safely away from the oligarch and his interests. Nicko assumed that the man had got what he wanted from his meeting with Tim and hoped that it was also true of the latter. He had certainly seemed pleased with how smoothly things had gone, when they had discussed it earlier. But now the conversation had a stilted, set-up feel to it and he just wanted to escape. He was also finding Ludmilla's facial semaphore a strain.

"Time, I think to settle the score," Nicko announced.

Tim declared himself ready and the bill was presented.

They parted immediately in the street, Tim taking his wife firmly by the hand, while Nicko pecked her discreetly on the cheek.

"You did well," she whispered into his ear in Russian. "Ochen harasho!"

"I'll ring you soon," he called to Tim. "There's a lot to talk through- the Gallery, I mean!"

"You do that."

Nicko disappeared into the Underground, leaving his friend looking out for a taxi. On the way home his thoughts flitted between the project that seemed to have made a promising start in the Sainsbury Wing and Oleg Dobrinin's appearance in the Pilsudski with Ludmilla, where they had run the risk of being found together by her husband. Had she and the oligarch been to the film together? Its theme would have been germane, though Oleg Dobrinin, as far as he knew, was no sex trafficker. But then there was no knowing how far his tentacles reached, or what the entirety of his interests was….

CHAPTER TWENTY-EIGHT

Viktor Forces the Pace

The following day Nicko was off to South Kensington once more, to see Vera. Arriving shortly after four, he was met at the door by Alyosha, who announced that Viktor Ilyich was back.

"When did he arrive?" asked Nicko.

"This morning - from New York." "Did you meet him?"

Alyosha shook his head. "He didn't tell anyone."

Nicko sighed. "I hope that doesn't mean more trouble."

Nicko went on into the house, where he met Kolya in the hall with Stenka.

"I hear Papa's back," he said to the boy.

Kolya shrugged his shoulders, saying nothing.

"Aren't you glad he's home again, safe and sound?"

Kolya mumbled something that he did not catch or pursue.

"Is Mama at home?"

The boy nodded in the direction of the sitting room.

"And Papa?"

"Upstairs in the study. He's busy."

"I'm sure he's got time to talk to me."

But Nicko first looked into the sitting room, where he saw Vera stretched out on the sofa.

"Don't move," he insisted as she tried to get to her feet.

"It's nice to see you, Nikoshka," she said.

As she sat up she took his hand, which he pressed to his chest.

"You don't look happy," he said.

Vera sighed. "You've heard?"

"You mean the wanderer has returned?"

"And he's cut his hair off."

"What? I hope he hasn't shaved it all off, like a zek - or a night club bouncer."

"Not quite, but it's very short."

"Does it suit him?"

"Not at all. It looks terrible." She sounded as if she did not care very much about it.

"He's not in trouble again is he? Alyosha told me that he arrived without letting anyone know."

"I've really no idea. He hasn't told me anything yet. He went straight upstairs and shut himself in his study. He didn't even speak to Kolochka."

"Shall I go and have a word with him?"

"If anyone can, you can, Nikoshka."

What a turnaround from of old, thought Nicko, Vik now a haunted man, and yet with such a beautiful wife and child!

He went up to the study and, before knocking, put his ear to the door, but heard nothing.

He knocked twice before he got an answer.

"Da?" said a listless voice.

"Vik? It's Nick here."

Something was muttered in Russian, followed by a pause. Nicko was about to call again, when the door opened.

If he had seen him elsewhere, he might not have immediately recognised his friend. His once thick, dark hair was cropped close to his skull and the New Russian, who had once fancied fogeyish tweeds, was clad now in a T-shirt bearing an image of Elvis Presley - of all the unlikely ikons - and a pair of washed out jeans, which in Nicko's eyes were about the most depressing item in the modern wardrobe.

"Christ, Vik, I would never have known it was you. Where's all your lovely hair gone to?"

Viktor ran a finger across the top of his head. "It's cooler this way."

"God, Vik, you don't have to talk like a teenager as well! And why Elvis, for Christ's sake? Is he cool as well?"

Nicko advanced into the room, which, despite his friend having only just got back, was already a mess.

Viktor sat heavily in one chair and Nicko settled opposite him. "Well," Nicko said. "Spill the beans."

But, before saying anything, Viktor fished inside the bottom drawer of his desk for a glass which he set beside one that was already in use.

"Da?" he said, holding a half-empty bottle of Stolichnaya over the fresh glass.

"Spasibo," Nicko replied, "but let's not turn this into a binge. We have some serious talking to do, I can see." He sounded almost as if he was addressing a pupil.

Viktor filled the glass to its rim and topped up his own. He sighed and shrugged his shoulders.

Nicko shook his head. "Why the makeover? What kind of a signal are you trying to send out?"

"I know it isn't your style, Nick. You don't have to tell me that."

"It certainly isn't my style. And didn't used to be yours either."

Viktor drained half the contents of his glass and rubbed a hand across the stubbly crown of his head. "After what so bloody nearly happened here - with Dobrinin, I mean - I feel safer like this. Less conspicuous somehow." He hardly sounded convincing.

"You think dressing up like a teenager makes you less conspicuous? Do you know the English expression 'mutton dressed as lamb'? Did I ever explain that one to you?"

Viktor grinned- for a second the old Vik. "Piss off. You may have done, but I think I know what it means anyway."

"Is that really the reason, Vik? Not to show up in the crowd? And bloody Elvis of all people! Can't you manage a bit more style than that? I mean something more like Mark Isaacs. When he was washed up on the beach at least he was wearing a decent dressing gown."

Viktor re-filled his glass and grinned broadly. "With serpents on it."

"In the Garden of Eden, Eve wouldn't have been the one he was after," Nicko said.

Viktor chuckled and their discourse appeared to be assuming a lighter tone. They fell silent, but when Viktor eventually spoke he had resumed a more solemn one.

"There's something I need to tell you, Nick," he said.

"That's what I'm here for. Sorry, I don't mean to sound like a shrink."

"I'm in love."

"That's exactly what we need."

"I know it sounds cheesy to you, Nick. I wouldn't expect anything else."

"So who is she? Assuming that it is a she."

"Of course it's a she. This leopard doesn't change his spots, so piss off!"

He grinned and gave Nicko a playful punch which was returned.

"Well go on then. Tell me all about her."

Viktor paused, apparently assembling his thoughts, a process perhaps not helped by the vodka he had already consumed.

"Well?" demanded Nicko. "I'm agog- all ears. Is she a nymph of sixteen? Which might account for the outfit?"

"She's a bit more than that."

"Not that can always tell these days." Nicko realised that he needed to adopt less flippant tone. Viktor's situation seemed to have a bearing on his own, but it was too early to consider seriously what that might be.

"She's nineteen. Or at least that's what she told me."

"Christ, Vik, you aren't even sure!"

Viktor laughed. "Her great grandparents on her father's side were Russians- from the south of the country, but she couldn't say where exactly."

"And what about her?"

"Her own folks moved from Detroit to New York back in the Sixties. Her dad's a management consultant, or something of that kind, with the name of Marionoff, which sounds Russian enough. She's an art student."

"Ah."

"Why 'ah'?"

So you came across her in the way of business- with your chum who supplies the Constructivist masterpieces?"

"She's got nothing to do with that."

"I'll believe you, but no doubt she's the one who's put you up to the sartorial adjustments? I won't call them improvements."

"Piss off, Nick. I had to dress up for a party."

"A fancy dress one?"

"Christ, Nick, you were born with one of your feet already in the grave."

"Quite likely. But what have you told Verochka? I suppose she fits into the equation somewhere."

Viktor drained the vodka bottle into their glasses.

"Go easy," Nicko said.

"You're my oldest and dearest friend… Nick. And I'm asking you for your help. You see - I know…. what she feels about you. Vera, I'm talking about."

Without thinking, Nicko reached out and gripped his friend's hand.

"You're a silly old fucker, Vik…" The vodka had got through by now and there was the beginning of a lump in his throat. "But isn't this something you have to tell her yourself?"

Viktor shook his head, almost as if trying to clear it, and then put it in his hands, slightly overplaying it Nicko felt.

"It's never been like this before, Nick. It's eating me up…"

Nicko sighed, sensing his own inadequacy in the situation, as he had never felt the same way himself. Empathy was out of his reach.

"You met her through your new dealer friend," he eventually came out with.

Viktor nodded. "He throws parties all the time- many of them for his young painter friends. He's on the lookout for fresh talent all the time, he tells them, and most of them buy into it. They want the celebrity that they feel ought to be theirs."

"And can this guy deliver it? Maybe he can offer them a career knocking up Rothkos and de Koonings? That shouldn't be too hard to do. Sorry, Vik, we're drifting. Tell me about… what's she called?"

"Svetlana."

"God, it has to be, hasn't it?"

"What's wrong with that? It's a perfectly good Russian name."

"Yet another drifting Russian soul by the sound of it."

"Isn't that a case of the pot calling the kettle black?"

"Did I tell you that once?"

Viktor grinned back at him.

"O.K. you win this time, just for once, you pisser."

"She's a stunner, Nick," Viktor said. "If you'd set eyes on her… even you Nick…"

"But I haven't, have I?"

"And Verochka…" A tear trickled down Viktor's face.

God, we are getting Slavic tonight, thought Nicko. Suddenly he hardened.

"For Christ's sake, don't turn on the taps," he told his friend. "Think of your wife and child. You have to face them yourself."

Viktor shook his head vigorously, gave a big sob and rubbed his eyes. He gazed hard at Nicko.

"Well?" the latter said. "You still love them, don't you? In spite of all you're telling me about your nymphet?"

"If you'd met her, you wouldn't use that word."

"Just think of the boy - your boy - and what the future might be holding for him! Frankly, at school they say he's bloody good - he's got his father's brains, there's no doubt about it. Already he's well ahead of his peers in most things, in spite of coming late to the language."

"He hardly needs me then - as long as the money lasts."

"God Vik, you are an utter shit!"

"And you're a silly old woman."

They had raised their voices, but caution prevailed and they dropped them again.

"This is no good," Viktor said. "I'm sorry about Verochka… of course I am…" He looked hard at Nicko. "About Verochka…"

"What about her? You have something more to tell me."

"She loves you, Nick and Kolochka does too. You're the one they really want, while my role will be to supply the money to give the boy his chance. Don't you see, Nikoshka, that something like this was meant to happen ever since we first met as thirteen-year-olds at that famous English public school?"

His frankness left Nicko lost for words.

"And like I said, Kolochka… he loves you too, the way a son loves his own father!"

"Don't say that Vik! You know that can't be true!"

"But I hope he'll keep a place for me as well. It doesn't need to be a very big one - but as a kind of uncle. We just swop parts."

For a moment he seemed about to break down in tears, while his words ran through Nicko like a hot iron.

"You must speak to Verochka first," he eventually came out with, "if you're really quite sure, that is. After that, I will. It has to happen that way round."

Viktor assented with a sigh.

"We'd better strike while the iron's hot," Nicko said. "You know what that one means?"

"Kaneshna." Viktor stood up, rubbed his hand across the unfamiliar stubble on his scalp and opened the door.

Nicko stood to one side. "Lead on McDuff."

Together they went downstairs, Nicko going into the breakfast room and leaving his friend to go by himself into the sitting one.

As he joined Kolya, he could hear words being spoken in Russian across the hall.

Better to have it out in their native tongue, he thought somewhat patronisingly. But at the same time he was concerned about passionate voices being raised and overheard by the boy.

Kolya was watching a DVD and Nicko was gratified to see that it was 'The Lion, the Witch and the Wardrobe'- in his opinion a well-nigh perfect adaptation of the original C.S. Lewis tale.

"I love this film," he said, settling on the sofa next to the boy.

Kolya nodded, but said nothing, while Nicko tried to put his mind to the thing he was watching and to keep the boy's attention away from what was going on across the hall.

"Do you mind turning the sound up a little?" he asked.

Kolya worked the handset and they went on watching the film without a further word passing between them.

No raised voices could be heard coming from the sitting room and Kolya seemed to be totally absorbed in the film.

After about ten minutes, Nicko heard a door opening, words spoken softly in Russian and then Viktor put his head round the breakfast room door. His son did not bother to look round.

Quietly Nicko stood up and went out into the hall, closing the door behind him. "Well?"

Viktor shrugged his shoulders, spread his hands and gave him a large grin.

"Just as I thought," he said. "Pravda?"

"Pravda."

Nicko looked closely at friend. "You're making it sound too easy."

"Like I said. It's what she wants."

"For you to clear out? And what about Kolya?"

"That's no problem. I'll go on paying his costs - school fees and the rest - so he can grow up to be an English gentleman - with a Russian name - like you, of course."

"What are you saying exactly?"

"Christ, it's staring you in the face, isn't it? She wants to marry you! You're to set the seal on it - your Englishness, which is being passed on to the boy, pretty successfully, by the look of it. But…" he paused and looked at his friend, wistfully.

"Go on."

"I would like to see him occasionally, to see how it works out. It seems such a far cry from the camps of Kolyma to what he's turning into."

"For God's sake, Vik, aren't you leaping to some pretty massive conclusions? Who says I'm going to marry Verochka for a start? And there's no way I'd ever come between you and your own child. Put that right of you mind, straight away!"

Viktor hugged him tightly. "Go in and speak to her," he said.

As Nicko entered the room, Vera smiled at him from where she lying stretched out on the sofa. She appeared relaxed, as if nothing of much moment had just passed between her husband and herself. Shifting her feet, she made a space for Nicko to sit beside her.

When he had sat down she pointed to a picture on the wall beside her. "You remember that, Nikoshka?"

"Of course I do."

"I could never have trusted my husband with a thing like that."

Nicko frowned, feeling mildly affronted on his friend's behalf. "That's a bit hard, isn't it?"

For a few seconds they contemplated the Schwitters in silence.

"How would I know if it was genuine or not?" Vera eventually came out with.

Nicko shrugged. "I was acting on a hunch and in the end we had to take the man's word for it - which seemed convincing, but you can never be absolutely sure."

"Vitya and I have been talking." "I know you have."

"He wants me to divorce him so that he can start a new life in America. And he knows I don't want to do that - to live in America, I mean." She smiled and looked at the picture again. "You chose well, Nikoshka. For some reason - which I still can't explain - I like it."

"Thank you, but you helped."

"I trusted your judgement, Nikoshka, that's all. And I still do."

"Your husband wants a divorce. What do you feel about it?"

"Just relieved, Nikoshka! Just relieved! And with no trouble either. No passion and no blaming each other!"

"Well, if it's what you both want and the boy's quite happy when the time comes, I'm not the one to raise any doubts, am I? But all the same I'll feel a bit sad. Vik's probably my oldest friend and you're a very dear one."

"Which is all the more reason to do what we're doing - if it makes everyone happier. We can all stay good friends."

Nicko scrutinised the Schwitters. "Yes," he said deliberately, "I think we got it right."

"Of course you did, you silly malchik!"

"And it looks right in that frame and where you've hung it." He glanced at the other walls which were sparsely covered- with a set of Monet reproductions.

"You can teach me so much, Nikoshka - about art, I mean. And Kolochka too - he worships the ground you walk on."

"But my feet are made of clay, the same as anyone else's."

They did not speak for a moment. Nicko suspect that Vera was waiting for him to come out with something important, but inwardly he was in a state of turmoil, and not sure what he wanted to say, let alone how he was going to say it.

"Vik seems to have made his mind up," he came out with, "and is very happy that you've agreed. I suppose he spoke to you about Svetlana?"

Vera laughed mockingly. "Of course he did. She's - how do I say it? the pretext?" Then she suddenly leaned forward and hugged him. "Oh Nikoshka! It could end so well, for all of us! For you too, Nikoshka! The way is open! There are many things I still have to teach you, but first there are some that you must do for yourself! You know what I'm telling you, Nikoshka?" She paused, biting her lower lip.

He took her hand. "It's all a bit sudden," he said. "You must give me a little time to think it over. Naturally you and Kolya will play a very big part in my life… that goes without saying…but… I still must have time to think." He pressed her closer to his chest.

"Oh Nikoshka, don't think for too long. It will only mean that you'll end by doing nothing."

"I'll try not to. He closed his eyes and kissed her in the middle of her forehead, and in the same instant an image flashed through his mind: Miguel, the nemesis of Mark Isaacs. "But Vik must get things started and then you must file for your divorce," he went on to say. "Everything must be done in the right order."

It was suddenly very alarming, terrifying almost, and he felt he was being forced into a decision which, left to himself, he would probably never have got round to making. He did not add anything to what he had just said, but kissed Vera's forehead for a second time, in a rather chaste manner. Then he rose to his feet and stood by the Schwitters, peering at it closely. He still wasn't sure quite why he liked the picture and questioned himself for assuming that he did. Was it simply a matter of the man's reputation? Or his family's unlikely brush with the artist in Norway? But then if he himself had assembled a collage, using newsprint and a few well-judged brushstrokes, might he not have achieved a similar result without the world ever taking notice of it? Talk about the flower that blooms in the forest unseen… all this raced through his mind in the minute between rising and turning back to Vera.

"I have to do a lot of thinking, Verochka," he told her, "but I'm pleased that you and Vik seem to be settling things so easily between yourselves, and I don't have to tell you that Kolya has to come first, whatever you decide to do." He bent down and kissed her.

"And it must be right for you too."

"For me too. I care deeply about both of you, not forgetting Vik either. I'll let myself out, and I'll be back very soon. God bless you, Verochka!"

Walking to the Underground station, Nicko felt that events were running on too fast for his own comfort. He felt himself being boxed into decisions that he would much rather have postponed indefinitely. The truth was that Nicko was emotionally lazy and reluctant to commit himself to any step that might radically alter the course of his life. The idea of being drawn into a closer relationship - he was reluctant to define it more precisely than that - with Verochka and Kolya, especially as Vik seemed to want it that way, had an obvious appeal to him, but it alarmed him as well. Was it something that he could sustain over time?

And then there was Miguel who kept re-appearing, like some spirit of the night. He preferred to think that he had seen the last of the youth, but his recent disclosures about Mark Isaacs showed what a lethal sting he had. Nicko tried to persuade himself that his relationship with the Mexican boy was now a thing of the past.

But he knew that he had to give Verochka a clear answer, even if no direct question had yet been put to him. By the time he had reached the station he had decided to consult Tim.

He rang him and spoke to Ludmilla, who knew nothing of Vik's sudden return and he felt reluctant to tell her. He needed to speak to her husband, he informed her.

Ludmilla fetched Tim, but with her hovering in the vicinity Nicko did not like to divulge his business, so at the risk of sounding unduly secretive, he convinced his friend that he had to speak to him privately about a very important development in his life.

* * * * * *

Supplied with malt whiskies in their usual nook, Nicko told Tim what had passed between himself and the Nikishovs.

"Vik's back," he began by telling his friend. "He's cut all his hair off and looks a proper oik."

"Good God, so where do we go next?"

"He claims to have hooked up with some arty bird in New York. She's called Svetlana and is an acquaintance of his new dealer chum."

"It just has to be, hasn't it? I mean the name - Svetlana."

"My own feeling a bit too. But the upshot is that he wants Vera to give him a divorce, which she is happy to do."

"Well that's all right then. As long as he forks out to keep her and the boy in the style they're used to."

"He says that's all part of the deal."

"What could be better? It would make life such a lot simpler if more people could settle their differences so easily." He eyed Nicko. "But there a bit more to it than that, isn't there?"

"I fear there is and that's where I'd like your opinion."

Tim sipped his whisky and raised his eyebrows expectantly.

"You're married to a Russian," Nicko began, "so perhaps you won't think I'm being a fool."

Tim smiled. "Why would I think such a thing?"

There was a pause.

"I think I know what you're trying to say to me," Tim eventually came out with. "Vera wants to marry you."

"Yes, I think so, but she hasn't quite said it."

"Because she's waiting for you to say it first, you prat! The man is usually the one who pops the question." Tim shook his head and smiled indulgently at Nicko's apparent naivety.

"Of course."

"So what am I supposed to tell you?"

"You have a Russian wife, Tim, and I don't want something to happen that any of us might regret."

"You mean I'm an authority on Slavic femininity, who is able to share the fruits of his wisdom with you? Well, for a start I know nothing of the particular chemistry that may exist between you and Vera and in any case my own experience in the field is not exactly extensive. Have you made love to her?"

"A couple of times when I confess she rather set the pace."

Tim laughed outright. "That's probably what you need."

"You make me sound almost deviant," Nicko said. "But there was nothing like that about it. Quite simply, she knows how to move things along better than I do. After all, she's had a lot more practice."

"Well that sounds pretty satisfactory to me. As long as each party has got his or her eyes open and the boy is happy about his new stepdad."

"That won't be a problem."

Tim smiled. "No, I'm sure it won't."

"Anyway, thanks Tim, You've told me what I needed to hear."

"Drink up then. Your turn to pay for the next one. We might have something to celebrate."

"Not so fast. I could be tempting fate."

"Which is what you should be doing with it."

Nicko fetched fresh drinks and they clinked their glasses in silence.

"How's Ludochka by the way?" Nicko asked.

"Working bloody hard and being a broody Russian." A shadow crossed Tim's face. "You come asking me for my advice, Nick, yet she baffles me."

Nicko said nothing, but assumed a sympathetic expression.

"Some days she hardly says a word. If she's not scribbling in her notebook, she seems locked up in a dream."

"She's not losing her marbles, is she?"

"I don't think so. When I suggested a break in Petersburg together, she perked up at that idea."

"Probably that's what she needs. Maybe she's pining for Mother Russia and the Black Earth or whatever."

"Bloody Slavic souls! Sorry, you're supposed to have one and to be marrying another."

"My own's somewhat diluted, I fear."

"I like that idea- a diluted soul. Anyway, Nick, you take the bull by the horns. Do what Verochka wants you to do. The lad'll love having you as his stepdad, while Vik lives out his days blissfully locked in the arms of his sprite, Svetlana. And they all lived happily ever after. Bloody Russians - everywhere you look these days!"

"Nasdorovia!" announced Nicko, raising his glass.

Their talk wandered off into politics and the shape of things to come, with inevitable speculation about where the tale of Lord Isaacs would lead to next.

"Dobrinin's yacht was a floating pleasure dome," Tim said.

"But it's what Isaacs might have had in his own house that interests me more," observed Nicko.

CHAPTER TWENTY-NINE

Tale End

Tim went for his holiday in St Petersburg with Ludmilla, while the pace of Nicko's life began to quicken. The fresh developments had to run beside his commitment to his work. After the success of 'The Pardoner's Tale', he was eager to follow it with something else and was toying with a number of ideas. In the meantime, Viktor and Vera were wasting no time untying the knot that bound them.

Nicko saw Kolya at school, and the boy showed no sign of concern at what was unfolding in his own home. Now that the decision had been taken, the atmosphere no doubt was less tense and Nicko found the boy as trusting as ever. Sometimes at the end of a lesson, after he had been teaching him, he would come and lean on Nicko's shoulder and repeat the Narnia story he was currently reading with the encouragement of his godfather.

When Nicko rang Thurloe Square, Vera spoke frankly about her husband, now that she was detaching herself from him. His teenage outfit aroused a contemptuous amusement in her, but nothing more. Solicitors had been approached and the matter was to be handled under the English legal system. She told him that Viktor was ready to act out the role of guilty party, but she did not press Nicko about his own intentions, though he knew that he had to say something before too long.

He decided to write her a letter, which was a general statement of his deep affection for them all, not omitting his old school chum, who was being so accommodating. But reading it through, he concluded that it sounded pompous and evasive. He knew that soon he would have to speak more directly. Put simply, Vera was expecting to marry him once her divorce from Viktor was through. The supply of money was to be assured and the continued education of her son in an English school confirmed. The matter of the boy's national status would be resolved with the new marriage. And Nicko's own aspirations? It was tempting to think that the financial settlement, reached by Vera with Viktor, would provide the economic base from which he might fulfill his own literary aspirations. But there was also a sense of pride and a reluctance to be a kept man- a position which could only be justified by a positive literary achievement.

And then what was his mother going to say? His visits to her had become even more perfunctory. It seemed that both parties preferred it that way, but he knew that if he broke off completely, umbrage would be taken. The notion of her son marrying a divorced New Russian already with a child was hardly going to appeal to Mrs Orloff, who continued to think wistfully of him bonded to an English rose. The irony was that his mother, with her fiercely English prejudices and Russian-sounding surname, was not so very different from Vera and her hopes for her descendants.

Nicko would leave his mother out of the picture until the thing was buttoned up. Likewise his sister and her family, with whom he had little contact anyway.

So he waited on events, being in no particular hurry to force them. He kept up a steady stream of hopeful signals to Vera and got down to writing a new play in his spare time.

This time he settled on the form of a morality play of the late Middle Ages. He liked the use of concrete images to express abstract ideas, which this early type of drama had employed, and decided to call his play 'One Man's Soul', where the soul, which was to be fought over by the forces of Good and Evil, would be given physical form as a mucky-looking rag, like a pocket handkerchief. It was a kind of update of the medieval play 'Everyman', addressing a number of modern themes. But it hadn't to be too solemn and portentous: its message had to lie within reach of an intelligent twelve or thirteen year old.

Nicko became so engrossed in it and had to force himself to think of Vera, while she, for her part, was waiting patiently for him to do the manly thing. Indeed, it was clear to him that she was carrying a stereotype of an English gentleman in her mind which he was expected to live up to.

But it was Viktor who nudged matters forward. He rang Nicko, mildly rebuking him for his hesitation and joshing him in the familiar fashion. Nicko's riposte was to tease him about his absurd adolescent appearance and they had good chuckle together, before telling each other to piss off.

Nicko nevertheless realised that it was time to gird up his loins and not to shelter behind his artistic creativity for too long. Viktor had informed him that Vera was already filing for his alleged adultery with Svetlana in the Big Apple, while he, of course, was not going to contend it. So the way was being cleared for Nicko to step up and declare his troth, while, at the same time, to begin the business of naturalising Kolya. The house in Thurloe Square, it went without saying, was part of the settlement. Viktor seemed perfectly confident about the extent of his own resources, expressing no misgivings about his future. Nicko had no idea of how extensive they actually were, but then Viktor was a Nikishov and they had been working hard at it ever since Stalin's time.

Tim, who was back from what had turned into an extended stay in Russia's second city, rang Nicko and there was a note of anxiety in his voice.

"All well?" enquired Nicko, suspecting that it wasn't.

"I'm not sure," his friend replied. "How so?"

"It all went a bit Slavic."

"What? Plot by Dostoyevski?"

"Not quite yet. But that might be on the cards. May I come and talk to you?"

"Kaneshna. There's something I'd like to ask you too. It's also Slavic."

"I hope you're heeding my advice."

"We'll pool our problems. I'm sure it'll be of mutual benefit."

A pair of clucking old chickens, Nicko reflected, that's what we're turning into.

* * * * * *

"How's Ludochka?" he demanded to know, as soon as Tim was through the door.

Tim shrugged. "She didn't want to come home."

"Home being here? Setting foot in Mother Russia again was almost too much for her?"

"She knows all sorts of people. I'd never met a quarter of them when we were there before. But that was a honeymoon, I suppose."

"What kind of people?"

"Academic types for the most part. They all spoke good English."

"Anything the matter with that?"

"Nothing at all. One of them was a lecturer in Balkan history who banged on a great deal about the Montenegran royal family, but there was another guy with a straggly beard - a kind of a cross between Tolstoy and

Rasputin, if you ask me - whom she seemed particularly drawn to. In fact they went off for an entire afternoon by themselves."

"I hope it wasn't Rasputin. Tolstoy might have been safer."

"She said he was a theologian."

"A kind of starets? A holy man out of the Siberian taiga - that kind of thing?"

"My own impression exactly. And it was after that, that she expressed herself reluctant to come back. But anyway, she did and now it's nose into the laptop once more."

Tim broke off to quiz Nicko about his own affair and told him to push ahead, when he had heard him out, though with a hint of circumspection.

"Marrying a Russian is a big step," he pointed out portentously. "But I don't think it will be quite such a big one for you as it was for me."

"I'm taking on a child at the same time," Nicko reminded him.

"That's the easy part - for you at least."

Nicko smiled, but did not reply immediately. Invariably people came to the same conclusion about him. They never expressed it openly, but it was plain enough - he was a man-child - and the world of children was his proper place. His occupation only seemed to confirm that. And even now, he was itching to get back to his new play and to enjoy once again the bond that the previous one had established between himself and those placed in his charge.

"You'll make a great stepdad," Tim came out with at length. "And if the boy's own father is happy enough with that, who am I to say otherwise?"

The ironic twists of Russian history, and the way it seemed to be turning back on itself since the tragedy of October 1917, struck Nicko forcibly in his talks with Tim. The link that was now being forged between himself, the direct descendant of a White Russian monarchist, and the descendant of one of Stalin's most notorious gulag satraps was a curious example. The enormity of it made it a tale worth telling. But it was a positive development, a reconciliation, a coming together after the horrors of the twentieth century, on terms that Nicko approved. For, broadly speaking, Vera wanted the things that he did.

Though he could sense Tim's reservations- resulting probably from his increasingly baffling relationship with a Russian wife, Nicko knew that it was time to make himself plain to Vera.

"Tomorrow," he declared, "I will take the bull by the horns."

"You do just that," Tim said, then sighed. "I wish my case was that simple. You see, as well as Ludochka's personal needs - her literary or academic career or whatever - behind her is what I can only describe as the Dobrinin factor. Sorry if that sounds a bit like the title of an airport thriller."

"I rather like it," said Nicko. "I might even snitch it from you."

"But seriously, Nick, it has got its problems- I mean locking ourselves in with a man like that. I'm talking, of course, from a business perspective. There's a potential killing to be made, maybe in more ways than one."

"Have you got any evidence to back such a supposition?" Nicko asked.

"Perhaps my imagination is getting a bit overheated, after those fearsome intellectuals in Petersburg," Tim said. "But now's not the moment to dwell on it. Have we time for one more?"

They settled down to plot their next museum excursion - to the V and A this time - after which Nicko ventured onto the territory of his new play. Tim seemed more than politely interested. Politics as usual rounded their evening off: Isaacs, it went without saying, and the Media's current perception of him. Regardless of his sexual proclivities, his body washing up in a silk dressing gown on a Greek strand had generated some sympathy for him, adding a Byronic lustre to his demise in the eyes of a couple of the posher broadsheets. The topic exhausted, for the moment at any rate, they turned finally to something more general, an attempt on the part of each to define his own particular brand of Toryism. Nicko felt that he belonged to the One Nation School, since it best reflected his romantic paternalism, while in Tim's case, working in the cut and thrust of the London property market, made his brand more hard-edged. But as usual the thread was lost as they grew more sleepy and incoherent.

* * * * * *

When Nicko rang Thurloe Square, it was Viktor who answered the phone, sounding bouncy. He and Vera were agreed on the shape of their case and were ready to proceed. Solicitors were being consulted and the question of their Russian citizenship being addressed. So far Kolya had not been told anything, but no doubt the less strained atmosphere in the house was beneficial, and when the final break came he could be eased without trauma into the new circumstances of his life. He was still full of his dog and Viktor fetched him to the phone to talk to Nicko about him.

Nicko did not speak to Vera, but informed his friend that there was something that he needed to say to her, which met with a ribald response. That it was his own wife who was being referred to appeared to matter not at all. Viktor then went on to mention that a deal involving an important cache of modernist paintings was coming to a head, which evoked a predictable sigh from Nicko.

"Don't fuck it up this time," he warned him.

"There're no Rothkos," Viktor assured him, "but we won't talk about it now."

On Saturday Nicko was to pay his visit and in the meantime he had to go over in his mind what he was going to say to Vera.

He decided to be down to earth and practical. Vera, he hoped, would approach it in the same pragmatic fashion and that there would be no extravagant displays of emotion, that would be out of keeping with the kind of Englishness which she was expecting her son to grow into. A gentlemanly reticence had to be the order of the day.

In the evenings remaining to him before his momentous expedition, Nicko marked school work and fiddled with his upcoming play. And when Saturday arrived, he presented himself in Thurloe Square, to be greeted at the door in the usual way by Alyosha, who had a discreetly confidential air as if he knew perfectly well what was afoot.

"Everybody at home, Alyosha?" Nicko asked in a conventional fashion.

"Kolya is out with his father. They've gone with Stenka to the Gardens."

"So there's only Vera?"

"Da." Alyosha eyed him conspiratorially.

"No trips to Mother Russia planned?" Nicko enquired breezily as he passed into the hall.

"Later in the year, maybe. She's in the kitchen."

Nicko went through and found Vera sitting at the table with her hands folded in front of her. Somehow it seemed easier to say what he had to say to her over the kitchen table, rather than in the more formal setting of the sitting room.

Vera did not rise, but remained seated, with a mildly expectant expression on her face. She was wearing an apron and looked rather homely. Nicko leaned over and kissed her on the cheek. She took his hand and squeezed it.

"I've been waiting for you, Nikoshka," she said softly. "Tea?"

"Please."

She turned on the ring on the stove and put cups and saucers on the table. Nicko watched her, without speaking. Then she looked at him squarely, waiting for him to say something.

"I've spoken to Vik," he came out with eventually. "I know you have."

"And everything appears to be going to plan. Da?"

"Da. Kaneshna." There was the merest hint of impatience in her answer.

"So when it's all settled, Verochka, will you marry me?"

She rose and spooned tea into the pot.

"Well?" said Nicko.

Vera came round the table and placed her arms round his neck. "I thought you were never going to ask me." "Well, I'm asking you now."

"You really mean it, Nikoshka?"

"Of course I mean it." He attempted to sound more masculine and assertive.

"You really do, Nikoshka?"

"Do I have to repeat myself?"

She gave him a hug. "We'll be so happy and Kolochka too."

"And Vik."

"And Vitya."

"But we must be patient," he reminded her. "There's all that legal work first. But I'm quite sure Vik'll play his part."

Vera heaved a large sigh.

"He'll still be a very dear friend," went on Nicko. "After all, he's the oldest one I've got. And he must be allowed to see his son. There can be no doubt about that."

"Kolochka will be happier," she said. "You can see that he already loves you."

"But he's Vik's son- a Nikishov, and not an Orloff. I will cherish him, but he must always put his own father first."

Instead of saying anything she stroked his hair, massaging the locks gently between her fingers.

"You're such a beautiful English boy," she murmured, "and Kolochka is going to be one like you."

"Don't build your hopes too high," he warned her. "But I'm sure that between the four of us we'll manage something."

"Of course we will." She hugged and kissed him before attending to the tea.

For a few moments they sat in silence. Everything that needed to be seemed to have been said. And anyway, Nicko felt it was hardly the moment for love play or a display of sentimentality. But eventually he took Vera's hand and squeezed it in his own, while she purred like a contented cat.

"Alyosha said that Kolya and his father had gone to the Gardens with the dog," he said. "They'll be back shortly?"

Vera glanced at the kitchen clock. "Shortly."

"Will that be the time to say something?"

She shook her head. "We'll speak to Kolochka in the morning- Vitya and I."

"And Alyosha and Tsina?"

"They know everything. Alyosha's helping Vitya with his paperwork."

"What does he think? Where's it going to leave him?"

Vera shrugged. "He'll be all right. He's a Russian and, anyway, Vitya won't forget him." She recharged their cups. "I'm sorry- you'd like a biscuit. I hope Kolochka hasn't eaten them all."

As they waited nervously for the walk party to return, their talk grew more stilted. So it was a relief almost when they heard the front door open and the dog bounded into the kitchen, ahead of the others.

"He wants his tea." Kolya declared in English as he followed hard on his heels. "And I do too."

Then he threw his arms round Nicko's neck and hugged him.

"You'll choke me," the latter protested.

"Stenka chased another dog," the boy announced. "It was bigger than him."

"A Great Dane," said Viktor, coming into the kitchen. "I nearly lost Kolochka in the chase."

"What's for tea, Mum?" demanded the boy, sounding utterly English.

Vera frowned, not quite sure yet how to take the English 'mum' in place of the Russian 'mama', despite her Anglophilia.

"Wash your hands first," she ordered him.

The boy scowled and went to the sink.

"Go to the cloakroom, Kolochka," said his mother sternly.

Obediently, he left and his father sat down at the table. Viktor looked at Nicko who nodded back to him.

"All done?" Viktor whispered across the table, while Vera went on slicing bread with her back to them.

Then she turned to them and stroked her husband's stubbly head. "Nikoshka and I have had our talk," she said. "Everything's fine." She repeated it in Russian, as if to ratify it. "I'll speak to Kolochka in the morning," she added.

Viktor seized her hand and squeezed it. "Harasho," he said. "Spasibo."

Meanwhile the boy returned and opened the fridge and took out a bottle of Coca-Cola.

"Out of there," his mother commanded him brusquely. "And sit at the table properly."

Without a word, he did as he was told.

"You had a great time in the Gardens?" Nicko said. "And apart from chasing a dog twice his size, did Stenka behave himself?"

Viktor watched his friend making inconsequential chat to his son, but said nothing, simply looking on with a benevolent smile.

To Nicko it felt awkward, but it was better than it could have been. Viktor showed no sign of resentment that his role was being usurped, but, on the contrary, that things were moving in exactly the direction he wanted them to go.

They talked in this light vein, until Nicko rather pointedly looked at the clock.

"I must be away," he declared.

"Aren't you staying for supper, Uncle Nicko?" Kolya said, with a note of disappointment in his voice.

"Not tonight, I'm afraid. I've got to meet a friend," lied his godfather.

"What sort of friend?"

"Don't be rude, Kolochka!" his mother said. "It's none of your business!"

"It's all right," Nicko assured her. "There's no harm done. A friend who's helping me to write a book, as a matter of fact."

"What sort of a book?"

"That's my secret. You'll know soon enough."

"Why can't I know now?"

"Kolochka, stop it at once! Do you want to be sent to your room?"

Viktor was smiling broadly, quite content, it appeared.

407

Nicko left the boy and his father at the table, while Vera came to see him to the door. On the step he turned and kissed her, pressing his lips tight against hers and searching out her tongue in the manner that they enjoyed. Then she tapped his nose in her admonitory fashion.

"Next weekend, Nikoshka. Vitya will probably be back in New York."

"It all seems a bit too easy. Aren't we tempting fate?"

She tapped his nose again. "Don't say things like that, Nikoshka."

"The weekend, then." He kissed her cheek and left her on the step.

As he strolled towards Knightsbridge, Nicko's mind was racing. It had all been uncannily straightforward and awaited only Kolya's seal of approval, which looked like a given. And Viktor was like a man liberated. Nicko wondered about Svetlana and the power she seemed to have over his friend. He could only hope for the best, as he waited to find out.

But at the same time he felt nervous. Though Vera could clearly take him for what he was, having already put him through his paces, marriage seemed to be an awesome transitional step. What would it be like in ten years' time, with them both advancing into middle-age and Kolya turning into a young man, no longer a bouncy boy in a green school blazer and grey flannel shorts? On reflection, it seemed quite daunting, but just then, as he was cutting through Pelham Place, a young man, dark, possibly Latino, though it was difficult to tell, brushed against him. Despite the generous width of pavement, their bodies touched. It seemed deliberate, as if the young man had been trying to pass a message of some kind on to him

Nevertheless, he was resolved to pursue the course he had set for himself. It was going to take time, he knew, until the legal settlement was wrapped up. In the coming weeks he would be seeing a good deal of Vera and her son and doubtless Viktor, too, during his toing and froing between continents. His friend appeared be throwing himself back into the art market in a big way and Nicko wondered what part, if any, his Slavic siren, Svetlana, was playing in it all. He just hoped that Viktor knew what he was up to. His slide into juvenile mode was hardly encouraging, and Nicko wondered if he would next see him in a beltless pair of jeans, its seat sagging down to the back of his knees. The paradox of Vik was his trusting nature, which was at odds with his entrepreneurial energy and ready knack for make money. Was there something particularly Russian about it? And this outfit in New York - what were they really up to? And over it all, there still hung the shadow of the oligarch, Oleg Pavlovich

Dobrinin, with whom Vik had already fallen out a couple of times, though apparently being forgiven on each occasion.

* * * * * *

The next few evenings Nicko devoted to his play, swiftly losing himself in the task. When he paused to think about it, he believed that it was the kind of thing that he had been sent into the world to do. It absorbed him so completely, that when he broke off he felt a twinge of conscience for putting other matters so firmly out of sight, including, of course, his proposal of marriage to Vera. His job too required a steady commitment, though that was largely a matter of routine. And he hadn't to forget his intention of writing his children's guide, either - a scheme that Tim appeared eager to pursue with him. But the duel between the representatives of Good and Evil for the possession of One Man's soul had eclipsed that for the time being.

It was Tim who broke into his reverie. He rang with fresh gossip about the Dobrinin yacht. An old school chum, who was a rising star in Conservative Central Office, had been on the very trip that had turned into Isaacs' last. He had said nothing to anyone about it until now, for fear of the possible political repercussions for his own party. But while the central event remained a mystery, some of the high jinks going on the same occasion did not. That the yacht was indeed a floating bordello was plain and it appeared that the oligarch even supplied a range of specialists to cater for the different appetites of his guests. It had all the decadence of the court of a Nero or a Heliogabalus, Tim said, and that Mark Isaacs' particular needs had been catered for. He suggested that it might have been on board the Anastasia that he had met Miguel in the first place.

Miguel in the employ of Dobrinin. That was an interesting thought for Nicko to conjure with, though he had, of course, assumed that the Mexican Boy had accompanied the Government Minister on most of his maritime romps. Tim was keen for him to meet his political chum, so that he could have it directly from the horse's mouth and Nicko readily assented, while at the same time remonstrating with himself for his lingering interest in the youth. He remembered to tell Tim about Vera and duly received his formal congratulations. Then he enquired after Ludmilla and Tim's tone clouded over.

"Hm," Tim faulted. "Dark forces."

"Oh God. Not as bad as that, is it?"

"Sorry, I don't mean to sound apocalyptic. You remember that character she met up with in Petersburg? The cross between Rasputin and Tolstoy? A sort of Old Believer from the taiga?"

"Go on."

"Well, he's got a website and prophesies, guess what? The end of the world!"

"That sounds par for the course."

"Apparently a rogue planet called Nibiru is heading in our direction and shortly there's going to be an almighty collision."

"Is that all? It's nothing new. After all, it is Russia- isn't it? where they watch the U.F.O.s landing and taking off again through the bottom of their vodka bottles."

"The trouble is my wife seems to have bought into it. There are times, I tell, you when I wish we could uninvent the bloody Internet."

Nicko concurred. "Of course it's a fact that Russian intellectuals are some of the most gullible when it comes to aliens and indeed conspiracy theories in general. It baffles me how they manage to accommodate such rubbish in otherwise rational minds. But then I suppose there are plenty of Americans who do the same."

"Meanwhile I've got to listen to it."

"What happened to the last King and Queen of Montenegro? Where've they gone to?"

"Probably off in a spaceship to the outer reaches of the Solar System." Tim sighed.

"She's not saying that surely, is she?"

"Not yet, but wherever they are, I'd welcome them back with open arms, rather than having to listen to this other drivel. Mind you, the Good Ship Anastasia provides a welcome distraction. Far better than any spaceship."

"I wonder what Dobrinin thinks about it? the planetary collision, I mean?"

"Keeping ahead of the game, I expect- building a spacecraft in Siberia- as a kind of intergalactic pleasure dome."

"And who's going to be allowed to book a passage in it? I expect only the great and the good."

Tim promised to fix a meeting with his Tory chum and bring him along to the Cock and Hen.

* * * * * *

Five days had gone by before Nicko spoke to Vera again. She was full of hope about the course things were taking, though she had nothing fresh to report since their last meeting. She was bubbling with schemes for Kolya's future, which she wanted to talk through with his stepfather-in-waiting- about which school should follow Bailey's, and so on. Some the London ones were very good, she had been told, and the Khlebnikovs were toying with Eton, so she wondered about a trip down to Windsor, where she had not yet been to anyway. What did Nikoshka think?

Nicko remembered Vik saying how he would like his son to follow in his own and Nicko's footsteps. Nicko reminded her of this and said he was broadly sympathetic to the idea, but that it was something that didn't need to be settled immediately.

He then passed on to Vera what Tim had been telling him about Ludmilla and her guru.

She did not sound greatly concerned. "Russians always talk like that," she told him. "I have a cousin in Ekaterinburg - I don't know if he's still there or not - and he once told me something of the same kind. About a prophet who had come from the taiga and was talking about the end of Time."

"But you don't take any of it seriously yourself, do you, Verochka? It's superstitious bunk out of the Middle Ages. Mind you, Marx and Lenin talked just as much bunk."

"You're probably right, Nikoshka. But I really don't know what I believe anymore."

"Kolya mustn't grow up to believe in smelly prophets, who crawl out of the taiga, preaching the imminent end of Time and God's wrath being brought upon anyone who's unwilling to take their word for it. You're not spending a fortune on his education for that to happen, Verochka."

"I trust you, Nikoshka."

"I'll get across at the weekend. I've been bloody busy. As well as schoolwork, I'm writing a new play."

"You can tell me all about it."

Nicko kissed the mouthpiece of his phone and she did the same.

* * * * * *

Friday evening was pleasantly spent in the Cock and Hen, getting chapter and verse about the high jinks on board the good ship 'Anastasia' from

Tim's Tory chum, Robin. Apparently there was a madame, a large Ukrainian lady, who organised things with a team also recruited in that country. Everything ran smoothly, as it should in any well-run brothel. Discreet cabin assignments were provided with the devushkas on request, but their living space and that of the guests was kept apart, so there was no overt intrusion on the decorous tone that Oleg Pavlovich still liked to maintain. In addition to the devushkas were the cabin boys, housed among the crew and including members of it, who met the needs of the likes of Mark Isaacs. A number of these were lads in their teens and of a variety of nationalities, ranging from Russians to Philippinos or Latinos. Robin, told them that most things, short of necrophilia, went.

"And what of Tatiana Yurievna herself?" enquired Nicko. "How did she fit into it all?"

"Perfectly happily," Robin replied. "I think for her, it's a bit like living over the shop. There was even a suggestion that she and Madame from Ukraine might have been cousins. Mind you, Yurievna liked to keep her distance. She held her own court in a separate cabin, where she was quite the Empress. It was rumoured that even the Great Man himself only attended by appointment."

"And she's a handsome woman in her own right?" asked Nicko.

"She was in her time certainly, but somewhat passé. Mind you, there was talk - very discreet of course, that Oleg's fortune did not emerge entirely from under the permafrost."

"But Isaacs felt quite at home?" put in Tim.

"Absolutely. Madame seemed particularly to take him under wing. He of course was an assiduous attender at the Royal boudoir, always ready to flatter the Tsarina."

"Though not one to offer her much else?" Nicko said, "despite being the direct descendant of Eve's tempter."

"Mind you," Robin went on," when I met him there, he was on the run from his exposure in the Media and of course didn't have his own acolyte in tow. So while he waited on Madame in her boudoir, he larked about with some of the matelots, but didn't really want to face the rest of us."

But how much of all of this, the full account of what went on aboard the ship of delights, would come to light in the enquiry into the peer's death? Indeed it was rather surprising that it wasn't in the public domain already, given all the speculation about Russia's oligarchs that went on. Nicko thought about Miguel. He must have a lot still to tell, reaping an enormous harvest from it. Was he biding his time? No doubt he was already in the hands of an agent. His first foray might have been revenge taken on his former master and tormentor, but having set such a chain of events in motion, the temptation to push on still further must be irresistible.

Tatiana Yurievna was back in London and, according to Tim, his wife had already spoken with her. He could not say what had passed between them, because Ludmilla had not divulged it, except to make a general observation about the woman's state of mind. Apparently she was perfectly calm and unfazed by anything that had happened. It seemed that nothing at all surprised her, least of all the suicide of a former British Government minister on board her husband's yacht. Ludmilla would say no more and Tim had been left wondering about the true nature of the friendship that appeared to exist between his own and the oligarch's wife.

Naturally when he next saw Vera, Nicko passed on to her what he had learned from Robin in the Cock and Hen. She merely laughed and said she was not in the least bit surprised.

"Have you heard anything from Vik?" he asked her.

"He's coming next week to talk to the solicitor," she said. "He said a lot about the pictures he's hoping to sell. Someone else he's discovered."

"I lose track. What happened to those Constructivists?"

Vera shrugged.

"And what about Svetlana?"

"He said nothing to me, but then I suppose he doesn't want to talk to me about her. And anyway it's not really my business."

"He'll be wearing filthy jeans, sagging from his backside and carrying a plastic water bottle about with him wherever he goes," said Nicko.

Vera heaved a big sigh. "Poor Vitya. How is it going to end for him? He might make himself look very foolish, if he's not careful. And he has such a fine son too." She squeezed Nicko's hand earnestly.

The fine son arrived in the kitchen at that moment, with the dog Stenka and went straight to the fridge. As he yanked at the door his mother seized his hand and rapped it. The boy pouted.

"I've begun another play, Kolya," his godfather told him, in an attempt to forestall the coming skirmish. "Would you like a part in it when it's done?"

"Tell me about it," the boy said.

He appeared to be genuinely interested, so Nicko went on to explain what a morality play was and how he was adapting the idea. Vera looked on, nodding with a satisfied expression on her face.

* * * * * *

It was late that night when Nicko heard the news on the Twenty-Four Hour service. If it had not been for the rumoured link with the Isaacs affair it would have gone largely unnoticed. Miguel, the former Government Minister's catamite, had been murdered.

There was no room for doubt. He had been shot dead on the landing of an apartment in the Bronx, while his killer had slipped away unseen by any security cameras. His personal role in the Isaacs affair, news which was just about to break, provided the spice, indicating that the matter had not ended in the Ionian Sea.

Nicko felt numb, then a stab of pain, followed by an almost complacent sense of relief. The decks were being cleared at least and his own way made easier, but then, as his thoughts centred on the Mexican boy, there came a physical reaction. It was as if the Miggie's face was only an inch away from his own, as it had lain on his pillow, with lips parted awaiting the entry of Nicko's tongue… He tried to focus his attention on what the reporter was saying. The man of course was talking about the enquiry into Isaacs' death and the newspaper article, which had presumably triggered it. Dobrinin's name cropped up and the part certain oligarchs were starting to play in the political, as well as the economic, life of the country. It needed to be chewed over with Tim, but not right away. Miggie felt like a still-living presence, his head nestling against his shoulder, so that he could even smell him…

For the next two nights he watched the Twenty-four Hour News, hungry for any morsel that might throw light on the Mexican Boy's death. He had talked to Tim and even asked him for Ludmilla's take on it. She had dismissed it as little consequence: the kind of thing that so often happened to young men who trafficked in their own bodies.

"Well," Tim had concluded, "the pair of them can settle their scores in the Great Beyond. I don't think it's hard to guess where that shot came from. Someone was onto him pretty swiftly."

And what would Vik be making it, Nicko wondered, assuming that the shooting of one more Latino boy in the Bronx would even catch the New York media's attention? But the link with a leading member of the last British Government and the oligarch's yacht must be arousing some curiosity across the pond. The full story of the floating whorehouse, and its motley celebrity clientele, was a likely runner.

* * * * * *

Viktor arrived in London to see his solicitor and met Nicko in the Pilsudski Restaurant. Nicko was relieved to see that his friend was more soberly dressed this time. He had shaved properly and was allowing his hair to grow back again. Nicko was assured that everything was going to plan.

"Has the boy been told anything yet?" Nicko wanted to know. When he had last raised it with Vera she had informed him that there was no need to hurry.

"His mother will do that - at the right time. It should be no problem."

"And Svetlana? Who is she exactly? I'm still in the dark."

Viktor grinned. "Her father's a painter."

"And what about her? Is she an artist of any kind, herself?"

"She's a dress designer - or at least setting out to be one."

"So you know her dad? That's something, I suppose."

Viktor nodded. "A Belo-Russian- second generation in the States, but he paints - how do I put it? in the Russian manner?"

"I'm not sure what that means."

"Russians understand and appreciate his work."

"Might that by any chance include Oleg Dobrinin?"

Viktor winked at him and laughed. "It might, but it would depend on how it was served up to him." "Or his partner, maybe?"

Viktor shrugged his shoulders, but added nothing.

"I suppose you know about the things that have been taking place on the good ship 'Anastasia'? The Isaacs business looks like the tip of an iceberg."

"Kaneshna. You'd hardly expect anything else, would you?"

"And now Miguel's dead. Having finished off Isaacs, he's bought it as well."

Viktor shrugged his shoulders to signal his indifference.

"Don't you think it's sad, though? I know he was playing with fire, but the boy had emerged from nowhere and was just grabbing at anything that happened to come his way. We still don't know who killed him, though I can guess." There was a tremor in Nicko's voice which caused his friend to look at him sharply.

But Viktor just sighed and still said nothing. They each stared moodily into their own glasses for a moment.

"So tell me now," Nicko came out with eventually, "what's your Belo-Russian painter's name?"

"Kravchenko. Pavel Kravchenko."

"Never heard of him. And he's got a grown-up daughter who wants to be a fashion designer? But you say he's selling well in the Russian market?"

"I can show you a catalogue of his work, if you like," explained Viktor. "He's had a recent show in New York. There was quite a lot of interest."

"Don't get your fingers burned this time."

"Piss off. How many times are you going to say that to me? His name isn't Rothko."

"I never said that it was, so you can piss off as well!"

They grinned and clinked their glasses.

Nicko had already commended his friend on his partially-restored appearance- he had feared that tattoos and facial metalwork were imminent and was gratified to see that he had reigned back, though the baseball cap and T-shirt were not really in his line. They went on to discuss future family arrangements and Nicko was struck by his friend's detachment about it all. He insisted, nevertheless, that there should be no question of Vik not having as much access to his child as he wanted.

"He's your own flesh and blood," he told him portentously, "and you have every reason to be proud of him. You must see as much of him as you can."

"But he's to grow up an English boy," Viktor pointed out. "His mother is determined about that and that's where you come in."

"Surely you don't want him to forget he's a Russian one too, do you? After all I'm very proud of my Russian ancestors and my Russian name."

"And your Russian soul, Nikoshka! Never forget that Russian soul of yours! Nasdorovia!" Viktor raised his glass. "Piss off!"

They ordered their meal with a bottle of red wine and went on mulling over old times - which meant their schooldays - as if nothing had arisen since then to complicate the lives of either of them. Somehow, the perversity of their present circumstances seemed to be bringing them closer to one another again. Nicko hoped that there would be something in it for Vik in the end, cutting loose and taking up, as he appeared to be, with the daughter of a still little-known, and hopefully up-and-coming, painter with Belo-Russian roots, called Kravchenko.

"Do you intend marrying this girl?" Nicko asked.

Viktor smiled. "Give me time," he said. "There's no rush."

"You seem remarkably relaxed about it all - as if the future's in the bag. But, be honest, Vik, what's really in it for you?"

Viktor smiled and, taking up his glass, touched Nicko's.

"We'll drink to that. The future," he said.

"But you haven't answered my question."

"Love," replied Viktor. "Money too - let's not forget that - and a place in the Californian sun."

Christ, thought Nicko, it might be his grandfather all over again, the Despot of Kolyma.

They chewed their steaks in silence for a few minutes.

"Tell me," Viktor came out with at length. "Tell me about Tim and how he's getting on with his Russian wife."

"You know Ludmilla, I think," Nicko said.

Viktor frowned and took a big pull at his wine. "Who knows Ludmilla? I once thought I did, but then I discovered I didn't. And of course the Kolyma business put a whole new light on it. Who would ever have thought of that connection? I suppose it explains some of what happened."

"We just have to keep our fingers crossed about it - that it's buried along with the Kolyma dead. But it's a funny business. Tim getting swept off his feet like that. He didn't know what he was letting himself in for."

"You mean by marrying a Russian?" "That one, especially."

"She's like a sleeping volcano."

"What an unsettling thought."

"I'd like to have a word with Tim," Viktor said. "But without his wife."

"It shouldn't be a problem."

They left the topic and turned to Kolya's education instead.

"He's taking to it like a duck to water, as I've told you so many times before," Nicko assured his friend, "so I don't have to say it again. It's exactly the right school for him. Honestly, Vik, you have to be bloody proud of your son."

"And you must carry on with the good work and see it through to the end. It's what his mother wants and that's what matters."

There was a note of finality in Viktor's manner, as if he was shutting the topic down.

Nicko tried to draw his friend on the subject of Svetlana and, though he issued an appropriately languid sigh or two, it was evident that he did not want to talk about that either, so it was dropped.

After brandies and coffee they went their separate ways - Viktor home to Thurloe Square and Nicko to Finchley, having agreed to arrange a session together with Tim at the Cock and Hen.

When Nicko spoke to Tim, he seemed agitated.

"Anything the matter?" he asked.

"It's Ludochka. She's stuck in front of her fucking computer from the moment she comes in, talking to that fucking lunatic, Vadim, in Russia - the one who's spouting the crap about the collision of Earth and a rogue planet. And after, that she's hard at it, trying to press his fucking junk on me. You do realise, don't you, that a date has been set for the Apocalypse? The planetary collision is due to occur on August the Fifteenth Two Thousand and Fifteen, at five o'clock in the morning, Moscow time. So don't say you haven't been warned."

"Vik's back in town to settle the divorce," Nicko informed him. "It's going smoothly apparently and he says he'd like to meet you for a chat." "It seems a pity that the End of the World is going to kibosh his plans, now that things are starting to work out so well, though he still has a couple of years grace before anything happens," said Tim. "But sure- I'd like to talk to Vik- especially about the future of the art market, especially in view of the end of things."

"The usual place at the usual time and then maybe we can go on for a bite somewhere. Have you any suggestions?"

Tim mentioned 'The Verona' in Covent Garden, which sounded suitable.

* * * * * *

Nicko picked up Vik at home and took him along to the Cock and Hen. He still felt protective about him, especially when they were out after the dark. In the tube he eyed their fellow passengers and regretted - unreasonably perhaps - that they did not have Alyosha with them.

Tim was already waiting for them in their familiar corner. It was a while since he had last set eyes on Vik and he looked at him closely. Mercifully the recent regression into adolescence - no doubt because of the need to appear as a rational being to his solicitor - having been put on hold, he struck up his old bonhomie with Tim, beginning with a lighthearted reference to Ludmilla Mikailovna, while trying not appear too nosy. It was Tim who pushed the matter further, saying that he was anxious to talk about his wife with another Russian, Nicko, despite his name and ancestry, not quite filling that bill.

He explained Brother Vadim's prophesy of the cataclysm involving the earth and the rogue planet, Nibiru, from outside the solar system, the presence of which, according to Ludmilla, had been credited by several leading academicians.

"Ludochka is convinced it's true," he said. "Have you heard anything about it?"

Viktor smiled and shook his head. "We Russians have always liked this crazy kind of rubbish," he explained, "especially after the end of Communism, another crazy idea, by the way. Lenin was the biggest fool prophet of them all."

"Agreed," said Tim, "but what baffles me is that someone who seems so rational in every other respect should be so easily taken in by it. Ludochka's obsessed and screams at me for not taking her seriously - though God alone knows what any of us can do about it, if it is going to happen."

Viktor laughed. "Sod all."

"All of which is very trying," went on Tim. "I wish to God she'd get back to her Montenegran royal family- or even the other fad of hers, Ripley and Patricia Highsmith. Quite honestly, Brother Vadim sounds like one of Dostoyevski's less inspired creations."

Viktor laughed and shook his head. There was not much he could say to ease Tim's burden, but the reference to criminal fiction provided Nicko with an opening of sorts.

"That was going to be her field, wasn't it?" he said. "Criminals in fiction. A comparison, maybe, between Ripley and Raskolnikov - though someone could have done that already."

"It's a big historical topic," mused Tim, "and in my opinion all that's happened in Russia in the last century and since makes it a very germane one. I mean the parameters and definition of criminality in a Russian context. Plenty there for anyone to get their teeth into. It raises philosophical considerations."

Nicko glanced at Viktor, who for some reason had a smirk on his face.

"I'm sure Vik here could dig up some fascinating material from his own ancestral archives," he said, but then, recalling the alleged atrocity committed in Kolyma, he felt that it was better left untouched.

But it was the consensus of their discussion that Ludmilla should somehow be weaned off the ravings of Brother Vadim and back to a serious academic study of fictional crime. With that settled, they turned to the less sombre topic of the good ship 'Anastasia'.

Nothing more had been heard from the tycoon since his quayside appearance. He was still abroad, apparently, while a verdict on the death of a former British Government minister was still awaited in Greece, where the wheels of such matters turned slowly. And now, to cap it, there was also Miguel's murder: the Mexican Boy being ferried swiftly across the Styx in the wake of his former master…

"My God, that really is one for a criminologist to get his - or her - teeth into," said Tim.

Viktor smiled. "Maybe, but maybe not- if they want to stay alive."

They fell silent for a minute and Nicko fetched a fresh round of drinks.

"We've got time for a last one, haven't we?" "

"The table's booked for eight-thirty." Tim reminded them.

The evening in the Verona proved congenial. They were able to linger over their meal - which was a simple one, the interstices of which were filled with a perfectly drinkable Chianti, followed by cognacs with their coffee. The mood was lighthearted- if not a little lightheaded- and Nicko was pleased to see Vik and Tim hitting it off so well. They had not had anything to do with each other since the time of settling into Thurloe Square and it was good to see them so relaxed together now. In Tim's case, there was a sense of escape, of being released from the bondage of his spouse's obsessions. But if anything, it was Vik who was the more ebullient of the pair. Was it perhaps his inborn Russian capacity for letting his hair down? Or was it the forthcoming family settlement, with its astonishingly amicable terms and the prospect of a new life in the United States in the arms of his Belo-Russian beauty that was lifting his spirits? The spat with Dobrinin was now something to be mulled over and joked about among friends.

Tim was now the one with the problem - how to handle his wife's lurch into dottiness - reminiscent, in its way, of the last Tsarina's obsession with another starets out of Siberia, with such fearful consequences. Could she be guided back to the path of rationality, to pursue a serious academic career and enjoy a proper relationship with her English husband? But for the moment, at least, the paroled prisoner was able to relax and probe Vik on the state of the art market in New York. The latter talked large on the subject, and in a way that Nicko felt was not informed in the best sense, but he seemed to have unbounded optimism in the continuing boom in the Russian market and the part that some expat Russians and Ukrainians were able to play in it. Quite what part his own should be, he did not elaborate, and Nicko recalled with some misgivings the Novgorod venture. However he left the matter in the air, while joining in the conviviality.

It was after eleven when their evening drew to its close. Indeed, they were the only customers left in the restaurant.

"My God!" Nicko exclaimed. "I've got to work tomorrow and I expect you have too, Tim."

They walked to the Covent Garden Underground station. It was a mild night and the streets pleasantly quiet. Their easy-going chat continued and they were in no hurry to part. In Tim's voice there was a regretful note that his parole was drawing to its close and that he was returning once more to the bondage of his precipitate marriage.

In the station there was a scattering of people passing through, eager to catch the last trains home, but with none of the daytime push and shove. The three friends rode down the escalator to where Nicko and Tim were to part from Vik, who took each of them by their hands, pressing them warmly to his chest. Then he hugged Nicko and kissed him.

The passion of his embrace took his old chum a little by surprise, while Tim looked on, somewhat bemused by its fervour.

When he stood back again, Nicko saw a tear running down his Russian friend's cheek and the sight of it stirred the same effect in himself. He wiped away his tear and looked at Tim.

"It must be the drink," he said.

"Shall I shed one too?" replied Tim, half in jest. "That will make it a truly Russian occasion."

Viktor laughed. "Time for bed," he declared, cutting onto the westbound platform.

"I'll give you a ring," Nicko called after him. "And my love to Verochka!"

The rumble of a train approaching the westbound platform could be heard and a few figures could be seen hastening down the escalator, in the hope of catching it. They looked to be young people - as might be expected - and a couple of them had hoods pulled down over their faces. It struck Nicko how sexless the hoods made them look and he remarked on it to Tim, as they turned onto the eastbound platform.

Meanwhile the train drew into the opposite side of the station, with the usual squeal of brakes. But mingled with the usual broadcast sounds about standing clear of the doors and minding the gap was another one: a medley of hysterical cries and exclamations. - "Did anyone see it happen?"….. "Christ, can no one get him out of there?"… "Did he fall or was he pushed?"…."Is he dead?"…. "He must be dead!"…

Nicko knew what had happened, without having to cross the concourse. Several passengers, including a slim figure in a hooded beige anorak, whom he had noticed coming down the escalator a minute or two earlier, were departing back up it, while Underground staff were descending hastily at the same time. The uproar continued while Nicko and Tim stood passively on the other platform. Neither of them spoke a word. What was running through Tim's mind, Nicko could not guess; but one thing he knew for certain, without having to venture onto the westbound platform: the chum of his schooldays had perished under the wheels of an incoming train…. And it seemed to have happened in a similar way to what had happened in another story he had once read… in that same collection as the one about the young man who had been forced to execute his twin brother…

* * * * * *

In the following days Nicko and Tim answered all the questions that were put to them, regarding Viktor to the best of their ability. They had not witnessed the accident, so they could offer no explanation- apart from the rather charged parting just before it had occurred, when it had almost been as if Vik had been setting a seal on their friendship.

Had he taken his own life? Or had someone pushed him into the path of the train? Or could he possibly have just slipped, helped, maybe, by the pressure of people, crowding behind him from the concourse? No one, it seemed, was able to offer a clear explanation.

Then there was another development which might have had some bearing on the tragedy. Early next morning, Tim phoned to say that he had got home to find a letter from Ludmilla, telling him that she had left him. She had filled a large suitcase and apparently set out for Heathrow. Clearly she had arranged it well in advance, booking her flight and so on. She had left a few odds and ends behind, including a scruffy blue tracksuit top hanging on a peg on the landing. When Tim provided that detail, Nicko recalled seeing her once or twice in a beige anorak which had not been left behind….

But Tim seemed mightily relieved, despite the weight of the tragedy that had befallen Nicko's friend.

"Every cloud has its silver lining," he said to his friend, while pondering, at the same time, on whether Ludmilla's rapid and furtive flight might have had anything to do with Vik's untimely death.

But the mystery remained unsolved. It was a strange fact that among all the people crowding the platform when Vik died, there was not one who could provide a clear answer as to how he might have fallen from the platform into the path of an incoming train.

But life had to go on. Nicko was deeply involved in the tragedy's aftermath. Interestingly, no kin from Russia itself came forward and he recalled that in the entire time he had spent there with him there, Viktor Nikishov had introduced him to no one of that description, alluding to their existence only in the most general terms. What had happened to the rest of the clan? Indeed, were any of them still left?

It was left to Nicko with Vera to arrange the last rites for his friend, once the authorities had released his body. Vera was stoical and Nicko felt that she got it right - if only for the boy's sake. It was not the way she had wanted things to work out, but at least this was a means of keeping the father's memory untarnished in his son's eyes. Indeed, at the burial, as Viktor Nikishov was laid to rest among the mortal remains of other exiles from their Russian homeland, it was Nicko who shed a tear and had to fight down the sob that was threatening to stifle him.

There were not many at the funeral: Alyosha and Tsina were there, of course, the Trubshaws, Ivor Wills, the solicitor who had been handling the divorce, Tim and Kolya, impeccably turned out for the occasion in his school blazer, cap and freshly pressed grey flannel shorts. His expression was solemn and perfectly composed as he stood at the graveside, holding his mother's hand while the Orthodox priest intoned the final obsequies.

"Well done, Kolya," his headmaster whispered in his ear as they retreated to the cemetery gate. "You handled that very well."

"Thank you, sir."

Meanwhile the spectre of Miguel was eclipsed in Nicko's thoughts, which were centred on his lost Russian friend. Now that he was dead, the strangely amicable arrangement, that had been hammered out between them was to go ahead, though in a more sacred glow. In Nicko's eyes, his paramount duty was to do everything that lay within his power to advance the fortunes of the son Vik had left behind him, and in that way to honour his friend's memory. To Nicko, Vik lived on in the lad - which, of course, was a biological fact.

No word of Ludmilla came from Russia. Tim had no idea where she had gone, after taking the plane to Moscow. Nor did he try to find out. His friends didn't either. He told them that she had set off back to her homeland and there was no speculation about a corpse decomposing beneath the floor tiles of a North London kitchen. Tim realised, of course, that should he elect for a fresh marriage there would be complications, but for the time being he was content simply to let sleeping dogs lie.

And the inquest into the death of Lord Isaacs finally reached its conclusions: death by drowning, almost certainly by his own hand. No suspicious roles were attributed to Oleg Dobrinin or anyone else on board the 'Anastasia'. The suicide was put down to the revelations made by the ex- Minister's catamite and the good ship 'Anastasia' continued to ply the Mediterranean waters, to the gratification of its passengers. The mystery of the Mexican Boy's death remained unresolved and it was probable that the New York police were not greatly interested in it anyway. After all, he was just one among the many of his tribe who came to a sticky end. Only a couple of British papers made discreetly phrased references to his links with the Dobrinin outfit.

* * * * * *

And finally, four months after Vik had been laid to rest, Nicko married Vera. Because in the end there had been no need for a divorce, the event went forward with the full Orthodox nuptials. Tim acted as Nicko's support, and enjoyed the irony of his friend's and his own relative situations.

The obdurate Mrs Orloff even graced the occasion and turned out to be surprisingly approving. She rapidly warmed to her new daughter-in-law, seeing in her a lot of good sense and approving wholeheartedly of her desire to embrace English ways. Kolya she took to also. She liked the look of him and his manners.

"I wish more of our own were like him," she observed to her son.

"But, Ma, he is one of our own," pointed out Nicko.

She did not try to cap that and nor did she want to. Relief that her son had at last got himself hitched and might shortly be in the business of raising a brood of his own, alongside this agreeable half-brother, was sufficient for her. She whispered something in Nicko's ear about school fees, but was assured that Viktor's means would easily cover that.

And that was the plan: Kolya would move on to his father and stepfather's old school after his time was up at Bailey's. And in due course he was to be followed by Vitya the Second, and then there was Sophie, who was destined for one of London's more famous girls' schools, one with an excellent academic record, which lay no great distance from where the Orloffs and the scion of the House of Nikishov continued to live, and where Alyosha and Tsina - now the proprietors of a popular Russian restaurant - remained in the basement flat, for which they paid a nominal rent.

In the short term 'One Man's Soul' had capped the success of 'The Pardoner's Tale' and other plays followed, while Orloff and Mumford eventually made it onto the bookstalls of London's leading museums and art galleries, where it continues to sell, making a modest, if not spectacular, return.